Praise for

THE MADNESS OF LORD IAN MACKENZIE

"Ever-versatile Ashley begins her new Victorian Highland Pleasures series with a deliciously dark and delectably sexy story of love and romantic redemption that will captivate readers with its complex characters and suspenseful plot."
—*Booklist*

"Ashley's enthralling and poignant romance . . . touches readers on many levels. Brava!" —*Romantic Times*

"Mysterious, heartfelt, sensitive, and sensual . . . Two big thumbs up." —*Publishers Weekly*'s Beyond Her Book

"A story of mystery and intrigue with two wonderful, bright characters you'll love . . . I look forward to more from Jennifer Ashley, an extremely gifted author." —*Fresh Fiction*

"Brimming with mystery, suspense, an intriguing plot, villains, romance, a tormented hero, and a feisty heroine, this book is a winner. I recommend *The Madness of Lord Ian Mackenzie* to anyone looking for a great read."
—*Romance Junkies*

"Wow! All I can say is *The Madness of Lord Ian Mackenzie* is one of the best books I have ever read. [It] gets the highest recommendation that I can give. It is a truly wonderful book." —*Once Upon A Romance*

"When you're reading a book that is a step or two—or six or seven—above the norm, you know it almost immediately. Such is the case with *The Madness of Lord Ian Mackenzie*. The characters here are so complex and so real that I was fascinated by their journey . . . [and] this story is as flat-out romantic as any I've read in a while . . . This is a series I am certainly looking forward to following."
—*All About Romance*

D0004171

Berkley Sensation Titles by Jennifer Ashley

THE MADNESS OF LORD IAN MACKENZIE
LADY ISABELLA'S SCANDALOUS MARRIAGE
THE MANY SINS OF LORD CAMERON
PRIDE MATES
PRIMAL BONDS

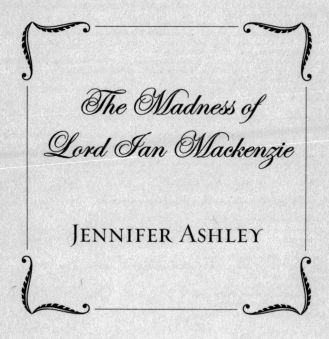

The Madness of
Lord Ian Mackenzie

JENNIFER ASHLEY

BERKLEY SENSATION, NEW YORK

THE BERKLEY PUBLISHING GROUP
Published by the Penguin Group
Penguin Group (USA) Inc.
375 Hudson Street, New York, New York 10014, USA

Penguin Group (Canada), 90 Eglinton Avenue East, Suite 700, Toronto, Ontario M4P 2Y3, Canada
(a division of Pearson Penguin Canada Inc.)
Penguin Books Ltd., 80 Strand, London WC2R 0RL, England
Penguin Group Ireland, 25 St. Stephen's Green, Dublin 2, Ireland (a division of Penguin Books Ltd.)
Penguin Group (Australia), 250 Camberwell Road, Camberwell, Victoria 3124, Australia
(a division of Pearson Australia Group Pty. Ltd.)
Penguin Books India Pvt. Ltd., 11 Community Centre, Panchsheel Park, New Delhi—110 017, India
Penguin Group (NZ), 67 Apollo Drive, Rosedale, Auckland 0632, New Zealand
(a division of Pearson New Zealand Ltd.)
Penguin Books (South Africa) (Pty.) Ltd., 24 Sturdee Avenue, Rosebank, Johannesburg 2196,
South Africa

Penguin Books Ltd., Registered Offices: 80 Strand, London WC2R 0RL, England

This is a work of fiction. Names, characters, places, and incidents either are the product of the author's imagination or are used fictitiously, and any resemblance to actual persons, living or dead, business establishments, events, or locales is entirely coincidental. The publisher does not have any control over and does not assume any responsibility for author or third-party websites or their content.

THE MADNESS OF LORD IAN MACKENZIE

A Berkley Sensation Book / published by arrangement with the author

PRINTING HISTORY
A Leisure Book mass-market edition / May 2009
Berkley Sensation mass-market paperback edition / August 2011

Copyright © 2009 by Jennifer Ashley.
Excerpt from *Lady Isabella's Scandalous Marriage* by Jennifer Ashley copyright © 2010
by Jennifer Ashley.
Cover design by George Long.
Cover illustration by Gregg Gulbronson.
Cover hand lettering by Ron Zinn.
Interior text design by Laura K. Corless.

ISBN: 978-0-425-24446-3

BERKLEY® SENSATION
Berkley Sensation Books are published by The Berkley Publishing Group,
a division of Penguin Group (USA) Inc.,
375 Hudson Street, New York, New York 10014.
BERKLEY® SENSATION and the "B" design are trademarks of Penguin Group (USA) Inc.

PRINTED IN THE UNITED STATES OF AMERICA

10 9 8 7 6 5 4 3 2

Acknowledgments

I'd like to thank the original editor for this book, Leah Hulten-schmidt, for encouraging me throughout this difficult project. Thanks also go to Kate Seaver at Berkley, who graciously acquired the book for rerelease. Also thanks to my critique partner, who read the early drafts and helped shape this book. I'd also like to thank the many, many fans of Lord Ian Mackenzie, whose encouragement kept me going during some tough times. As always, thanks go to my husband, who endured me reading him the entire revised manuscript and who tirelessly acted as my sounding board. More information on the Mackenzie family and the Highland Pleasures series can be found on the series page at my website, www .jennifersromances.com.

Chapter 1

"I find that a Ming bowl is like a woman's breast," Sir Lyndon Mather said to Ian Mackenzie, who held the bowl in question between his fingertips. "The swelling curve, the creamy pallor. Don't you agree?"

Ian couldn't think of a woman who would be flattered to have her breast compared to a bowl, so he didn't bother to nod.

The delicate vessel was from the early Ming period, the porcelain barely flushed with green, the sides so thin Ian could see light through them. Three gray-green dragons chased one another across the outside, and four chrysanthemums seemed to float across the bottom.

The little vessel might just cup a small rounded breast, but that was as far as Ian was willing to go.

"One thousand guineas," he said.

Mather's smile turned sickly. "Now, my lord, I thought we were friends."

Ian wondered where Mather had got that idea. "The bowl is worth one thousand guineas." He fingered the slightly chipped rim, the base worn from centuries of handling.

Mather looked taken aback, blue eyes glittering in his overly handsome face.

"I paid fifteen hundred for it. Explain yourself."

There was nothing to explain. Ian's rapidly calculating mind had taken in every asset and flaw in ten seconds flat. If Mather couldn't tell the value of his pieces, he had no business collecting porcelain. There were at least five fakes in the glass case on the other side of Mather's collection room, and Ian wagered Mather had no idea.

Ian put his nose to the glaze, liking the clean scent that had survived the heavy cigar smoke of Mather's house. The bowl was genuine, it was beautiful, and he wanted it.

"At least give me what I paid for it," Mather said in a panicked voice. "The man told me I had it at a bargain."

"One thousand guineas," Ian repeated.

"Damn it, man, I'm getting married."

Ian recalled the announcement in the *Times*—verbatim, because he recalled everything verbatim: *Sir Lyndon Mather of St. Aubrey's, Suffolk, announces his betrothal to Mrs. Thomas Ackerley, a widow. The wedding to be held on the twenty-seventh of June of this year in St. Aubrey's at ten o'clock in the morning.*

"My felicitations," Ian said.

"I wish to buy my beloved a gift with what I get for the bowl."

Ian kept his gaze on the vessel. "Why not give her the bowl itself?"

Mather's hearty laugh filled the room. "My dear fellow, women don't know the first thing about porcelain. She'll want a carriage and a matched team and a string of servants to carry all the fripperies she buys. I'll give her that. She's a fine-looking woman, daughter of some froggie aristo, for all she's long in the tooth and a widow."

Ian didn't answer. He touched the tip of his tongue to the bowl, reflecting that it was far better than ten carriages with matched teams. Any woman who didn't see the poetry in it was a fool.

Mather wrinkled his nose as Ian tasted the bowl, but Ian had learned to test the genuineness of the glaze that way. Mather wouldn't be able to tell a genuine glaze if someone painted him with it.

"She's got a bloody fortune of her own," Mather went on, "inherited from that Barrington woman, a rich old lady who didn't keep her opinions to herself. Mrs. Ackerley, her quiet companion, copped the lot."

Then why is she marrying you? Ian turned the bowl over in his hands as he speculated, but if Mrs. Ackerley wanted to make her bed with Lyndon Mather, she could lie in it. Of course, she might find the bed a little crowded. Mather kept a secret house for his mistress and several other women to cater to his needs, which he loved to boast about to Ian's brothers. *I'm as decadent as you lot,* he was trying to say. But in Ian's opinion, Mather understood pleasures of the flesh about as well as he understood Ming porcelain.

"Bet you're surprised a dedicated bachelor like myself is for the chop, eh?" Mather went on. "If you're wondering whether I'm giving up my bit of the other, the answer is no. You are welcome to come 'round and join in anytime, you know. I've extended the invitation to you, and your brothers as well."

Ian had met Mather's ladies, vacant-eyed women willing to put up with Mather's proclivities for the money he gave them.

Mather reached for a cigar. "I say, we're at Covent Garden Opera tonight. Come meet my fiancée. I'd like your opinion. Everyone knows you have as exquisite taste in females as you do in porcelain." He chuckled.

Ian didn't answer. He had to rescue the bowl from this philistine. "One thousand guineas."

"You're a hard man, Mackenzie."

"One thousand guineas, and I'll see you at the opera."

"Oh, very well, though you're ruining me."

He'd ruined himself. "Your widow has a fortune. You'll recover."

Mather laughed, his handsome face lighting. Ian had seen women of every age blush or flutter fans when Mather smiled. Mather was the master of the double life.

"True, and she's lovely to boot. I'm a lucky man."

Mather rang for his butler and Ian's valet, Curry. Curry produced a wooden box lined with straw, into which Ian carefully placed the dragon bowl.

Ian hated to cover up such beauty. He touched it one last time, his gaze fixed on it until Curry broke his concentration by placing the lid on the box.

He looked up to find that Mather had ordered the butler to pour brandy. Ian accepted a glass and sat down in front of the bankbook Curry had placed on Mather's desk for him.

Ian set aside the brandy and dipped his pen in the ink. He bent down to write and caught sight of the droplet of black ink hanging on the nib in a perfect, round sphere.

He stared at the droplet, something inside him singing at the perfection of the ball of ink, the glistening viscosity that held it suspended from the nib. The sphere was perfect, shining, a wonder.

He wished he could savor its perfection forever, but he knew that in a second it would fall from the pen and be lost. If his brother Mac could paint something this exquisite, this beautiful, Ian would treasure it.

He had no idea how long he'd sat there studying the droplet of ink until he heard Mather say, "Damnation, he really is mad, isn't he?"

The droplet fell down, down, down to splash on the page, gone to its death in a splatter of black ink.

"I'll write it out for you, then, m'lord?"

Ian looked into the homely face of his manservant, a young Cockney who'd spent his boyhood pickpocketing his way across London.

Ian nodded and relinquished the pen. Curry turned the bankbook toward him and wrote the draft in careful capitals.

He dipped the pen again and handed it back to Ian, holding the nib down so Ian wouldn't see the ink.

Ian signed his name painstakingly, feeling the weight of Mather's stare.

"Does he do that often?" Mather asked as Ian rose, leaving Curry to blot the paper.

Curry's cheekbones stained red. "No 'arm done, sir."

Ian lifted his glass and swiftly drank down the brandy, then took up the box. "I will see you at the opera."

He didn't shake hands on his way out. Mather frowned, but gave Ian a nod. Lord Ian Mackenzie, brother to the Duke of Kilmorgan, socially outranked him, and Mather was acutely aware of social rank.

Once in his carriage, Ian set the box beside him. He could feel the bowl inside, round and perfect, filling a niche in himself.

"I know it ain't me place to say," Curry said from the opposite seat as the carriage jerked forward into the rainy streets. "But the man's a right bastard. Not fit for you to wipe your boots on. Why even have truck with him?"

Ian caressed the box. "I wanted this piece."

"You do have a way of getting what you want, no mistake, m'lord. Are we really meeting him at the opera?"

"I'll sit in Hart's box." Ian flicked his gaze over Curry's baby-innocent face and focused safely on the carriage's velvet wall. "Find out everything you can about a Mrs. Ackerley, a widow now betrothed to Sir Lyndon Mather. Tell me about it tonight."

"Oh, aye? Why are we so interested in the right bastard's fiancée?"

Ian ran his fingertips lightly over the box again. "I want to know if she's exquisite porcelain or a fake."

Curry winked. "Right ye are, guv. I'll see what I can dig up."

⌒⌒⌒

Lyndon Mather was all that was handsome and charming, and heads turned when Beth Ackerley walked by on his arm at Covent Garden Opera House.

Mather had a pure profile, a slim, athletic body, and a head of golden hair that ladies longed to run their fingers through. His manners were impeccable, and he charmed everyone he met. He had a substantial income, a lavish house on Park Lane, and he was received by the highest of the high. An excellent choice for a lady of unexpected fortune looking for a second husband.

Even a lady of unexpected fortune tires of being alone, Beth thought as she entered Mather's luxurious box behind his elderly aunt and companion. She'd known Mather for several years, his aunt and her employer being fast friends. He wasn't the most exciting of gentlemen, but Beth didn't want exciting. *No drama,* she promised herself. She'd had enough drama to last a lifetime.

Now Beth wanted comfort; she'd learned how to run a houseful of servants, and she'd perhaps have the chance to have the children she'd always longed for. Her first marriage nine years ago had produced none, but then, poor Thomas had died barely a year after they'd taken their vows. He'd been so ill, he hadn't even been able to say good-bye.

The opera had begun by the time they settled into Sir Lyndon's box. The young woman onstage had a beautiful soprano voice and an ample body with which to project it. Beth was soon lost in the rapture of the music. Mather left the box ten minutes after they'd entered, as he usually did. He liked to spend his nights at the theatre seeing everyone of importance and being seen with them. Beth didn't mind. She'd grown used to sitting with elderly matrons and preferred it to exchanging inanities with glittering society ladies. *Oh, darling did you hear? Lady Marmaduke had three inches of lace on her dress instead of two. Can you imagine anything more vulgar? And her pleats were limp, my darling, absolutely limp.* Such important information.

Beth fanned herself and enjoyed the music while Mather's aunt and her companion tried to make sense of the plot of *La Traviata*. Beth reflected that they thought nothing of an outing to the theatre, but to a girl growing up in the East End, it was anything but ordinary. Beth loved music, and imbibed it any way she could, though she thought herself only a mediocre musician. No matter, she could listen to others play and enjoy it just fine. Mather liked to go to the theatre, to the opera, to musicales, so Beth's new life would have much music in it.

Her enjoyment was interrupted by Mather's noisy return to the box. "My dear," he said in a loud voice, "I've brought you my *very* close friend Lord Ian Mackenzie. Give him your hand, darling. His brother is the Duke of Kilmorgan, you know."

Beth looked past Mather at the tall man who'd entered the box behind him, and her entire world stopped.

Lord Ian was a big man, his body solid muscle, the hand that reached to hers huge in a kid leather glove. His shoulders were wide, his chest broad, and the dim light touched his dark hair with red. His face was as hard as his body, but his eyes set Ian Mackenzie apart from every other person Beth had ever met.

She at first thought his eyes were light brown, but when Mather almost shoved him down into the chair at Beth's side, she saw that they were golden. Not hazel, but amber like brandy, flecked with gold as though the sun danced on them.

"This is my Mrs. Ackerley," Mather was saying. "What do you think, eh? I told you she was the best-looking woman in London."

Lord Ian ran a quick glance over Beth's face, then fixed his gaze at a point somewhere beyond the box. He still held her hand, his grip firm, the pressure of his fingers just shy of painful.

He didn't agree or disagree with Mather, a bit rudely, Beth thought. Even if Lord Ian didn't clutch his breast and declare Beth the most beautiful woman since Elaine of Camelot, he ought to at least give some polite answer.

Instead he sat in stony silence. He still held Beth's hand, and his thumb traced the pattern of stitching on the back of her glove. Over and over the thumb moved, hot, quick patterns, the pressure pulsing heat through her limbs.

"If he told you I was the most beautiful woman in London, I fear you were much deceived," Beth said rapidly. "I apologize if he misled you."

Lord Ian's gaze flicked over her, a small frown on his face, as though he had no idea what she was talking about.

"Don't crush the poor woman, Mackenzie," Mather said jovially. "She's fragile, like one of your Ming bowls."

"Oh, do you have an interest in porcelain, my lord?" Beth grasped at something to say. "Sir Lyndon has shown me his collection."

"Mackenzie is one of the foremost authorities," Mather said with a trace of envy.

"Are you?" Beth asked.

Lord Ian flicked another glance over her. "Yes."

He sat no closer to her than Mather did, but Beth's awareness of him screamed at her. She could feel his hard knee against her skirts, the firm pressure of his thumb on her hand, the weight of his *not*-stare.

A woman wouldn't be comfortable with this man, she thought with a shiver. *There would be drama aplenty.* She sensed that in the restlessness of his body, the large, warm hand that gripped her own, the eyes that wouldn't quite meet hers. Should she pity the woman those eyes finally rested on? Or envy her?

Beth's tongue tripped along. "Sir Lyndon has lovely things. When I touch a piece that an emperor held hundreds of years ago, I feel . . . I'm not sure. *Close* to him, I think. Quite privileged."

Sparks of gold flashed as Ian looked at her a bare instant. "You must come view my collection." He had a slight Scots accent, his voice low and gravel-rough.

"Love to, old chap," Mather said. "I'll see when we are free."

Mather lifted his opera glasses to study the large-bosomed soprano, and Lord Ian's gaze moved to him. The disgust and intense dislike in Lord Ian's unguarded expression startled Beth. Before she could speak, Lord Ian leaned to her. The heat of his body touched her like a sharp wave, bringing with it the scent of shaving soap and male spice. She'd forgotten how heady was the scent of a man. Mather always covered himself with cologne.

"Read it out of his sight."

Lord Ian's breath grazed Beth's ear, warming things inside her that hadn't been touched in nine long years. His fingers slid beneath the opening of her glove above her elbow, and she felt the folded edge of paper scrape her bare arm. She stared at Lord Ian's golden eyes so near hers, watching his pupils widen before he flicked his gaze away again.

He sat up, his face smooth and expressionless. Mather turned to Ian with a comment about the singer, noticing nothing.

Lord Ian abruptly rose. The warm pressure left Beth's hand, and she realized he'd been holding it the entire time.

"Going already, old chap?" Mather asked in surprise.

"My brother is waiting."

Mather's eyes gleamed. "The duke?"

"My brother Cameron and his son."

"Oh." Mather looked disappointed, but he stood and renewed the promise to bring Beth to see Ian's collection.

Without saying good night, Ian moved past the empty chairs and out of the box. Beth's gaze wouldn't leave Lord Ian's back until the blank door closed behind him. She was very aware of the folded paper pressing the inside of her arm and the trickle of sweat forming under it.

Mather sat down next to Beth and blew out his breath. "There, my dear, goes an eccentric."

Beth curled her fingers in her gray taffeta skirt, her hand cold without Lord Ian's around it. "An eccentric?"

"Mad as a hatter. Poor chap lived in a private asylum most

of his life, and he runs free now only because his brother the duke let him out again. But don't worry." Mather took Beth's hand. "You won't have to see him without me present. The entire family is scandalous. Never speak to any of them without me, my dear, all right?"

Beth murmured something noncommittal. She had at least heard of the Mackenzie family, the hereditary Dukes of Kilmorgan, because old Mrs. Barrington had adored gossip about the aristocracy. The Mackenzies had featured in many of the scandal sheets that Beth read out to Mrs. Barrington on rainy nights.

Lord Ian hadn't seemed entirely mad to her, although he certainly was like no man she'd ever met. Mather's hand in hers felt limp and cool, while the hard pressure of Lord Ian's had heated her in a way she hadn't felt in a long time. Beth missed the intimacy she'd felt with Thomas, the long, warm nights in bed with him. She knew she'd share a bed with Mather, but the thought had never stirred her blood. She reasoned that what she'd had with Thomas was special and magical, and she couldn't expect to feel it with any other man. So why had her breath quickened when Lord Ian's lilting whisper had touched her ear; why had her heart beat faster when he'd moved his thumb over the back of her hand?

No. Lord Ian was drama, Mather, safety. She would choose safety. She had to.

Mather managed to stay still for five minutes, then rose again. "Must pay my respects to Lord and Lady Beresford. You don't mind, do you, m'dear?"

"Of course not," Beth said automatically.

"You are a treasure, my darling. I always told dear Mrs. Barrington how sweet and polite you were." Mather kissed Beth's hand, then left the box.

The soprano began an aria, the notes filling every space of the opera house. Behind her, Mather's aunt and her companion put their heads together behind fans, whispering, whispering.

Beth worked her fingers under the edge of her long glove

and pulled out the piece of paper. She put her back squarely to the elderly ladies and quietly unfolded the note.

Mrs. Ackerley, it began in a careful, neat hand.

I make bold to warn you of the true character of Sir Lyndon Mather, with whom my brother the Duke of Kilmorgan is well acquainted. I wish to tell you that Mather keeps a house just off the Strand near Temple Bar, where he has women meet him, several at a time. He calls the women his "sweeties" and begs them to use him as their slave. They are not regular courtesans but women who need the money enough to put up with him. I have listed five of the women he regularly meets, should you wish to have them questioned, or I can arrange for you to speak to the duke.

I remain,
Yours faithfully,
Ian Mackenzie

The soprano flung open her arms, building the last note of the aria to a wild crescendo, until it was lost in a burst of applause.

Beth stared at the letter, the noise in the opera house smothering. The words on the page didn't change, remaining painfully black against stark white.

Her breath poured back into her lungs, sharp and hot. She glanced quickly at Mather's aunt, but the old lady and her companion were applauding and shouting, "Brava! Brava!"

Beth rose, shoving the paper back into her glove. The small box with its cushioned chairs and tea tables seemed to tilt as she groped her way to the door.

Mather's aunt glanced at her in surprise. "Are you all right, my dear?"

"I just need some air. It's close in here."

Mather's aunt began to fumble among her things. "Do you need smelling salts? Alice, do help me."

"No, no." Beth opened the door and hurried out as Mather's aunt began to chastise her companion. "I shall be quite all right."

The gallery outside was deserted, thank heavens. The soprano was a popular one, and most of the attendees were fixed to their chairs, avidly watching her.

Beth hurried along the gallery, hearing the singer start up again. Her vision blurred, and the paper in her glove burned her arm.

What did Lord Ian mean by writing her such a letter? He was an eccentric, Mather had said—was that the explanation? But if the accusations in the letter were the ravings of a madman, why would Lord Ian offer to arrange for Beth to meet with his brother? The Duke of Kilmorgan was one of the wealthiest and most powerful men in Britain—he was the Duke of Kilmorgan in the peerage of Scotland, which went back to 1300-something, and his father had been made Duke of Kilmorgan in the peerage of England by Queen Victoria herself.

Why should such a lofty man care about nobodies like Beth Ackerley and Lyndon Mather? Surely both she and Mather were far beneath a duke's notice.

No, the letter was too bizarre. It had to be a lie, an invention.

And yet . . . Beth thought of times she'd caught Mather looking at her as though he'd done something clever. Growing up in the East End, having the father she'd had, had given Beth the ability to spot a confidence trickster at ten paces. Had the signs been there with Sir Lyndon Mather, and she'd simply chosen to ignore them?

But, no, it couldn't be true. She'd come to know Mather well when she'd been companion to elderly Mrs. Barrington. She and Mrs. Barrington had ridden with Mather in his carriage, visited him and his aunt at his Park Lane house, had him escort them to musicales. He'd never behaved toward Beth with anything but politeness due a rich old lady's companion, and after Mrs. Barrington's death, he'd proposed to Beth.

After I inherited Mrs. Barrington's fortune, a cynical voice reminded her.

What did Lord Ian mean by *sweeties*? *He begs them to use him as their slave.*

Beth's whalebone corset was too tight, cutting off the breath she sorely needed. Black spots swam before her eyes, and she put her hand out to steady herself.

A strong grip closed around her elbow. "Careful," a Scottish voice grated in her ear. "Come with me."

Chapter 2

Before Beth could choke out a refusal, Lord Ian propelled
her along the gallery, half lifting, half pulling her. He
yanked open a velvet-draped door and all but shoved her
inside.

Beth found herself in another box, this one large, heavily carpeted, and filled with cigar smoke. She coughed. "I
need a drink of water."

Lord Ian pushed her down into an armchair, which welcomed her into its plush depths. She clasped the cold crystal glass he thrust at her and drank deeply of its contents.

She gasped when she tasted whiskey instead of water,
but the liquid burned a fiery trail to her stomach, and her
vision began to clear.

Once she could see again Beth realized she sat in a box
that looked directly onto the stage below. From its prime
position she judged that it must be the Duke of Kilmorgan's
box. It was very posh indeed, with comfortable furniture,
gaslights turned low, and polished inlaid tables. But apart
from herself and Lord Ian, the box was empty.

Ian took the glass from her and seated himself on the chair next to hers, far too close. He put his lips to the glass where Beth had just drunk from it and finished off the contents. A stray droplet lingered on his lower lip, and Beth suddenly wanted to lick it clean.

To drag her mind from such thoughts, she slid the paper from her glove. "What did you mean by this, my lord?"

Ian didn't even look at the letter. "Exactly what it said."

"These are very grave—and quite distressing—accusations."

Ian's expression said he didn't give a damn how grave and distressing they were. "Mather is a blackguard, and you would be well rid of him."

Beth crumpled the letter in her hand and tried to organize her thoughts. It wasn't easy with Ian Mackenzie sitting half a foot from her, his powerful presence all but making her fall off the chair. Every time she drew a breath, she inhaled the scent of whiskey and cigar and dark maleness she wasn't used to.

"I have heard that collectors envy one another to the point of madness," she said.

"Mather isn't a collector."

"Isn't he? I've seen his porcelain. He keeps it locked away in a special room and won't even let the servants in to clean."

"His collection isn't worth a damn. He can't tell the difference between the real thing and a fake."

Ian's gaze roved over her, as warm and dark as his touch. She shifted uncomfortably.

"My lord, I've been betrothed to Sir Lyndon for three months, and none of his other acquaintances have mentioned any peculiar behaviors."

"Mather keeps his perversions to himself."

"But not from you? Why are you privileged with this information?"

"He thought it would impress my brother."

"Good heavens, why should such a thing impress a duke?"

Ian lifted his shoulders in a shrug, his arm brushing Beth's. He sat too close, but Beth couldn't seem to make herself rise and move to another chair.

"Do you go about prepared with letters such as these in case they're wanted?" she asked.

His gaze moved swiftly to her, then away again, as though he wanted to focus on her and couldn't. "I wrote it before I came tonight, in case when I met you I thought you'd be worth saving."

"Should I be flattered?"

"Mather is a blind idiot and sees only your fortune."

Exactly what her own little voice had just told her. "Mather doesn't need my fortune," she argued. "He has money of his own. He has a house in Park Lane, a large estate in Suffolk, and so forth."

"He is riddled with debt. That's why he sold me the bowl."

She didn't know what bowl, but humiliation burned in her stomach along with the whiskey. She'd been so careful when the offers had come thick and fast after Mrs. Barrington's death—she liked to laugh that a young widow who'd just come into a good fortune must be, to misquote Jane Austen, in want of a husband.

"I'm not a fool, my lord. I realize that much of my charm comes from the money now attached to me."

His eyes were warm, their gold the same color as the whiskey.

"No, it doesn't."

The simple phrase thawed her. "If this letter is true, then I am in an untenable position."

"Why? You are rich. You can do whatever you like."

Beth went silent. Her world had turned topsy-turvy the day Mrs. Barrington had died and left her house in Belgrave Square, her fortune, her servants, and all her worldly goods to Beth, as Mrs. Barrington had no living relation. The money was all Beth's to do with as she liked.

Wealth meant freedom. Beth had never had freedom in her life, and she supposed another reason she'd welcomed Mather's proposal was that he and his aunt could help her ease into the world of London Society as something more than a drudge. She'd been a drudge for so very long.

Married women were supposed to look the other way at their husbands' affairs. Thomas had said this was balderdash, rules thought up by gentlemen so that they could do as they liked. But then, Thomas had been a good man.

The man sitting next to her couldn't be called good by any stretch of the imagination. He and his brothers had terrible reputations. Even Beth, sheltered by Mrs. Barrington for the last nine years, knew that. There were whispers of sordid affairs and stories of the scandalous separation of Lord Mac Mackenzie from his wife, Lady Isabella. There had also been rumors five years ago about the Mackenzies' involvement in the death of a courtesan, but Beth couldn't remember the details. The case had gained the attention of Scotland Yard, and all four brothers had removed themselves from the country for a time.

No, the Mackenzies were by no means considered "good" men. Then why should a man like Lord Ian Mackenzie bother to warn nobody Beth Ackerley that she was about to marry an adulterer?

"You could always marry me," Lord Ian said abruptly.

Beth blinked. "I beg your pardon?"

"I said, you could marry me. I don't give a damn about your fortune."

"My lord, why on earth should you ask me to marry you?"

"Because you have beautiful eyes."

"How do you know? You've not once looked at them."

"I know."

Her breath hurt, and she wasn't sure whether to laugh or cry. "Do you do this often? Warn a young lady about her fiancé, then turn about and offer to marry her yourself? Obviously the tactic hasn't worked, or you'd have a string of wives dogging your footsteps."

Ian looked away slightly, his hand coming up to massage his temple, as though he had a headache coming on. He was a madman, she reminded herself. Or at least, he'd grown up in an asylum for madmen. So why did she not fear to sit here alone with him, when no one in the world knew where she was?

Perhaps because she'd seen lunatics in Thomas's charity work in the East End, kept by families who could barely manage them. Poor souls, they'd been, some of them kept roped to their beds. Lord Ian was a long way from being a poor soul.

She cleared her throat. "It is very kind of you, my lord."

Ian's hand closed to a tight fist on the arm of his chair. "If I marry you, Mather can't touch you."

"If I married you it would be the scandal of the century."

"You would survive it."

Beth stared at the soprano on the stage, suddenly remembering that gossip painted the large-bosomed lady as a paramour of Lord Cameron Mackenzie, another of Ian's older brothers. "If anyone has seen me dive in here with you, my reputation is already ruined."

"Then you will have nothing to lose."

Beth could stand up in a huff, point her nose in the air as Mrs. Barrington had taught her, and march out. Mrs. Barrington had said she'd slapped a good many would-be suitors in her time, though Beth would leave off the slap. She couldn't imagine Lord Ian being fazed by any blow she could land, anyway.

"If I said yes, what would you do?" she asked in true curiosity. "Balk and try to talk your way out of it?"

"I would find a bishop, pry a license out of him, and make him marry us tonight."

She widened her eyes in mock horror. "What, no wedding gown, no bridesmaids? What about all the flowers?"

"You were married once before."

"So that ought to have satisfied my need for white gowns and lilies of the valley? I must warn you that ladies are quite particular about their weddings, my lord. You might want to know that in case you decide to propose to another lady in the next half hour."

The touch had her heart pounding and heat washing to every limb. He sat too close, his fingertips so warm through his gloves. It would be a simple thing to tilt her head back and kiss him.

"You are ten times higher than I am, my lord. If I married you it would be a misalliance never to be forgotten."

"Your father was a viscount."

"Oh, yes. I had forgotten about dear, dear Father."

Beth knew exactly how real her father's claim to be a viscount had been, exactly how well her father had acted the part.

Lord Ian drew a thin curl between his fingers, straightening it. He let it go, his eyes flickering as it bounced against her forehead. He drew the curl out again, watching it bounce back, and again. His concentration unnerved her; the closeness of his body unnerved her still more. At the same time, her own wanton body was responding.

"You shall take all the spring out of it," she said. "My maid will be so disappointed."

Ian blinked, then returned his hand to the arm of his chair as though having to force it.

"Did you love your husband?"

This bizarre encounter with Lord Ian was the sort of thing she would have had a good laugh over with Thomas. But Thomas was gone, years ago, and she was alone.

"With all my heart."

"I wouldn't expect love from you. I can't love you back."

Beth plied her fan to her hot face, her heart stumbling. "Hardly flattering, my lord, for a woman to hear a man won't fall in love with her. She likes to believe she will be the center of his abject devotion."

Mather had said he'd be devoted. The crumpled letter burned her again.

"Not *won't*. I can't love you."

"I beg your pardon?" She'd been using the phrase so often tonight.

"I am incapable of love. I will not offer it to you."

Beth wondered what was more heartbreaking, the words

themselves or the flat tone of voice with which he delivered them. "Perhaps you simply haven't found the right lady, my lord. Everyone falls in love sooner or later."

"I have taken women as lovers, but never loved them."

Beth's face heated. "You make no sense, my lord. If you don't care about my fortune or whether I love you, why on earth do you wish to marry me?"

Ian reached for the curl again as though he couldn't stop himself. "Because I want to bed you."

Beth knew in that instant that she was not a true lady, and never would be. A true lady would have fallen out of her chair in a gentle swoon or screamed down the opera house. Instead, Beth leaned into Ian's touch, liking it. "Do you?"

His hand loosened more curls, rendering the maid's work useless. "You were a vicar's wife, respectable, the sort to be married. Otherwise, I would offer a liaison."

Beth resisted rubbing her face against his glove. "Have I got this right? You want me to come to your bed, but because I was once a respectable married lady, you must marry me in order to get me there?"

"Yes."

She gave a half-hysterical laugh. "My dear Lord Ian, don't you think that a bit extreme? Once you'd had me in your bed, you'd still be married to me."

"I planned to bed you more than once."

It sounded so logical when he said it. His deep voice slid through her senses, tempting her, finding the passionate woman who'd discovered how much she loved touching a man's body and having that man touch her.

Ladies were not supposed to enjoy the marriage bed, so she'd been told. Thomas had said that was nonsense, and he'd taught her what a woman could feel. If he'd not taught her so well, she reflected, she'd not be sitting here boiling with need for Lord Ian Mackenzie.

"You do realize, my lord, that I am engaged to another man? I have only your word that he is a philanderer."

"I will give you time to make inquiries about Mather

and put your affairs in order. Would you prefer to live in London or at my estate in Scotland?"

Beth wanted to lay her head back on her chair and laugh and laugh. This was too absurd, and at the same time dismayingly tempting. Ian was attractive; she was alone. He was rich enough not to care about her little fortune, and he made no secret that he wanted to enjoy carnal knowledge of her. But if she truly knew so little about Lyndon Mather, she knew nothing at all about Ian Mackenzie.

"I'm still puzzled," she managed to say. "A friendly warning about Sir Lyndon is one thing, but to warn me and then offer me marriage in the space of minutes is another. Do you always make up your mind so quickly?"

"Yes."

" 'If it were done when 'tis done, then 'twere well it were done quickly'? That sort of thing?"

"You can refuse."

"I think I should."

"Because I'm a madman?"

She gave another breathless laugh. "No, because it is too enticing, and because I've drunk whiskey, and I should return to Sir Lyndon and his aunt."

She rose, skirts rustling, but Lord Ian grasped her hand. "Don't go."

The words were harsh, not a plea. The strength left Beth's limbs and she sat down again. It was warm here, and the chair was oh, so comfortable. "I shouldn't stay."

His hand closed over hers. "Watch the opera."

Beth forced her gaze to the stage, where the soprano was singing passionately about a lost lover. Tears gleamed on the singer's face, and Beth wondered if she were thinking about Lord Cameron Mackenzie.

Whoever the woman thought of, the notes of the aria throbbed. "It's beautiful," Beth whispered.

"I can play this piece note for note," Ian said, his breath warm in her ear. "But I cannot capture its soul."

"Oh." She squeezed his hand, hurt for him welling up inside her.

Ian almost said, *Teach me to hear it as you do*, but he knew that was impossible.

She was like rare porcelain, he thought, delicate beauty with a core of steel. Cheap porcelain crumbled to dust or shattered, but the best pieces survived until they reached the hands of a collector who would care for them.

Beth closed her eyes to listen, her enticing curls trembling at her forehead. He liked how her hair unraveled, like silk from a tapestry.

The soprano ended the piece on another long, clear note. Beth clapped spontaneously, smiling, eyes glowing with appreciation. Ian had learned, under Mac's and Cameron's tutoring, how to applaud when a piece stopped, but he never understood why. Beth seemed to have no trouble understanding, and responding to, the joy of the music.

When she looked up at him with tears in her blue eyes, he leaned down and kissed her.

She started, her hands coming up to push him away. But she rested her hands on his shoulders instead and made a soft noise of surrender.

He needed her body under his tonight. He wanted to watch her eyes soften with desire, her cheeks flush with pleasure. He wanted to rub the sweet berry between her legs and make her wet, he wanted to drive into her until he released, and then he wanted to do it all over again.

He'd wake with her head on his pillow and kiss her until she opened her eyes. He'd feed her breakfast and watch her smile as she took food from his hand.

He drew his tongue across her lower lip. She tasted of honey and whiskey, sweet spice. He felt her pulse pounding beneath his fingertips, her breath scalding his skin. He wanted that hot breath on his arousal, which was already hard and aching for her. He wanted her to touch her lips to it like she touched them to his mouth.

She wanted this—no maidenly vapors, no shrinking away from him. Beth Ackerley knew what it was to be with a man, and she liked it. His body throbbed with possibilities.

"We should stop," she whispered.

"Do you want to stop?"

"Now that you mention it, not really."

"Then why?" His lips brushed her mouth as he spoke. She tasted whiskey on his tongue, felt the firm brush of his lips, the roughness of his chin. He had a man's mouth, a commanding mouth.

"I'm sure there are a dozen reasons why we should stop. I confess I can't think of any good ones at the moment."

His fingers were strong. "Come home with me tonight."

Beth wanted to. Oh, she wanted to. Joy shot through her entire body, a painful ache she'd thought she'd never feel again.

"I can't," she almost moaned.

"You can."

"I wish . . ." She imagined the newspapers blazing the gossip all over London tomorrow. *Heiress Abandons Fiancé for Sordid Affair with Lord Ian Mackenzie.* Her origins were murky—would anyone be surprised? *Blood will out,* they'd say. *Wasn't her mother no better than she ought to be?*

"You can," Ian repeated firmly.

Beth closed her eyes, trying to press aside sweet temptation. "Stop asking me. . . ."

The door of the box banged open, and harsh, gravelly tones cut through the audience's thunderous applause.

"Ian, damn it, you were supposed to be watching Daniel. He's down dicing with the coachmen again, and you know he always loses."

Chapter 3

A giant walked into the box. He was bigger than Ian and had the same dark red hair and eyes like chips of topaz. His left cheek bore a deep, angry scar, a gash made long ago. It was easy to imagine this man fighting with fists or knives, like a thug.

He had no trouble pinning Beth with his gaze. "Ian, who the devil is *she*?"

"Lyndon Mather's fiancée," Lord Ian answered.

The man stared at Beth in amazement, then burst out laughing. The laugh was large, like he was, deep and booming. Some of the audience looked up in annoyance.

"Good on you, Ian." The man clapped his brother on the back. "Absconding with Mather's fiancée. You do the lass a favor." He looked Beth over with bold eyes. "You don't want to marry Mather, love," he said to Beth. "The man's disgusting."

"It seems everyone knows that but me," Beth said faintly.

"He's a slimy bastard, desperate to get into Hart's circle. Thinks we'll like him if he tells us he enjoys reliving his days of schoolboy punishments. You're well rid of him, lass."

Beth could hardly breathe. She should leave in a huff, not listen to things no ladies should listen to, but Ian's hand was still laced firmly through hers. Besides, they didn't try to comfort her with banalities, tell her pretty lies. They could be making up all this to part her from Mather, but why the devil should they?

"Ian will never remember to introduce us," the giant said. "I'm Cameron. And you are?"

"Mrs. Ackerley," Beth stammered.

"You don't sound certain of that."

Beth fanned herself. "I was when I came in here."

"If you're Mather's fiancée, why are you in here kissing Ian?"

"I was just asking myself that same question."

"Cam," Ian said. The quiet word cut through the noise as the crowd waited for the next act. There was no drama on the stage now, but plenty in Ian Mackenzie's box. "Shut up."

Cameron stared at his brother. Then his brows rose and he dropped into a chair on Beth's other side. He pulled a cigar from the box next to him and struck a match.

A gentleman should ask a lady's leave before he smokes. Mrs. Barrington's tones rang in her head. Neither Cameron nor Ian seemed worried about Mrs. Barrington's rules.

"Didn't you say someone called Daniel was dicing with coachmen?" Beth asked him.

Cameron touched the flame to the end of the cigar and puffed smoke. "Daniel, my son. He'll be all right if he doesn't cheat."

"I should go home." Beth started to rise again, but Ian's hand on her arm stopped her.

"Not with Mather."

"No. Heavens, no. I never want to see the man again."

Cameron chuckled. "She's a wise woman, Ian. She can go home in my coach."

"No," Beth said quickly. "I'll have the porter fetch me a hansom cab."

Ian's fingers clamped down. "Not in a hansom. Not alone."

"Me climbing into a coach with the pair of you would be the scandal of the year. Even if you two were the archbishops of Canterbury and York."

Ian's gaze fixed on her as though he had no idea what she was talking about. Cameron threw back his head and laughed.

"She's worth stealing, Ian," he said around his cigar. "But she's right. I'll lend you the coach and my man will take care of you, if I can find him. My own fault for employing a Romany as a manservant. They're blasted hard to tame."

Ian didn't want her to go alone; she saw that in his eyes. She thought of how he'd played with her curls—proprietary, possessive, like Mather with his Chinese pottery.

She'd check on the information in Ian's letter. She'd send Mrs. Barrington's wheezing, gossipy butler around to pry tales out of other gossipy servants. The Mackenzie brothers *could* be part of some mad and improbable conspiracy to ruin Mather, but she had the awful feeling they told the truth.

Below them the next act started with a fanfare. Ian rubbed his temple as though it gave him a headache. Cameron stubbed out his cigar and noisily exited the box.

"My lord? Are you all right?"

Ian's gaze remained remote as he continued to absently rub his forehead. Beth put her hand on his arm. Ian didn't respond, but he stopped rubbing his temple and rested his large hand on hers.

He didn't follow the action on the stage, didn't try to continue his conversation with Beth, didn't move back to kissing her. It was as though his mind had moved somewhere she couldn't follow. His body was very much present, though, his hand heavy and strong. She studied the sharp profile of his face, the high cheekbones, the square jaw. A woman would want to run her hands through his thick hair when she held him in bed. It would be warm, damp with sweat as he lay heavy-limbed on top of her. Beth dared to reach up and smooth his hair back from his forehead.

Ian's gaze snapped to her. For one instant, he pinned her with his stare. Then his eyes slid sideways. Beth stroked his hair again. He sat still under her touch, quivering with tension like a wild animal.

They sat this way, Beth lightly smoothing his hair, Ian's body tight, until Cameron returned with a dark-complexioned man in tow. Cameron looked at Ian in surprise, and Ian rose in silence, forcing Beth's hand to slide away.

Beth scanned the theatre before Ian led her out, followed by Cameron. In a box across the vast room, Mather sat deep in conversation with Lord and Lady Beresford. He never noticed Beth or saw her leaving the box.

~~~

"Mackenzie! I'll kill you. Do you hear me?"

Ian scooped up warm bathwater and sloshed it over his hair and down his neck. He thought of Beth's hand on his hair, her soothing fingers. Ian didn't always like to be touched, but with Beth he'd stilled, willing to take her offering. He imagined her stroking his hair while she lay next to him in bed, her warm scent all over him. He wanted Beth's lush body tangled in his sheets, her hair unwinding from its tight curls, her blue eyes half closed in pleasure. He wanted her with a deep intensity that hadn't gone away, and even now his organ stiffened under the water.

The annoying voice outside shattered his fantasy. The threats got louder the nearer they came until the bath chamber door burst open to reveal Lyndon Mather struggling against two of Ian's footmen. They were Scots lads who'd come with Ian to his hired house in London and looked pleased that at last they had someone against whom to strain their muscles.

Ian shifted his gaze over the three of them and returned it to the muscular calf he'd rested on the side of the tub. The footmen released Mather but hovered warily beside him.

"You cheated me out of that bowl, but it wasn't enough for you, was it, Mackenzie? Beth Ackerley is worth a hundred thousand guineas, man. *One hundred thousand.*"

Ian studied the twisting dark hairs that wound down his leg. "She's worth a damned sight more than that."

"You mean she has more?" the idiot Mather asked. "I'll sue you. I'll have you for cheating me out of all that money."

Ian closed his eyes, seeking his visions of Beth. "Write to Hart's solicitor."

"Don't hide behind your brother, you coward. I'll ruin you. London will be too hot to hold you. You'll be running back to Inverness with your tail between your legs, you dung-eating, sheep-buggering, Scots pig."

The footmen growled in unison. Mather yanked a small object out of his pocket and hurled it at the bathtub. Something plopped into the water and sank to the bottom with a soft clink.

"I'll sue you for the price of that, too."

Ian flicked his fingers at the footmen, sending droplets of water over the marble floor. "Throw him out."

The lads whirled on Mather, but he turned on his heel and stomped away. The two footmen followed, and when they'd gone, Curry slunk into the bathroom and closed the door.

"Whew," the valet said, wiping his brow. "Thought 'e would shoot you for certain."

"Not here. He'd do it in a dark alley, in my back."

"Maybe you should leave town for a spell then, guv."

Ian didn't answer. He thought of the short letter from Mrs. Ackerley he'd received this afternoon.

My lord, I thank you for your kind intervention that saved me from a step that would have caused me great regret. As you may no doubt soon read in the newspapers, the betrothal between myself and the other party concerned is at an end.

I also wish to thank you for condescending to propose marriage to me, which I now realize was to keep my reputation from ruin. I know you will understand and not be offended when I say I must I decline your generous offer.

*I have decided to use the fortune that fate bestowed
upon me to travel. By the time you receive this letter, I
will have departed for Paris with a companion, where
I intend to make a study of painting, a skill I have
always wished to learn. Thank you again for your kindness to me and for your advice.*

I remain yours sincerely,
Beth Ackerley

"We're going to Paris," Ian said to Curry.

Curry blinked. "Are we, guv?"

Ian fished out what Mather had thrown into the bathtub,
a narrow gold band with tiny diamonds on it. "Mather is
cheap. She should have a wide band filled with sapphires,
blue like her eyes."

He felt the pressure of Curry's stare. "I'll take your
word, m'lord. Shall I pack?"

"We won't leave for a few days. I have some business to
attend to first."

Curry waited for Ian to indicate what business, but Ian
returned to studying the ring in silence. He lost himself
contemplating the sparkle of every facet on each tiny diamond until the water turned cold, and Curry worriedly
pulled the plug on the drain.

⟞⟝

Detective Inspector Lloyd Fellows paused before he rang
the bell of the Park Lane home of Sir Lyndon Mather.
Detective *Inspector*, Fellows reminded himself, recently
risen from the subordinate gloom of sergeant despite the
last chief's determination to keep Fellows humble.

But all good chief inspectors were called to peaceful
retirement, and the incoming chief had found it incredible
that Fellows had languished so long as a mere sergeant.

So why had Fellows risked all by rushing to Park Lane
at Mather's summons? He'd read the note in rising excitement, burned it, then left the office. He'd grated his teeth at

the slowness of hansom cabs until he stood on the doorstep of the palatial house.

Fellows hadn't bothered to mention the journey to his chief. Anything to do with the Mackenzies was verboten to Detective Fellows, but Fellows reasoned that what his chief didn't know would not hurt him.

A stiff butler with his nose in the air answered the door and directed Fellows into an equally stiff reception room. Someone had crammed the room with draped tables and costly objets d'art, including photographs in silver frames of stiff people.

The reception room said, *We have money*, as though living in Park Lane hadn't already conveyed the same. Fellows knew, however, that Sir Lyndon Mather was a bit up against it. Mather's investments had been volatile, and he needed a large infusion of cash to help him out. He'd been about to marry a widow of means, which ought to have kept him from bankruptcy. But a couple of days ago, a notice had appeared in the newspaper that the wedding was off. Mather must be feeling the pinch of that.

The butler returned after Fellows had paced for half an hour, and he led him to a lavish sitting room across the hall. More draped tables, gilded knickknacks, and people in silver frames.

Mather, a blond and handsome man that the French might call debonair, came forward and stuck out his hand.

"Well met, Inspector. I won't invite you to sit down. I imagine that when you hear what I've got to say, you'll want to hurry out and make arrests."

Fellows hid his annoyance, hating when other people told him his job. The average man obtained his knowledge of Scotland Yard from fiction or the newspapers, neither of which was very accurate.

"Whatever you say, sir," Fellows said.

"Lord Ian Mackenzie's gone to Paris. Early this morning. My butler had it from my footman, who walks out with a girl who worked in Lord Ian's kitchen. What do you make of that?"

Fellows tried to conceal his impatience. He knew Ian Mackenzie had gone to Paris, because he made it his business to know exactly what Lord Ian Mackenzie was doing at all times. He had no interest in servants' gossip, but he answered, "Has he indeed?"

"You know about the murder in Covent Garden last night?" Mather watched him carefully.

Of course Fellows knew about the murder. It wasn't his case, but he'd been briefed on it early this morning. Body of a woman found in her room at a boardinghouse near the church, stabbed to death with her own sewing scissors. "Yes, I heard of it."

"Do you know who went to that house last night?" Mather smiled triumphantly. "Ian Mackenzie, that's who."

Fellows's heart started to race, his blood tingling as hotly as when he made love to a woman. "How do you know that, sir?"

"I followed him, didn't I? Bloody Mackenzies think they can have everything their own way."

"You were following him? Why was that, sir?" Fellows kept his tone calm, but he found breathing difficult. *At last, at long last.*

"Why isn't important. Are you interested in the details?"

Fellows removed a small notebook from his coat pocket, opened it, and retrieved a pencil from the same pocket. "Go on."

"He got into his coach in the wee hours of the morning and went to Covent Garden. He stopped at the corner of a tiny lane, coach too big to go into it. He went down the lane on foot, entered a house, stayed maybe ten minutes, then hurried out again. Then he goes to Victoria Station and takes the first train out. I returned home to hear my butler say that Mackenzie had gone to France, and then I opened my morning paper and read about the murder. I put two and two together, and decided that rather than tell a journalist, I should consult the police."

Mather beamed like a schoolboy proud to tattle on

another schoolboy. Fellows digested the information and put it with what he already knew.

"How do you know Lord Ian entered the same house where the murder was committed?"

Mather reached into his frock coat and pulled out a piece of paper. "I wrote down the address when I followed him. I wondered whom he was visiting. His fancy piece, I thought. I wanted to give the information to Mrs. . . . to another person."

He handed the paper to Fellows. *Number 23 St. Victor Court.* The very address at which a former prostitute called Lily Martin had been found dead early this morning.

Fellows tried to keep his excitement in check as he slid the paper into his notebook. He'd been trying to land Ian Mackenzie in the dock for five years, and maybe this new development would let him.

He calmed himself. He'd have to pursue this carefully— no mistakes, make certain everything was proved beyond the shadow of a doubt. When he presented the evidence to his chief, it would have to be something that Fellows's superiors couldn't dismiss, couldn't ignore, couldn't keep quiet, no matter how much weight the duke, Hart Mackenzie, tried to throw around.

"If you don't mind, sir," Fellows said, "please keep this information to yourself. I will act upon it, rest assured, but I don't want him warned. All right?"

"Of course, of course." Mather tapped his nose and winked. "I'm your man."

"Why did you quarrel with him?" Fellows asked, putting away his notebook and pencil.

Mather's hands balled in his pockets. "That's rather personal."

"Something to do with breaking your engagement with Mrs. Ackerley?" Who had also gone to Paris, Fellows knew from checking up on Mather.

Mather went scarlet. "Blackguard stole her out from under my nose, telling her some pack of lies. The man is a snake."

Likely the lady had found out about Mather's longing for his old school days of corporal punishment. Fellows had learned that Mather kept a house of ladies where he indulged in that sort of thing. Inspector Fellows liked to be thorough.

Mather looked away. "I shouldn't like that to get about. The newspapers . . ."

"I understand, sir." Fellows tapped his nose in imitation of Mather. "It will be between us."

Mather nodded, his face still red. Fellows left the house in great spirits, then returned to Scotland Yard and requested leave.

After five long years, he at last saw a chink in the armor that was the Mackenzie family. He would put his finger in the chink and rip their armor to shreds.

~~~

"How very vexing." Beth carried the newspaper to better light at the window, but the tiny print said the same thing.

"What is, ma'am?" Her newly hired companion, Katie Sullivan, a young Irish girl who'd grown up in Beth's husband's parish, looked up from sorting the gloves and ribbons Beth had bought from a Parisian boutique.

Beth threw down the newspaper and lifted her satchel of art things. "Nothing important. Shall we go?"

Katie fetched wraps and parasols, muttering darkly, " 'Tis a long way up that hill to watch you stare at a blank piece of paper."

"Perhaps today I will be inspired."

Beth and Katie left the narrow house Beth had hired and climbed into the small buggy her French footman had run to fetch. She could have afforded a large carriage with a coachman to drive her, but Beth was frugal by habit. She saw no reason to keep an extravagant conveyance she didn't need.

Today she drove distractedly, her gloved hands fidgety, much to the horse's and Katie's annoyance.

The newspaper she'd been reading was the *Telegraph*

from London. She took several Paris newspapers as well, her father having taught her to speak and read French fluently, but she liked to keep up with what was going on at home.

What vexed Beth today was a story about how lords Ian and Cameron Mackenzie had nearly come to blows in a restaurant, fighting about a woman. The woman in question was a famous soprano, the very one who'd enchanted Beth at Covent Garden the week before. Many people had witnessed the event and related it to the newspapers with glee.

Beth shook the reins impatiently, and the horse tossed his head. While Beth didn't regret turning down Lord Ian's proposal, it was a bit galling to find that he'd been quarreling with his brother over the heavy-bosomed soprano shortly after Beth had refused him. She'd have liked him to feel a *little* bit sorry.

She tried to forget the story and concentrated on maneuvering through the wide Parisian boulevards that became the jumbled streets of Montmartre. At the top of the hill she found a boy to watch the horse and buggy, and she trekked to the little green she liked, Katie grumbling behind her.

Montmartre still had the feeling of a village, with narrow, crooked streets, window boxes bursting with summer flowers, and trees dotting slopes down to the city. It was a far cry from the·wide avenues and huge public parks of Paris, which, Beth understood, was why artists and their models had flocked to Montmartre. That and the rents were cheap.

Beth set up her easel in her usual place and sat down, pencil poised over a clean piece of paper. Katie plopped onto the bench next to her, listlessly watching the artists, would-be artists, and hangers-on who roamed the streets.

This was the third day Beth had sat here studying the vista of Paris, the third day her paper had remained blank. She'd realized after her initial excitement of purchasing pencils, paper, and easel that she had no idea how to draw. Still, she'd come up the hill each afternoon and set out her things. If nothing else, she and Katie were getting plenty of exercise.

"Do you think she's an artist's model?" Katie asked.

She jerked her chin at a lovely red-haired woman who strolled with several other ladies on the other side of the street. The woman wore a pale gown with a gossamer overskirt pulled back to reveal a beribboned underskirt. Her small hat was tastefully trimmed with flowers and lace and tipped provocatively over her eyes. Her parasol matched her dress, and she carried it at a becoming angle.

She had an air of allure about her that made heads turn when she passed. It wasn't anything she did on purpose, Beth decided with a touch of envy. Everything about her enticed. She was simply a joy to look at.

"I couldn't say," Beth replied after an all-over surveillance. "But she certainly is very pretty."

"I wish I were beautiful enough to be a model." Katie sighed. "Not that I would. Me dear old mother would whip the skin off me. Dreadful wicked ladies they must be, taking off their clothes to be painted."

"Perhaps." The woman disappeared around the corner with her cluster of friends, lost to sight.

"And what about *him*? He looks like an artist."

Beth glanced to where Katie indicated, and she froze.

The man didn't have an easel—he lounged on a bench with one foot on it and moodily watched a twitchy young man glob paint on a canvas. He was a big man, barely fitting on the delicate stone bench. He had dark hair touched with red, a square, hard face, and enticingly broad shoulders.

Beth's breath poured back into her lungs as she realized the man was not, in fact, Lord Ian Mackenzie. He looked very much like Ian, though; the same forbidding face, the same air of power, the same set of jaw. But this man's hair shone redder in the sunlight, he having set his hat on the bench next to him.

He was definitely another Mackenzie. She'd read that Hart, the Duke of Kilmorgan, had traveled to Rome on some government business, she'd met Lord Cameron in London, so by process of elimination, this must be Lord Mac, the famous artist.

As though he felt her scrutiny, Lord Mac turned his head and looked straight at her.

Beth flushed and snapped her eyes back to her blank paper. Breathing hard, she put her pencil to the page and drew an awkward line. She let herself become absorbed in the line and the next one, until a shadow fell over her paper.

"Not like that," a deep voice rumbled.

Beth jumped and looked up past a watered silk waistcoat and a carelessly tied cravat to harsh eyes very much like Ian's. The difference was that Mac's gaze fully met hers instead of shifting away like an elusive sunbeam.

"You're holding the pencil wrong." Lord Mac put a large gloved hand over hers and turned her wrist upward.

"That feels awkward."

"You'll get used to it." Mac sat himself down next to her, taking up every spare inch of the bench. "Let me show you."

He guided her hand over the paper, shading the line she'd already drawn until it looked like a curve of the tree in front of her.

"Amazing," she said. "I've never taken drawing lessons, you see."

"Then what are you doing out here with an easel?"

"I thought I'd give it a try."

Mac arched his brows, but he kept his hand on hers and helped her draw another line.

He was flirting with her, she realized. She was alone with only a female companion, she'd been blatantly staring at him, and this was Paris. He must have thought she wanted a liaison.

The last thing she needed was to be propositioned by yet another Mackenzie. Perhaps the newspapers would print reports of Ian and Mac fighting over *her*.

But the hand cupping hers didn't give her the same frisson of warmth that Ian's had. She dreamed about Ian's slow, sensual lips on hers every night, and then she'd jump awake, sweating and tangled in the sheets, her body aching.

She glanced sideways at Mac. "I met your brother Lord Ian at Covent Garden last week."

Mac's gaze snapped to her. His eyes were not quite so golden as Ian's, more copper-colored with flecks of brown. "You met Ian?"

"Yes, he did me a kindness. I met Lord Cameron as well, but only briefly."

Mac's eyes narrowed. "*Ian* did you a kindness?"

"He saved me from making a grave mistake."

"What kind of mistake?"

"Nothing I wish to discuss on top of Montmartre."

"Why not? Who the devil are you?"

Katie leaned around from Beth's other side. "Well, that's a bloody cheek."

"Hush, Katie. My name is Mrs. Ackerley."

Mac scowled. "I've never heard of you. How did you manage to scrape an acquaintance with my brother?"

Katie glared at Mac with Irish frankness. "She's a bloody heiress, that's who she is. And a kind lady what doesn't have to take rudeness from the likes of forward gentlemen in a French park."

"Katie," Beth admonished her quietly. "I beg your pardon, my lord."

Mac's sharp gaze flicked to Katie, then back to Beth. "Are you certain it was Ian?"

"He was introduced to me as Lord Ian Mackenzie," Beth said. "I suppose he could have been an impostor in an excellent disguise, but that never occurred to me." Mac didn't look impressed with her humor. "He never would look directly at me."

Mac released her hand, tension draining. "That was my brother."

"Didn't she just say so?" Katie demanded.

Mac looked away, studying the passersby and the would-be artists struggling to make sense of what they saw. When he switched his gaze back to Beth, she was startled to see moisture on his lashes.

"Put your terrier on a lead, Mrs. Ackerley. You say you don't draw. Would you like me to give you lessons?"

"As a reward for my rudeness?"

"It would entertain me."

She stared in surprise. "People demand your paintings left and right. Why would you give a novice like me drawing lessons?"

"For the novelty of it. Paris bores me."

"I find it quite exciting. If it bores you, why are you here?"

Mac shrugged, the gesture so much like Ian's. "When one is an artist, one comes to Paris."

"One does, does one?"

A muscle moved in his jaw. "I find people of true talent here and try to give them a leg up."

"I have no talent at all."

"Even so."

"It will also give you a chance to discover why Lord Ian would bother with someone like me," she suggested.

A smile spread over Mac's face, one so dazzling Beth imagined most women who saw it fell at his feet. "Would I do such a thing, Mrs. Ackerley?"

"I do believe you would, my lord. Very well, then. I accept."

Mac stood up and retrieved his hat from where he'd set it on the ground. "Be here tomorrow at two o'clock, if it's not raining." He tipped the hat to Beth and made a slight bow. "Good day, Mrs. Ackerley. And terrier."

He placed the hat on his head and swung away, his coat moving with his stride. Every female head turned to watch him as he passed.

Katie fanned herself with Beth's sketchbook. "He's a good-looking man, no doubt. Even if he is rude."

"I admit he is interesting," Beth said.

Why the man wanted to find out all about her, she didn't know, but she intended to use him to learn all about Lord Ian.

You are entirely too curious, Beth my gel, Mrs. Barrington had said to her often. *A very unattractive trait in a young lady.*

Beth agreed with her. She'd vowed to have nothing

more to do with the Mackenzie family, and here she was accepting an appointment with Lord Mac in hopes of gaining more knowledge about his younger brother. She smiled to herself, knowing she looked forward to the next afternoon with too much interest.

But when Beth turned up at Montmartre again on the morrow, the sun sailed brightly in the sky, the clocks struck two, and Lord Mac was nowhere to be seen.

Chapter 4

"See what I mean?" Katie said after a quarter of an hour had gone by. "Rude."

Beth fought down her disappointment. She wanted to wholeheartedly agree with Katie and say a few choice phrases she'd learned in the workhouse, but she restrained herself.

"We can hardly expect him to remember such a thing. Giving me lessons must be a trivial matter to him."

Katie snorted. "You're a lady of consequence now. He has no call to treat us like this."

Beth forced a laugh. "If Mrs. Barrington had left me only ten shillings, you wouldn't consider me a lady of consequence."

Katie waved that aside. "Anyway, me father wasn't as rude as this lordship, and he were *drunk* as a lord all the time."

Beth, familiar with drunken fathers, didn't answer. As she gazed across the square again, she noticed the lovely young woman she and Katie had speculated about yesterday staring at them.

The lady looked at her for a long while from under her parasol, her gaze pensive. Beth returned the look with lifted brows.

The lady gave a determined nod and started for them. "May I give you a bit of advice, my dear?" she asked when she reached Beth. Her voice was English and very well-bred, no trace of the Continent about her. She had a pale, pointed face, finely curled red hair under a tip-tilted hat, and wide green eyes. Again, Beth was aware of her arresting quality, the indefinable something that drew all eyes to her.

The lady went on. "If you are waiting for his lordship Mac Mackenzie, I must tell you that he is extremely unreliable. He might be lying in a meadow studying the way a horse gallops, or he might have climbed to the top of a church tower to paint the view. I imagine he's forgotten all about his assignation with you, but that is Mac all over."

"Absentminded, is he?" Beth asked.

"Not so much absentminded as bloody-minded. Mac does as he pleases, and I thought it only fair that you know right away."

The lady's diamond earrings shimmered as she trembled, and she grasped her parasol so tightly Beth feared the delicate handle would break.

"Are you his model?" Beth didn't really think so, but this was Paris. Even the most respectable Englishwomen were known to throw propriety to the wind once they set foot on its avenues.

The lady glanced around and sat down next to Beth in the very spot Lord Mac had occupied yesterday. "No, my dear, I am not his model. I am very unfortunately his wife."

Now this was much more interesting. Lord Mac and Lady Isabella were separated, estranged, and their very public breakup had been a ninety-days scandal. Mrs. Barrington had savored every drop of the newspaper reports with malicious glee.

That had been three years ago. Yet Lady Isabella sat in agitated anger as she confronted a woman she thought had made a tryst with her husband.

"You misunderstand," Beth said. "His lordship offered to give me a drawing lesson because he saw how ignorantly I did it. But he became interested in me only when I told him I was a friend of Lord Ian's."

Isabella looked at her sharply. "Ian?"

Everyone seemed surprised Beth had even spoken to him. "I met him at the opera."

"Did you?"

"He was very kind to me."

Her brows arched. "*Ian* was? You do know, my dear, that he is here."

Beth quickly scanned the green but saw no tall man with dark red hair and unusual eyes. "Where?"

"I mean here in Paris. He arrived this morning, which is likely why Mac didn't come. Or possibly why. One never knows with Mac." Isabella peered at Beth with new interest. "I mean no offense, my dear, but I can't place you. I'm sure Ian has never spoken of you."

"My name is Mrs. Ackerley, but that will mean nothing to you."

"She's an heiress," Katie broke in. "Mrs. Barrington of Belgrave Square left her one hundred thousand guineas and an enormous house."

Isabella smiled, radiating beauty. "Oh, you're *that* Mrs. Ackerley. How delightful." Isabella ran a critical eye over Beth. "You've come to Paris on your own? Oh, darling, that will never do. You must let me take you under my wing. Granted, my set is a bit out of the ordinary, but I'm sure they will be enchanted with you."

"You're very kind, but—"

"Now, don't be shy, Mrs. Ackerley. You must let me help you. You come home with me now, and we shall chat and know all about each other."

Beth opened her mouth to protest, then closed it again.

The Mackenzies had stirred her curiosity, and what better way to learn about Lord Ian than from his own sister-in-law?

"Certainly," she amended. "I shall be delighted."

~

"So, Ian, who is this Mrs. Ackerley?"

Mac leaned across the table and spoke over the strains of the orchestra scraping out a raucous tune. On the stage above Ian and Mac, two women in corsets and petticoats showed their knickers and patted each other's bottoms to the lively music.

Ian drew a long drag of his cigar and followed it with a sip of brandy, enjoying the acrid bite of smoke and the smoothness of the liquor. Mac had a brandy as well, but he only pretended to drink it. Since the day Isabella had left him, Mac hadn't touched a drop of spirits.

"Widow of an East End parish vicar," Ian answered.

Mac stared at him, his copper-colored eyes still. "You're joking."

"No."

Mac watched him a moment longer before he shook his head and took a pull of his cigar. "She certainly seems interested in you. I'm giving her drawing lessons—or I will be once I finish with this damned painting. My model finally turned up out of the blue this morning, gushing about some artist she's been holed up with. I'd use someone else, but Cybele is perfect."

Ian didn't answer. He could easily contrive to be in the studio when Beth's drawing lessons commenced. He would sit next to her and breathe her scent, watch the pulse flutter in her throat and perspiration dampen her skin.

"I asked her to marry me," he said.

Mac choked on cigar smoke. He pulled the cheroot out of his mouth. "Damn it, Ian."

"She refused."

"Good Lord." Mac blinked. "Hart would have apoplexy."

Ian thought of Beth's quick smile and bright way of speaking. Her voice was like music. "Hart will like her."

Mac gave him a dark look. "You recall what happened when I married without Hart's royal blessing? He'd thrash you within an inch of your life."

Ian took another sip of brandy. "Why should he care if I marry?"

"How can you ask that? Thank God he's in Italy." Mac's eyes narrowed. "I am surprised he didn't take you with him."

"He didn't need me."

Hart often took Ian on his expeditions to Rome or Spain, because Ian was not only a genius at languages, but he could remember every single word of every single conversation that went on during negotiations. If there were any dispute, Ian could recall the transaction word for word.

"That means he's gone to see a woman," Mac predicted. "Or on some political venture he doesn't want the rest of us to know about."

"Possibly." Ian never pried too closely into Hart's affairs, knowing he might not be comfortable with what he found.

Ian's thoughts strayed to Lily lying dead in her sitting room, her scissors through her heart. Curry had remained in London at Ian's request, and Ian expected his report any moment.

"You get yourself to Paris, guv," Curry had said as he'd shoved Ian's valise onto the seat of the first-class carriage. "Anyone asks, you left by an earlier train."

Ian had looked away, and Curry slammed the door, exasperated. "Damn it, m'lord, one of these days you're going to have to learn to *lie*."

Mac broke into Ian's thoughts. "So, you followed Mrs. Ackerley to Paris? That speaks of a man who won't take no for an answer."

The words of the letter Beth had sent him ran through his brain once more, overlaid with the taste of her lips. "I intend to use persuasion."

Mac burst out laughing. Heads craned at the noise, but the girls danced on, oblivious, palms firmly on each other's backsides.

"Damn it all, Ian, I must know this woman. I'll have her

start her lessons—you wouldn't know where I can send word to her, do you?"

"Bellamy says she's staying with Isabella."

Mac sat upright, dropping his cigar. Ian rescued it before it could catch the tablecloth on fire and dropped it into a bowl.

"*She's* in Paris?"

For the last three years, since Isabella had departed Mac's house while he lay in a drunken stupor, Mac had not spoken Isabella's name. Nor had he used the words *my wife*.

"Isabella came to Paris four weeks ago," Ian said. "Or so your valet says."

"Hell. Bellamy never told *me*. I'll wring his neck." Mac looked off into the distance, planning his valet's execution. Bellamy was a former pugilist, so it was doubtful Mac's rage would have any impact. "Damnation," Mac said, very softly.

Ian left him alone and watched the dancers. The women had progressed to prancing around without corsets, their breasts small, their nipples the size of pennies. Gentlemen around Ian laughed and applauded.

Ian wondered what Beth's breasts looked like. He remembered the rather plain opera gown she'd worn, dark gray taffeta that covered her to her shoulders.

She'd worn a corset, because all respectable women did, but Ian imagined what a pleasure it would be to unlace it with slow hands. Her corset would be a functional garment, plain linen over whalebone, and she'd blush as it fell away to bare her natural beauty.

Ian felt himself harden, and he lounged back in his seat and closed his eyes. He didn't want to sully the image of Beth with the half-naked dancers, but his thoughts did not allow his erection to go down for quite some time.

~~~

"The things I do for you, guv." Curry dropped his valise on the floor of Ian's hotel bedroom the next morning and collapsed in a chair.

Ian stared into the fire, a cigar in his sweating fingers.

He'd had a bad night after he'd left Mac, the nightmares returning to pull at his brain until he awoke, screaming in the dark.

The French servants had tumbled in, clutching candles and babbling in fear as Ian rocked on the bed, his head in his hands as it throbbed with hideous pain. The pinpoints of light had stabbed in through his eyes, and he'd shouted at them to take the candles away.

He needed Curry and the concoctions he mixed to soothe the headaches and let Ian drift back to sleep. But Curry had been on a train heading through the night toward Paris, and Ian had lain back, sweating and nauseous and alone.

He'd heard what the French servants whispered about him: *Sweet Mary, help us, he's a madman. What if he murders us in our beds?*

He'd got through the rest of last night by thinking erotic thoughts about Beth Ackerley. He thought some now as he closed his eyes and waited for Curry to recover himself. Beth at the opera, her lips under his. The flick of her tongue in his mouth, the press of her fingers against his cheek. The curve of her sweet bottom swaying as he'd helped her into Cameron's coach.

Ian looked up at Curry, whose face was gray with exhaustion. "Well? Did you find out who killed Lily?"

"Oh, certainly, guv. The culprit gave hisself up to me, and I dragged him off to the magistrate. And daisies are growing in the streets and London will never see fog again."

Ian let Curry's words go by, not bothering to understand them. "What did you find out?"

Curry heaved a sigh and hoisted himself out of the chair. "You expect miracles, you know that? So do your bleeding brothers, begging your pardon. I know that when Lord Cameron sent me off to tend you in that joke of an asylum, he expected me to cure you and bring you home."

Ian waited, aware that Curry liked to run on before he got to the point.

Curry snatched up Ian's frock coat from the back of a

chair and started brushing it off. "Gawd, what will you have done to your suits while I was gone?"

"The hotel man looked after them," Ian said, knowing Curry could wail about Ian's clothes for hours. For a man born in the gutters of the East End, Curry was extremely snobbish about Ian's state of dress.

"Well, I hope he hasn't had you wandering the streets in lavender with spotted waistcoats. These frogs have no sense of taste."

"What did you find out?" Ian prompted.

"I'm coming to it. I did just like you said and got into the house like I was common trash looking for a souvenir. There wasn't nothing to find. All ordinary as could be."

"Lily was stabbed to death with her own scissors. That isn't ordinary."

"She didn't fight. I got the constable on watch to tell me that. Looked surprised, not scared."

Ian had thought the same thing. "She knew who it was. Let him in like a regular customer."

"Exactly." Curry rummaged through his pockets and pulled out a paper. "I drew the room like you asked and wrote down everything in it. It was quite a job, trying to do it with the Old Bill following me about."

Ian glanced at Curry's drawing and the lists. "Is this all?"

"Is it all?" Curry demanded of the air. "I drag myself across the continent of Europe, traveling in trains and musty cabs to be his eyes and ears, and he says, 'Is this all?'"

"What else did you find out?"

"A little sympathy wouldn't be amiss, guv. What I put up with, working for you. Any rate, I went all the way to Rome. He's there, has been there for a month, never left."

"He didn't see you?" Ian asked sharply.

"No. I made sure of it. He almost did, but I managed to slip away. That wouldn't have done, would it?"

Ian gazed at the fire, rubbing his temple. Damn headache. He knew bloody well that a man could stay in the Italian states and pay someone to do things for him back in London, just as Ian had done with Curry.

Ian wanted to know the truth, but truth was so dangerous. He rubbed his temple until the tight pain lessened. Thinking of Beth's eyes helped.

"Beth thought you were a detective," Ian remembered.

"Beth?" Curry said sharply.

"Mrs. Ackerley."

"Ah, yes, her. Fiancée of Sir Lyndon Mather. Former fiancée, I should say, after your timely intervention. You call her *Beth*, now, do you? What does she call you?"

"I don't know."

"Ah." Curry nodded sagely. "A bit of advice, guv. Stick with fancy ladies—Paris has dozens of 'em, as you know. You always know where you are with tarts."

Curry was right, and Ian knew it. Courtesans loved Ian, and he never had to worry about being without female companionship. But all the charms of Parisian courtesans couldn't pull him away from his desire for Beth. He thought again of Beth's lips under his, the soft sound she'd made in her throat when he'd kissed her. If he could feel Beth's warmth beside him every night, he wouldn't have the nightmares and the migraines. He was sure of it.

He'd have her in his bed if he had to recruit Curry, Isabella, Mac, and every other person in Paris to get her there.

~

Five mornings after Beth had agreed to share lodgings with Lady Isabella Mackenzie, she was writing letters in her bedchamber when she heard the strains of music below.

Isabella never rose before one—*darling, it's impossible to open one's eyes before that hour.* No one had come up to tell Beth that a visitor had arrived, but she couldn't imagine a thief breaking in to belt out a Chopin sonata in the drawing room.

Beth slid her half-written letter into a drawer and made her way downstairs, liking how the shutters and curtains had been thrown open to let sunshine stream in. Mrs. Barrington had kept the drapes shut tight and the gaslights low, so Beth and the servants had groped their way through the dark, day and night alike.

The double doors to the drawing room stood ajar, and pure, sweet Chopin floated out through the crack. Beth pushed the doors open and paused on the threshold.

Ian Mackenzie sat at Isabella's polished piano, staring at the empty music stand in front of him. His wide shoulders moved as his hands found and played notes, and his booted foot flexed as he worked the damper pedal. Sunlight caught on his dark hair, burning it red.

I can play this piece note for note, he'd said at the opera house. *But I cannot capture its soul.*

He might not think he could capture the soul of this piece either, but the music wove around Beth and drew her to him. She walked across the room to the piano as the notes floated around her, loud and sweet. She could bathe in them.

The music made a little run high on the keyboard, then ended with a low chord that used all of Ian's fingers. He let his hands stay in place, sinews stretching, as the last undulations died away.

Beth pressed her hands together. "That was splendid."

Ian snatched his fingers from the keys. He looked quickly up at Beth and away, then placed his hands back on the keyboard, as though he drew comfort from the feel of the ivory.

"I learned it when I was eleven," he said.

"Quite a prodigy. I don't think I'd even seen a piano when I was eleven."

Ian didn't do all the things a gentleman ought to do: rise when she entered the room, shake hands with her, make sure she sat somewhere comfortable. He should ask after her family, seat himself, and chat about the weather or something equally banal until a quiet and efficient servant brought in a tray of tea. But he remained on the bench, frowning as though trying to remember something.

Beth leaned on the piano and smiled at him. "I'm certain your teachers were impressed."

"No. I was beaten for it."

Beth's smile died. "You were punished for learning a piece perfectly? Rather a strange reaction, isn't it?"

"My father called me a liar because I said I'd only heard it once. I told him I didn't know how to lie, so he said, 'Better be thought a liar, because what you've done is unnatural. I'll teach you never to do it again.'"

A gruff note entered Ian's voice as he echoed the man's timbre as well as his words.

Beth's throat tightened. "That's horrible."

"I was often beaten. I was disrespectful, evasive, difficult to control."

Beth imagined Ian as a boy, his frightened gold eyes looking everywhere but straight at his father while the man shouted at him. Then closing his eyes in pain and fear as the cane came down.

Ian began another piece, this one slow and sonorous. He kept his head half bent, his strong face still as he focused on the keys. His thigh moved as he worked the pedal, his entire body playing the music.

Beth recognized the piece as a piano concerto by Beethoven, one the tutor Mrs. Barrington had hired for Beth had liked. Beth had been a mediocre player, her hands too work-worn and stiff to learn the skill. The tutor had been haughty and mocking of her, but at least he'd never beaten her.

Ian's large fingers skimmed the keyboard, and slow notes filled the room, the sound rich and round. Ian might claim he couldn't find the music's soul, but the strains of it called too vividly to mind the dark days Beth had suffered after her mother's death.

She remembered sitting in a corner in the hospital ward, her arms around her knees, watching as her mother's consumption stole her last breaths. Her beautiful mother, always so frail and frightened, who'd clung to Beth for strength, was now ripped from the life that had terrified her.

The hospital had turned her out after they laid her mother in a pauper's grave. Beth had not wanted to return to the parish workhouse, but her feet had taken her there. She'd known she had nowhere else to go.

They at least had given her a job, since she could speak

well and had a modicum of manners. She'd taught younger children and tried to comfort herself by comforting them, but all too often they fled the workhouse to return to the more lucrative life of crime.

It was only the in-between people like Beth who were trapped. She didn't want to resort to selling her body to survive, feeling nothing but disgust for men who could lust after fifteen-year-old girls. Nor could she find respectable employment as a governess or nanny. She had little education, and middle-class women didn't want someone from a Bethnal Green workhouse taking care of their precious tots.

She'd finally persuaded one of the parish women to find her a typing machine. The woman had eventually produced a thirdhand one whose B and Y keys stuck, and Beth had practiced and practiced on it.

When she got a little older, she reasoned, she could hire herself out as a typist. Perhaps people wouldn't mind her background as long as she worked quickly and efficiently. Or she might write little stories or articles and try to persuade newspapers to buy them. She had no idea how this was done, but it was worth a try.

And then one day, while she was pounding away at the machine, the new vicar of the parish came to call. Beth had been soundly cursing the B key, and Thomas Ackerley had looked at her and laughed.

A tear rolled swiftly down her cheek. She put a quick hand on Ian's, and the piece stumbled to a halt.

"You don't like it," he said, his voice flat.

"I do—only, could you play something a little happier?"

Ian's gaze skimmed past her like a beam of sunlight. "I don't know whether a piece is happy or sad. I just know the notes."

Beth's throat squeezed. If she wasn't careful, she'd start blubbering all over him. She whirled to the music cabinet and dug through sheets until she found something that made her smile.

"How about this?" She brought it back to the piano and spread the music across the stand. "Mrs. Barrington hated the opera—she couldn't understand why anyone wanted to listen to people bellow for hours in a foreign tongue. But she loved Gilbert and Sullivan. They at least speak plain English."

Beth opened the music to the ditty that had made Mrs. Barrington laugh the most. She'd made Beth learn it and play it over and over. Beth had tired of the bouncy rhythms and the absurd words, but now she was grateful for Mrs. Barrington's tastes.

Ian looked at the paper without changing expression. "I can't read music."

Beth had leaned over him without thinking, and now the rosette at her bosom was level with his nose. "No?"

Ian studied the rosette, his eyes taking in every facet of it. "I have to hear it. Play it through for me."

He shifted slightly, giving her about five inches of space on the bench. Beth sat down, her heart hammering. He wasn't about to move, and his body was like a solid wall. This close she felt the hard muscle of his biceps, the length of his thigh against hers.

His amber eyes glittered behind thick lashes as he half turned his head to watch her.

Beth drew a breath. She stretched her arm across his abdomen to reach the lower notes, clumsily played through the intro, and then sang in a shaky voice.

"I am the very model of a modern major-general . . ."

Chapter 5

Ian studied Beth's nimble fingers as they tripped across the keyboard. Her nails were small and rounded, neatly trimmed, her only adornment a silver ring on the little finger of her left hand.

Her soothing alto flowed over him, though he didn't bother to make sense of the words: "I'm very good at integral and differential calculus; I know the scientific names of beings animalculous . . ."

The blue rosette at her bosom rose and fell as she sang, and her elbow slid across his waistcoat as she reached up and down the keyboard. Light blue silk flowed across her lap—no more drab gray for Beth Ackerley. Isabella must have taken her in hand.

One curl fell across her cheek as she sang. He watched it bounce against her skin, watched her mouth pronouncing the lively words. He wanted to take the curl between his lips and pull it straight.

At last the tune lilted upward with her voice: "I am the

very model of a modern major-general." A few tinkling chords, and that was the end.

Beth smiled at him, out of breath. "I haven't practiced in a while. I have no excuse now, since Isabella has this excellent piano."

Ian laid his fingers on the keys where Beth's had been. "Is the song supposed to make sense?"

"Do you mean to say you've never seen *The Pirates of Penzance*? Mrs. Barrington dragged me to it four times. She'd sing along with the entire performance, to the dismay of the audience around us."

Ian went to the theatre or opera when Mac or Hart or Cameron took him along, and he didn't much care what he saw there. The thought of taking Beth to this show and having her explain it appealed to him.

He recalled the notes exactly as she'd played them, and they came tripping out of his fingers. He sang the words, not caring about meaning.

Beth smiled as he performed his trick, and then she joined in. "With many cheerful facts about the square of the hypotenuse . . ."

They ran through it, Beth singing in his ear. He wanted to turn and kiss her, but he couldn't stop in the middle of a piece. He had to play it to the end.

He finished with a flourish.

"That was—" Ian cut off her praise by cupping the nape of her neck and taking her mouth in a hard kiss.

Beth tasted brandy, felt the burn of his whiskers. He laced his fingers through the hair at the base of her neck, fingertips finding sensitive skin.

He kissed her like a lover, as if she were his courtesan. She imagined glittering, overly sensual ladies melting like ice on a hot sidewalk when Ian touched them. He feathered kisses onto Beth's cheekbones. His breath was hot, and she felt her body loosening, flowing like water.

"I shouldn't let you do this," she whispered.

"Why not?"

"Because I think you could break my heart."

He traced his finger around her lips, outlining the cleft of the top lip and the roundness of the lower. His gaze remained on her lips as his large hand moved to her thigh.

"Are you wet?" Ian whispered, teeth on her earlobe.

"Yes." She tried to swallow. "If you must know, I am quite, quite damp."

"Good." His hot tongue circled the shell of her ear. "You understand such things. Why you need to be wet."

"My husband explained on our wedding night. He thought that ignorance on the woman's part was the cause of much unnecessary pain."

"An unusual vicar."

"Oh, Thomas was quite the radical. A thorn in the side of his bishop, with all his modern views."

"I would like to explain even more," Ian whispered. "Someplace more private than here."

"That's a mercy." Beth laughed a little. "It is fortunate I am not a delicate, shielded lady. If I were, I'd be on the ground in a state of unconsciousness, with Isabella's servants trying to fan me."

His eyes flickered. "Does what I say anger you?"

"No, but never speak like that in a drawing room full of ladies and fine china, I implore you. There would be quite a mess."

He nuzzled her hair. "I've never been with a lady before. I don't know the rules."

"Fortunately, I'm an unusual sort of woman. Mrs. Barrington did her best to change that, but she never succeeded, bless her."

"Why should she want to change you?"

Beth warmed. "My lord, I do believe you are the most flattering man of my acquaintance."

Ian paused, his expression unreadable. "I state truths. You are perfect as you are. I want to see you bare, and I wish to kiss your cunny."

The heat there flared. "And as always, I don't know

whether to run away from you or stay and bask in your attention."

"I know how to answer that." He snaked his strong fingers around her wrist. "Stay." His hand was heavy and warm, and he traced a circle on the inside of her arm.

"I must confess that your plain speaking is refreshing after the acrobatics I must perform to keep up with Isabella's friends."

"Tell Isabella's gentlemen friends to keep far from you. I don't want them touching you."

His fingers clamped down, and she glanced pointedly at his large hand still wedged into her skirts. "Only you can touch me?"

He nodded, brows together. "Yes."

"I don't think I mind that," she said softly.

"Good."

He moved her deftly onto his lap, her bustle not letting her sit quite against him. Disappointing things, bustles.

The blue rosette at her bosom crushed against Ian's waistcoat, and he cupped his hand around her bottom. She didn't argue, didn't gasp at him for taking a liberty.

She wanted to take even more of a liberty with him. She wanted to undo the buttons of his trousers and put her hand inside. She wanted to work through layers of cloth until she could stroke his swollen organ, to feel it against her hand. Never mind that they sat in Isabella's front drawing room; never mind that the curtains were wide open to the busy Paris street.

"I am a wicked, wicked woman," she murmured. "Kiss me again."

Without a word he swiftly slanted his lips over hers. His tongue stabbed inside her mouth, and he pressed his fingers to the corners of her lips, opening her wider.

These weren't the kisses of a man flirting. They were the kisses of a man who wanted to lie with her, damn the timing and damn the circumstances. Every part of her that touched him throbbed.

"We should stop," she whispered.

"Why?"

Beth couldn't think of a reason. *I am a widowed lady, well past the age of innocence. Why should I not kiss a handsome man in a drawing room? A little carnality won't hurt me.*

She snaked her wanton hand between his thighs, finding the hard ridge behind his trousers.

"Mmm." One corner of his mouth turned up. "Do you want to touch it?"

Yes, please, said the wicked lady. "I can hear the china breaking now."

"What?" His brow furrowed.

"Never mind. You are a rogue and a scoundrel, and I love every single second of it."

"I don't understand you."

She cupped his face. "Never mind, never mind. I'm sorry I spoke."

Her lips felt raw, swollen from his kisses. She kissed the curve of his lower lip, tasting the corners of his mouth as he'd done with her. He chased her tongue, pinning it inside her mouth before he proceeded to lick every inch of it.

He wants me to welcome him into my bed and not be ashamed.

This was a world she didn't know, one she'd only glimpsed through half-closed curtains behind which diamond-bedecked women smiled at cigar-smoke-wreathed gentlemen. So many houses, so many windows, so much warmth inside, and this was the first time she'd been invited in.

The door suddenly banged open, and Isabella strolled into the room in a blue silk dressing gown. Beth tried to jump away from Ian, but he was holding her too tight. She ended up half sitting on, half sliding off his knee.

Isabella peered blearily about. "Ian, darling, what are you doing here playing Gilbert and Sullivan at the crack of dawn? I thought I was having a nightmare."

Beth finally slid to her feet, her face flaming. "I beg your pardon, Isabella. We didn't mean to wake you."

Isabella's eyes widened. "I see. I beg *your* pardon for interrupting."

Thank heavens for corsets, Beth thought distractedly. Her nipples were hard little points against the fabric, but the thick boning would hide it.

Ian didn't rise. He leaned one elbow on the piano and studied the moldings behind Isabella.

"Will you stay to breakfast, Ian?" Isabella asked. "I'll try to prop my eyes open long enough to join you."

He shook his head. "I came to deliver Beth a message."

"Did you?" Beth asked. How ridiculous, she'd never thought to ask why he'd suddenly appeared in Isabella's drawing room.

"From Mac." Ian continued to stare across the room. "He says he'll be ready to start your drawing lessons in three days. He wants to finish the painting he's working on first."

Isabella answered before Beth could. "Really? My husband was always so good at doing two things at once." Her voice was strained.

"The model is Cybele," Ian answered. "Mac doesn't want Beth there while Cybele is."

Pain flashed through Isabella's eyes. "He never bothered about such things with me."

Ian didn't answer, and Beth couldn't help asking, "Is this Cybele so awful?"

"She's a foulmouthed tart," Isabella said. "Mac introduced me to her to shock me when we first married. He loved to shock me. It became his raison d'être."

Ian had turned his head to stare out the window, as though the conversation no longer interested him. Isabella's delight evaporated, and her face looked pinched and tired.

"Oh, well, Ian, if you aren't staying for breakfast, I'll drag myself back to bed. Good morning to you." She drifted out, leaving the door open behind her.

Beth watched her go, not liking how unhappy Isabella looked. "*Can* you stay to breakfast?" she asked Ian.

He shook his head and rose to his feet—did he regret leaving or was he happy to go? "Mac expects me at his studio. He gets worried if I don't appear."

"Your brothers like to look after you." Beth felt a pang. She'd grown up so alone, with no sisters or brothers, and no friends she could trust.

"They're afraid."

"Of what?"

Ian kept his gaze out the window, as though he didn't hear her. "I want to see you again."

A hundred polite refusals Mrs. Barrington had drilled into her flitted through her head and out again. "Yes, I'd like to see you, too."

"I will send you a message through Curry."

"Ever resourceful, is your Mr. Curry."

He wasn't listening. "The soprano," he said.

Beth blinked. "I beg your pardon?" She remembered the newspaper article that had bothered her so much the day she'd met Mac. "Oh. That soprano."

"I asked Cameron to pretend to argue with me about her. I wanted people to focus on the soprano and forget about you. He was happy to oblige. He enjoyed it."

People must have seen Beth enter the Mackenzie box, perhaps had seen Ian spirit her away to Cameron's coach. He'd created a public argument with Cameron to divert attention from Beth to the Mackenzies, famous for their sordid affairs.

"Pity," Beth said. "It was such a well-done story."

"It is not what happened."

"I realize that. I'm overwhelmed."

"Why should it overwhelm you?"

"My dear Lord Ian, the paid companion is the last person anyone thinks to spare gossip about. She is drab and faded—her own fault, really, that no one wanted to marry her."

"Who the devil told you that?"

"Dear Mrs. Barrington, although she didn't put it quite like that. I should be demure and forgettable, she said. She had the best of intentions. She was trying to protect me, you see."

"No." He stared at her, his gaze resting on a curl over her ear. "I don't see."

"That's all right. You don't need to."

Ian went silent again, lost in his own thoughts. Then he looked at her abruptly, crushed her to him, and pressed a swift kiss to her mouth.

Before Beth could gasp, he stood her bodily aside and strode out of the room. Beth stood still, her lips burning, until the cold draft from the slamming front door announced that he'd gone.

"Darling, how lovely," Isabella said that evening, holding out her arm so her maid could slide a glove up it. "You and Ian." Her green eyes danced, but shadows stained her face. "I am so pleased."

"Nothing lovely about it," Beth said. "I am being horribly scandalous."

Isabella gave her a knowing smile. "Whatever you say. I shall wait avidly for further news on the subject."

"Do you not have a ball to attend, Isabella?"

Isabella kissed Beth's cheeks, bathing her in a wash of perfume. "Are you sure you don't mind me running off, my dear? I hate to leave you alone."

"No, no. Go and enjoy yourself. I'm rather tired tonight, and I don't mind time to gather my thoughts."

Beth wanted a quiet night, not feeling up to the scrutiny of Paris this evening, even with Isabella's protection. Isabella knew "absolutely everyone," and had introduced Beth around with enthusiasm. Isabella hinted that Beth was a mysterious heiress from England, which seemed to go over well with the artists, writers, and poets that flocked to Isabella.

Tonight Beth was willing to forgo the glamour. She would write about her day in her journal, then retire and indulge in fantasies about Ian Mackenzie. She had no business indulging in fantasies about him, but she didn't care.

Once Isabella had gone, Beth asked the butler to serve her a cold supper in her chamber. Then she took up a pen and turned to her diary.

She'd begun an account of her adventures in Paris, which she scribbled about whenever she had a moment. As she chewed leftover meat pie, she flipped to clean pages at the end of the notebook.

I'm not certain how he makes me feel, she wrote. *His hands are large and strong, and I wanted too much for him to lift them to my bosom. I wanted to press my breasts inside his palms. I wanted to feel the heat of his bare hands against my nipples. My body shouted for it, but I refused its wishes, knowing it was impossible in that time and place.*

Does that mean I wish him to do such things in another time and place?

I want to unbutton my frock for him. I want him to unlace my stays and ease them from my body. I want him to touch me as I haven't been touched in years. I ache for it.

I do not think of him as Lord Ian Mackenzie, aristocratic brother of a duke and well beyond my reach; not as the Mad Mackenzie, an eccentric people stare at and whisper about.

To me, he is simply Ian.

"Madam," Katie bleated from the doorway.

Beth jumped and slammed her notebook closed. "Good heavens, Katie, you startled me. Is something wrong?"

"Footman says a gentleman's called to see you."

Beth rose. Her skirt caught a spoon and sent it clattering to the floor. "Who? Lord Ian?"

"I would have said so right away if it was him, wouldn't I? No, Henri says it's a gent from the police."

Beth's brows rose. "The police? Why should the police want to see me?"

"I don't know, madam. Says he's an inspector or something, and he's English, not a frog. I promise you, I haven't stolen a thing since you caught me when I was fifteen. Not a bleedin' thing."

"Don't be ridiculous." Beth retrieved the spoon with a

shaking hand. "I don't think stealing oranges in Covent Garden ten years ago would warrant an inspector chasing you to Paris tonight."

"I hope you're right," Katie said darkly.

Beth locked her notebook away in her jewelry case and pocketed the key before she made her way downstairs. The French footman bowed to her as he opened the door, and Beth thanked him in his own language.

A man in a faded black suit turned from the fire as she entered. "Mrs. Ackerley?"

He was tall, though not as tall as Ian. He wore his dark hair slicked back from his forehead, and his eyes were hazel. He was in his thirties and nearly handsome, though his luxuriant mustache didn't hide the grim set to his mouth.

Beth stopped just inside the door. "Yes? My companion says you are from the police."

"My name is Fellows. I've called to ask you a few questions, if you don't mind."

He held out an ivory card that had seen better days. *Lloyd Fellows, Insp., Scotland Yard, London.*

"I see." Beth gave the card back to him, not liking how it felt in her hand.

"May we sit down, Mrs. Ackerley? There is no need for you to be uncomfortable."

He gestured her to a plush armchair, and Beth perched on the end of it. Inspector Fellows took the hard chair from the desk, turned it around, and sat, looking utterly composed.

"I won't stay long, so you may dispense with the usual polite offering of tea." He eyed her keenly. "I've come to ask you how long you have known Lord Ian Mackenzie."

"Lord Ian?" Beth stared in surprise.

"Youngest brother of the Duke of Kilmorgan, brother-in-law to the lady who owns this house."

His tone was brutal and sarcastic, but the look in his eyes was . . . odd. "Yes, I do know who he is, Inspector."

"You met him in London, I believe?"

"Why is that your business? I met him in London, and

I met his brother and his sister-in-law here in Paris. I don't believe any of this is against the law."

"Today you spoke to Lord Ian here in this house."

Her heart beat faster. "You've been watching me?" She thought of the drapes pulled back from the windows of this very room, and of herself perched on Ian's knee, kissing him madly.

Fellows leaned forward, his expression unreadable. "I've not come here to accuse you of anything, Mrs. Ackerley. My visit is in the nature of a warning."

"Against what? Speaking to my friend's brother-in-law in her home?"

"Mixing in the wrong company could prove your downfall, young woman. You mark my words."

Beth shifted in annoyance. "Please be plain, Mr. Fellows. The hour grows late, and I would like to retire."

"No need to get haughty. I have your best interests at heart. Tell me, have you read of a murder in a boardinghouse near St. Paul's, Covent Garden, about a week ago?"

Beth frowned and shook her head. "I was busy traveling about a week ago. I must have missed the story."

"She was not an important woman, so the English newspapers wouldn't have made much of it, and the French ones nothing at all." He rubbed his finger and thumb over his mustache. "You speak French fluently, do you not?"

"It seems you know much about me." His manner and arrogance, in Isabella's own drawing room, irritated her. "My father was French, so yes, I speak the language rather well. It is one reason I decided to visit Paris, if you must know."

Fellows pulled a small notebook from his pocket and turned over the pages with a quiet rustle. "Your father called himself Gervais Villiers, Viscount Theriault." He glanced at her. "Funny thing, the Sûreté have no record of such a person ever living in France."

Beth's pulse sped. "He left Paris a long time ago. Something to do with the revolution in 'forty-eight, I believe."

"Nothing to do with it, madam. Gervais *Villiers* never existed. Gervais *Fournier*, on the other hand, was wanted for petty theft, fraud, and running confidence games. He fled to England and was never heard of again." Fellows flipped another page. "I believe both you and I know what happened to him, Mrs. Ackerley."

Beth said nothing. She couldn't deny the truth of her father, but she had no desire to break into hysterics about it in front of Mr. Fellows.

"What has all this to do with Lord Ian Mackenzie?"

"I'm coming to that." Fellows consulted the notebook again. "I have here that your mother was once arrested for prostitution. Can that be right?"

Beth flushed. "She was desperate, Inspector. My father had just died, and we were starving. Thank heavens she was very bad at it, and the first approach she made was to a detective constable in plainclothes."

"Indeed, it seems the magistrate was so moved by her pleas for mercy that he let her go. She promised to be a good girl and never do it again."

"And she never did. Will you please not discuss my mother, Inspector? Let her rest in peace. She was doing the best she could in difficult circumstances."

"No, Mrs. Villiers wasn't lucky like you," Fellows said. "You have been uncommonly lucky. You married a respectable gentleman who took care of you. Then you became a companion to a wealthy old lady, so ingratiating yourself with her that she left you her entire fortune. Now you're the guest of English aristocrats in Paris. Quite a rise from the workhouse, isn't it?"

"Not that my life is any of your business," Beth said stiffly. "But why is it of such interest to a detective inspector?"

"It isn't, not in itself. But murder is."

Every limb in her body stiffened, like an animal that knew it was being stalked.

"I haven't done any murders, Mr. Fellows," she said, trying to smile. "If you are suggesting I helped Mrs. Barrington to her grave, I did not. She was old and ill, I was very fond of her, and I had no idea she meant to leave everything to me."

"I know. I checked."

"Well, isn't that a mercy? I confess, Inspector, I can't imagine what you are trying to tell me."

"I bring up your mother and father because I want to speak frankly with you about topics that might cause a lady to swoon. I am establishing that you are a woman of the world and not likely to faint at what I have to say."

Beth fixed him with an icy stare. "Rest assured, I am not prone to swooning. I might have the footmen throw you out, yes, but swoon, no."

Fellows held up his hand. "Please bear with me, madam. The woman killed at St. Paul's, Covent Garden, was called Lily Martin."

Beth looked at him blankly. "I don't know anyone called Lily Martin."

"Five years ago, she worked in a brothel in High Holborn."

He waited expectantly, but Beth shook her head again. "Are you asking whether my mother knew her?"

"Not at all. Do you recall that there was a murder of a courtesan at this High Holborn house five years ago?"

"Was there?"

"There was indeed. The details are not pretty. A young woman called Sally Tate, one of the ladies of the house, was found dead in her bed one morning, stabbed through the heart, then her warm blood deliberately smeared on the wallpaper and the bedstead."

Beth's throat tightened. "How dreadful."

Fellows sat forward, on the very edge of the chair now. "I know—I *know*—that Lord Ian Mackenzie did that murder."

Beth felt the floor dropping from under her feet. She tried to drag in a breath, but her lungs wouldn't work, and the room began to ripple.

"Now, Mrs. Ackerley, you promised me you wouldn't swoon."

She found Fellows at her side, his hand on her elbow. Beth gasped for breath.

"It's absurd." Her voice grated. "If Lord Ian had done a

murder, the newspapers would have been full of it. Mrs. Barrington wouldn't have missed that."

Fellows shook his head. "He was never accused, never arrested. No one was allowed to breathe a word to the journalists." He returned to his chair, his face betraying impatience and frustration. "But I know he did it. He was there that night. By morning, Lord Ian had disappeared, nowhere to be found. Turns out he'd left for Scotland, out of my reach."

Beth grasped at the straw. "Then perhaps he was gone beforehand."

"His servants tried to tell me he'd returned home before two in the morning, gone to bed, and left for Scotland by an early train. They were lying. I know it in my bones, though his brother the duke did his best to block me from finding what Ian really did do. I wanted to arrest Ian, but I had no evidence to please my guv, and the Mackenzies are high-and-mighty lords. Their late mother was a personal friend of the queen. The duke has weight with the Home Office, and he made my superiors put me off it. Ian's name was never mentioned—not in the newspapers, not in the halls of Scotland Yard. In other words, he got clean away with it."

Lights spun at the edges of Beth's vision as she stood up and walked away from Fellows. She thought of Ian, his quick, flickering gaze, his intense golden eyes, his hard kiss, the pressure of his hands.

It occurred to her that this was the second time in a few weeks that a man had warned her away from another gentleman. But when Ian had told her about Mather, she'd easily believed him, whereas she wanted to deny all that Inspector Fellows said about Ian.

"You have to be wrong," she said. "Ian would never do such a thing."

"You say this when you've known him only a week? I've watched the Mackenzie family for years. I know what they're capable of."

"I've seen my share of violent men in my life, Inspector, and Ian Mackenzie is not one of them."

Beth had grown up among men who solved their

problems with their fists, her own father included. Her father could be perfectly charming when sober, but once he had gin inside him he became a monster.

Fellows looked unconvinced. "The girl, Lily, who died in Covent Garden worked in that High Holborn house five years ago. She disappeared after the murder, and I couldn't find her no matter what. Turns out she'd moved into this Covent Garden boardinghouse, and a protector was paying her handsomely to live alone and keep quiet. Housekeeper says a gentleman used to visit her in the night from time to time, well after dark. She never saw him. But there was an eyewitness who saw a man visit the house the night Lily got scissors stuck into her chest, and that man was Lord Ian Mackenzie."

The floor wavered again under Beth's feet, but she held her head high. "Your speculation isn't proof. What if the witness had faulty eyesight?"

"Come, come, Mrs. Ackerley. You will admit that Lord Ian is most distinctive."

Beth couldn't deny that. She also knew that policemen could lead people into believing they'd seen what said policeman wanted them to have seen.

"I can't think why you've come here tonight to tell me this story," she said icily.

"Two reasons. One is to give you warning that you've befriended a murderer. The second is to ask you to watch Lord Ian and pass to me any information you think is relevant. He did both of these girls, and I intend to prove it."

Beth stared at him. "You wish me to spy on the brother-in-law of the woman who has befriended me? On a family that so far has shown me nothing but kindness?"

"I am asking you to help me catch a cold-blooded killer."

"I am not employed by Scotland Yard or the French police, Inspector. Have someone else do your dirty work."

Fellows shook his head in mock sadness. "I am sorry for this attitude, Mrs. Ackerley. If you refuse to help me, I will have you as an accessory when I nick Lord Ian."

"I have a solicitor, Mr. Fellows. Perhaps you should consult him. I will even give you his address in London."

Fellows smiled. "I like that you don't take kindly to bullying. But consider this—I am certain you won't want your new highborn friends tumbling to the fact that you're a fraud. The daughter of a confidence trickster and a prostitute, worming your way into the bosom of the aristocracy. Dear, dear." He clicked his tongue.

"I don't take kindly to blackmail, either. I will take your warning as a concern for my safety, and we'll speak no more of the matter."

"Just so we understand each other, Mrs. Ackerley."

"You may go now," Beth said in freezing tones that would have made Mrs. Barrington proud. "And we don't understand each other at all."

Fellows refused to look cowed. In fact, he gave her a cheerful grin as he gathered up his hat and made his way to the drawing room door. "If you change your mind, I'm staying at the hotel at the Gare du Nord. Good evening."

Fellows dramatically shoved open the pocket doors, only to find himself facing the wall that was Ian Mackenzie. Before Beth could say a word, Ian took Fellows by the throat and shoved him back inside the room.

Chapter 6

Ian's vision filmed red with fury. Through it he saw Beth, her hair in the same sleek, complex curls she'd worn this morning, Fellows in his black suit crinkled with wear, and Beth's blue eyes filled with dismay.

Fellows had told her. Damn him, he'd told her everything.

Fellows clawed at Ian's hands. "Accosting a police officer is an offense."

"Everything about you is an offense." Ian shoved the man away. "Get out."

"Ian."

Beth's voice made him turn. She stood like a flower, fragile and vulnerable, the only color in a world of gray.

He'd wanted Beth to remain apart from the sordid business at High Holborn and everything Ian had strived to hide the last five years. Beth was unsoiled by it, innocent.

Fellows had ruined that. The bloody man ruined everything he touched. Ian didn't want Beth looking at him and wondering what others did—whether Ian had plunged a knife into the warm body of a courtesan, then smeared the walls with her blood. He wanted Beth to keep looking at him in soft wonder, to smile her little smile when she made a jest Ian didn't follow.

Ian sometimes wondered himself whether he had, in his rage, killed Sally. He sometimes didn't remember things he did in his muddles. But he also remembered what he'd seen that night, things he'd never revealed to anyone, not even to Hart.

Fellows fingered his collar, his face red. Ian hoped he'd hurt the man. Fellows's purpose in life was to turn public opinion against Hart, against Ian, against anything Mackenzie. Fellows had harassed Hart and Ian so much that he'd been pulled off the High Holborn case five years ago and warned that he risked his job pursuing it further.

Now Fellows was back. That meant he'd learned something new.

Ian thought of Lily Martin lying in the parlor where he'd found her a week ago, her sewing scissors through her heart. He remembered the anger he'd felt, and the sorrow. He'd meant to protect her, and he'd failed.

"Get out," he repeated to Fellows. "You aren't welcome here."

"This house has been hired by Lady Isabella Mackenzie," Fellows said. "And I have not been cautioned against speaking to Mrs. Ackerley. She's not a Mackenzie."

Ian's gaze slid over Fellows's self-satisfied face. "Mrs. Ackerley is under my protection."

"Your protection?" Fellows smirked. "A fine way to phrase it."

"I certainly don't like *that* implication," Beth broke in. "Please go, Inspector. You've said what you need to say, and I'd be obliged if you'd leave."

Fellows bowed, but his eyes glittered. "Of course, Mrs. Ackerley. Good evening."

Ian wasn't satisfied with watching Fellows exit the

drawing room—he followed Fellows down to the foyer and instructed the footman to not let him back in under any circumstances. Ian stood in the doorway watching until Fellows walked away down the busy street, whistling.

He turned back to find Beth behind him. She smelled like flowers, faint perfume clinging to her skin. Her face was flushed, her cheeks damp, her breath rapid.

Damnation. Her smile was gone, her brow puckered. Ian had difficulty reading people's expressions, but Beth's worry and uncertainty screamed at him. Damn it all, if she'd believed Fellows . . .

Ian took Beth's elbow and steered her back up the stairs to the drawing room. He slammed the doors behind him, and Beth walked away from him, holding her arms tight across her chest.

"Don't trust him," Ian said, his voice grating. "He's been harassing Hart for years. Have nothing to do with him."

"It's a bit late for that." Beth made no move to sit down, but she didn't pace either. She stood very still, save for where her thumbs moved restlessly on her elbows. "I'm afraid the good inspector knows many secrets."

"He knows far less than he thinks. He hates my family and will do anything to discredit them."

"Why on earth should he?"

"I don't know. I never did know."

Ian scrubbed his hands through his hair, his frustrated rage boiling to the surface. He hated that rage, the one that had so infuriated Ian's father and had earned young Ian many beatings.

It rose in him when he wanted to explain things but couldn't find the words, when he couldn't understand the nonsense everyone around him was babbling. As a child he'd done the only thing he could—lashed out with fists and screaming until two footmen had to hold him down. The screaming would stop only when Hart came. The little boy Ian had worshiped Hart Mackenzie, ten years his senior.

Ian was old enough now to control his impulses, but the anger still came, and he fought the demon of it every day. He'd fought it the night Sally Tate had been murdered.

"I don't want you to be part of this," he repeated.

Beth simply looked at him. Her eyes were so blue, her lips lush and red. He wanted to kiss her until she forgot all about Fellows and his revelations, until that look in her eyes was gone.

Ian wanted her under his body, his heat meeting hers, to hear her gasp when he fitted himself inside her. He needed the oblivion of coupling with her until they both dissolved with the passion of it. He'd wanted her as his refuge ever since he'd seen her sitting next to Lyndon Mather at Covent Garden Opera House.

He'd taken her away from Mather by betraying the man's secrets. Mather had been right that Ian had stolen her, and Ian didn't care. But now Beth knew Ian's secrets, and she was afraid.

"It should be simple enough to establish that you committed neither crime," she was saying. "Surely your coachman and valet and so forth can account for your whereabouts."

She thought it was so, so simple.

Ian went to her and cupped her cheek, loving her petal-soft skin beneath his palm. "I don't want you to know about this. It's base and dirty. It will soil you."

He wasn't certain what all Fellows had told her, though he could guess. But Fellows had dug up only the barest part of the incident. The reality went miles deep, secrets so nasty they could ruin all of them.

Beth waited, expecting him to clear it up in a sentence or two, to reassure her. Ian couldn't, because he knew the stark truth. His damned memory wouldn't blur, wouldn't let go of what he'd seen, what he'd done. Both ladies had been involved, and they'd both died.

Would Beth?

"No," he said sharply.

"Ian."

Her whisper cut him to the heart. Ian released her, the shaking rage pouring to the surface again.

"You shouldn't have anything to do with Mackenzies," he said harshly. "We break whatever we touch."

"Ian, I believe you."

Her fingers closed on his sleeve and held tight. He wished he dared stare into her eyes, but that was impossible.

Beth spoke rapidly. "You're afraid that Fellows has turned me away from you. He hasn't. He obviously has a bee in his bonnet. He said himself he had no evidence, and there was never a case against you."

That was partly true, but would it were that simple. "Let it alone," he snapped. "Forget."

Ian wished *he* could forget, but he forgot nothing in his life. The events were as vivid to him as was sitting here playing the piano with her this morning. As vivid as every "experiment" the quack doctor had performed on him in the private asylum.

"You don't understand." Beth let go of his sleeve only to close her hand on his arm. "We are friends, Ian. I don't hold friendships lightly—goodness knows I've had few enough of them in my life."

Friends. Ian didn't think he'd ever heard that term applied to him. He had his brothers, no one else. Courtesans liked him and liked him well, but he was under no illusion that they'd like him if he didn't give them so much money.

Beth's gaze was intense. "What I mean is, I will not flounce off in a huff because Inspector Fellows turned up and made accusations."

She still wanted him to clear it up, to declare his innocence at the top of his voice. Ian had difficulty with lies, not understanding the point of them, but he also knew that the truth was tricky.

"I didn't see Sally Tate die," he said, his gaze fixed on the door frame. "And I didn't drive the scissors into Lily."

"How did you know it was scissors?"

He darted his gaze over her face, watching her eyes sharpen. "I saw her that night. I went to visit her and found her dead."

A swallow moved in Beth's slender throat. "You didn't report this to the police?"

"No. I left her and caught the train to Dover."

"Inspector Fellows says a witness saw you go to the house."

"I didn't notice anyone there, but I didn't look. I had the train to catch, and I didn't want to draw a connection between me and Lily and High Holborn."

"The inspector drew it anyway."

Ian's rage began to rise again. "I know. I tried to protect her from him. I failed her."

"A footpad or a cracksman might have killed her. That can't be your fault."

Lily hadn't struggled. She'd known and trusted whoever had driven the scissors deep into her chest. His own observation and Curry's confirmed that.

"I couldn't protect her. I can't protect you."

Her little smile returned. "You have no need to protect me."

Lord, could the woman be any more innocent? Beth was associated with Mackenzies now. That marked her in the eyes of the world. "Fellows will use you to get to us. It's his way."

"Does he use Isabella?"

"He tried. He failed." Fellows had thought Isabella would hate all things Mackenzie once she'd walked out on Mac. He'd assumed she'd tell Fellows all their secrets, but Fellows had been so very wrong. Isabella was the daughter of an earl, blue-blooded through and through, and she refused even to speak to a mere policeman. Her loyalty remained with Mac's family.

"There you are, then," Beth said. "He'll fail with me as well."

"If you throw in your lot with us, you'll regret it."

"I told you, it's too late for that. I've come to know

Isabella well, and I know she wouldn't speak so fondly of you if she thought you capable of murder."

It was true that Isabella retained affection for Ian, Hart, and Cam, God knew why. Ian had liked Isabella right away when Mac had presented her the day after their elopement. She'd been incredibly innocent, but she'd taken her plunge into their masculine world with aplomb.

"Isabella believes in us."

Beth's touch softened. "If she does, I do, too."

He felt his red anger lessening, the despair easing. Beth believed him. She was a fool to, but the fact that she did wormed its way into the empty spaces inside him.

"You'd take the word of a madman?" he asked.

"You're not a madman."

"I was put into that asylum for a reason. I couldn't convince the commission that I was sane."

She smiled. "One of my husband's parishioners firmly believed she was Queen Victoria. She wore black bombazine and mourning brooches and talked constantly of her poor, deceased Albert. I can't believe you are as eccentric as she."

Ian turned from her, forcing her to let go of his arm. "When I was first released from the asylum I wouldn't speak for three months."

He heard her stop behind him. "Oh."

"I hadn't forgotten how—I simply didn't want to. I didn't know it distressed my brothers until they told me. I can't read hints from others. A person has to tell me a thing plainly."

She gave him a shaky smile. "Which is why you don't laugh at my little jokes. I thought I'd lost my knack for it."

"I learn what to do by watching others, like applauding at the opera when the rest of the audience starts. It's like learning a foreign language. And I can't follow a conversation when I'm with a crowd."

"Is that why you didn't speak much when you came to Mather's box at Covent Garden?"

"One-on-one is much easier." He spoke a fact. He could focus on what one person was saying, but trying to follow several people's contributions to a conversation led to confusion. As a youth he'd been punished for not answering at the table or not joining in a discussion. *Sullen*, his father had labeled him. *Look at me when I'm talking to you, boy.*

Beth's eyes were tight. "My dear Ian, then we are birds of a feather. Mrs. Barrington had to teach me how to behave in society from the ground up, and I still don't understand all the rules. For instance, do you know it is considered vulgar to eat ices with a spoon? One must use a fork, which seems rather ridiculous. The most difficult is to leave a few morsels of food on the plate, so as not to seem overzealous in eating. I had so many hungry days in my youth that I consider this beyond perplexing."

Ian let her words wash over him without bothering to follow them. He liked her voice, smooth and cool, like the mountain stream he fished from in the wilds of Scotland.

"You call me *Ian* now," he said.

She blinked. "Do I?"

"You've said it five times since I arrived."

"You see? I do consider us friends."

Friends. He wanted so much more than that.

Beth gave him a glance from under her lashes. "Ian, there's something I've been meaning to ask you."

He waited, but she took a step back, toying with the silver ring on her left hand. He knew jewels well enough to see that the ring was cheap, the one stone in it the merest chip. Someone poor had given it to her, but she'd kept it with care. She'd returned Mather's diamond ring without hesitation, but this one was precious to her.

"Ian, I wonder if perhaps . . ."

Ian focused his attention on her words with difficulty. He'd rather listen to her flowing voice, watch the rise and fall of her breasts, study the movement of her lips.

"Since you seem to like me a little," she said, "I wonder

whether you would be interested . . . in having a liaison with me."

The last words came out in a rush, and Ian's attention snapped to her.

"Have carnal relations, I mean," Beth continued. "On occasion, when we mutually agree."

Chapter 7

Pleasure bubbled through Ian's tension. "Carnal relations," he repeated.

"Yes," she said, her voice shy. "If it would interest you."

If it would interest me?

"You mean bed," he said bluntly.

Her blush deepened, her fingers twisting the ring around and around. "Yes, that is exactly what I mean. Not like a mistress, you understand, but just two people enjoying . . . that side of life. We like each other well enough, and I don't foresee that I will marry again. Mather frightened me off that, goodness knows. But perhaps we can be . . . lovers, at least while we are in Paris. I'm babbling, I know, but I can't help myself."

Did she know how beautiful she was? Her cheeks were flame red, her look both defiant and uncertain.

He gazed into her eyes for one fleeting instant and said, "Yes."

Beth let out a breath that turned to a shaky laugh. "Thank you for not leaving in disgust."

Disgust? What man could be disgusted with a lady with eyes like hers, who'd just stammered out that she wanted to be his paramour?

Ian took a step back to have a full view of her. She wore a simple frock of mauve broadcloth, the overskirt pleated, the underskirt soft ruffles. A row of buttons shaped like blackberries marched up her bodice to her chin. The damn collar was too high, closing her off instead of exposing her lovely neck.

"We will start now," he said.

She jumped. "Right now?"

"Before you have second thoughts."

Beth pressed fingers to her mouth, as though trying to stop her smile. "Very well, what did you have in mind?"

"Unbutton your frock." He came to her and touched the button at the hollow of her throat. He wanted to take it between his teeth and see if it truly tasted of blackberries. "Down to there."

"Only that?"

"For now."

She gave him a surprised look but began to undo her buttons. Her pale throat came into view, the hollow damp with perspiration. It was a beautiful throat, long and slender, unmarred.

Ian slid his hands around her waist. She looked up at him, lips parted, but he didn't kiss her. He gently pushed open the placket, then leaned down and kissed her neck.

"Ian."

"Shh."

He licked the hollow of her throat, then pulled her soft skin between his teeth.

"What are you doing?"

"Giving you a love bite."

"A love—"

Ian bit down, and Beth inhaled sharply. He suckled, keeping it tender. He tasted the salt of her skin, felt her pulse flutter beneath his lips.

Strip for me, he wanted to say. He wanted to see his

Beth with her skirts up, her fingers untying the waistband of her pantalets. He wanted her to pull the pantalets down so he could see her triangle of hair glistening with moisture. His already hard erection gave a throb.

He wondered if her nipples would taste the same as her neck. He wanted to unbutton the bodice and remove the damned corset so he could feast on her breasts. He wanted to open his mouth over one, grip the other with his hand.

Go slowly with her. Savor this.

Ian raised his head. He let his gaze brush hers, catching a flash of blue before he lowered it to the safety of her lips again.

Very kissable lips. The bottom one curved slightly, as though she liked to smile; the top one was ever so slightly bowed. Her eyes were half closed, her hair mussed, a dark mark on her throat where he'd suckled her.

"Your turn now," he said.

Ian slid off his frock coat, pulled off his tie and collar. Beth watched him intently as he bared his throat.

She approached him tentatively, keeping her gaze fastened to his neck. Her curls tickled his chin as she leaned into him, her balled hands resting on his shoulders.

Her lips touched his throat, warm and firm. Then he felt the tiny prick of her teeth.

He couldn't stifle his groan as she caught a fold of his skin. The slight pain as she began to suckle made him want to spill his seed. Lay her on the floor, part her legs, send it inside her. Never since he'd been seventeen years old and first excited by the attentions of a rosy-cheeked maid had he come so close to losing control.

He wanted to open his shirt all the way and have Beth apply her mouth to his nipples. Then let her sink down to her knees to take his staff into her clever mouth and practice giving him love bites there.

Have carnal relations, she'd said in her sweet voice. *On occasion, when we mutually agree.*

Oh, yes, there would be many occasions, and he would make certain they always agreed.

Beth eased away and looked up at him, her eyes blue enough to break his heart. "Is that right?"

He couldn't talk anymore, the words jumbling up without meaning. He took her mouth in a wild kiss and scraped her hard against him.

So many occasions, every day, anyplace they happened to be. His mind spun with possibilities. He liked games, and this one he'd never tire of.

It took all his strength to press her away. If he didn't end this now, he truly would have her on the floor, or maybe straddling him on the convenient straight-backed chair.

Both ways. He'd take her all night and not tire.

He kissed her forehead, not hearing whatever it was she was saying. He wished he had Mac's charm, so he could find the right words to thank her, to propose another tryst, to continue the play. Instead Ian cupped her face in his hands and gave her another kiss on the mouth.

"I said, will you send another message through the very useful Curry?" she asked.

"Yes." How easy it was to be with her, when she answered questions so he didn't have to. "That will do."

He retrieved his coat, thrusting his collar and tie into the pocket, and turned for one last look.

Beth stood upright in the middle of the room, where he'd found her when he'd first stormed in. Now her dress gaped to her throat to expose the dull red mark he'd left on her skin. Her eyelids were heavy, her lips swollen with his kisses. She was the most beautiful thing he'd ever seen in his life.

"Good night," she whispered.

He made himself turn away and thrust open the doors, ignoring the footman and Katie, who suddenly scuttled away down the hall. He snatched hat, gloves, and scarf from hooks in the foyer and banged out of the house before he could give in to temptation and stay.

He would soon arrange it so he never had to leave. He'd marry her for a very basic reason: to have her with him every night, every day, every afternoon, and every time in between. He walked down the boulevard, something in him awakening and breaking free.

The night had turned foggy, which only enhanced Ian's ability to hear the footsteps that turned and followed him as he moved off down the avenue.

Sleep was impossible. Beth paced her bedchamber far into the night, wrapped in a dressing gown. She found herself unable to return to her journal or to go to bed. The events were too fresh to write about, and anytime she tried, her trembling hand spilled ink all over her journal pages.

She kept her dressing gown closed to her throat, though every so often, she'd stop in front of the mirror and ease it open. The red mark Ian had left stood out stark against her skin, almost a bruise, though not quite. Some of the game girls who'd come to the workhouse had had such marks, had laughed at Beth when she asked about them in concern.

Beth pressed her hand against the love bite. She'd had no idea why anyone would want to do such a thing. Now she remembered the warm tingle in her veins when his breath touched her throat, the throbbing of her opening when his teeth closed on her neck. His hair had touched her chin, warm and soft and smelling of soap.

She heard Isabella come home and hoped her friend wouldn't race in for a late-night chat. Beth had come to like Isabella, but she knew she wouldn't be able to hide her agitation, her excitement. Isabella would crack Beth open like an egg.

Isabella was uncharacteristically quiet as she came down the hall and soon closed her door. Through the wall, Beth heard the low voice of her maid, readying Isabella for bed. Then the maid departed and all was silence.

Beth still couldn't settle down. Her body was keyed up, angry at her for not completing what she'd started with Ian. She had feared he'd laugh at her suggestion that they have a liaison—she'd shared a man's bed and knew of orgasm, but Ian Mackenzie was decadence itself. A completely different thing.

He'd given her his slow half smile, had met her gaze for the briefest instant, and had said yes. He'd not been amused, bored, indifferent, embarrassed. The smile had set her body aflame.

As Beth turned to make another agitated pass through her room, she heard a muffled sound through the walls. She knew the sound, had heard it often from herself after Thomas had died. She'd lain alone in her plain bedroom in Mrs. Barrington's house and wept.

Drawing her wrapper around her, Beth hurried next door to Isabella's room. Tapping on the door brought no response, so she pushed her way in.

The gaslights had been turned low, and a weak yellow glow filtered through the room. Depressing. Beth turned up a light to reveal Isabella on a chaise longue, her head in her hands. Isabella's long hair poured over her back like a scarlet curtain, and she wept in choked, heaving sobs.

Beth slid next to her, her hand on Isabella's satiny hair. "Darling, what is it?"

Isabella jerked her head up. Her face was blotchy and tear-streaked. "Go away."

"No." Beth lifted a curl from Isabella's cheek. "I've cried alone like this before. It's a terrible thing."

Isabella regarded her with streaming green eyes before she flung her arms around Beth's neck. Beth held her close, stroking her hair.

"Mac was at the ball tonight," Isabella sobbed.

"Oh, dear."

"The comtesse invited us both to see what would happen when we saw each other. The bitch."

Beth agreed. "What did happen?"

Isabella raised her head. "He utterly ignored me. Pretended he didn't see me, and I pretended I didn't see him." She made a sound of anguish. "But, oh, Beth, I love him so much."

"I know, dearest."

"I want to hate him. I wish I could hate him. I try so hard, but I can't. I'm usually brave about it. But when I saw him tonight . . ."

Beth rocked her a little. "I know."

"You can't know. Your husband died, but it's not the same. You know he loved you, and he's always in your heart. But whenever I see Mac, the knife twists so hard. He loved me once, before it all went wrong."

The last word elongated into a sob. Beth held her close, resting her cheek against Isabella's hair. Beth's heart ached. She'd seen the strain in Isabella's eyes, and she'd seen the hard weariness in Mac's. It was none of her business, but she wished she could put it right.

Isabella raised her head again and wiped her eyes. "I want to show you something."

"Later, Isabella. You should rest."

"No. I want you to understand."

Isabella rose, pushing back her hair, and padded across the room to her wardrobe. She opened it and extracted a small picture wrapped in cloth. Isabella carried it to her bed, laid it reverently on the mattress, and stripped off the cloths.

Beth caught her breath. The painting showed Isabella sitting on the edge of a tumbled bed. A sheet slid provocatively down her shoulder, baring one prefect breast, and a swirl of hair peeped from the join of her thighs. Isabella was looking away from the painter, her red hair caught in a loose knot at the base of her neck.

Despite the subject—a woman just rising from the bed of her lover—the portrait was in no way lewd or indecorous. The muted colors were elegantly cool, with Isabella's hair and a sprig of bright yellow roses the only vivid colors.

It was the portrait of a beloved, painted by a man who regarded his wife as his lover. It was also, if Beth was any judge, an amazingly good painting. The light, the shadows, the composition, the colors—so much captured on one small canvas. The painter had signed the corner with a flourish: *Mac Mackenzie.*

"You see?" Isabella said softly. "He really is a genius."

Beth pressed her hands together. "It's absolutely beautiful."

"He painted that the morning after we married. He did the sketch right there in the bedroom, then painted it in his studio. Slapdash, he called it, but he said he couldn't stop himself."

"You are right, Isabella. He did love you."

Silent tears slid down Isabella's cheeks. "You should have seen me at my debut ball—I was a silly ninny, and he was the most decadent man I'd ever seen. He wasn't even invited to the ball; he 'crashed,' as they say, for a wager. He made me dance with him, said I was too afraid to. He teased me and made fun of me until I wanted to strangle him. He knew it, drat him. He played me like a fish, knowing all he had to do was scoop me into his net." She sighed. "And he did. I married him that very night."

Beth studied the painting again. Mac might have begun the night as a lark, but it had ended quite differently. The picture was the work of a man inspired, all tenderness and soft colors. The work of a man in love.

"Thank you for showing me," Beth said.

Isabella smiled. "You need to understand about Mackenzies. I am so happy you've caught Ian's attention, but I might have done you a disservice, my dear. Loving a Mackenzie can tear you to pieces. Be careful, darling."

Beth's heart throbbed. She knew as she looked again at the beautiful woman painted with love by Mac Mackenzie that it was already far too late for caution.

~~~

Beth didn't see Ian for a week after their encounter. She waited for the promised message setting up their next liaison, but nothing came. She tried not to start every time the bell rang downstairs, every time she heard a footman or maid hurrying toward her chamber. She tried not to feel the sting of disappointment as the days passed without a word.

There could be a hundred reasons why he didn't seek her out, she told herself, the foremost of which was that Ian had business to attend to. Isabella explained that Hart had Ian read political correspondences and treaties for him and commit them to memory, then alert Hart to those with particular phrases Hart told him to watch for.

Ian also had great mathematical skill and kept his eyes on all the Mackenzie brothers' investments. Like a cardsharp who knew every card on the table, Ian followed the ups and downs of markets with uncanny precision. In the years since Ian had left the private asylum, he'd nearly doubled the Mackenzies' already large fortune.

"I wouldn't be a bit surprised if that was the reason Hart got Ian released from the asylum," Isabella said when she'd explained. "That's a bit unfair of me, but Hart does put Ian's astonishing brain to much use. No wonder Ian gets headaches."

Beth felt indignant on Ian's behalf. Perhaps Ian liked working for his brother, though he'd never mentioned it. But it would explain his absence during the week.

On Saturday, Isabella took Beth to another whirlwind ball, this one at the palatial home of a duchess. Beth danced with gentlemen who regarded her with predatory eyes. If she'd been a vain young woman, she might believe they were dazzled by her, but she knew better. Many of Isabella's bohemian friends lived far beyond their means, and a widow with a large bank account was just what they needed. *French peasants pretending to be quality*, Mrs. Barrington would have said with a sniff. She'd disapproved of the entire nation of France, forgiving it only slightly for producing Beth.

Beth fanned herself in a corner after a rigorous waltz with such a gentleman. He ran on about the cost of keeping a carriage and decent servants. *But one has to, my dear, or one appears gauche.* The sweet nothings a lady wanted to hear.

A servant saved her from the conversation by bringing her a note. Beth excused herself from the spendthrift gentleman and unfolded the paper.

Most urgent I see you. Top of the house, first door. Ian.

Beth's pulse leapt. She crumpled the note in her pocket and sped through the house and up the winding staircase. At the top she found a recessed door trimmed with gold. She opened it to an ornate little room with Ian Mackenzie in the middle of it. He scowled at a pocket watch in his hand and didn't look up when she entered.

"Ian," she said, trying to catch her breath. "What is it? What's wrong?"

Ian clicked his watch closed and tucked it into his waistcoat. "Close the door. We don't have much time."

Chapter 8

Beth closed the door and stood with her back against it. "Time for what? Are you all right?"

"Come over here."

Beth lifted the satin skirts of her ball gown and picked her way delicately toward him. Delicately because her feet were already swollen in her too-tight shoes, and the four-story climb had left her wincing.

Ian caught her hand and pulled her the last couple of steps. She landed against his hard body, and his strong arms came around her. "What . . . ?"

He stopped her words with his mouth. His tongue stroked hers, stirring embers that hadn't quite gone out since their last encounter. This man could kiss.

Beth eased away from him with difficulty. "If we haven't much time, perhaps you'd better tell me what's wrong."

"What are you talking about?"

"The note." She took it from her pocket. "Did you not send it?"

Ian glanced once at it, his amber eyes meeting hers for an instant. "I did."

"Why?"

"So you would come to me."

"Are you saying you summoned me up here, saying it was most urgent, just to kiss me?"

"Yes. To continue our liaison."

"Here. *Now?*"

"Why not?"

He bent to kiss her again, and she tried to step away. Her heel snagged on the carpet, and he caught her squarely in his arms.

Ian smiled. It was a feral smile, the smile of a predator who'd caught his prey. Her thundering heart told her she didn't mind much.

"This is someone else's house," she tried.

"Yes." His tone said, *What of it?*

Beth had imagined them conducting their affair in her bedroom, secretly, after she'd made sure everyone was out of the house. It would be clandestine and hole-and-corner—not that she knew much about having affairs.

"Someone could come in," she said. "And there's no bed."

Ian laughed softly. She'd never heard him laugh before, and she liked it, all smooth and throaty and dark.

Ian crossed the room to turn a little key in the lock, then laced his arms around her from behind. "We don't need a bed."

"None of these chairs look quite comfortable."

He nuzzled beneath her hair. "You are not used to this."

"I confess, this is my first liaison."

He kissed her neck as he slid his hands up her tightly cinched waist to her breasts. Beth closed her eyes and leaned into his warm palms.

"You are right," she whispered. "I am not used to this at all. What do you wish to do?"

"Touch you," he said in her ear. "Learn you. Have you touch me."

Beth's heart jumped. "You said we didn't have much time."

"No."

"Then what do I do?"

Ian licked her neck, bared by the low-cut gown. "Pull up your skirt."

Did he expect to do this standing up? Beth wasn't quite certain it would work, especially not with her corset smoothing down to her hips. *Dratted underthings.*

Ian took hold of her skirts and started shoving them upward. Beth curled her fingers in the fabric and helped him. It was quite a task, and Beth reflected that if she'd known he'd planned this, she'd have worn fewer petticoats.

But she'd wanted the line of her gown to look well, vain creature that she was. At least in this gown made for dancing she'd been able to leave off the bustle.

While she held her skirts bunched in her hands, Ian scraped a curve-backed chair in front of her and sat down. This put his face on a level with her pantalets. She wore a new pair, ivory silk, quite thin, adorned with lovely little embroidered flowers. Beth had never owned such frivolous, feminine undergarments in her life, but Isabella had insisted Beth purchase them.

Ian untied the tapes of the pantalets. With her hands full of skirts, Beth could scarcely stop him, but she did let out a tiny squeak when he yanked the drawers down. From the softening of his eyes, Beth concluded that he could see everything.

He touched the swirl of hair between her legs. A hot tingle flushed through her body, and she made a soft sound in her throat.

"Beautiful," he murmured.

Beth could barely breathe. "I am happy not to disappoint you."

"You could never disappoint me."

He sounded grave, as though he took her flippant words seriously. He leaned forward and touched his lips to the nub that was swelling with all its might.

"You are wet for me." Ian's breath brushed her where no man's breath should in someone else's sitting room. "So wet."

His tongue flicked out and tasted it.

I am going to drop over dead right here.

Mrs. Barrington would meet her at the gates of heaven and laugh herself silly. *This is what happens when you give in to base lust, my gel,* she'd say.

Then again, if Beth died of giving in to base lust, would heaven's gate open for her at all?

I'm sorry, Saint Peter, but I hadn't felt the caress of a man in such a long, long time. You took my Thomas away from me; could I not have some bodily pleasure to compensate?

Ian grasped her right ankle and lifted it free of the pantalets crumpled on the floor. He planted her foot on the chair next to his thigh, which opened her legs to him. He slid his hands around her buttocks, leaned forward, and pressed his tongue into her cleft.

She wanted to scream. It had been *far* too long. She'd been secretly sorry for women who looked upon bedding their husbands as a burden, because she'd known what a joy it could be. But the knowledge had another edge— she'd known what it was she missed during her long years alone. Ian's talented tongue freed her at last.

The position with her foot on the chair let him spread her as much as he liked. And he seemed to like it. His thumbs massaged her as his tongue probed her depths. He was right: She was wet, and Ian lapped up every drop.

Ian tortured her for a long time, drinking her until she couldn't contain her cries any longer. Beth felt her hips gyrating, her hands locking around her skirts. A sob burst from her, feminine joy that had been denied her for so long. Tears rained down her face.

Ian drew back and looked up, his eyes burning her. She felt herself falling, but Ian caught her and pulled her to his lap, safe in his strong arms. "Did I hurt you?"

Beth buried her face in his fine-smelling shoulder. "No. It was wonderful."

"You're crying."

Beth lifted her head. "Because I never thought I'd feel such bliss again." She put her hand on his cheek, tried to turn his gaze to her, but she couldn't make him look at her. "Thank you."

He nodded once, and then his feral smile returned. "Would you like to feel such bliss again?"

Beth pressed her lips together, but her smile wouldn't be contained. "Yes, please," she said.

Ian eased her onto the chair, then slid to his knees in front of her. He pushed her legs open, then leaned down and showed her that he'd done only half of what he could do with his gifted mouth.

              ~

"Now, where did you get to, darling?" Isabella pulled Beth with her through a whirl of bright skirts in the ballroom. "You have a look in your eye. What have you been doing?" Her tone was disapproving.

Beth caught sight of Ian in the marble-lined foyer outside the ballroom and felt her cheeks flush. Isabella saw her look and gasped in delight.

"You were kissing, Ian, weren't you? My darling, how wonderful."

Beth didn't answer. If she spoke, she might burn up from the inside out. *Is this me, Beth Ackerley? Dressed in satin and glittering with diamonds, having a wicked affair with the most decadent man in Paris?*

She thought of her hungry days of childhood, of grime-filled streets and thin children, of drunken men, of women desperate and exhausted. She'd never dreamed her life could change so dramatically.

Ian paused to speak to another gentleman, then turned away with him, walking back through the darkened hall. Of course he wouldn't enter the ballroom. He hated crowds.

Beth swallowed her pang of disappointment. She couldn't expect him to dance attendance. Or was it part of what he'd told her, that he couldn't engage his heart? More fool Beth.

She kept up lighthearted chatter with Isabella and her friends, but her attention kept straying to the outer hall. Ian never reappeared.

Fog was gathering as Beth and Isabella left the house much later. As they crossed the small space of pavement to Isabella's waiting carriage, Beth saw a man in the shadow between lampposts. He moved away when he caught her gaze, and the lamplight briefly shone on his thick, luxuriant mustache.

~~~

"Mrs. Ackerley."

Beth turned sharply the next morning on her walk through the Tuileries Gardens. The burned-out remains of the Tuileries Palace loomed across the park, a reminder of violence in this beautiful place.

Katie walked next to her, surly because Beth had insisted on coming out early after such a late night. Isabella remained in bed, fast asleep, but Beth felt energetic and restless.

"*Fashionable* ladies never rise before noon," Katie growled under her breath. "I thought now we were fashionable, too."

"Hush, Katie," Beth said. She bade Katie walk ahead and waited for the tall man in black to catch up to her.

"Well?" she asked when Katie was out of earshot. "I know you've been following me about, Inspector. Please tell me why."

"Just doing my duty."

The wind blew in from the river, bringing with it the musty stench of water and the sound of bells from Notre Dame.

"Does Scotland Yard know you're in Paris?" she asked. "Looking into murders that you've been forbidden to investigate?"

"I took a leave of absence. I'm in Paris on holiday."

"Then I take it you will not be making any arrests."

Fellows shook his head, his hazel eyes hard. "If I feel there's reason to arrest anyone, I'll go through the proper channels. I'll inform the Sûreté and assist them any way I can."

Beth gave him a cold look. "I've already told you that I'll not spy on my friends."

"I've not come to renew that suggestion."

"Because you know it is useless?"

"Because I realize you have integrity, Mrs. Ackerley. Surprising, considering your background."

"You've made your point. My mother was gently bred, despite her unfortunate marriage, please remember."

"Yes, I've made inquiries and found one country squire from Surrey called Hilton Yardley. Very respectable, very English. Died of grief when his daughter married a frog of dubious origins."

"No, he died of a liver complaint four years later," Beth said. "You will no doubt say it was brought on by the shock of his daughter marrying my father."

"No doubt," Fellows answered dryly.

Beth turned and walked away at a pointedly brisk stride, but Fellows easily kept pace with her. "I approached you about a different matter, Mrs. Ackerley."

"I have no interest, Inspector."

"You will."

Beth halted so abruptly that her skirts swung. She held her parasol firmly and bathed him in a glare. "Very well, what is it?"

He looked her up and down, his hazel gaze raking her in a most insulting manner. His mustache twitched.

"Mrs. Ackerley, I want you to marry me."

Chapter 9

Beth stared at Inspector Fellows until she realized this wasn't a joke. "I beg your pardon?"

"Marry me, Mrs. Ackerley," Fellows repeated. "I am a respectable man with a job and income, although I know you no longer need to worry about money. But you're in deep waters, too deep for your own good."

"And you fear that I'll drown?"

Fellows grasped her elbow. His fingers were strong, like Ian's. "The Mackenzies will pull you under. Look what they did to Lady Isabella. She was an innocent debutante, and now she's not received by her own family. You have even less social position than she does, and once you've lost public regard, you will have nothing. Doesn't matter about all your money."

Fellows's words rang with sincerity. But there was something behind the sincerity, a watchfulness that she couldn't quite place.

"It is the best offer you'll have," he said. "I've seen the gigolos here running after you, panting after your fortune.

They'll ruin you. I care nothing for your money—I am happy being a detective, and I will continue to forge ahead at Scotland Yard."

Beth clutched her parasol's handle until her knuckles hurt. "You amaze me. Why should you worry so much about my reputation?"

True anger blazed from his hazel eyes. "Because the Mackenzies destroy everything they touch. Any lady who goes nigh that family comes to grief. I'd like to save one, at least."

"One?" she asked sharply. "There have been others?"

"Do you not know the stories?"

Fellows's eyes glittered. It was obvious he wanted to tell her, and Beth was cursed with wanting to know.

She studied the sad ruin of the palace, which the Parisians had already started to knock down. Clearing out the past, ridding itself of its ghosts.

"Please tell me, Inspector," she said. "You are going to anyway."

"I am talking about the wives of Hart and Cameron Mackenzie. Hart married a slip of a girl, a marquess's daughter. This was after another young woman jilted him—came to her senses in time, most like. But the poor thing His Grace married was terrified of him by all accounts. He shut her up in that great house in Scotland and never let her out. She died trying to give him the heir he wanted. It's said he took five minutes out to bury her in the family mausoleum, then went back to his houseful of fancy women."

"You're very certain of this information."

"I have my sources. The duke now won't talk about his wife and refuses to have her name mentioned."

"Perhaps he is grief-stricken."

Fellows snorted. "Unlikely. Did you forbid all and sundry to speak your husband's name when he passed, Mrs. Ackerley?"

"No." She remembered the emptiness of her life after Thomas had gone. "You're right. I didn't want people to forget him. I wanted his name mentioned everywhere. Thomas Ackerley was a good man."

Ian closed hard fingers around her hand. "I am asking *you*. Yes or no?"

"You don't know anything about me. I might have a sordid past."

"I know everything about you." His gaze went remote, and his hand closed more tightly around hers. "Your maiden name is Villiers. Your father was a Frenchman who appeared in England thirty years ago. Your mother was the daughter of an English squire, and he disowned her when she married your father. Your father died a pauper and left you destitute. You and your mother were forced into a workhouse when you were ten years old."

Beth listened in astonishment. She'd made no secret of her past to Mrs. Barrington or Thomas, but to hear it come out of the mouth of a lofty lord like Ian Mackenzie was unnerving.

"Goodness, is this common knowledge?"

"I told Curry to find out about you. Your mother died when you were fifteen. You were eventually employed by the workhouse as a teacher. When you were nineteen the vicar newly in charge of the workhouse, Thomas Ackerley, met you and married you. He died of fever a year later. Mrs. Barrington of Belgrave Square hired you as her companion."

Beth blinked as the drama of her life unfolded in the brief sentences. "Is this Curry a Scotland Yard detective?"

"He is my valet."

"Oh, of course. A valet." She fanned herself vigorously. "He looks after your clothes, shaves you, and investigates the pasts of obscure young women. Perhaps you should be warning Sir Lyndon about *me* instead of the other way around."

"I wanted to discover whether you were genuine or false."

She had no idea what that meant. "You have your answer, then. I'm certainly no diamond in the rough. More like a pebble that's been polished a little."

Ian touched a lock of hair that had drifted to her forehead. "You are real."

"You see? Lord Cameron's wife died equally as tragically, though she was a much more spirited woman. She was a firebrand her own family couldn't handle. Then after she had her son, she went crazy with a knife, tried to kill the baby and Lord Cameron both. No one knows quite what happened in that room, but when Lord Cameron came out, his face was cut up, and his wife lay dead on the floor."

Beth blenched. "How dreadful." She'd seen the scar on Cameron's face, a deep gash on his cheekbone.

"Yes," Fellows agreed. "If they'd left those ladies alone, they'd be alive today."

"Were either of them friends of yours?" Beth asked him. "Are you persecuting the family to avenge their deaths?"

Fellows looked surprised. "No, I never knew them. The ladies in question were well above my class."

"But someone you cared about was hurt by the Mackenzies."

His look told her she was right. "They've hurt so many, I doubt they'd even remember."

"And because of this slight, whatever it is, you want to blame Ian for the High Holborn murder."

Fellows reached out and clutched Beth's elbow. "Ian killed her, Mrs. Ackerley. You mark my words. He never should have been let out into the world—he's completely mad, and I intend to prove it. I will do anything to prove he murdered Sally Tate and Lily Martin, and I'll lock him away forever. He deserves it."

His face was red with fury, his mouth shaking. The anger went deep, nursed for years, and Beth was suddenly consumed with curiosity. What on earth could the Mackenzie family have done to a police inspector to make him so determined to destroy them?

She heard shouting and looked behind her to see the tall bulk of Ian Mackenzie running toward them. He had a walking stick in his hands and rage in every step. The wind carried Ian's hat to the ground at the same time he dropped the stick and jerked Fellows from Beth.

"I told you to stay away from her."

"Ian, no."

Last time, Ian had shaken the man and pushed him off. This time, Ian's strong hands closed on his throat and didn't let go. "Leave her alone, or I'll kill you."

"I'm trying to save her from you, you filth."

Ian roared, his rage so bright that Beth backed up a step.

"*Ian.*" Mac Mackenzie sprinted across the grass and grabbed his brother's arms. "Curry, help me, damn you."

A lean, wiry man wrapped his hands around Ian's huge arm, but it was like a small dog trying to drag down a tree. Mac was shouting in Ian's ear, but Ian ignored him.

A crowd began to gather. Upper-class Parisians out for their morning stroll, nannies with their children, and beggars alike moved closer to get a look at the mad Englishmen brawling in the middle of the park.

Mac spewed foul language as he pried Ian's hands from Fellows's neck. Released, Fellows fell to his knees, then hauled himself up again, trousers stained with wet grass. His throat was red, his collar ripped.

"I'll have you," Fellows snarled. "By God, I'll have you swinging for the hangman before you know where you are." Foam flecked his lips. "I'll destroy you, and I'll put my heel in your brother's face when he begs me for mercy."

"*Fuck you,*" Ian screamed.

Beth pressed her hands to her face. Katie stared, open-mouthed, as Curry and Mac laced their arms around Ian's middle and dragged him away from Fellows.

Ian's face was purple, tears tracking his cheeks. He coughed as Curry jerked a fist against his breastbone.

"You have to stop, guv," Curry said rapidly. "You have to stop or you won't breathe sweet air anymore. You'll be back in that hellhole, and you'll never see your brothers again. What's worse is I'll be stuck in there with you."

Ian coughed again, but still fought like an animal not understanding it had been caught. Mac stepped in front of Ian and grabbed his face.

"Ian, look at me."

Ian tried to pull away, to do anything but look his brother directly in the eye.

"Look at me, damn you."

He swiveled Ian's head, forcing Ian's eyelids open until finally, Mac's eyes and Ian's met.

Ian stopped. He gasped for breath, tears shining on his face, but he stilled, staring, mesmerized, into Mac's eyes.

Mac's hold on him softened, and Beth saw that Mac's own eyes were wet. "That's it. You're all right." His grip on Ian's cheek turned to a caress, and then Mac leaned forward and kissed Ian on the forehead.

Ian's breath was hoarse and audible. He dropped his gaze and looked away across the park, seeing no one.

Curry still had hold of his arms. Ian shook him off, then turned his back and started toward the carriage that had stopped in the lane.

Its coachman was standing on the ground, holding the horses and looking agitated. Beth guessed that Ian and Mac had been riding by, and Ian had leapt from the coach when he'd seen Beth with Fellows.

She realized then that Mac and Ian both wore rumpled evening dress, Ian in the same suit he'd worn the night before. They weren't up early; they were still returning from the night's revelries.

Ian never looked at Beth. Curry retrieved Ian's hat from the ground, dusted it off, and strode after him.

Mac turned to Fellows, his eyes like cold copper. "Go back to London. If I see you again, I'll thrash you until you can't stand."

Fellows was breathing hard, rubbing his throat, but he wasn't cowed. "You can hide Lord Ian behind the duke as much as you want, but in the end, I'll get him. That terrifies you, doesn't it?"

Mac growled. Beth pictured another outburst of violence in this quiet, sunny park, and she stepped between them.

"Do as Mac says," she begged Fellows. "Haven't you caused enough trouble?"

Fellows turned hard hazel eyes to her. "One last warning,

Mrs. Ackerley. Don't throw in your lot with them. You do, and I won't be merciful."

"Didn't you hear her?" Katie said, planting her hands on her hips. "Be off or I'll call the police on you. Wouldn't that be a laugh? A Scotland Yard 'tec arrested by the French coppers?"

Mac put his hand on Katie's shoulder and pushed her toward Beth. "Get your mistress home and make her stay there. Tell my . . . Tell *her* she needs to look after Mrs. Ackerley better."

Katie opened her mouth to snap at him, but she took one look into Mac's eyes and quieted. "He's right, Mrs. A," she said meekly. "Best we go home."

Beth gave Ian's retreating back one last look, and then gazed up at Mac. "I'm sorry," she said, her throat tight.

Mac said nothing. Beth ignored Fellows and let Katie turn her toward the lane that led to the Rue de Rivoli. She felt Mac's eyes on her all the way, but when she glanced back, Ian had entered the coach and was sitting with his head turned from her. He never once looked out at her, and she walked away with Katie, the garden's brilliance blurred by her tears.

━━━━⁓

"I've lost her, haven't I?" Ian grated.

Mac landed next to him in the carriage with a thump, and slammed the door himself.

"You never had her, Ian."

Ian let familiar numbness flow over him as the coach started. He rubbed his temple, the rage having brought on his headache.

Damn the demon inside him. Seeing Fellows reach out and touch Beth—and worse, Beth do nothing to stop him—had unleashed the beast. All he'd wanted was to wrap his hands around Fellows's throat and shake him. Just like Father—

Mac sighed, cutting through the memory. "We're Mackenzies. We don't get happy endings."

Ian wiped his eyes with the back of his hand and didn't answer.

Mac watched him a moment. "I'm sorry. I should have sent the bastard packing the minute you told me he was in Paris."

Ian sat back, unable to speak, but his thoughts spun, words tumbling over words until he had to keep mute. He looked out the window, but instead of the passing streets, he saw Beth reflected in the glass, her hands white lines on her beautiful face.

"I'm sorry," Mac repeated wearily. "Damn it all, Ian, I am so sorry."

Still gripping Ian's arm, Mac rested his forehead on Ian's broad shoulder. Ian felt Mac's distress, but he couldn't move or say a word that could offer any comfort.

~~~~

Mac's studio was not what Beth expected. He'd rented a shabby apartment in the Montmartre area, two rooms to live in on the first floor and a studio at the top of the house. A far cry from what she pictured a wealthy English aristocrat would live in.

A man built like a pugilist with iron gray hair and hard brown eyes opened the door. Beth stepped back in alarm, clutching her satchel to her bosom. This was a man one would find in a wrestling match or a brawl in a pub, not answering doors in Paris.

But no, he seemed to be Mac's valet. Isabella had told her that the four brothers picked up their unconventional valets off the streets, thus saving them time and expense at the agencies. Curry had been a pickpocket, Bellamy a pugilist, Cameron's valet a Roma, and Hart's a disgraced clerk to a London financier.

The sneer left Bellamy's thuglike face when Beth said who she was. Looking almost polite, he directed her up three flights of stairs to the door at the top.

The studio covered the entire floor, with two huge skylights letting in the gray Paris sky. The view, on the other hand, was breathtaking. Beth saw across rooftops down the steep hill to the flat plain of Paris and cloud-bedecked hills in the distance.

Mac was perched on a ladder in front of an enormous canvas, his hair covered by a red kerchief that made him look like a Gypsy. He held a long paintbrush in his hand and scowled bleakly at his canvas. Paint splattered his hands, face, painter's smock, and the floor around him.

On the eight-foot canvas that reared in front of him, the figures of a pillar and a plump naked woman had been roughed in. Mac was concentrating on the folds of a drape that just missed the woman's intimate parts, but the model kept twitching.

"Stay still, can't you?"

The model saw Beth and stopped wriggling. Mac glanced over his shoulder and also went still.

Ian moved out of the shadows. His hair was rumpled, as though he'd been scraping his hands through it, perhaps massaging one of his temples, as he often did. His gold gaze darted over Beth, and then he deliberately turned to look out the window.

Beth cleared her throat. "The porter at your hotel said you'd come here," she told Ian's back.

Ian didn't turn.

"Cybele," Mac snapped, "go downstairs and tell Bellamy to give you tea."

Cybele squeaked, then spoke in a heavy accent. "I'll not go near Bellamy. He frightens me so much. He looks at me like he wishes to lock his hands around my throat."

"Can't imagine why," Mac muttered, but Beth broke in.

"It's all right. It doesn't matter. I only came here to apologize. To both of you."

"What the devil do you have to apologize for?" Mac said. "Fellows is to blame, blast the man. He was told to stay away from us."

Beth walked to the window, her gloved fingers closing tightly on the handle of her satchel. She looked up at Ian reflected in the glass, his face utterly still.

"You were quite right, Ian," she said softly. "I should have sent the inspector away with a flea in his ear. I didn't because I was curious about things that were none of my

business. Mrs. Barrington always said curiosity was my
besetting sin, and she was right. I had no call to pry into
your family's history, and for that I soundly apologize."

"Very pretty," Cybele sneered.

Mac leapt from his stepladder, threw a dressing gown at
Cybele, took her by the ear, and pulled her with him out of
the room. Cybele shrieked and swore in French. The slam
of the door shook the walls, and then everything went silent.

Beth studied the unfinished painting as she gathered her
wits. The painted woman gazed at the bowl of water at her
feet. Patches of wetness suggested she'd just stepped out of it.
She held a thin scarf across her back as though she'd been
drying off.

It was a sensual painting, like the one Isabella had
shown her, but Beth understood the difference right away.
The woman in this picture was a thing, a curve of colored
flesh. She was no more a person than was the bath at her
feet or the pillar behind her.

The woman in Isabella's picture had been Isabella. Mac
had painted his *wife*, every stroke lovingly placed, every
shadow carefully laid. Any woman could have modeled for
this bather—only Isabella could have been the woman in
her painting.

Beth turned from the easel and faced the solid upright
that was Ian. "I bought you a present."

He still didn't move. Beth unlocked her satchel and
pulled out a small box.

"I saw it while I was shopping with Isabella. I wanted
you to have it."

Ian continued to stare sightlessly away from her, the
shape of his broad shoulders reflected in the grimy window.

Beth laid the box on the windowsill and turned away.
If he didn't want to speak to her, there was nothing she
could do.

Ian pressed his hand flat against the windowpane, still
not looking at her. "How can you be to blame?"

Beth dropped the skirt she'd caught up in preparation for
leaving. "Because if I'd refused to speak to Inspector Fellows

yesterday in the park, you'd never have seen him. I should have had him thrown out when he came to Isabella's house and began those awful accusations, but I'm too curious for my own good. Both times, I wanted to hear what he had to say."

Ian finally turned his face to her, keeping his hand on the window. "Don't protect me. They all try to protect me."

Beth went to him. "How can I possibly protect you? It was wrong of me to poke and pry, but I fully admit I wanted to speak to Fellows to find out all about you. Even his lies."

"They aren't lies. We were there."

"Fellows's interpretation of the truth, then."

One hand fisted on the windowsill. "Tell me what he said to you. Everything." His gaze rested on her mouth as he waited for her words.

She told him what Fellows had told her, including the man's abrupt proposal of marriage. She did keep Fellows's speculations about her father to herself, something she'd have to explain to Ian someday, but not now.

When Beth got to the proposal, Ian pivoted to the window again. "Did you accept?"

"Of course not. Why on earth should I want to marry Inspector Fellows?"

"Because he'll ruin you if you don't."

"Let him try." Beth glared. "I'm not a hothouse flower to be sheltered; I know a thing or two of the world. My new fortune and Mrs. Barrington's approval have done much for my standing—I'm no longer the girl from the workhouse, or even the poor vicar's widow. The wealthy get away with much. It's disgusting, really."

She realized, when she ran out of breath, that Ian hadn't registered a word. "I beg your pardon. I do run on sometimes, especially when I'm rattled. Mrs. Barrington often remarked on it."

"And why the devil do you drag Mrs. Barrington into every conversation?"

Beth blinked. He sounded more himself. "I don't know. I suppose she had great influence on me. And opinions. Many, many opinions."

Ian didn't answer. He reached to the windowsill and picked up the package, his strong fingers making short work of the paper. He opened a wooden box and stared into it, then lifted out a flat gold pin embossed with stylized curlicues.

"For your lapel," Beth said. "I'm sure you have dozens of them, but I thought it was pretty."

Ian continued to stare at it as though he'd never seen such a thing.

"I had it engraved, on the back."

Ian turned the pin over, his eyes flickering as he read the inscription Beth had mulled over for so long in the shop.

To Ian, In friendship. B.

"Put it on me," he said.

Beth slid the pin through the cashmere with a trembling hand. His body was hard beneath his coat, and she let her fingers rest a moment on his chest.

"Do you forgive me?" she asked.

"No."

Her heart beat faster. "I suppose I shouldn't expect too much."

"There is nothing to forgive." Ian caught her hand in a crushing grip. "I thought you would leave Paris after you saw me in the park."

"I can't possibly. Your brother hasn't given me drawing lessons yet."

A line appeared between his brows. Beth amended quickly, "I was joking."

His frown deepened. "Why did you stay?"

"I wanted to make sure you were all right."

Ian's gaze flicked past hers. "You saw."

Beth remembered his nearly purple face, his hoarse curses, his hands in hard fists, his brother and Curry dragging him away.

"It stays away most of the time. But when I saw him touch you, my Beth, it rose like a fire. I frightened you."

"You did, rather." But not in the way he meant. Beth's

father had been prone to violent rages when drunk. She'd run from him and cowered behind whatever would hide her small body until he'd slammed out of the house.

With Ian, she'd not wanted to flee. That he could have hurt Fellows she had no doubt, but she hadn't been afraid Ian would hurt her. She'd known he wouldn't. She'd been more afraid that he'd hurt himself or that a passing policeman would decide to arrest him.

Beth rested her cheek against the stiff white fabric of his shirtfront. "You told me not to protect you, but I don't want anything to happen to you."

"I don't want you to lie for me." His voice rumbled under her ear, overshadowing the strong beat of his heart. "Hart lies for me. Mac and Cam lie; Curry lies."

"Sounds like verbal conjugation. I lie; you lie; he, she, it lies. . . ."

Ian fell silent, and she looked up. "I'm a very truthful person, Ian. I promise."

He ran the backs of his fingers down her cheek.

Beth felt an insane need to keep talking. "Those clouds are thick. It might rain."

"Good. Then it will be too dark to paint, and Mac will send that bloody girl home."

"He isn't her lover, is he?" Beth put her fingers over her lips. "Oh, dear, I can't stop asking questions. You don't have to answer."

"She's not his lover."

"Good." She hesitated. "Are *we* lovers?"

"The pin says 'in friendship.' "

"Only because I was too put off by the shopkeeper to have him engrave 'to my love.' Besides, Isabella was standing right next to me."

Ian went silent for a long time, looking at her and avoiding her gaze at the same time. She saw his eyes flicker back and forth, restless, never wanting to settle.

"I told you I can't fall in love," he said. "But you have."

Her heart thumped. "Have I?"

"With your husband."

So many people wanted to talk about Thomas Ackerley. "I did. I loved him very much."

"What was it like?" His words were so low she barely caught them. "Explain to me what loving feels like, Beth. I want to understand."

Chapter 10

He waited, his golden eyes burning, for her to explain the mysteries of the world. "It is the most divine thing imaginable," she tried.

"I don't want to hear about divinity. I want to hear about flesh and bone. Is love like desire?"

"Some people think so."

"But you don't."

Sweat trickled down Beth's back, despite the clouds cutting the sun's heat. The trouble with Ian Mackenzie's questions was that he asked the unanswerable. And yet she should know how to answer—everyone should. But they couldn't, because everyone simply *knew*. Everyone except Ian.

"Desire is part of it," she said slowly. "The love for another's body. But also love for their heart and their mind, and for all the silly things they do, no matter how absurd. Your world brightens when they walk into a room, dims when they leave it again. You want to be with the beloved so you can see him and touch him and hear his voice, but you want his happiness as well. It's selfish, but not entirely so."

"I can feel desire and wanting. I find you beautiful, and I want you."

She warmed. "I must say, you are quite good for my pride. But when you don't desire a woman, you feel nothing for her?"

"Nothing at all."

Beth heaved a sigh. "And that, Ian Mackenzie, is why I said you'll break my heart."

His gaze strayed out the window to cloud-strewn Paris. "Wanting is not enough? Desire so strong you'll do anything to fulfill it?"

"It's lovely in the moment, but in the long view, I think, no."

"In the asylum, I learned to take the short view."

She imagined a younger Ian, lanky and not yet grown into his man's body, bewildered and alone. The bewildered boy reminded her of the girl who found herself abandoned at fifteen with predators roaming, waiting for her to become their victim. Even now, with a respectable name and a fortune, Beth never felt entirely safe.

"I admit that I, too, have learned to take the short view," she said.

"You feel the wanting." Ian took her fingers between his, pressing their palms together. "You felt it at the duchesse's."

Her face heated. "Of course I felt it. You had me in that sitting room with my skirts up to my ears. How could I not?"

"Do you want to feel it again?"

Excitement whispered through her. "If I were a lady, I'd protest that of course I don't want to feel like that ever again. But I do, actually. Very much."

"Good, because I want to see your body."

Beth swallowed. "You've already seen a good portion of it."

He sent her a dark smile. "And it was fine. I wish to see the rest. Right now."

Beth darted a glance to the door. "Mac might return any minute."

"He'll stay away until we leave."

"How do you know that?"

"I know Mac."

"The window . . ."

"Too high for anyone to see in."

Beth had to admit that he'd answered her most basic objections. She knew she should have other objections, but she couldn't remember them right now.

"And if I decide I'd rather run away?"

"Then we'll wait."

Beth hesitated, her legs feeling like water, but at the same time, she knew nothing would induce her to leave this room short of a fire. A very large fire.

"I'll need help with the buttons," she said.

Beth's clothes came off layer by layer, like a complicated wrapping peeling back to reveal simple beauty. One by one, her garments fell across the studio's sofa in a multi-colored layer: rich blue bodice and overskirt, a brighter blue underskirt, the fabric light for summer. Two silk petticoats, both white, then her corset cover, until at last Ian unlaced the linen corset himself.

Ian's arousal throbbed, and he knew he wouldn't be happy until he saw her bared in her entirety. He untied her lacy pantalets, then unbuttoned the chemise. The silk garments floated gracefully to the floor, and Beth stepped out of them, nude for him. She reached for him, but Ian stepped away, and Beth stopped, confused.

Her hair was mussed from undressing, little ringlets falling from the mass of curls on top of her head. Her arms were soft and round, her thighs also, her waist nipped in by years of wearing a corset.

From her waist her hips softly flared to smooth and firm buttocks. He'd seen her vee of dark hair when he lifted her skirts in the little gilded room, but it was even more beautiful now touched by daylight.

Under his close scrutiny, she blushed and folded her arms over her breasts.

Ian leaned against the back of a chair and basked in her beauty. "You don't need to hide from me."

Beth hesitated, then gave a little laugh and spun around, arms outstretched. She was so beautiful, with her curls every which way, her mouth laughing, her blue eyes flashing in the fading sunlight. The clouds thickened and rain began to fall, but that didn't dampen the glow inside the room.

Beth laughed again. "How strange is life?" she asked. "One moment you are a dowdy companion without a shilling, the next you are a wealthy bohemian in Paris. One moment a drudge, the next you are buying gifts for your paramour."

Her words slid over him like water. He'd remember each one in its precise order later, but he would never understand them any better than he did now.

Beth caught up the drape Cybele had dropped and spun it around herself. The gauzy folds caught her hips and breasts, not hiding her in the slightest. She spun around and around, laughing.

Ian grasped the drape when she whirled by, and used it to haul her against him. She stumbled into his arms, still laughing. His first kiss parted her lips, stopping the laughter as she melted to him.

Beth had seen him at his worst, and yet she'd come here today, bleating an apology and handing him a gift. He caught the glint of the gold pin on his chest and his heart warmed beneath it.

Other parts of him were plenty warm, too. He lifted her against him, loving her pliant, bare body in his arms. If she'd been a courtesan, Ian would have already bent her over the chair and taken her without further ado. But while Beth's husband might have taught her the pleasures of the bed, she'd know nothing of the crude coupling of courtesans. She smiled at him in perfect faith, a flower just opening.

Beth's fragile trust was in Ian's hands. He'd growled that he didn't want to be protected, but the instinct to protect *her* was strong. Beth was so alone in the world, so vulnerable, and she didn't even realize it.

Ian rubbed his hands over her warm body, wanting to gather her to him and not let go. The thought of anything happening to her, of other men demanding things from her, wound his thoughts into a frenzy.

"Kiss me," he said.

Beth smiled into his mouth. She wrapped her arms around him, the gauzy drape coming around his neck.

She tasted like warm honey, incredible sweetness. Something deep inside him responded. Ian recognized wanting, but it was more than that.

He slid his broad knee between hers, coaxing her forward as he kissed her. He boosted her with his hands on her buttocks until she trustingly straddled his thigh.

Ian loosened his hold a little, letting her slide against his rock-hard thigh. Beth looked surprised, and then a soft sound escaped her lips.

Ian held his hands loosely on her hips, rocking her against his hard leg, teaching her to pleasure herself. Her sweet and exciting scent surrounded him. He kissed her, then left her alone to enjoy the strange sensation of the fabric against her cleft.

Beth scraped back and forth, her breath coming faster, cheeks pink and damp with sweat. She'd never pleasured herself, he realized. This was new to her, astonishing, delightful.

Her head went back, and she closed her eyes. Wisps of hair trickled down her neck, her lips parting in desire.

"Ian," she whispered. "How do you know so well . . . what I want?"

He knew because her body told him. He liked a woman rising under his touch like Beth did now, eyes softening in delight. Women were more beautiful than ever when they gave in to pleasure. He loved how they smelled, how they tasted, the sound of their breathy sighs, the warmth of their bodies under his hands.

That meant that Ian could stand in Mac's studio, fully dressed, and have Beth go crazy with pleasure. He liked the power of it, and the joy of watching Beth's eyes widen and hearing her gasp turn to frenzied cries of delight.

Ian took a curl at her forehead between his lips. He wanted her in every way possible, but he was enjoying slowly spinning out the seduction, giving her one taste at a time, watching her learn to want him.

One night, he would have her. By then, Beth would want him so much he could make her his forever. Ian didn't understand love, by his own admission, but he knew having Beth in his life was something worth striving for. She'd said no the first time he'd asked her to marry him; she'd explained in her sensible manner that she had no inclination to marry. But Ian would change her mind. Ian Mackenzie had learned to be good at getting what he truly wanted.

Beth's cries rang against the studio's high ceiling. She clasped his face between her hands and kissed him, hard. "Thank you, Ian," she whispered.

Ian sank his fingers into her bottom and returned the kiss, tasting her as her orgasm wound down. She'd thanked him in the duchesse's tiny sitting room, yet she was the one who stilled the beast inside him. He should be thanking her for giving him this peace, if only for a few precious moments.

I have become a truly wicked woman, Beth wrote in her journal a few days later. *I find myself looking forward every day to what naughtiness Ian and I might do together.*

> *Yesterday he escorted Isabella and me to Drouant's, that very fashionable new restaurant where everyone goes to see who is there and with whom. Ian doesn't speak much in company and never minds that Isabella and I gossip like magpies—or rather, Isabella tells me all about the people she sees, and I inhale it with too much enjoyment.*
>
> *Ian held my hand under the table the entire meal. Isabella knew—of course she did. She seems quite enchanted with Ian's attentions to me. But if she knew* how *Ian held my hand, she might not be so sanguine.*
>
> *Ian cannot do something so simple as hold a woman's hand. He moves his thumb up my wrist and under my glove, finding points that shoot wild heat through my*

body. He caresses the inside of my palm with soft fingers, and then he threads his fingers through mine and holds hard, as though teaching me that my hand belongs there with his.

He calmly eats his sole meunière, or whatever exotic concoction Isabella has insisted we try, and says not a word.

Ian and I are lovers—how strange for me to pen the word. And yet, we have not consummated our affair, not in the way of the marriage bed. I had thought, in Mac's studio, that he would remove his clothes and couple with me on the couch. But he did not. He didn't take off one stitch, not even loosening his collar, while I lay against him in my altogether. Quite disappointing.

However, my bare skin against the fabric of his coat was a strange but pleasing sensation. I never thought myself so depraved, but it made me feel rather wild and wanton. I would have done anything in that room, anything he wanted me to, but he gently suggested I dress and go before Isabella worried where I was.

I did, but the way he kissed me before I departed promised more adventures at a later time. And good heavens, did I have an adventure today. . . .

Beth paused in her writing to listen to the rain beating at the windows. Paris had come in for a series of summer storms, rain and wind gusting endlessly through the city. It had ruined Beth's morning walk and put paid to her and Isabella strolling along looking at shops.

Ian had said he'd take Isabella and me driving in the park today, and he arrived at the appointed hour. Isabella took one look at the slate gray sky and flatly refused to go. If we wanted fresh air so much, she said, Ian and I could go without her. Ian didn't look as though he minded one way or another, so I found myself climbing into the carriage alone with him.

Was Isabella a bit too easily put off by the weather? Did she too readily press her hand to her head and declare she felt a migraine coming on? She seems to want me to be improper—perhaps to encourage Ian to propose?

But Ian and I are grown-up people—he is twenty-seven, Isabella tells me, which puts him two years younger than I. I am not a virginal debutante sheltering behind her mama's skirts, and he is not a dark villain. We are simply a widow and a bachelor of the same age enjoying each other's company.

When the carriage began moving around the park at a fair clip, I boldly told Ian how much I'd liked feeling his clothes against my body in Mac's studio. He smiled that warm, melting smile of his and said that if I liked that sort of sensation, I could pull down my drawers then and there and sit bare-buttocked on his lap.

The thought aroused me instantly, and Ian knew it, drat the man. I believe he delights in putting me in this state.

I did not obey, because I could imagine the coach having an accident and me scrambling to safety with my lacy drawers about my ankles. Paris is a more permissive place than London, but I think even here I'd never live it down.

Ian smiled at my fears and told me that nearly getting caught was part of the fun. I countered by mentioning that he had seen quite a lot of my bare skin, while I hadn't seen a bit of his.

He then asked me which bit I had in mind.

I, of course, want to see all of him. The feel of hard muscle beneath his suits suggests a body well honed, and the thought of viewing any part of it makes me pulse with excitement.

Unfortunately we were in a moving carriage, and Ian removing all his clothes, then resuming them wouldn't have been practical. He told me I could view any bit I wished, but I'd have to open that part of his clothing myself.

Depraved thing that I am, I reached over and began to unfasten his trousers.

Ian sat back and let me, his eyes closing to slits of gold. He spread his legs but refused to help me. This vexed me, because men's clothes are wretched things. I don't know how they manage. I had to unbutton and untie and move several pieces of fabric before I finally found what I sought. Ian was shaking by the time I finished—with laughter, I believe.

At last his clothes parted, and I was able to reveal that part of a man's anatomy that is the cause of so much wickedness. I am pleased to say I felt no embarrassment or timidity as I closed my hand around it and drew it forth.

Ian did not need to be embarrassed either. He is perfectly shaped. His shaft is smooth and dark, very warm in the cool carriage. It ends in a wide tip, like a cap with a tiny slit in its middle. I stroked my finger over this slit, and Ian made a hungry noise.

Realizing he liked this, I moved my thumb over the tip in a circular motion until he groaned again. I played with him thus, enjoying my power. I varied my technique, grasping his shaft and stroking my fingers up and down it, or tickling my way around the flange.

Ian put his hand over his face and wrapped his other arm tightly around me. I rested my cheek on his chest and kept up my play with his fascinating appendage.

After a while, I wanted more. The carriage was moving smoothly, so I slid from the seat to my knees. I studied him a little while at eye level, enjoying looking over every part of him. Then I leaned over and took him into my mouth.

Ian jumped like I'd stung him. I feared I'd hurt him, but when I tried to back away, he laced his fingers through my hair and pulled me to him again.

I'd never tasted a man's shaft before, and I licked it, assessing what it was like. I found the taste faintly salty, but darker, different from his lips.

I speculated whether I could put a love bite on him here, and when I began to try, he moaned out loud. He moved his legs farther apart while I worked, and his feet flexed in his boots. I heard him whisper my name, but I couldn't reply, my mouth being far too full of him.

I couldn't quite leave a love bite, though I tried for a long time. When I finally gave up, I pushed my mouth back over his shaft, as though I meant to swallow it entirely.

The thought excited me. I wanted to devour him. I

didn't understand the wanting, but I pushed him into my mouth as far as he could go.

I know he liked this, because he wrapped his legs around my middle, and the sounds that came out of his mouth were incoherent. His hips moved, making him rise out of the seat. I felt gleeful that I could torment him this way, just as he'd tormented me. I now knew how to give him such pleasure he couldn't keep still.

I dipped my hand between his spread legs to find the round firmness of his balls, and entertained myself moving them gently in my palm. I felt him shudder, felt the pulsing inside him, and then suddenly he let out a loud groan and filled my mouth with his seed.

I was surprised and nearly pulled away, but my heart beat swiftly, and I decided I wanted to stay put. Ian tasted like fine cream with a little bite, not at all a bad concoction. I slid my tongue around my mouth as he eased himself out, and I swallowed him, happy to keep some part of him for myself.

Ian dragged me up into the seat without bothering to refasten his trousers. He kissed me hard, despite what I'd just done, as though he wanted to taste what lingered on my lips.

He looked at me and said nothing at all, but his grip on my face softened. I saw his gaze try to meet mine and fall short every time.

Finally he growled a little and gathered me into his arms. He held me thus, stroking and kissing my hair, until the carriage slowed again in front of Isabella's house.

Ian refused to come in, which I understood, though he'd of course fastened his trousers again. I expected him to say some good-bye, to let me know when we might meet again and continue our wanton entertainment, but he remained silent. He was breathing hard, though, and I believe he'd not had a chance to compose himself.

Isabella greeted me without the slightest trace of the headache she'd affected before I left. In fact, the deceptive young woman raced upstairs and dressed to attend a salon, even though the rain hadn't slackened one whit.

*I declined to attend with her, because Ian wasn't escort-
ing us, and I couldn't imagine any delight that could match
what I'd experienced in Ian's closed carriage on this wet
day.*

~

The hotel room was hot and close, despite the window
thrown open to coax in the summer breeze. The suite had
been fitted with a fan that spun lazily overhead, propelled
by compressed gas. But it worked in fits and starts and did
nothing to move the still Italian air.

"There is another one, Your Grace."

The Duke of Kilmorgan's whippet-thin valet laid a newspaper across the volume of papers on the duke's desk. Hart
scanned the page Wilfred had folded open for him, but the
relevant story was obvious. A society paper sketch portrayed
Ian Mackenzie alongside a lovely young woman with dark
hair at a crowded theatre. Behind the young woman, his
sister-in-law, Isabella, beamed. Stark capitals, with many
exclamation marks, blazoned in French across the page:

> *A new amore for a duke's brother? The mysterious En-
> glish heiress, Mrs. A——, accompanies Lady I——M——
> and her brother-in-law to a production of* La Bonne
> Femme, *the latest and most scandalous musical comedy
> to open in Paris. Naughty, naughty Mrs. A——.*

"Who the devil is this woman?" Hart growled. He'd
never heard of her, never seen her before.

"Lord Ian is quite rich, Your Grace," Wilfred said in his
creaking voice. "Perhaps she seeks to double her invest-
ment."

"I find no humor in it, Wilfred." Hart bent the pen in his
hand until the slender instrument snapped. Ink splattered
across the newspaper.

"Of course not, Your Grace."

"Damn it all, what is Isabella playing at?"

"You think she has a hand in it, Your Grace?"

"Both hands. Damnation."

"Is it such a danger?" When Hart glared up at Wilfred, the man flushed. "I mean, sir, that if her ladyship likes this Mrs. Ackerley, approves of her, perhaps all is well? If your brother, his lordship, enjoys her company . . . well, he is getting to be of an age where he should think about settling down."

Hart watched him steadily until Wilfred trailed off. "You've been in my employ ten years, Wilfred. You know Ian, and you know what he's capable of."

"I do, Your Grace."

"Isabella isn't aware of certain facts. Neither are you."

"Yes, Your Grace."

"Trust me when I say Ian must be kept away from this woman, whoever she is." Hart studied the drawing, the woman's round, pretty face and dark curls on top of her head. She looked innocent and harmless, but Hart knew better than anyone how much looks could deceive. This was the fifth time a Parisian newspaper had chosen to print such a tidbit about Ian and this Mrs. Ackerley. "Whatever her motives are, they can't be good."

"No, Your Grace."

"Have a packed valise standing by for me at all times, Wilfred. I want to be able to leave at a moment's notice."

"Of course, Your Grace. Shall I dispose of the newspaper?"

"Not yet." Hart put his hand on it. "Not yet."

Wilfred bowed and left him. Hart studied the picture again, noting the way Ian was half turned to look at Mrs. Ackerley. An artist's interpretation, yes, but it likely wasn't far off the mark. Mrs. Ackerley must know Ian's history by now, his eccentricities, his headaches, his nightmares. The latter depended on whether she'd yet wormed her way into his bed.

Hart clenched his fists and rested them on the newspaper. Ian wasn't even supposed to be in Paris. Ian was to stay in London, returning to Scotland when Hart finished his business on the Continent. There had been no mention of Ian visiting Mac or Isabella in Paris.

"I don't know who you are," Hart said, tracing the outline of the laughing Mrs. Ackerley. "But you have taken one step too far."

Hart slowly crumpled the page in his hands, then tore it apart in long, ragged strips.

～

In the week between Ian's interesting carriage ride with Beth and his next planned encounter with her, he saw nothing of Inspector Fellows. He had Curry watch out for the man, but Curry couldn't find him either.

"'E must 'ave run off 'ome," Curry declared, "'is tail between 'is legs."

Ian didn't think so. Inspector Fellows was canny and smart, and he wouldn't run because Ian threatened him. If he'd returned to London in truth, it would be for a very good reason. Ian wished he knew what the man was planning.

Isabella asked Ian to accompany her and Beth to an outing on Wednesday, and though another summer storm had come up to drench Paris, Isabella still insisted on going.

"It's a den of iniquity, darling," Isabella said to Beth as the three of them descended in front of an ordinary-looking house on the edge of Montmartre. "You'll love it."

Ian had been here before with Mac, but entering the house was much more satisfying with Beth on his arm. She was dressed in dark red taffeta tonight, rosettes at her bosom. Everything she wore shimmered and whispered in some way.

He kept her hand tight in the crook of his arm, not letting go when she tried to pull away. He was glad Isabella had been wise enough to ask Ian to escort them, because he'd be damned if he'd let Beth into this place alone.

"Den of iniquity?" Beth asked, peering around the dim, dusty shop they entered. "I believe someone's having you on."

Isabella laughed. "This way, darling. It's a dead secret."

She led the way through the shop to an unmarked door at the back. Light and noise and the stench of cigar smoke and perfume poured up a carpeted staircase.

Not so secret, Ian thought as he let Beth precede him down the stairs. The Parisian police were aware of this illegal gambling den, but took money to look the other way. The wealthy Parisians thought they were getting away with something, excited like mischievous children.

The staircase spilled them into a glittering palace. The room ran the length of several houses upstairs, and crystal chandeliers marched across the ceiling. A rich red carpet covered the floor, and the walls were lined with walnut. People hovered around tables, talking, laughing, shouting, groaning. The click of dice, the slapping of cards, and the whir of a roulette wheel floated above it all.

Too many people pressed around Ian. He didn't like it. They crushed him, stared at him, talked all at the same time until he couldn't hear what they were saying. He felt the need to flee winding like an insidious vine, and he looked around for the nearest retreat.

"Ian?" Beth glanced up at him, faint perfume clinging to her. Her curls on top of her head were level with his nose. He could bury his face in her hair, kiss her. He didn't have to run.

His hand tightened on hers. "I don't like crowds," he said.

"I know. Should we go?"

"Not yet," Isabella said. She looked back at them with shining eyes and stopped in front of a roulette table. The wheel's brass finial gleamed as it spun, the wooden slats of the base beautifully inlaid. Piles of counters rested on numbers on the green baize tabletop.

Ian watched the ball whizzing around the wheel, in the opposite direction the wheel spun. Roulette wheels were precisely balanced, floating on their bases, the nearest thing to a perpetual-motion machine. Ian wanted to snatch up the ball and start the wheel again, to count how many times the ball could glide around the circumference before friction had its way.

The wheel slowed. Ian stared closely, predicting how many turns were left before the ball dropped. Fifteen, he predicted, or twenty.

The ball danced across the double row of slots before finally coming to rest. "*Rouge quinze*," the partially dressed lady behind it announced. Red fifteen.

There were groans and sighs. The croupier raked counters toward herself, and hands reached for winnings or left them to ride.

"I love roulette." Isabella sighed. "It's banned in France, but you can find it if you know where to look. Saves the bother of traveling all the way to Monte Carlo. Give me your money, and I'll change it to markers for you."

Beth looked questioningly at Ian. He nodded. The tightness had eased from his throat, and he breathed more easily.

Isabella handed Beth markers, and Beth reached to put a stack on one of the numbers.

"Not there," Ian said quickly.

"Does it matter?" Diamonds glittered on Beth's gloved wrist as her hand stilled.

Ian took the markers from her and placed one on the lines between four numbers. "Odds are better here."

Beth looked doubtful, but she withdrew her hand to the edge of the table. The croupier spun the wheel, muscles in her bare shoulders working.

The wheel whirred, all eyes fastened on it. The ball spun in its enticing motion until it clicked softly into its slot. "*Noir dix-neuf.*" Black nineteen.

Beth rapped the table in frustration as the croupier scraped away her counters.

"The same again," Ian said.

"But I lost."

"The same again."

"I do hope you know what you're doing, Ian."

She obediently put her marker in the same place. The wheel spun, and the ball dropped. "*Rouge vingt et un.*" Red twenty-one.

Beth squealed and did a little victory hop. The croupier shoved a pile of counters onto Beth's number.

"I won. Gracious, shall I do it again?"

Ian's large hand shot out, and he scraped Beth's winnings to her. "Roulette is a fool's game. Come with me."

Isabella grinned at them, reaching to put her marker where Beth's had been. "It's all rather fun, isn't it? You're so lucky, darling. I knew you would be." She laughed and spun back to the table.

Ian kept Beth's hand in his as they moved to a long table where a portly man shook a cup of dice. Bettors up and down the table shouted encouragement, and the gentleman's face shone with sweat. The lavishly dressed lady next to him hung on his arm and bounced excitedly.

"She'll ruin his throw," Beth hissed.

"She might, if she is employed by the house," Ian murmured back.

"Isn't that cheating?"

He shrugged. "It's the risk of coming into such places as this."

"Isabella seemed so keen."

"She likes danger." After all, she'd married Mac.

"Shall I place a bet?" Beth asked.

Hazard had so many odds, so many different combinations that the dice could produce. Predicting which would come up or waiting for a precise throw seemed futile to Ian. People found that risk exciting, which baffled him.

Beth's eyes sparkled as she watched the gentleman nerve himself to throw. "What bet shall I place?"

Ian rubbed his thumb over his forehead, numbers flowing through his brain in mathematical precision. "Here, and here," he said, pointing to squares on the table.

The man finally threw the dice, establishing the number he had to match, a ten. Then he threw again. Everyone groaned when the dice read twelve.

"I lost," Beth said, disappointed.

"You won." Ian retrieved the counters. "You bet that he would overreach on an early throw."

"Did I?" Beth looked at the counters, then back at the table. Her cheeks were pink, lips shining red. "I think I shouldn't wager if I have no idea what I'm betting on."

"You're a rich woman." Ian placed the counters in her hands. "You have the money to lose."

"I won't be rich for long if I wager on hazard and roulette. What would have happened if you hadn't been here?"

"If I'd not been here, you wouldn't have come."

"No?"

She raised her brows at him, dove's wings across her face. Ian wanted to lean down and kiss them, here in the middle of the crowd. Beth, his lover, his mistress. He wanted everyone to know she belonged to him.

"Ian?"

She'd asked him a question. "Mmm?"

"I said, how do you know I wouldn't have come without you?"

Ian took her elbow and steered her to a less crowded part of the room. "I wouldn't have let you."

"Really? Would you follow me about, like Inspector Fellows?"

"This is a dangerous place," he said grimly. "Isabella understands. You don't."

Beth's bosom rose. "You're very protective." She leaned in to whisper to him. "I thought we agreed that our *relations* were between two people who enjoyed that side of life. Nothing more."

Ian didn't remember agreeing to that. She'd said, *We like each other well enough, and I don't foresee that I will marry again.* Ian hadn't responded, and he didn't respond now.

Having the affair with her would never be enough. He wanted more than playing with her in Mac's studio, the bliss of having her go down on him in the carriage. He wanted it again and again, the joy of her forever. Not Beth as his courtesan, not a love affair that ended when he left Paris. He wanted Beth for always.

The problem was how to do it. Beth didn't wish to marry, she said. Her engagement to the snake Mather had left her shy, and she'd already turned Ian down once. He would have to think of a way, but the task didn't bother him. Ian was good at focusing his attention on a problem until he solved it, to the exclusion of everything else.

A slender young man with thick blond hair stepped out in front of him, and Ian's thoughts fell in shards.

"I thought that was you." The man's eyes lit up, and he stuck out his hand. "Ian Mackenzie, as I live and breathe. How are you, old man? I haven't seen you since they sprang you from prison."

Chapter 11

Beth studied the young man with interest. About thirty, well-bred voice, slim hands, manicured nails. The man continued to hold out his hand, his smile wide. "Well met."

Ian hesitated, then took the proffered hand as though reminding himself of the appropriate response.

A darker man loomed behind the first and looked at Ian with dislike. "Who is this, Arden?"

The slender man laughed. "This is Lord Ian Mackenzie. Be nice to him, old chap. He once saved my life."

The other man didn't look mollified. Arden released Ian's hand and clapped him on the arm. "You look uncommonly well, Mackenzie. What has it been, seven years?"

"Seven years," Ian agreed. "And two months."

Arden burst out laughing. "He always has to be precise. So very, very precise. They let me out, too. My pater kicked off a few years after you left our happy home, and my foul brother went next. He got drunk as a lord and drowned in his bath, thank God. I wouldn't blame his wife one whit if she'd held him under."

Beth hid a gasp, but Ian nodded. "I am pleased."

"Not as pleased as me, I'll wager. So there I was, sole heir to the bulk of my father's fortune. Good Dr. Edwards was rubbing his greedy hands, but my sister got my commission of lunacy reversed, bless her down to her rosette-laden slippers. She and I fled the morbid climes of England and now inhabit a rather drafty house in the French countryside. This is Graves. He lives there, too."

The dark-haired Graves nodded tersely. Arden chuckled. "He's jealous as a wet hen; don't mind him. Is this your wife?"

"This is Mrs. Ackerley," Ian corrected.

"A friend," Beth said quickly, extending her hand.

Arden looked as impressed as if he'd been introduced to the queen. "Well met, Mrs. Ackerley. Lord Ian is a fine man, and I'll never forget him." His words were glib, but his eyes shone with emotion. He glanced at his glowering friend and laughed. "Don't worry, Graves. I'm all yours. Shall we?"

Graves turned away at once, but Arden lingered. "Excellent to have seen you again, Mackenzie. If you're ever near Fontainebleau, look us up." He waved, beamed a final smile, and turned away. "Yes, yes, I'm coming, Graves. Stop a moment, do."

Ian watched them go without expression. "The card games are much more lucrative," he said to Beth. "I will teach you how to play."

"Ian Mackenzie." Beth set her heels as Ian tried to lead her away. "What did he mean, you saved his life? You cannot simply close up without telling me the story."

"I didn't save his life."

"Ian."

She walked to an empty alcove where chairs had been placed for weary gamers. She plumped down on a chair and folded her arms. "I refuse to move until you tell me."

Ian sat down next to her, his golden eyes unreadable. "Arden was in the asylum with me."

"So I gathered. He doesn't look insane."

Disgust flickered across Ian's face. "His father had him

committed, wanted the doctors to cure him of his affliction any way possible."

Beth glanced to where Arden was speaking to Graves by the hazard table. They had their heads together, Arden's nose almost on Graves's cheek. Graves clamped a gloved hand on Arden's elbow, then softened his grip and moved his hand to Arden's back.

"Mr. Arden prefers the company of gentlemen," Beth concluded.

"Yes, he's an unnatural."

Beth studied the two men with interest. She'd known youths in the slums who sold themselves to men with certain perversions, but she'd never seen two men obviously in love with each other. At least, none who admitted it, she amended. Such things didn't last long in the rough neighborhoods of the East End.

"So his father sent him to an asylum," she said. "How awful."

"Arden shouldn't have been there. It was hard for him."

"He is adamant that you saved his life."

"He means I took a punishment for him."

Beth dragged her attention from Arden and Graves. "Punishment?"

"He was caught with a book of erotic drawings. Men with men. I remember how frightened he was. I claimed it was mine."

Beth's mouth popped open. "That was brave of you. Why would they believe that?"

"My brother Cam used to smuggle me erotic books. I told the attendants that this one had been in the last bundle Cam had brought me."

"Quick thinking." Beth's eyes narrowed. "Wait a moment, you told me you didn't know how to lie."

Ian absently stroked his thumb across the back of her hand. "I have trouble saying things that aren't the truth. I let them ask questions, and I nodded at what I wanted them to believe."

She couldn't help smiling. "Sly devil."

"They sent Arden off and had me take the treatment."

Her smile died. "What sort of treatment?"

"An ice bath first. To dull the heat of the perversions, they said. Then electric shocks." He swirled his fingertip over his temple. "So many of them."

Beth had a sudden vision of the long-limbed young Ian sitting in ice water, his eyes closed, his lips blue as he shivered. And then stretched on a bed hooked to an infernal machine she'd once seen a picture of in a journal, coils and wires fastened to manacles.

The marvels of modern medicine, the caption had read. *Patients treated by new and improved methods of electric current.*

They'd have sent shocks through Ian's body while he tried not to scream. Perhaps that explained why he always massaged his temples, was prone to headaches.

Beth squeezed his hands between hers, tears filling her eyes. "Oh, Ian, I can't bear to think of you like that."

"It was a long time ago."

She looked at Arden again, angry this time. "The coward. Why on earth did he let you do that for him?"

"Arden was frail. The treatment might have killed him. I was strong enough to bear it."

She squeezed his hand harder. "It still wasn't right that they should do that to you. It's horrible."

Ian caressed her fingertips. "I could bear it. I was used to it."

She heard the echoes of Ian's screams in her head. Beth pressed her forehead to his hands, her heart wrenching. Ian's hands were large, sinews hard under his kid-leather gloves. Yes, he was strong. In the Tuileries Gardens, it had taken both Mac and Curry to pull him away from Fellows.

That didn't mean others could try to tear at that strength, try to defeat him. The doctors in the horrible asylum had done it, and now Fellows was trying to.

I'm falling in love with you, she wanted to say into their clasped hands. *Do you mind awfully?*

Ian was silent, but she sensed when his attention moved from her. His body tensed; his head turned. She looked up.

Ian stared across the room at the door that had admitted them. He rose slowly, like an animal sensing danger. The door burst open, and shouts and screams filled the room.

"Hell," Ian said.

He jerked Beth to her feet and started dragging her toward the back of the room. Beth craned to see what was going on as Ian propelled her at a rapid pace to the rear of the casino. People ran every which way, and the female croupiers scrambled to grab money and stuff it into their corsets.

"Wait." Beth clutched his sleeve. "We can't leave Isabella."

"Mac's here. He'll see to her."

Beth scanned the room and saw Mac's large body breaking through the swarming people. Isabella's red head stopped when Mac grabbed her arm.

"Why didn't you tell her he was coming?"

"He made me promise not to."

"Mac wanted to watch out for her, didn't he?" Her hopes rose. "He came to protect her."

"Yes. It's dangerous."

"So you said. It's a police raid, isn't it? Funny how they chose tonight of all nights."

"Not funny. It was Fellows."

"Yes, I wondered. . . ."

Beth trailed off as Ian shoved aside a black curtain, yanked open a door that blended into the paneling, and pulled Beth up a narrow staircase that reeked of cigar smoke. The stair led to a dingy back hall and a rickety door that spilled into a tiny yard. The yard was inky black and filthy, and torrents of rain poured down on them.

"A shame our wraps are back there," Beth said, shivering. "I don't suppose the police would be polite enough to return them?"

Ian didn't answer. He pulled her through an open gate

and hurried with her down an alley, Ian's arm firmly around
Beth's waist.

Lightning flared overhead, for an instant illuminating
the wet, refuse-strewn alley and the faceless walls on either
side. Beth saw movement at the mouth of the alley, and Ian
swung her down another, even darker passage.

"That was the way out." Her teeth chattered.

"Fellows and the Sûreté will have blocked it."

"I do hope you know where you're going."

"I do."

Beth went silent again. It was just like Ian to commit the
maze of alleys of Montmartre to memory. She wondered if
he'd explored them or simply looked at a map.

"Fellows is quite a thorn in our side, isn't he?" Beth said
over the pounding rain. "Blast the man. This was my best
frock."

The narrow alley ended at another street, but Beth couldn't
say where they were. The crooked lanes of Montmartre ran
every which way. Ian held Beth close as they hurried along
the street, drenched in rain. Thunder rolled overhead, the
lightning too close.

Ian knew they were on the opposite end of the town
from Mac's dingy studio. Fellows would look for them
there, in any case. Beth was shivering, soaking wet. He had
to get her out of the rain.

The word *Pension* caught Ian's attention as they ran past
a house. He grabbed the doorknob of a dusty glass door
and pushed his way inside.

"Monsieur." A man with lank black hair looked Ian and
Beth up and down, took in their fine clothes, and straightened his shoulders. In a torrent of French, he offered them
the best room in the pension, which he tried to tell them
was superb.

Ian piled a stack of gold coins in the man's hand and
demanded the room plus a hot bath for the lady. Thunder
rocked the house as they hurried up the stairs.

The pension had no gaslights, and a maid hurriedly lit

candles throughout the small bedroom, pinpoints of yellow in the gloom. Beth stood by the tiny stove, rubbing her arms.

She shivered too much, Ian thought. Ian curtly reminded the maid about the bath, and presently two men came in lugging a large tub. Ian stripped off his coat while the maid and a younger girl filled the tub with steaming water.

When they'd all gone, Ian turned Beth around and began unbuttoning her sodden bodice. Beth wiped rain from her face while Ian pulled off the bodice and unhooked her skirts.

Undressing her was a pleasure, even when he worried about getting her warm. She tried to help him strip off her petticoats and bustle, then the corset and chemise, but her fingers shook too much.

Ian went down on one knee to untie her drawers and slide them down her legs. Her stockings came off in clumps, heaps of wet silk on the floor.

Ian ran his hands up her cold legs, over her hips, and up her sides. As he stood he cupped his hands around her breasts, then bent his head and kissed her. Her tongue moved in his mouth, and he circled his thumbs over her nipples, teasing the points to stand.

Rain splashed against the bare window, coating the glass with water. Lightning flashed outside, followed by a boom of thunder.

Ian lifted Beth, still kissing her, and lowered her into the steaming bath. Beth's eyes closed in relief as the warm water engulfed her. Ian stripped off his waistcoat and collar, then his shirt, letting them fall in heaps of wet fabric.

Beth opened her eyes as he kicked off his boots and stepped out of his trousers. He rubbed his bare skin with a towel the maid had left, then stepped into the end of the tub, sliding his feet on either side of hers.

Hot water covered his calves, the bite of its heat soothing. He hadn't liked hot baths as a child—he'd screamed that the water burned him, even when it was only mildly warm. His father had never believed him and shouted at the footman to plunge Ian into the water and be damned.

"There isn't enough room for both of us." Beth gave Ian a lazy smile, her blue eyes slits.

"I just need to get my feet warm."

Ian toweled his wet hair, and Beth leaned back against the curved end of the copper tub to watch him. He'd have to send word to Curry to bring them fresh clothes, but not now. None of the poor sods in this house needed to be running out in the storm.

"This hotel is rather seedy," Beth murmured. She made little figure eights with her hands in the water, watching the ripples spread. "Not the sort in which respectable ladies and gentlemen stay."

"Does it matter?" One room was much like another as far as Ian was concerned.

"Not really. It's another wickedness in a night of so much wickedness. I never knew I'd like wickedness so much, Ian. Thank you for showing it to me."

Her gaze roved his body and came to rest solidly on his erection. That organ pointed stiffly at her, and how could it help it?

Beth was beautiful. Her limbs were white against the tub's copper bottom, her nipples pinched tight with cold and desire. Strands of dark hair floated around her shoulders, and the twist of hair between her thighs was darker still.

Her face flushed with heat, her red lips curved into a smile, and her blue eyes gleamed. She lazily licked a droplet of water from her lower lip.

The storm raged through Montmartre like cannon fire. No one, not even Curry, knew where they were. Tonight, Beth belonged to him.

Ian's life was dictated by other people—events and conversations swirled past him before he could follow them; other people decided whether he'd live in an asylum or out of it, whether he'd go to Rome or wait in London. Events flowed and ebbed, and as long as they didn't interfere with his interests, like finding elusive Ming pottery, he let them happen.

Now Beth had landed in the swift stream of his life, and she'd stuck there like a rock. Everything else swirled past him, but like an anchor, Beth stayed.

He needed her to stay forever.

Ian bent and hauled her to her feet. Her body was slippery, sliding in a fine way against his.

"You're still cold," she said.

"You'll warm me."

He snatched another towel from the pile and wrapped it around her before she could start shivering again. The heat of her body was better than a fire, better than all the hot water in the world.

Ian lifted her, stepped carefully from the bath, and carried her to the narrow bed near the stove. The maid had and inserted hot bricks wrapped in cloth under the worn but clean linens.

Ian laid Beth on the warmed bed. She looked up at him, not in the least worried as Ian dropped his towel and stretched out beside her. He pulled the covers over them both, cocooning them in warmth. The heat of the bricks and Beth's body permeated the bed, driving away the cold.

Beth wrapped her arms around Ian as he turned onto his side to face her. "What naughtiness are you going to teach me now?" She smiled.

She still didn't understand.

"No games tonight."

"Oh." She sounded disappointed.

Ian smoothed her wet hair back from her face and leaned so he was half on, half off her. Her breath touched his mouth, fragrant and sweet.

"Promise me," he said.

"Promise you what?"

"Promise you'll tell me to stop."

She gave him an arch look. "That all depends on what you start."

Beth still thought he was playing. *Don't let me hurt you.* "Promise me."

"Very well," she said, still smiling.

Ian smoothed her eyes closed, brushed kisses down her nose and across her lips. Her mouth moved, her tongue darting out to catch his, but he moved out of reach.

"I want you," she whispered. A blush spread across her face. "But it's been a very long time. Perhaps I won't be able to."

Ian reached between her legs and sank his fingers into hot moisture. "You will."

"How do you know?"

She pretended to have so much experience, but sharing a bed with a sedate husband and intense coupling with a lover were two different things. One was duty, the other . . . wildness. Perhaps her husband had made duty enjoyable, but what Ian wanted was not a dutiful wife lying on her back for her husband.

He wanted to show Beth every nuance of pleasure, from the incredibly gentle to the crazed and rough. He wanted them falling to the bed afterward, bruised and spent, both of them sated. He wanted everything with her, and he didn't want it tame.

"Let me," Ian whispered against her mouth as he slid his fingers inside her.

Beth gasped, and her hips rocked up. Ian stroked two fingers into her, then swirled them around her sleek tuft of hair. She was hot, wet, ready.

He'd been ready for weeks. He slid his knee between hers and let his tip part her opening.

Beth moaned deep in her throat. "Please, Ian."

"Please stop?" he murmured, excitement gripping him. "No."

He smiled into her lips. "Please what, Beth? What do you want me to do?"

"You know."

"I am not good at hints. You have to tell me straight out."

"You're teasing me now."

Ian licked her mouth. "You like being teased. You like ducking into private rooms with me and pulling up your skirts when I tell you."

"Is that what you call teasing?"

"You like fellatio and cunnilingus."

"I do, truth be told. I'd never done either before."

"No?" he murmured. "I thought you a woman of the world."

"I thought I was rather clumsy at it."

"You were beautiful. You are beautiful now."

She bit her lip, making it red and enticing. Shy Beth, blushing while he lay naked on top of her. She always filled him with laughter.

"Please, Ian," she whispered. "I want you inside me."

His entire body tightened. "Yes."

~~~~~~~~~

He was too big. It had been nine years since a man had entered her, and she was too tight. She couldn't take it.

Ian groaned softly as he pushed all the way in. He took a long breath, his chest pressing hers. He wouldn't look at her, turning his head so Beth stared directly at his cheekbone and rain-wet hair slicked to his skull.

"Am I hurting you?" he asked.

"No."

"Good." He thrust once. "*Good.*"

Beth squeezed her eyes shut as he thrust again. The thickness of him pushed so deep inside her she thought it would tear her apart.

And it felt *good.*

"Ian," she groaned. "I am wicked. I'm a wicked, sinful woman, and I don't want you to ever stop."

Ian didn't answer. He moved slowly inside her, full and hard. *Deeper, faster. Please.*

She rocked her hips up as he came down. He held himself up on one hand while he fisted her hair in his other. He tickled the ends of her hair along her breasts, and her overly sensitive nipples rose and tightened.

He leaned down and licked one areola, teasing the point into his mouth. She watched his teeth play, his tongue swirl over the nipple, the pink skin rising into his mouth. He closed his eyes as though he were savoring some rich dish, his lashes soft points against his cheeks.

Beth ached where they joined. The friction burned on her petals too long untouched, fire that made her want to open her legs wide. She did, sliding her feet on the covers, letting her hips arch upward.

"Do you feel it?" Ian asked.

A dozen phrases went through Beth's head, but she gasped out, "Yes."

"Your cunny is tight, my Beth. Squeezing me so hard." He smiled when he said it, feral and raw.

No man had ever done bawdy talk with her. Game girls had told her of it, but she'd never dreamed she'd hear it hot in her ear, spoken by a beautiful man.

"Squeeze me some more, love," he murmured. "You feel so damn good."

"Good," Beth echoed. She tightened her muscles, and he groaned.

He felt good. All full and hard and moving inside her. She tried to tell him, to give him bawdy talk in return, but she couldn't form words.

"I wanted you in Covent Garden," he said. "I wanted you straddling me in the dark while I came up inside you."

"In the theatre?"

"Right there in the damn box, with the opera blaring on. I'd take you, make you my own." He put his hand on her neck over the spot where he'd given her the love bite. "I branded you."

Beth smiled. "You, too." She touched his neck. "I branded *you*."

He laced his fingers hard through hers and pressed her hand to the bed. "Belong to me."

"No one here to dispute that at the moment."

"Always mine. Always, Beth." Thrusts punctuated the words.

Always. Her body jerked in rhythm with his, the bed creaking. It was a solid bed, thick mahogany, made to take men like Ian loving their women.

She was his lover. Beth laughed for the delight of it. Being with Ian was decidedly unrespectable, and she felt freer than she'd ever felt in her life. Under him, she could spread her wings.

Beth laughed again. She was spreading herself as far as she could. Ian's eyes were closed, his face twisted in pleasure. His thrusts accelerated, his hips pounding as if it were the last coupling he'd ever have.

He drove her into the mattress, his body heavy on hers, his sweat dripping onto her skin. Rain streamed against the windows, and a boom of thunder swallowed Beth's sudden cry of ecstasy.

Ian shouted, not waiting for thunder. Lightning flared, bathing the room in white. The light outlined Ian's body, his sharp-lined face, burning his hair red.

In that moment, Ian opened his eyes, like twin suns coming into view, and let his gaze directly meet Beth's.

Chapter 12

Beth stopped breathing. For the first time since she'd met him, Ian's gaze fully connected with hers.

His eyes were golden, as she'd known, but she'd not known that his black pupils were ringed with green. His body slowed as he studied her, as though looking at her arrested all his attention. He didn't blink, didn't move, just let his gaze rest on hers.

She touched his face in wonder. "Ian."

Ian started and turned his head, and when he looked back, his eyes drifted sideways, not meeting hers.

Beth's heart wrenched. "No, please don't look away."

Ian closed his eyes and bent to kiss her.

"Why won't you look at me?" she asked. "What's wrong with me?"

He opened his eyes again, but his gaze didn't meet hers. "Nothing. You are perfect."

"Then why?"

"I can't explain. Don't ask me to explain."

"I'm sorry," she whispered. She stroked his hair as tears leaked from her eyes.

"Don't cry." He kissed her wet cheek. "This is the time for joy."

"I know."

He was still inside her, full and hard, spreading her marvelously.

Don't hunger for what you can't have, she admonished herself. *Take pleasure in what you can*. Such thoughts had got her through the worst days.

She wanted all of Ian, body and soul, when she knew she couldn't have that. He was giving her what he could: bodily pleasure and momentary joy. She'd asked him to have a purely carnal affair with her. If she hurt because she couldn't have more, it was her own fault.

"Ian, you are so bad for me," she said.

He gave her a half smile. "I'm the Mad Mackenzie."

Beth pressed his face between her hands, anger suddenly rising. "That is other people's explanation, because they don't understand you."

He looked away. "You always try to be kind to me."

"It isn't kind. It's the truth."

"Shh." Ian kissed her. "Too many words."

Beth agreed. Ian kissed her again, occupying her mouth with something much more satisfying.

He began to move inside her again. Ian's body was hot and tense, the noises he made exciting her beyond what she thought she could feel.

This is bliss, her mind whispered as he took her to cresting waves of pleasure. She came beneath his body, twisting and arching against his hips. She moved and moaned until the black waves subsided, and Ian crashed down against her, their bodies melding into one line of heat.

Thunder cracked right overhead, and Beth jumped awake. Ian lay beside her, propped on one elbow, watching her sleep.

"Hello," she murmured.

Ian gave her a slow smile. She couldn't tell if he'd slept or not, but he didn't look tired at all.

"I thought the storm would be over by now," she said. "What time is it?"

"I don't know. Early morning."

Beth grimaced. "Isabella will be worried."

"She knows I will take care of you."

"And she might be with Mac." Beth grinned at him. "Maybe he's gone home with her."

Ian's look told her he didn't agree. "Tonight was the first time he'd spoken to her in three years."

"That's good, isn't it?"

"He was very angry when I told him she wanted to go to the casino. I don't think their reunion will be pleasing."

"You're a pessimist, Ian. Isabella has been such a dear friend to me, and I want to see her happy again."

"She chose to leave Mac," Ian pointed out.

"I know. But she regrets it."

Ian's body was like a warm wall, his touch amazingly gentle. "When they were married they were either wildly happy or fighting tooth and nail. No in-between."

"I suppose such drama would be tiring."

Beth could imagine herself deliriously happy with Ian, so happy she couldn't bear it. She also saw that she could be completely miserable. Her heart had certainly never flip-flopped so much in her life as after she'd met Ian Mackenzie.

Ian stroked her hair, and she closed her eyes. How lovely to stay here for always in this bubble of contentment, floating away in quiet happiness.

"I should go home." She hadn't meant for her voice to sound so sad.

"Curry will have to fetch more clothes for you before you can leave. Yours are ruined."

"Does Curry even know where we are?"

"No."

Then no one knew, Beth thought. She and Ian were utterly alone. Her heart squeezed with joy.

"He'll worry, won't he?" she murmured.

"He's used to me disappearing. I always turn up again. He knows that."

Beth studied him. "Why do you disappear?"

"Sometimes it gets too much for me. Trying to follow what people say, trying to remember what I'm supposed to do so people will think I'm normal. Sometimes the rules are too hard. So I go."

Beth traced his muscular arm with her fingernail. "Where do you go?"

"Most times to the wilds around Kilmorgan. It's a vast place, and I can lose myself for a long time. You'll like it there."

She ignored this. "What about other times?"

"Courtesans' houses. As long as I pay, they leave me be. I don't have to think of conversation there."

Beth had grown used to Ian's bluntness, but that didn't mean she wanted to hear about his being with other women. She imagined that courtesans were happy to give Ian sanctuary whenever he wanted it. He was rich, had the body of a god, and possessed devastating charm, especially when he smiled. Even his sideways look gave him a roguish quality. If she were a courtesan, she'd give Ian a special rate.

"Anywhere else?"

"Sometimes I take a train to a place I've never been or hire a horse and ride into the countryside. To find somewhere I can be alone."

"Your family must go wild with worry."

Ian propped himself on his arm and drew his finger between Beth's breasts. "They did at first. Hart never wanted to let me out of his sight."

"But he eventually did, obviously."

"He used to be furious when I went. Threatened to have me locked up again."

Beth's anger stirred. "His Grace the duke sounds a great bully."

One corner of his mouth turned up. "He realized I was going, no matter what. Curry took my side. Told Hart to fuck himself."

Beth's eyes widened. "And Curry is still alive?"

"As you see."

"Good for Curry."

"Hart worries, that's all."

Beth frowned. "He let you out of the asylum and got your commission of lunacy reversed. Why, so you could help him win at high finance?"

"I don't much care why he did it. I only care that he did."

Beth grew suddenly angry with Hart. "It's not fair. He shouldn't use you so."

"I don't mind."

"But—"

Ian put his fingers on her lips. "I'm not a servant. I help when I can but take something for myself."

"Like when you disappear for days at a time."

"Hart could have let me rot in that asylum. I'd be there now if not for him. I don't mind reading his treaties and moving around his stocks if that's what it takes to pay him back."

Beth twined her fingers through his. "I suppose I can be grateful to him for letting you out, at least."

Ian stroked the backs of her fingers, not listening. His warmth covered her like a blanket, and his breath burned as he kissed the line of her hair. "Tell me about your husband," he murmured.

"Thomas?" *Now?* "Why?"

"You loved him desperately. What was that like?"

Beth lay quietly, remembering. "When he died, I thought I would die, too."

"You hadn't known him very long."

"That didn't matter. When you love, especially with all your heart, it comes upon you so fast, you don't have time to resist."

"And then he died," Ian said. "And you can never love that deeply again."

"I don't know."

Liar. Beth knew she was falling stupidly in love with Ian, and she had no idea how to stop herself. *What is the matter with me?*

She answered her own question when Ian suddenly gave her a bruising, punishing kiss. Her tension dissolved and she gladly slipped her arms around him, holding him close.

Ian made it evident he didn't want to talk anymore. He shoved her legs apart with a strong hand and pushed his way inside her again, no argument.

Mrs. Barrington would say that only a very loose woman would let a man have his way with her without protest. Beth rocked back on the pillows and spread her thighs, happily violating Mrs. Barrington's strictures in every way.

~

Beth slept again. When she woke, the window was a dim gray square. Ian stood to one side of it, looking out.

Rain still beat down, but the thunder had abated. Ian was naked, and he rested one hand on the wall, his glorious backside half turned to her.

In the gloomy light that played on his powerful muscles, he reminded Beth of the perfect male sculptures she'd seen in the Louvre. But those sculptures had been marble and alabaster; Ian was like living bronze.

When she stirred, Ian put a finger to his lips.

"Is someone out there?" she whispered in alarm. They were on the second floor in the front of the pension, the nicest room, the landlord had assured them. But the windows had no curtains, and Beth felt queasily exposed.

"Inspector Fellows is watching the house," Ian said. "He's brought along some police."

Beth pulled the covers to her chin. "Oh, dear, how embarrassing."

"I think it's worse than that."

"How can it be worse? They can't arrest us for spending the night in a pension, can they? Goodness, if lewd behavior is illegal, they'll have to arrest half of Paris."

The newspapers would get hold of it. They always did somehow, and the story would leak across the Channel to London. *English Heiress up before the French Magistrates for Fornicating in a Questionable Parisian Hotel. This after Playing at the Evil and Illegal Roulette.*

A soft knock on the door made her sit up straight.

"It's me, guv," came a Cockney voice from the other side. Curry. Beth heaved a sigh of relief.

Ian didn't bother to cover himself as he let Curry into the room. Curry didn't pay any attention to Ian's state of nudity, and he laid the garments he'd brought with him over the back of a chair. He calmly unfastened a leather bag and took out a razor, shaving cup, and brush.

"Any hot water to be had in this benighted place, guv?"

"Ring for the maid. Did you bring Mrs. Ackerley's things?"

"That I did." Curry kept his gaze on Ian, pretending he didn't see Beth cowering in the bed. "Her companion wanted to come, but I convinced her it wouldn't be prudent."

Ian only nodded. He pulled on the drawers Curry held out to him, hiding his lovely anatomy, and sat down to be shaved. He might be at the luxurious Langham Hotel in London, rising after a night of leisure.

Beth realized with a jolt that Curry had done this before. He seemed comfortable with the routine of slipping in the back way to bring Ian fresh linens and shave him after he'd spent the night with a woman.

Beth hugged her knees. *My own stupid fault if I'm jealous.*

"Did they see you?" Ian asked Curry.

Curry answered as he stropped the razor. "No, I came up the back alley to the kitchen. The staff are all keeping mum. They don't want the police in any more than we do."

"This is too absurd," Beth said. "Why is Fellows persecuting you like this? And me?"

"It's his way," Ian answered.

Not much of an answer, but Ian closed his mouth and

leaned his head back as Curry finished sharpening the razor. The maid of the night before slipped quietly into the room bearing a ewer of steaming water, and Curry told her in broken French that she should dress Beth.

The girl curtsied, and while Ian and Curry faced the other way, the maid laced Beth into the clothes Curry had fetched from Isabella's.

The maid's face glowed with excitement. "He must be very rich, madame," she breathed.

Beth didn't correct her assumption that Ian was her protector. Last night Beth had been amused that the landlord and servants had supposed her Ian's kept woman, though it didn't seem as funny now.

"I suppose we shall have to flee out the back way as well," she said to Ian. "Mr. Fellows is getting to be an absolute bother."

"We'll not go yet," Ian said.

"Good, because it is still pouring rain." Beth glanced at the windows. "I do hope the inspector and all his friends from the Sûreté are soaked."

Ian tilted his head back, face covered with lather. "Did you send for it?" he asked Curry.

"I did like you said, m'lord. Now please stop talking so I don't slice you open."

Ian went silent, and Curry drew the razor up his throat. Beth sat down on the bed she'd enjoyed such a night in and wished for something to eat.

The maid bustled about and shook out Beth's clothes from the night before, laying them before the fire to dry. Curry shaved Ian in silence, the only sound the scrape of the razor across Ian's skin and the maid's pattering footsteps.

Ian seemed in no hurry. When Curry finished, Ian asked the maid to bring him a newspaper and coffee, and tea for Beth. Just after the maid returned with the requested things, someone else knocked on the door. Curry held the razor tightly while he answered it.

Mac stood on the threshold. He came inside, and Curry quickly closed the door behind him.

"Fellows looks like a drowned rat. Don't worry, Ian. I took care."

"It is kind of you to come fetch us," Beth said, trying not to sound impatient. "How is Isabella?"

Mac looked blank. "How the devil should I know?"

"You saw her home last night."

Mac turned a wooden chair around and straddled it back to front. "I got her into her carriage and paid her coachman to ensure she arrived home and didn't leave again."

Beth frowned at him. "You didn't go with her?"

"No, I did not."

Most vexing of him. "She showed me the painting you did of her."

"Did she? That trifle?" Mac spoke casually, but he tensed.

"Not a trifle. It's beautiful. She travels with it—obviously, or she could not have shown it to me. She takes it everywhere, she says."

"Doubtless trying to find the perfect spot to throw it into the sea."

"Of course not."

Mac clenched the chair so tightly Beth feared he'd splinter the wood. "May we not speak of it?"

"As you wish." Beth frowned, but she dropped the subject.

By the time Curry had got Ian fully dressed and Beth had drunk a cup of tea, someone else knocked on the door.

Mac hastened to open it, but he slipped out into the hall without letting Beth see who it was. She heard a rapid exchange of French, and then Mac came back in with his pugilist valet, Bellamy, and a man in a long black-buttoned cassock and rosary.

"Good heavens," Beth bit out. "Are we having a fancy-dress party? So many more people to slip out the back."

Ian turned around. "We are leaving by the front door. Be damned to Fellows."

"I thought you said he was ready to arrest us."

"Why should he?" Ian's voice hardened, and he glanced at her with a look she didn't understand. "He has no reason to arrest a man for spending a night in a pension with his wife."

Beth stopped. "But I'm not your . . ."

She took in the priest, Mac's expression, Curry's innocently blank face.

"Oh, no," she said, her heart sinking. "Oh, Ian, no."

Chapter 13

They all stared at her, Curry with amusement, the priest with a worried frown, Bellamy nonplussed, Mac in impatience. Only Ian remained expressionless. He could be a man waiting for someone to tell him whether or not there were any eggs for breakfast.

"Why the hell not?" Mac asked. "Ian likes you, you get on, and he needs a wife."

Beth squeezed her hands together. "Yes, but perhaps I don't need a husband."

"A husband is exactly what you need," Mac growled. "It will keep you and my wife from running about in illegal casinos."

"Mac." Ian's voice was quiet. "I'll talk to Beth alone."

Mac ran his hands through his russet hair. "Sorry," he said to Beth. "I'm a little on edge. Marry him, do. We need at least one sensible person in this family."

Without waiting for her reply, he got the priest, the maid, Bellamy, and Curry out of the room and shut the door.

Rain beat against the windows, the sound grainy in the silence. She was aware of Ian's gaze boring a hole in her head, but for once she couldn't look at him.

"I determined not to marry." Beth tried to sound determined, and failed. "I decided to live as a wealthy widow, traveling, enjoying myself, helping others."

Her words sounded feeble, even to herself.

"Once you are my wife, Fellows can't touch you," Ian said as though he hadn't heard her. "His superiors ordered him to stay away from my family, and when you marry me, you'll be my family, too. He can't arrest you or harass you. My protection, and Hart's protection, will extend to you."

"It hasn't much stopped him from bothering you, has it?"

"He won't be allowed on the grounds of Kilmorgan, and Hart will make trouble for him if he tries to approach you anywhere else. I promise you this."

"Didn't you say Hart was in Rome? What if he doesn't want his protection extended to me?"

"He will do it. He hates Fellows and will do anything to thwart him."

"But . . ."

The suddenness of it all took her breath away, and she groped for arguments. She found one.

"Ian, there's something you *don't* know about me. My father was never a French aristocrat. He told people in England he was a viscount, and they believed him. He could ape the manners of the nobility very well indeed. But he was as lowborn as any in the slums of the East End."

Ian's gaze slid away from her. "I know. He was a confidence trickster fleeing arrest in Paris."

Beth's breath left her. "You know?"

"When I decide to learn about someone, I learn everything."

Her throat tightened. "Do your brothers know?"

"I saw no reason to tell them."

"And you still want to marry me?"

"Yes, why not?"

"Because I'm not the kind of woman a duke's son should

marry," she almost shouted. "My background is sordid—I was little better than a servant. I'd ruin you."

He lifted his shoulders in a very Ian-like shrug. "Everyone believes you the daughter of an aristocrat. That will be good enough for the stuffy English."

"But it's a lie."

"You and I know the truth, and the people who prefer the fiction will be satisfied."

"Ian, you will make me a confidence trickster myself, just like my father. I'm no better than he was."

"You are better. You are a hundred times better."

"But if someone found out . . . Ian, it could be horrible. Newspapers . . ."

He wasn't listening. "We don't fit in, you and me," he said. "We're both oddities no one knows what to do with. But we fit together." He took her hand, pressed her palm to his, then laced their fingers through each other's. "We fit."

He was saying, *We are adrift and no one wants us, not the real us. We might as well drift together.*

Not, *Please marry me, Beth. I love you.*

Ian had told her that first night at the theatre that he could never love her. She couldn't expect that.

On the other hand, as Mac pointed out, they got on. Beth had learned not to be startled at his abrupt speeches, not to be offended when he looked as though he hadn't heard a word she said.

"The priest is Catholic," she said. "I'm C of E."

"The marriage will be legal. Mac saw to that. We can have another ceremony when we return to Scotland."

"Scotland," she repeated. "Not England."

"We'll go to Kilmorgan. You'll be part of it, now."

"Do stop trying to make me feel better, Ian."

He frowned, Ian always taking her words literally.

She went on. "A lady likes to be wooed a bit before she's thrust into marriage. Offered a diamond ring and so forth."

Ian's grip tightened. "I'll buy you the largest ring you ever saw, covered with sapphires to match your eyes."

Her heart skipped a beat. His gaze was so intense, even when he couldn't meet hers directly.

She remembered the breathless moment when he'd actually looked at her when they'd made love. His eyes had been so beautiful, fixed on her as though she were the only person in the world. The only person who mattered.

What would she give to have him look at her like that again?

Everything she had.

"Blast you, Ian Mackenzie," she whispered.

Someone tapped on the door, and Curry stuck his head around it. "The rain's slackened, and the good inspector's getting impatient."

"Beth," Ian said, his grip crushing.

Beth closed her eyes. She hung on to Ian's hands as though he were the only thing between her and drowning. "All right, all right," she said, her voice shaking as much as her body. "We'd better do it quickly, before the inspector storms the battlements."

And it was done. Beth's eyes were heart-wrenchingly blue as she repeated the vows. Then the marriage was sealed by the priest, witnessed by Curry, Mac, and Bellamy. Ian slipped a plain ring he'd instructed Curry to bring onto Beth's finger, a placeholder until he could buy her the wide sapphire band. When he kissed her, he tasted the heat left over from their lovemaking as well as her nervousness.

They walked out together, Ian holding an umbrella over both himself and Beth. Ian pointedly ignored Fellows and the crowd of Paris police and journalists who waited on the opposite side of the street.

Ian's carriage pulled forward as they emerged, blocking Fellows's view. The man strode around the carriage anyway as Ian was handing Beth in.

Fellows's eyes were grim, his mustache soaked with rain. His stance bore the furious exhaustion of a man who'd stalked his prey all night and now saw it slipping away.

"Ian Mackenzie," he said heavily. "My friends in the Sûreté have come to arrest you for abducting Mrs. Beth Ackerley and holding her hostage in this inn."

Beth gazed out of the carriage, a warm, lighted haven from the rain. "Oh, don't be so ridiculous, Inspector. He didn't abduct me."

"I have witnesses who saw him drag you out of that gambling den and hustle you here."

Ian slowly folded his umbrella, shook it out, and stowed it inside the carriage. "Mrs. Beth Ackerley is no longer here," he said, focusing on the pension they'd just left. "Lady Ian Mackenzie is."

He turned and climbed into the carriage before Fellows could begin to splutter. Mac came out of the pension, a wide grin on his face, followed by Curry with a valise, and Bellamy with a basket of wine and bread Ian had bought from the hotelier.

"You lost that round, Fellows," Mac said, clapping the inspector on a soggy shoulder. "Better luck next time."

He climbed up into the carriage and thumped down opposite Beth and Ian, smiling broadly at them. Bellamy climbed up with the coachman, but Curry sprang into the coach and slammed the door in Fellows's face.

The inspector's eyes were hard as agates, and Ian knew he'd thwarted the man only briefly. The battle had been won, but the war would rage on.

~

They left immediately for Scotland. Beth had only a few hours to pack and say good-bye to Isabella, because Ian was suddenly in a tearing hurry.

"Oh, darling, I'm so happy." Tears wet Isabella's lashes as she gathered Beth in a tight hug. "I've always wanted a sister, and you are the best I can think of." She held Beth at arm's length. "Make him happy. Ian deserves to be happy, more than any of them."

"I'll try," Beth promised.

Isabella's dimples showed. "When I move back to London,

you'll come down and stay with me, and we'll have scads of fun."

Beth clung to Isabella's hands. "Are you certain you won't come with us now? I'll miss you."

"I'll miss you, too, darling, but no. You and Ian need to be alone together, and Kilmorgan—" She broke off, pain in her eyes. "Too many memories for me. Not yet."

They hugged again. Beth hadn't realized how fond she'd grown of Isabella, the openhearted young woman who'd taken Beth under her wing and shown her a new and astonishing world.

Isabella hugged Ian as well, expounding upon how happy she was for him.

At last Ian and Beth made their way to the train station, with Curry and Katie and another carriage full of boxes and bags. Beth quickly learned how much aristocrats took for granted when Ian guided her into the first-class compartment and left Curry to see to the baggage, the tickets, and Katie.

For all Ian's assertions that he didn't fit anywhere, he was still a lord, a duke's brother, rich and lofty enough to ignore the tiny details of life. He had people to pay attention to those details for him.

Mrs. Barrington's voice in Beth's head had grown fainter in the last days, and Beth heard it only weakly now. *You've got well above yourself, my gel. See that you don't make a meal of it.*

She wondered what Thomas would have said, and found his voice completely gone. Tears blurred the ponderous station that slid past the windows as the train began to move.

Ian hadn't even bothered to wonder whether Curry made it aboard before they went. Beth compared this leaving to her own departure from Victoria Station: Mrs. Barrington's wheezing, elderly butler trying to help but dropping everything he picked up, Katie convinced their luggage would be stolen and never seen again, and the lady's maid Beth had hired having hysterics about "foreign parts" and running off at the last minute.

Of course, Curry had no such problems. He appeared

calmly at the door of their compartment as they glided through Paris to tell them he'd ordered tea and squared the tickets, and he asked if they wanted anything else. Very efficient, very calm, as though his master hadn't just rushed into a marriage and a journey of hundreds of miles on top of it.

Beth also discovered, as they left Paris behind and chugged across rain-soaked France, how restless Ian could be. After only half an hour in their private compartment, Ian left to roam the train, walking up and down, up and down. When they reached Calais and boarded the boat for England, he paced the deck above while Beth slept alone in their private cabin.

Finally, during the journey from Dover to Victoria Station, Beth stuck out her foot when Ian again rose to leave the compartment.

"Is anything the matter?" she asked. "Why don't you want to sit?"

"I don't like to be confined." Ian opened the door to the corridor as he spoke, fine beads of sweat on his upper lip.

"You don't mind carriages."

"I can make carriages stop whenever I like. I can't step off a train or boat whenever I please."

"True." She touched her lip. "Perhaps we can find something to take your mind from it."

Ian abruptly closed the door. "I also leave because keeping my hands off you is a strain."

"We'll be on the train for a few more hours," Beth continued. "And I'm certain Curry will ensure we're not disturbed."

Ian pulled down the curtains and turned to her. "What did you have in mind?"

Beth hadn't thought they could do very much in a small railway carriage, but Ian proved to be quite resourceful. She found herself half-undressed with her legs wrapped around him as he knelt in front of her. In that position they were face-to-face, and Beth studied his eyes, hoping he'd look at her fully again. But this time, when climax hit him, Ian closed his eyes and turned his head.

Only a few minutes later, Beth was dressed again and sitting breathlessly on the seat while Ian went out to pace the train.

When Beth had shared a bed with Thomas, they'd been less exuberant and more conventional, but at the end, there had been quiet kisses and whispered *I love you*s. Now Ian wandered the train, and Beth sat alone, watching the green countryside of England rush by. She heard the echo of Ian's matter-of-fact statement from weeks ago: *I wouldn't expect love from you. I can't love you back.*

The luggage made it to the station intact, but when they entered an elegant coach outside—hired by Curry—it took them toward the Strand instead of Euston Station.

"Are we stopping in London?" Beth asked in surprise.

Ian answered with a brief nod. Beth peered through the window at gloomy, rainy London, which looked grimier and duller now that she'd seen the wide boulevards and parks of Paris. "Is your house near here?"

"My London household was packed and sent to Scotland while I was in France."

"Where will we stay, then?"

"We are going to visit a dealer."

Enlightenment came when Ian led her into a narrow shop in the Strand filled floor-to-ceiling with Oriental curiosities.

"Oh, you're buying more Ming pottery," she said. "A vase?"

"Bowl. I know nothing about Ming vases."

"Aren't they much the same?"

His look told her she'd lost her mind, so Beth closed her mouth and fell silent.

The dealer, a portly man with dull yellow hair and a limp mustache, tried to interest Ian in a vase that was ten times the price of the small, rather chipped bowl Ian asked to see, but Ian ignored his maneuverings.

Beth watched in fascination as Ian held the bowl between his fingertips and examined it in minute detail. He missed nothing, not a crack or anomaly. He smelled it, he touched his tongue to it, he closed his eyes and rested the bowl against his cheek.

"Six hundred guineas," he said.

The burly dealer looked surprised. "Good lord, man, you'll ruin yourself. I was going to ask three hundred, I must be honest. It's chipped."

"It's rare," Ian said. "It's worth six hundred."

"Well." The dealer grinned. "Six hundred it is then. I've done well for myself. You wouldn't want to appraise the rest of my collection, would you?"

Ian laid the bowl reverently on the velvet bag the dealer placed on the counter. "I don't have time. I'm taking my bride to Scotland tonight."

"Oh." The good-natured dealer looked at Beth with new interest. "I beg your pardon, my lady. I didn't realize. My felicitations."

"It was all rather sudden," Beth said faintly.

The dealer raised his brows and glanced at Ian, who had returned his broad fingertips lovingly to the bowl. "I am pleased you had time to stop and look at my offering."

"Rather lucky we found you in," Beth said. "And the bowl still here."

The dealer looked surprised. "Not luck, my lady. Lord Ian wired me from Paris and told me to hold it for him."

"Oh." Beth's face grew warm. "Yes, of course he would have."

Beth had been with Ian constantly since their hasty marriage, except when he paced the trains and boat. The all-efficient Curry must have sent the wire from some station along the way. More details Ian didn't have to worry about.

The dealer's assistant packed the bowl under Ian's watchful eye. Ian said that his man of business would be along with the money, and the dealer bowed. "Of course, my lord. Congratulations again. My lady."

The assistant held the door for them, but before they could take two steps, Lyndon Mather stepped out of a carriage in front of them. The blond, handsome man stopped dead in his tracks and went a peculiar shade of green.

Beth had her hand in the crook of Ian's arm, and Ian pulled her so abruptly against him that she fell into his side.

Mather glared at the box under Ian's arm. "Damnation, man, is that my bowl?"

"The price would have been too high for you," Ian returned.

Mather's mouth hung open. He stared at Beth, who wanted very much to leap headfirst into the closest hansom cab and flee. She lifted her chin instead, standing her ground.

"Mrs. Ackerley," Mather said stiffly. "Have a care for your reputation. People might put it about that you're his mistress."

By *people*, Mather likely meant himself.

Before Beth could answer, Ian said quietly, "Beth is my wife."

"No." Mather's face started to go purple. "Oh, you bastard. I'll sue you both. Breach of contract and all that."

Beth imagined the humiliation of court, solicitors digging into her past, revealing what a horrible misalliance was her marriage with Ian.

"You came to sell," Ian interrupted Mather.

"Eh?" Mather clenched his fists. "What do you mean?"

"The proprietor said he expected a bowl to come in as well as go out. You wanted to exchange yours for this one."

"What of it? This is a collector's shop."

"Let me see it."

Mather's dithering was almost comical. He opened and shut his mouth a few times, but Beth watched greed and desperation take over indignation. Mather snapped his fingers, and his manservant handed him a satchel from the carriage.

Ian jerked his head toward the shop, and they all went back inside.

The proprietor looked surprised to see them return, but he had his assistant fetch another square of black velvet, and Mather removed the bowl from the satchel.

This one was different, with red camellia blossoms dancing around the outside. It was not as chipped as the other, and the glaze shone in the lamplight.

Ian lifted it, examining it as carefully as he had the first one. "It's worth twelve hundred," he announced.

Mather's mouth became a round O. "Yes," he spluttered. "Of course it is."

Beth swallowed. If she understood aright, Mather had been about to exchange a twelve-hundred-guinea bowl for one worth six hundred. No wonder Ian derided him. That Ian's assessment was the correct one, Beth had no doubt.

"I'll buy it from you," Ian said. He nodded at the proprietor. "Will you handle the sale?"

"Ian," Beth whispered. "Isn't that an awful lot of money?"

Ian didn't answer. Beth pressed her lips together and watched Ian coolly transact a twelve-hundred-guinea sale, with another hundred pounds to the proprietor for doing nothing but standing next to them. Beth had lived with frugality for so long that to watch someone who didn't know what frugality meant left her shaky. Ian didn't even break a sweat.

Mather did, though, when he clutched Ian's note in his hand. No doubt he'd rush to the bank right away.

Ian left the shop without telling Mather good day, and he helped Beth into the carriage. Curry handed in both boxes with a cheeky grin on his face.

"Well, that was an adventure," Beth said. "You just gave Lyndon Mather twelve hundred pounds."

"I wanted the bowl."

"How the devil did you even know the first bowl was there? Or that Mather was bringing the other? You've been in Paris for weeks."

Ian looked out the window. "I have a man in London who keeps an eye out for pieces for me. He wired me the evening we went to the casino that there was a bowl here that Lyndon Mather had his eye on."

Beth stared at him, feeling her life spinning out of control. "That means you would have left Paris the next morning, whether you married me or not."

Ian looked at her briefly, then returned his gaze to the passing streets. "I would have brought you with me, no matter what. I'd not have left you alone. Marrying you was the best way of thwarting Fellows."

"I see." She felt cold. "Thwarting Mather was a bonus, was it?"

"I intend to thwart Mather out of everything."

Beth studied him, his strong profile turned away, his large hand resting easily on the box next to him. "I'm not a porcelain bowl, Ian," she said softly.

He looked at her with a frown. "Are you joking?"

"You didn't want Mather to have the bowls, and you didn't want him to have me."

He stared a moment. Then he leaned to her, suddenly fierce. "When I saw you, I knew I had to take you away from him. He had no idea what you were worth, just like he can't price the damn bowls. He's a philistine."

"I think I feel marginally better."

Ian's gaze wandered back to the window, as though the conversation were over. She studied his broad chest, the long legs that filled up the carriage. Her thoughts strayed to what it felt like to have his legs stretched next to hers in bed.

"I suppose it will be good to stay a few nights in London," she said. "I'll have to buy things for Scotland—I imagine the weather is quite a bit cooler."

"We're not staying a few nights in London. We're taking the night train out. Curry has arranged the tickets."

Beth blinked. "I thought when you said 'stopping in London' you meant stopping for a night or two. Not whizzing in and out."

"We need to get to Kilmorgan."

"I see." A cold knot formed in her chest. "What will we do once we get to Kilmorgan?"

"Wait."

"Wait for what?"

"Time to pass."

Beth stilled, but there was no more forthcoming. "You are maddening, Ian."

Ian said nothing.

"Well." Beth sat back, the tightness in her body cork-screwing. "I can see this will be a different sort of marriage than what I was used to."

"You'll be safe. The Mackenzie name will protect you. That's why Mac wouldn't divorce Isabella—so Isabella could retain her money and security."

Beth thought of the laughing, gregarious Isabella and the pain in her eyes. "How very thoughtful of him."

"I'll never ruin you."

"Even if I have to communicate with you via notes through Curry?"

His brows drew down, and Beth caught his hand. "Never mind, I was joking that time. I've never taken a night train to Scotland—well, any train to Scotland. It will be a new adventure. Will the bunks be as interesting as the compartment from Dover, I wonder?"

━━━

They arrived in the morning in Glasgow, and then the train went on to Edinburgh. When they rolled into Edinburgh, Beth looked about with hungry eyes. The city was bathed in fog but didn't lack in beauty for all that.

She barely had time to take in the castle on the hill and the avenue that led between castle and palace before she had to hurry, sandy-eyed, into another train that chugged slowly northward.

At long last, many miles and countless hours since they'd left Paris, the train pulled into a small station on an empty, rolling plain. A mountain ridge rose like a wall to the north and west, cool air flowing from it even in the height of summer.

Ian returned from his pacing up and down the corridor in time to hand her out of the train. The sign announced they'd arrived at Kilmorgan Halt, but other than that the platform was empty. A tiny station house crouched beyond the platform, and the station master scuttled back to it after he'd waved his flag for the train to move on.

Ian took Beth's arm and steered her down the steps past

the station house to the small drive beyond. A carriage waited there, a lush chaise with the top folded down to expose plum-colored velvet seats. The horses were well-matched bays, the buckles of the harness gleaming. The coachman, dressed in red livery with a brush in his hat, leapt from his box and tossed the reins to a boy who climbed up to take his place.

"Ye've arrived, then, m'lord," the coachman said with a broad Scots burr. "M'lady."

He opened the door and Ian boosted Beth in. She settled herself, marveling at the luxury of such a vehicle up here in the wild end of the world.

But Kilmorgan belonged to a duke, one of the most prominent dukes in Britain. In order of precedence, she'd learned from Isabella, the Duke of Kilmorgan came behind only the Duke of Norfolk and the Archbishop of Canterbury. Small wonder the coach that took them to the duke's seat would be the most sumptuous she'd ever beheld.

"I suppose Curry arranged this, too," she said to Ian as the coachman climbed back to his box.

"We have the telegraph even in Kilmorgan," Ian answered gravely.

Beth laughed. "You've made a joke, Ian Mackenzie."

He didn't answer. They rolled through a village of white-washed houses, an inevitable pub, and a long, low building that might be a school or a council house or both together. A stone church with a new roof and a spire stood a little way from the village with a steep path leading to it.

Beyond the village, the land dipped to a wooded valley, and the carriage thudded over a bridge that crossed a rushing stream. They rose up into hills again, the earth undulating in green and purple waves to the sharp mountains in the background. The hills were covered in mist, but the sun shone, the afternoon soft.

The carriage turned from the country road to a wide, straight lane lined with trees. Beth sat back and breathed the pure air. The pace Ian had kept since Paris exhausted her. Now, in this still place with birdsong overhead, she could at last rest.

The coachman turned through a wide gate to a lane that led to an open park. The gatehouse was small and square with a flag flapping above it—two lions and a bear on a red background. The lane sloped downward in a wide curve toward the house spread across the bottom of the hill.

Beth half rose in her seat, hands pressed to her chest. "Oh, my dear Lord."

The place was enormous. The building rose four stories in height, with tiny windows peeking out of round cupolas under the vast roof. Rambling wings reached left and right from the central rectangle of the house, like arms trying to encompass the entire valley. Windows glittered across the monstrosity of it, punctuated here and there by doors and balconies.

It was the largest house she'd ever seen, comparable only to the Louvre she'd just left in Paris. But this wasn't a remote palace she'd never be invited into. This was Kilmorgan. Her new home.

The coachman pointed at the pile of house with his whip. "Built just before the time of Bonnie Prince Charlie, m'lady. The duke then wanted no more drafty castles. Employed th' whole village and laborers for miles around. The bloody English burned the place after Culloden, but the duke, he built it back again, and his son after. Nothin' keeps down a Mackenzie."

The pride in his voice was unmistakable. The lad next to him grinned. "He's clan Mackenzie, too," the boy said. "Takes credit for it, like he was there."

"Shut it, lad," the coachman growled.

Ian said nothing, only adjusted his hat over his eyes as though he meant to doze off. The restlessness that had kept him roving the trains had vanished.

Beth clutched the edges of the seat and stared, drymouthed, as they approached the house. She recognized the Palladian elements—the oval windows wreathed with stone curlicues, the arched pediments, the symmetrical placement of every window and door across the enormous facade. Later generations had added things, like the stone balustrade that encircled the marble entranceway, the modern bellpull beside the front door.

Not that Beth had to ring to get in. As Ian handed her down, the double doors opened to reveal a tall, stately butler and about twenty servants waiting in a marble-tiled hall. The servants were all Scottish, all red-haired and big-boned, and all smiled with enormous pleasure as Ian led Beth through the door.

Ian didn't introduce her, but as one, every maidservant curtsied and every man bowed. The effect was marred by five dogs of various sizes and colors that barreled through the hall and headed straight for Ian.

Not used to dogs, Beth pulled back, but laughed as they reared up on Ian, burying him in paws and waving tails. Ian's face relaxed, and he smiled. And, to her astonishment, he looked directly at them.

"How are you, my bonny lads?" he asked them.

The butler ignored this, as though the canine welcome was commonplace. "M'lady." He bowed. "If I may say, on behalf of the entire staff, we are verra pleased t' see ye arrive."

From the smiles that beamed at her, the staff obviously agreed with him. No one had ever been this happy to see Beth Ackerley before.

Lady Ian Mackenzie, she corrected herself. Beth had known from the first moment she met Ian Mackenzie that her life would become entangled with his. She felt the tangle grow, winding around her.

"Morag will lead ye to your rooms, m'lady," the butler continued. He was tall and large-boned, like the rest of them, his red-blond hair going to gray. "We have a bath prepared and the bed made up so ye can rest after your long journey." He gave Ian a bow. "Your lordship, His Grace is waiting in the lower drawing room. He asked that ye see him as soon as ye arrived."

Beth had taken two steps with the beaming Morag, but she pulled up in alarm. "His Grace?"

"The Duke of Kilmorgan, m'lady," the butler said patiently.

Beth looked at Ian in panic. "I thought he was in Rome."

"No, he's here."

"But you told me . . . Wait, did Curry receive a telegram? Why didn't you warn me?"

Ian shook his head, his dark red hair spilling against his collar. "I didn't know until we rode through the gate. The flag was up. The ducal flag always flies when Hart's at home."

"Oh, of course. Why didn't I think of that?"

Ian held out his hand. "Come with me. He'll want to meet you."

Ian, as usual, didn't betray what he was thinking, but Beth sensed that he wasn't entirely happy with this turn of events. Despite his calmness in the carriage, he was now tense, wound tight, like when he paced the train.

Her own fingers were ice-cold when she slid them into Ian's warmer hand. "Very well. I suppose I had better get it over with."

Ian gave her the faintest of smiles, then held her hand tighter and led her off into the bowels of the house. The dogs, all five of them, followed, their nails clicking loudly on the slate floor.

Chapter 14

Hart Mackenzie, Duke of Kilmorgan, both resembled his brothers and at the same time looked nothing like them.

He sat behind a writing table near the fireplace, the desk long and ornately carved, as befitted the rest of the room. He was writing with great intensity and didn't look up when the door closed behind Ian.

The vast drawing room in which Beth and Ian awaited His Grace's attention looked as though it had once been three rooms, with the intervening walls removed. The ceiling rose higher than a ceiling had a right to, and it was covered with frescoes of frolicking gods and goddesses.

The walls were covered with paintings, too. They ranged from pictures of the Kilmorgan house in various stages to portraits of ladies and gentlemen—some in Scottish dress, some in whatever formal clothes were fashionable in their period. One could learn a history of clothing, Beth reflected, simply by studying the portraits in this room.

Ian had closed the door on the faces of the five dogs, and

they'd looked resigned, as though knowing they were never allowed in this grand sanctuary.

Hart was going to make Ian and Beth stand there like schoolchildren waiting to be dressed down, Beth thought irritably. "Your Grace," she said.

The duke glanced up sharply. His eyes glittered the same gold as Ian's but pierced Beth from across the room—hawk's eyes.

Ian said nothing, remaining in place without flinching. Hart's pen clattered to his pen tray and he rose.

He was tall, like all the Mackenzies, his hair a darker red-brown. Hart had the Mackenzie broad shoulders, powerful build, and square face. He wore a formal kilt, the Mackenzie colors, blue and green with red and white thread. His dark coat fit him like a second skin, likely made for him by the best tailors in Edinburgh.

Still, he wasn't a mirror image of the brothers she'd already met. Mac's face bore the restless brilliance of an obsessed artist. Cameron's face was heavier, more brutish, complete with scar. He looked like a ruffian.

So did Hart, but Hart's smooth confidence rolled off him in waves. This was a man who had no doubt that his slightest command would be fulfilled. It wasn't conceit, but cool certainty.

Hart overpowered every single thing in the room—except Ian. The waves of Hart's overweening confidence seemed to break and flow around Ian without Ian feeling the slightest effect.

Hart finally removed his knifelike gaze from Beth and switched it to Ian. "Was there no other way?"

He spoke as though they were in the middle of a conversation, but Ian nodded. "Fellows would have found some means to use her. Or turned her into an excuse to arrest me."

"The man's a pig." Hart's stare came back to Beth. "She was once a lady's companion? Why did Isabella befriend her?"

Beth pulled herself away from Ian and walked forward,

sticking out her hand. "I'm very well, thank you so much for inquiring. The journey was tiring but uneventful, no problems on the lines, and no Fenian bombs at any of the stations."

Hart shot Ian a scowl.

"She is fond of jokes," Ian said.

"Is she?" Hart answered, his voice cool.

"I am also fond of chocolate, and of raspberry fool." Beth curled her ignored hand at her side. "At the moment I'd be fond of a cool drink of water and a soft bed."

Hart spoke directly to her for a change. "I don't recall sending for you, Mrs. Ackerley. You'd even now be reclining on a soft bed if you'd gone upstairs with the maid."

Beth's heart hammered. "The only person I ever allowed to *send* for me, Your Grace, was Mrs. Barrington, and that was because she paid me wages."

Hart's brows drew fiercely together, and Ian said, "Leave her be, Hart."

Hart gave Ian a quick glance, then returned his scrutiny to Beth. The look told her Hart didn't know what to make of Beth or what she was to Ian.

Beth wasn't quite sure what she was to Ian either, but she saw that Hart didn't like not understanding. He wanted to instantly sum her up and put her in a slot—likely he had done so before she even arrived, and having to reassess her made him irritable.

Hart said coolly, "Now that we've established you're a woman of independence, will you indulge us a moment? I'd like to talk to Ian alone."

A man bound and determined to get his own way—always. Beth opened her lips to say a polite, "Of course," but Ian spoke again.

"No."

Hart's eagle gaze swung to him. "What?"

"I want to see that Beth gets upstairs and settled in. We can talk at supper."

"We have maidservants to help her."

"I want to do it."

Hart gave up, but Beth could see that it rankled. "The gong goes at seven forty-five and the meal is served at eight. We dress formally, Mrs. Ackerley. Don't be late."

Beth slid her hand through Ian's, trying to hide her nervousness. "Call me Beth, please," she said. "I am no longer Mrs. Ackerley and have become, to our mutual astonishment, your sister."

Hart froze. Ian raised his brows at him, then turned around and led Beth from the room. As they walked out, surrounded by the waiting dogs, Beth slanted a worried glance up at Ian, but Ian wore the broadest smile she'd ever seen.

She was a wonderful, amazing woman. Ian's heart warmed as Beth emerged from her dressing room in a gown of dark blue silk. The bodice bared her bosom, perfect for the necklet of diamonds he'd just given her. Beth gazed up at him serenely as he held out his arm to escort her down to dinner.

The necklet had belonged to his mother. Ian remembered his father's pride in her beauty, remembered his father's jealous rages when any other man so much as looked at her. He'd had uncontrollable rages, with dire consequences.

Any other woman would have fallen over in fear when Hart turned that famous stare on her. Hart's own wife had fainted on more than one occasion when Hart had looked at her. Not Beth. She'd stood straight and tall and told Hart what she thought of him.

Ian had wanted to laugh until the paintings of his illustrious ancestors rang with it. Hart needed a kick in his ass sometimes, and if Beth wanted to do it, Ian would let her.

Hart was quiet when they entered the dining room, and he pointedly remained standing until Ian seated Beth. Hart took the chair at the head of the table, and Ian and Beth sat across from each other a few feet down from him.

If Hart hadn't been there, Ian could have had supper served in the little dining room in his own wing of the house. He and Beth could have sat side by side and basked in the privacy.

He'd wanted to linger in the dressing room with her and help her dress for dinner, but Curry had arrived and insisted he bathe and shave Ian and get him sorted. Ian's Mackenzie kilt had been draped over Curry's arm.

When Ian and Beth retired tonight, Ian would dismiss the overly helpful staff and undress her himself. He was determined to fall asleep in her arms and wake up in them as well.

"Did you hear me?" Hart said sharply.

Ian dissected the sole on his plate and ran through the words Hart had poured out while Ian had focused on Beth. "The treaty you had drafted in Rome. You want me to read it and commit it to memory. I'll do that after dinner."

"Are many treaties with foreign nations stored in Ian's head?" Beth asked. Her voice was innocent, but her blue eyes danced.

Hart gave her a hard look. "Treaties have a way of reading a bit differently once committees get hold of them. But Ian will remember every word of the original."

Beth winked at Ian. "I'm certain it makes for fascinating teatime conversation."

Ian couldn't resist a grin. He'd not seen Hart this annoyed in a long time.

Hart bathed Ian in a cold stare, but Beth blithely ignored him. "Did your bowls survive the journey intact?" she asked Ian.

Ian's pulse quickened as he remembered the cool brush of porcelain against his fingers, the satisfaction of Mather's bewildered face. "I unpacked them and put them in their places. They fit well."

Hart interrupted. "You bought more bowls?"

Beth nodded after Ian had remained silent a moment. "They are both quite lovely. One is a white bowl with a blue flush and interlinked flowers. The other is red flowers and thinner porcelain. The wash and fineness of the porcelain indicate it might be Imperial Ware. Have I got that right?"

"Exactly right," Ian said.

"I found a book in Paris," she said with a cheeky smile.

Ian looked at her and forgot everything else in the room. He was aware of Hart's stare but only peripherally, as though an insect buzzed on the edges of his hearing.

How did Beth always know what words he needed and precisely when to say them? Even Curry didn't anticipate him like that.

She was taking everything in, the lavish room, the long table, the gleaming silver serving dishes. The paintings of Mackenzie men, Mackenzie lands, and Mackenzie dogs, and the white-gloved footmen hovering to wait on them.

"I was surprised you had no piper," she said to Hart. "I imagined we'd be escorted to dinner to the drone of bagpipes."

Hart gave Beth a deprecating look. "We don't have the pipes inside. Too loud."

"Father used to," Ian said. "Gave me raging headaches."

"Hence the ban," Hart returned. "We're not a storybook Scottish family with everyone wearing claymores and longing for the days of Bonnie Prince Charlie. The queen may build a castle at Balmoral and put on plaid, but that doesn't make her Scottish."

"What does make one Scottish?"

"The heart," the Duke of Kilmorgan said. "Being born to a Scottish clan and remaining part of the clan inside yourself."

"Having a taste for porridge doesn't hurt," Ian said.

He'd spoken seriously, wanting only to stop Hart from going on and on about what it meant to be Scottish, but he liked the reward of Beth's beautiful smile. Though Hart could speak English with no trace of a Scots accent, had been educated at Cambridge, and sat in the English House of Lords, he had firm ideas about Scotland and what he wanted to accomplish for his country. He could expound on it for hours.

Hart shot Ian a formidable frown and fixed his attention onto his food. Beth gave Ian another smile, which sent Ian's imagination dancing.

They continued the meal in silence, the only sound the

click of silver on porcelain. Beth was beautiful in the candle-light, her diamonds sparkling as much as her eyes.

When they finally rose, Hart rumbled something about his damned treaty.

"It's all right," Beth said quickly. "I'd love a turn in the garden before bed. I'll leave you to it, shall I?"

Ian walked her to the terrace door. The dogs sprang to their feet, tails wagging. Ian would prefer to have Beth join him in the billiards room, his imagination rife with things he could teach her about billiards. But if she wanted a walk, he wouldn't stop her. The garden could be just as entertaining.

Beth pressed Ian's arm before he could form the words, and she disappeared out the back door. The five dogs milled back and forth in front of her as she strolled down the walk.

Ian took the treaty from Hart and stalked with it into the billiards room, hoping the damn thing was short.

"You're a very clever young woman."

Beth turned at Hart's voice. She'd walked, escorted by the dogs, down a well-tended path to a fountain that sprin-kled merrily into a marble bowl. Plenty of light lingered in the sky, though it was already half past nine—Beth had never been this far north before, and she understood the sun barely dipped below the horizon here during the summer months.

She'd spent some time figuring out which dog was which. Ruby and Ben were the hounds, Achilles was the black set-ter with one white foot, McNab was the long-haired spaniel, Fergus the tiny terrier.

Hart stopped by the fountain, the end of his cigar glow-ing orange as he took in smoke. The dogs swarmed to him, tails moving furiously. When he didn't respond, they moved off to explore the garden.

"I don't think myself especially clever." Beth had thought the night warm, but now she wished she'd brought a wrap. "And I'm afraid I never went to finishing school."

"Cease with the flippancy. You obviously bamboozled Mac and Isabella, but I'm not so gullible."

"What about Ian? Are you saying I bamboozled him?"

"Didn't you?" Hart's voice was deadly quiet.

"I remember telling Ian quite plainly that I had no interest in marrying again. And then there I was, signing a license and repeating that I'd be with him until death do us part. I believe Ian bamboozled *me*."

"Ian is—" Hart broke off and swung away to stare into the multicolored sky.

"What? A madman?"

"No." The word was harsh. "He's . . . vulnerable."

"He's stubborn and smart and does exactly what he pleases."

Hart pinned her with his stare. "You've known him, what, all of a few weeks? You saw that Ian is rich and insane, and you couldn't resist taking down such an easy mark."

Beth's temper flared. "If you had paid more attention, you'd have realized that I have a fortune of my own already. Quite a large one. I don't need Ian's."

"Yes, you inherited one hundred thousand pounds and a house in Belgrave Square from a reclusive widow called Mrs. Barrington. Very admirable. But Ian is worth ten times that, and when you realized that, you wasted no time getting rid of Lyndon Mather and chasing Ian to the altar."

Beth clenched her hands. "No, I went off to Paris, and Ian came after *me*."

"Quite a good ploy to smarm up to Isabella. She's got too soft a heart for her own good, and I'm certain she thought it a fine scheme to push you together. Mac did, too. I can't think what got into him."

"*Smarm?* I don't smarm. I wouldn't know how to. I'm not even sure what the word means."

"I know your background, Mrs. Ackerley. I know your father was a lying blackguard and your mother fell into his trap. Her folly led her straight to the workhouse. I'm sure you learned much there."

Beth's face burned. "Goodness, so many people looking into my past. You ought to have asked Curry. Apparently he has quite a dossier on me."

Hart dropped his cigar and ground it out with his heel. He leaned close to Beth and spoke in a low voice, his breath tinged with sweet-smelling smoke. "I will not let a fortune hunter ruin my brother, if it's the last thing I do."

"I assure you, Your Grace, I've never hunted a fortune in my life."

"Don't mock me. I'll annul the marriage. I can do that, and you will leave. It never will have happened."

Beth summoned the courage to look straight into Hart's golden eyes. "Can you not consider that perhaps I fell in love with him?"

Deeply, dramatically, foolishly in love.

"No."

"Why not?"

Hart drew a breath but didn't speak. A muscle twitched in his jaw.

"I see," Beth said softly. "You believe he's mad, and you don't think any woman could love that."

"Ian *is* mad. The commission of lunacy proved it. I was there. I saw."

"Then why not leave him in the asylum if you think he's insane?"

"Because I know what they did to him." In the gentle twilight the powerful Duke of Kilmorgan looked suddenly haunted. "I saw what the damn quacks did. If he hadn't been mad when he went in, the place would have driven him so."

"The ice baths," Beth said. "The electric shocks."

"Even worse than that. Dear God, when he was twelve years old they had him bend bare-assed over his bed every night so they could strap him. To keep his dreams quiet, they said. My father did nothing. I *couldn't* do anything; I didn't have the power. The day my father fell off his horse and broke his damned neck, I went to the asylum and took Ian out."

Beth flinched at his vehemence, but at the same time, her heart warmed. "And Ian is grateful you did. Very grateful."

"Ian couldn't even speak. He wouldn't look up when we talked to him or answer questions put to him. It was as though his body was with us but his mind was far away."

"I've seen him do that."

"He did it for three months. Then one day when we were eating breakfast, Ian looked up and asked Curry whether there was any toast." Hart flicked his gaze away, but not before Beth saw the moisture in his eyes. "As though nothing had been wrong, as though it were the most natural thing in the world to ask Curry for toast."

The breeze of the dying afternoon stirred his hair, tugged at the curls on Beth's forehead. She watched as one of the highest dukes in the land blinked away tears.

"I'll send for my solicitor in the morning," he said abruptly. "We'll find a way to negate the marriage. You'll not be ruined."

"I know you don't believe me, but I would never hurt Ian."

"You are right. I don't believe you."

The wind freshened, scattering cool droplets from the fountain over Beth's face. Hart turned on his heel to stride back to the house, but Ian stood there like a solid wall.

"I told you to leave her be," he said quietly.

Hart's back went stiff. "Ian, she can't be trusted."

Ian took one step closer to Hart. Though he kept his eyes averted, there was no mistaking the anger in his stance and his voice. "She is my wife, under my protection. The only way I will let you do anything against this marriage is if you declare me a lunatic again."

Hart flushed dull red. "Ian, listen to me—"

"I want her as my wife, and she stays my wife." Ian softened his voice a notch. "She is a Mackenzie now. Treat her as one."

Hart stared at Ian, then at Beth. Beth tried to keep her chin up, but her heart raced, and the urge to run away from that predatory stare was strong.

Strange, when Ian had informed Beth they were marrying, she'd argued with him. Now that Hart looked grimly determined to part them, she knew she'd do anything to stay wedded.

"I am Ian's wife because I choose to be," she said. "Whether we live in a grand mansion or a tiny boardinghouse, it makes no difference."

"Or a vicarage?" Hart countered, scowling.

"A vicarage in the slums served me very well, Your Grace."

"It had rats in it," Ian said.

Beth looked at him in surprise. Curry's notes must have been thorough.

"Indeed, there was a family of them," she said. "Nebuchadnezzar and his wife, and their three children, Shadrach, Meshach, and Abednego."

Both men merely stared at her, the double golden gaze unnerving even if Ian's didn't touch her fully.

"It was our little joke, you see," she stammered. "Made having rats a bit more bearable if they had names."

"There are no rats here," Ian said. "You never have to worry about rats again."

"Not the four-legged kind, anyway," Beth went on. "Inspector Fellows reminds me a bit of Meshach—his eyes would glow and his nose would twitch when he set his sights on a particularly tasty bit of cheese."

Ian frowned, and Hart clearly didn't know what to make of her.

"I imagine you have snakes, though," she said, her tongue tripping. "This is the countryside, after all. And field mice and other creatures. I must confess I'm not used to the country. My mother was country born, but I lived in London from an early age and strayed outside the metropolis only when Mrs. Barrington saw fit to go to Brighton and pretend she liked the sea."

Ian half closed his eyes, taking on the expression he did when he'd stopped hearing her. She knew he wasn't listening, but a week from now he'd be able to come back to a particular phrase and drill her on it.

She closed her mouth with effort. Hart looked at her as

though he'd fetch a lunacy commission up here on the morrow to grill her.

Ian came out of his trance and reached for her. "Tomorrow I will show you everything about Kilmorgan. Tonight we sleep in our chamber."

"Have we got a chamber?"

"Curry fixed it up while we were at supper."

"The ten-times-resourceful Curry. Whatever would we do without him?"

Hart looked at Beth sharply, as though she'd said something significant. Ian slid his arm around her waist and turned her around to lead her to the house. His warmth cut the coolness of the evening and blocked her from the wind.

A safe harbor. In the turmoil of her life, she'd known so few of them. Now Ian drew her close, protecting her, but Beth felt the edge of Hart's gaze on her back all the way to the house.

The house swallowed Beth. Ian led her up the vast, ornate staircase, deeper and deeper into its maw.

There were so many pictures on the walls of the staircase hall that they obscured the wallpaper beneath them. Beth glimpsed the signatures on them as Ian rushed her up the stairs—Stubbs, Ramsay, Reynolds. A few paintings of horses and dogs were by Mac Mackenzie. Dominating the first landing was a portrait of the current duke, Hart, his eyes as golden and formidable in the picture as in person.

On the second landing hung the portrait of an older man who glared as haughtily as Hart did. He fiercely clutched a fold of Mackenzie plaid and sported a full beard, mustache, and side-whiskers.

Beth had noted him on their rush downstairs to dinner, but now she stopped. "Who is that?"

Ian didn't even glance at the painting. "Our father."

"Oh. He is quite . . . hairy."

"Which is why we all like to be clean-shaven."

Beth frowned at the man who'd caused Ian so much

pain. "If he was so awful, why does he have pride of place? Hide him in the attic and be done with him."

"It's tradition. The current duke at the first landing, the previous duke at the second. Grandfather is up there." He pointed to the top of the next flight. "Great-grandfather after that, and so on. Hart won't break the rules."

"So every time you go upstairs, Dukes of Kilmorgan glower at you at every turn."

Ian led her on up toward Grandfather Mackenzie. "It is one reason we all have our own houses. At Kilmorgan, I have a suite of ten rooms, but we'll want more privacy."

"A suite of ten?" Beth asked. "Is that all?"

"Each of us has a wing of the house. If we invite guests we put them in our wing and take care of them."

"Do you often have guests?"

"No." Ian led Beth back to the dressing room in which she'd changed for dinner. She'd thought the little room grand, but Ian now showed her that on its other side lay a bedroom the size of Mrs. Barrington's entire downstairs. "You are my first."

Beth gazed at the high ceiling, the enormous bed, the three windows with deep window seats. "If a person must marry you to get an invitation, I'm not surprised you haven't had more guests."

Ian's golden gaze swept over her and back to the bed. "Are you joking again?"

"Yes. Don't mind me."

"I never mind you."

Beth's heart thumped. "Is this your bedchamber?"

"It's our bedchamber."

She wandered nervously to the heavily carved walnut bedstead. "I'd heard that all aristocratic couples had separate bedrooms. Mrs. Barrington quite disapproved. A frivolous waste of space and money, she said."

Ian opened another door. "The boudoir in here is yours. But you will sleep with me."

Beth peered around him into an elegant room with

comfortable-looking chairs and a deep window seat. "My. I suppose it will do."

"Curry will help you fit it out as you like. Just tell him what you want and he will arrange it."

"I'm beginning to think Curry is a magician."

Beth waited for him to respond, but Ian said nothing, his gaze remote again.

"I think you take an awful risk," she said. "I read somewhere that sharing a bedroom with a woman is dangerous, because she exhales noxious fumes when she sleeps. Absolute balderdash, Mrs. Barrington said when I told her. Mr. Barrington slept beside her for thirty years and never once took sick."

Ian slid his arms around her, the warmth of his body distracting her from all other thought. "Quacks will say anything to attract money for their research."

"Is that what they did at the asylum?"

"They tried all kinds of experiments to cure my madness. I never saw where any of them worked."

"That was cruel."

"They thought they were helping."

Beth put her fists on his arms. "Don't be so bloody forgiving. Your father locked you away, and those people tortured you in the name of science. I hate them for it. I'd like to go to that asylum and give your doctor, whoever he is, a piece of my mind."

Ian put his fingers to her lips. "I don't want you part of that."

"Like you don't want me part of the High Holborn murder."

Coldness crept into his usually warm gaze. "It has nothing to do with you. I want you . . . apart. I want to remember only this, not you with the things of my past."

"You wish to create different memories," she said, thinking she understood.

"My memory is too damned good. I can't blot out things. I want to remember you alone here with me, or in that pension in Paris. You and me, not Fellows or Mather or my brother, or High Holborn . . ."

His words died and he began to rub his temple, frustration glinting in his eyes. Beth put her hand over his.

"Don't think of it."

"It plays over and over and over again, like a melody that won't stop."

Beth softly rubbed his temple, his hard fingers beneath hers.

He pulled her close. "Your being with me makes it stop. It's like the Ming bowls—when I touch them and feel them, everything stops. Nothing matters. You are the same. That is why I brought you here, to keep you with me, where you can please make . . . everything . . . stop."

Chapter 15

Beth stared up at him, her blue eyes wet. "Tell me how."

He held her face between his hands, her beautiful face that had jolted through the clamor in his head at the Covent Garden Opera House. She'd been the only thing real to him in Lyndon Mather's box; everything else had been shadowy and wrong.

"Stay with me."

"We're married," she whispered. "Of course I'll stay."

"You could decide to leave me." He leaned his forehead to hers, remembering the horrible day that he'd gone to Mac's house with the farewell letter Isabella had written. Ian had never forgotten Mac's devastation when he'd realized that Isabella was gone.

"I won't."

"Promise me."

"I have promised. I do promise."

Her voice rang with sincerity, her eyes wide and lovely. He kissed her lips so she wouldn't keep giving him reassuring lies. Isabella had loved Mac desperately, and yet she'd left him.

"Stay with me," he repeated.

She nodded into his kiss. He drew her body against his, fingers finding the buttons of her bodice. Her chest came into view, and he leaned down and kissed it. She made a soft noise, and he suckled her skin, branding her yet again.

He felt her hands parting his clothes, burrowing past the layers of fabric to find him. She put her mouth to his chest just below the hollow of his throat, and he inhaled sharply. The scent of her hair filled his nostrils, driving him a little bit mad.

Ian pulled her up to him and kissed her, parting her lips, pressing his thumbs to the corners of her mouth. She was his wife, and he wanted her. For now, for always.

He swiftly unbuttoned the rest of her bodice, then untied her stays in little jerks. He pushed them from her body, then unfastened her chemise, catching her bare breasts as they tumbled out. She arched back as he kissed her again, pressing her nipples tight against his palms.

Unlacing and pushing away her skirts and bustle and petticoats took some time, and he became impatient, tearing fabric while she squeaked a protest. He lifted her and carried her to the bed, then pulled off his own clothes with the same impatience. He climbed up with her, not bothering to pull back the bedclothes. When she started to speak, he silenced her with a deep kiss.

He pushed her legs apart and entered her, finding her plenty wet for him. Beth lifted her hips and met him thrust for thrust, already used to what felt best to her. He rode her quickly, then slowly, his arms braced on either side of her. He kissed her with swollen lips, put love bites on her neck, licked her sweating skin.

Once his initial frenzy was over, he became gentler, more playful. He draped her long hair over his body, stroking it, fisting it, kissing it.

He kissed her and loved her in utter silence. Nothing

else existed but this twilit room with Beth under him—not Hart, not Fellows, not the murders.

He sensed her trying to make him look straight into her eyes, but he evaded her. If Ian looked directly at her, he'd get lost, and he didn't want to distract himself from the physical reality of thrusting into her.

He loved her until the sky brightened, the short night rushing past. She smiled sleepily at him as he withdrew the final time, and he kissed her before dropping onto the bed beside her.

He slid his arm around her warm abdomen and spooned her back against him. Her shapely backside fit nicely against his hips, giving him ideas for the next round of loving.

He looked at his large, strong hand covering her slim waist, his arm brown against her white skin. Ian would keep her safe with him here, so safe she'd never, ever want to leave.

When Beth woke, she found the covers pulled around her and Ian still with her. Before she could ask about breakfast, his smile turned predatory. He pressed her back into the pillows and made love to her again, swift and hard, until she was breathless with it.

"We should get up now," she whispered when he lay still again, on top of her, idly kissing her neck.

"Why?"

"Won't your brother expect us for breakfast?"

"I told Curry to serve us in here."

Beth stroked his cheek. "I certainly hope you pay Curry high wages."

"He doesn't complain."

"He stayed in the asylum with you?"

"Cameron sent him to look after me when I was fifteen. Cam decided I needed someone to shave me and look after my clothes. He was right. I was a mess."

Curry came in at that moment bearing a tray heavy with silver and porcelain. Ian didn't get up, but made sure Beth was covered while Curry pulled a table to the bed and set the tray on it.

As he had in Paris, Curry pretended he couldn't see Beth as he set out the breakfast and poured fragrant tea into the waiting cups. He'd even brought newspapers from both London and Edinburgh, which he folded beside the plates. He also deposited a few letters.

Beth felt like a decadent lady, lolling about in bed while a servant brought her food and drink. Mrs. Barrington never held with breakfast in bed, even in her last, weak days.

Curry left them with a quick grin at Ian, and Ian decided he'd rather feed Beth in bed than have them rise and sit at the table.

He was quite good at it, giving her bits of bread and butter and feeding her eggs from a fork. She tried to take the fork from him and started laughing when he refused to give it to her.

Ian smiled, too, and then let Beth feed him. He liked her straddling his lap while she did it.

The whole day was like this—Ian making love to her, then the two of them lounging in the bed reading the newspapers while Curry brought them meals and drink and took away the remains.

"I like being an aristocratic lady," Beth said as the afternoon wore on. "I'm still getting used to not having to rise at dawn and wait on someone else."

"My servants will wait on you now."

"They seem very cheerful about it." The red-haired maids who'd come in to lay a fire and straighten the room had smiled broadly when Beth thanked them. Sunny, happy smiles, not sneering ones.

"They like you," Ian said.

"They don't know anything about me. I might be a termagant and scold them all hours of the day and night."

"Would you?"

"Of course not, but how do they know? Unless Curry has read them my dossier."

"They trust Curry's opinion."

"Everyone does, it seems."

"The family has served the Mackenzies forever. They're clan Mackenzie themselves and have always worked on our land. Fought beside us and looked after us for generations."

"There is so much I must get used to."

Ian said nothing, distracting her from chatter by sliding his hands under her breasts and kissing her.

~~~

Later that afternoon, Ian took her to his collection room.

Beth had the feeling of being ushered into a shrine. Shallow shelves with glass fronts had been built around the walls of the huge room, and more glass-shielded shelves ran through the middle. Ming bowls of all sizes and colors rested on small pedestals on the shelves, all labeled as to approximate year, maker, and other details. Some of the shelves were empty, waiting for the collection to grow.

"It's like a museum." Beth wandered the room in wonder. "Where are the ones you bought in London?"

The shelves all looked the same to her, but Ian walked unerringly to one and extracted the red-painted bowl he'd bought from Mather.

She thought all the bowls pretty, but she wasn't quite sure what it was about them that made Ian want to have a hundred. And he kept them so lovingly. Ian replaced the piece, walked to another seemingly random shelf, and removed another bowl. This one was flushed jade green and had three green-gray dragons around the outside.

Beth clasped her hands. "How lovely."

"It is yours."

She stilled. "What?"

His gaze moved away, though his hands were rock steady. "I give it to you. A wedding present."

Beth stared at the bowl, a fragile piece of the past, such a delicate object in Ian's large, blunt fingers. "Are you certain?"

"Of course I'm certain." His frown returned. "Do you not want it?"

"I do want it," Beth said hastily. She held her hands out for it. "I'm honored."

The frown faded, to be replaced by a slight quirk of his lips. "Is it better than a new carriage and horses and a dozen frocks?"

"What are you talking about? It's a hundred times better."

"It's only a bowl."

"It's special to you, and you gave it to me." Beth took it carefully and smiled at the dragons chasing one another in eternal determination. "It's the best gift in the world."

Ian took it gently back from her and replaced it in its slot. That made sense; in here it would stay safe and unbroken.

But the kiss Ian gave her after that was anything but sensible. It was wicked and bruising, and she had no idea why he smiled so triumphantly.

⁓

"Cam is here."

Ian saw his brother out of the window a few days later as he buttoned the shirt he'd just shrugged on. Behind him, Curry prepared the rest of Ian's clothes, while Beth, looking pretty bundled in a red silk wrapper, drank her morning tea at the little table.

Three days he and Beth had been here, and they'd spent all three days in Ian's apartments making love. They'd made forays through the house or garden so he could show them to Beth, but mostly they'd stayed in the bedroom. Ian knew they had to leave his wing eventually and return to Hart and the real world, but he'd never forget the joy of this cocoon. Whenever times got bad, and he had no doubt they would, he could remember this.

Cameron had brought a new filly, the horse about a year old, and Ian took Beth down to greet them both.

Cam was watching the unloading of the horse from its special cart as they approached. He cursed the handlers soundly, and then waded in and did the job himself.

"I've never seen a horse in its own carriage before," Beth

said as the spirited filly emerged. "Being pulled instead of pulling."

The horse's conformation was dainty, the pink edges of her nostrils sharp. She was a bay, and her black mane and tail flowed in falls of sable. She turned an interested brown eye to Beth.

"She's not a cart horse," Cameron said, his gruff voice even more gravelly from the dust on the road. "She's a fine beauty and will win dozens of races, won't you, love? Then she'll breed more racers." Cameron fondly stroked her nose.

"Why don't you marry her, Father?" Daniel asked, leaning against the van. "He's been crooning to the damn beastie all the way up. It's disgusting."

Cameron ignored his son and went to Beth. He leaned to kiss her cheek, then clapped Ian on the shoulder, the scents of horse and sweat clinging to him. "Welcome to the family, Beth. Cuff my son when he's rude. He's had no upbringing."

"That's because you brought me up, Father."

"Everything all right?" Cameron asked casually of Ian.

He was wondering how Hart had taken the news. "He'll come around," Ian said.

"We haven't seen much of Hart in the last few days," Beth said.

"Oh, no? Hiding from him, are you?"

"No, we—" Beth broke off and went bright red. Cam looked from her to Ian, who couldn't help grinning, and then Cam burst out laughing. Cameron's laugh could ring to the skies. The filly jerked her head back in irritation.

"What are you laughing at?" Daniel asked, frowning. "Oh, you mean you were in bed. Good on you, Ian. I'll have a little cousin soon, will I?"

"Unmitigated brat," Cameron growled in good humor. "You don't say such things to a lady."

"But laughing at them is all right?" Daniel countered.

"You see what I mean?" Cameron said to Beth. "He has a foul, impertinent mouth, and it's all my fault. Ignore him. Have you taken her riding, Ian? Got a good horse for her?"

Beth's face lost its color. "Oh, I don't ride."

All three Mackenzies stared at her. "You don't ride?" Daniel asked in shock.

Beth slipped her hand into Ian's. "Not much opportunity to prance down the Rotten Row as a poor vicar's wife. And Mrs. Barrington was beyond her riding years. I did hire a pony cart in Paris."

Both Cameron and Daniel gave her pitying looks.

"You are in luck," Cam said. "The compensation for marrying a Mackenzie is that your brother-in-law is the best horse master in the British Isles. I'll pick you out a horse and begin your instruction tomorrow."

Beth squeezed Ian's fingers tighter. "An elderly, placid nag, please. And really, I don't need to ride. I'm happy using my own two feet."

"Tell her, Ian."

Beth turned to him, her eyes wide. Ian forgot all about the conversation and didn't much care whether Beth rode like a master or stayed on the ground. He only wanted to put his arms around her, to hold her, to continue what they'd been doing before Cameron interrupted. He bent down and kissed her.

"I won't let him hurt you," he said.

"How reassuring," Beth answered faintly.

~~~~~

The horse Cameron chose for her wasn't exactly an elderly nag, but she was a gentle mare who had left her sporting days far behind. She was much larger than the sweet little pony Beth had pictured, towering above even Cameron, her feet like platters.

"She's half draft horse," Cameron said. "I breed them like that sometimes for jumping and stamina. She's a sweetheart. Up you go."

The saddle looked the size of a doily on the horse's great back. It had one stirrup and a groove that was to hold Beth's right leg.

"Why can't ladies ride like men?" Beth complained as Cameron boosted her up. She overbalanced and gave a little shriek as she went off the other side—to be caught in Ian's arms.

"With a horse between your legs?" Cameron's gold-flecked eyes went wide, and he touched his fingers to his mouth like a shocked, elderly maiden. "What kind of woman did you marry, Ian?"

"A practical one," Beth said. She fought the skirt of her new riding habit and flailed for the stirrup.

Ian's strong hand supported her back like a rock. Cameron grabbed Beth's ankle and pressed her foot into the stirrup. "There. Ready?"

"Oh, of course. Let's be off to the Derby." She reached for the reins, but Cameron wouldn't hand them to her.

"No reins today. I'll lead."

Beth looked at him in terror. Ian was on her other side, his bulk reassuring, but she sat at a heart-stopping height above him.

"I'll fall off without the reins," she protested. "Won't I?"

"You can't hold on by dragging at the horse's face," Ian explained. "You balance."

"Something I've never been good at."

"You'll be good at it now," Cameron said.

Without further ado, Cameron led the horse off at a very slow walk. Beth immediately slid off the horse's right side, but Ian caught her and pushed her back up into the saddle. He was smiling broadly. Laughing at his poor wife.

The stable hands and many of the mansion's staff gravitated out to watch. They either pretended to pass by the patch of park on their way somewhere else or blatantly hung on the fence that separated park from stable yard. They weren't above giving the new lady of the house words of advice or applauding when she managed to stay on when the mare broke into a trot.

By the end of the lesson, Beth had at least learned how to balance on the saddle and use her legs for support. The staff gave her a cheer when Ian lifted her down.

Their warm encouragement was a stark contrast to the chill of the dining table that evening. Hart sat in frigid silence. The footmen who'd shouted for Beth with Scots enthusiasm now looked subdued and chastised.

Beth's legs hurt, the muscles unused to such exercise. When she plopped into the dining room chair Ian held out for her, she jumped up again with a little cry.

Ian's strong hands closed around her. "Are you all right?"

"Perfectly fine." She bit her lip. "I believe Cameron needs to find me a softer horse."

Ian grinned, then burst out laughing. His laughter was warm and velvety, so fine she paused to drink it in.

Beth smiled at him and made a show of gingerly sitting down. "You may cease laughing at me, Ian Mackenzie. It was only my first lesson."

He leaned toward her. "You already have a very good seat, my Beth."

"Shall I take it you are referring to how I sit on a horse?"

Ian kissed her cheek and moved to his own chair, still smiling. He wiped his eyes with the back of his hand and sat down. "Beth likes to joke," he said without looking at the others.

Beth felt the frost of Hart's rigid stare. Daniel's mouth was open in surprise, and Cameron sat very still. Something had happened, and Beth wasn't certain what.

The rest of the meal was tense, though Ian didn't notice. He ate calmly, oblivious. Occasionally he'd look up at Beth, his smile hot, and once, when the others weren't looking, he curled his tongue at her. Beth turned beet red and stared down at her plate.

When the footmen finally cleared the last course, Hart rose and tossed down his napkin.

"Ian, I need you," he said, and stalked from the room.

Cameron reached for the humidor on the sideboard. Daniel joined him, neither of them acting surprised at Hart's abrupt departure. When Ian went to them, Beth leapt from her chair and sped out of the room.

"Beth . . ." she heard Ian say, and then she was down the

hall and inside Hart's private study. Hart swung around in the middle of the room.

"Ian is not your servant," Beth burst out.

Hart pinned her with his eagle's gaze. "What the devil?"

"You summon Ian the same way you'd summon a footman for your boots."

A muscle twitched in his jaw. "Mrs. Ackerley, you have been one of this family barely a week. Ian and I hammered out an understanding long before you appeared on the horizon."

"He is your brother, not your secretary."

"Don't try my patience."

"You love him. Why don't you show him?"

Hart came to her, lips tight, and gripped her shoulders. He was abominably strong. "Mrs. Ackerley—"

"My *name* is Beth."

The door banged open, and Ian stormed inside. He caught Hart and shoved him away from Beth. "Don't touch her."

Hart shook him off. "What is the matter with you?"

"Beth, get away from him."

Beth's heart thumped. "Ian, I'm sorry, I was just—"

Ian swung his head to her but wouldn't look at her. *"Now!"*

Beth stood for one more stunned instant, then sped out of the room.

Cameron looked startled as she passed him in the hall, then he said, "Hell," and marched to Hart's study. The slam of the door thundered down the passage.

Beth made it to the main stairs before she collapsed, lungs burning. She could barely breathe, her dratted corset too tight.

Someone thumped down next to her. "You all right, Auntie Beth? Want a drink or something?"

She wanted to laugh hysterically at "Auntie Beth," but she held herself together. "Yes, thank you, Daniel, a drink would be lovely."

"Oy," Daniel shouted over the banisters. "Angus. Bring a dram o' whiskey."

The burly footman who'd been passing through the hall turned on his heel and went back into the dining room.

"Are they always like this?" Beth asked, breathing carefully.

"At each other's throats? Oh, aye. Always shouting about something. You'll get used to it."

"Will I?"

"You'll have to, won't you? But they've been unhappy."

Beth blinked away the moisture in her eyes. "What about you? Are you unhappy?"

Daniel shrugged his lanky shoulders. "You mean because my mum tried to murder me and my dad and then offed herself? I never knew her, and Dad's done his best."

His matter-of-fact acceptance of his mother's violence twisted Beth's heart. It had been the same in the East End; ten-year-old girls whose prostitute mothers had been beaten by their men shrugged shoulders and said tightly, "She were a whore. What'd she expect?"

Unaware of her pity, Daniel took the cut-crystal glass that Angus brought and thrust it into her hand. Beth sipped, the smooth taste of whiskey curling pleasantly on her tongue. *Ladies don't drink spirits*, she heard Mrs. Barrington say. This despite the secret brandy bottle stashed in Mrs. Barrington's bedside table.

"Tell me something, Daniel," Beth said tiredly. "In the dining room, when Ian laughed at me, you all stared like the ceiling had come down. Why?"

Daniel wrinkled his forehead. "Why? 'Twas because Ian laughed. I don't think any of us have ever heard Uncle Ian laugh out loud before. At least not since he got sprung from the asylum."

Beth progressed on her riding lessons until, by the end of the week, she could ride unassisted as long as Cameron or Ian rode alongside her. She learned to use her legs to guide the horse and not flail or grab the reins to keep her balance.

The soreness began to slacken as her muscles became accustomed to the exercise. By the beginning of her second week of lessons, she could climb into bed with only a soft moan of pain. Ian proved amazingly capable at massaging the stiffness out of her.

Beth became fond of the old horse she rode. The mare had a mile-long pedigree name, but her nickname among the stable lads was Emmie. While Beth and Emmie plodded across the vast lands of Kilmorgan, Ian and Cameron raced or put their horses over fences. Ian was an excellent rider, but Cameron seemed to become part of his horse. When he wasn't giving Beth lessons, he worked at training the filly he'd brought, letting her run on a long line he held in competent hands.

"It's his gift," Ian said to Beth as they watched him one morning. "He can do anything with horses. They love him."

With people Cameron was harsh and often rude, and his language colored the air. At first he apologized to Beth, but after a while he forgot to. Beth remembered what Isabella had told her, that the Mackenzies had lived as bachelors for so long, they didn't think to soften their manners around ladies. Beth, used to East End toughs, decided she could bear it. As she'd told Inspector Fellows, she was not a wilting weed.

She learned to treasure Ian's conversations with her, like this one about Cameron, because she never saw him much outside of bed. Over the next two weeks, he closeted himself with Hart, or the two went riding alone, and neither would say where.

Cameron kept on with Beth's lessons without indicating that anything was unusual. Beth tried to ask Ian once what he and Hart were doing, and Ian answered laconically, "Business," before looking off into the distance.

It maddened her to not understand, but she hated to poke and pry. Hart had been right; she barely knew Ian, and perhaps this was what they always did.

I can't expect them to change their entire lives for me,

she chided herself. Another part of her would respond, *But he's my husband. . . .*

Things went on like this until one afternoon when Cameron took her riding beyond the park up into the hills.

It was a beautiful day, with a fine summer breeze dancing through the trees. Patches of snow lingered on the highest peaks of the mountains, the sun never quite warming it enough to melt it.

"There's a folly in the woods out here," Cameron said, riding beside her. His own horse was a glossy black stallion. The stable lads were afraid of the beast, but he obeyed Cam without fuss. "My father built it for my mother. There weren't enough ruined castles in the Highlands for him, so he decided to build a fake one."

The brothers never spoke much about their mother, or their father either, for that matter. The portrait of their much-bearded father glared at her every day from the top of the second-floor staircase, but she'd never seen a picture of their mother. She nudged Emmie to move faster, interested.

Behind her Cameron's horse stumbled. Beth turned in alarm to find Cameron already dismounted and anxiously examining the stallion's hoof.

"Is he hurt?"

She spoke to Cameron's broad back. "No, he's all right. Threw a shoe, didn't you, old lad?" He patted the horse's neck. "Go on up to the folly. Emmie knows the way."

Beth swallowed, never having ventured out by herself, but she decided she had to sometime. She nudged Emmie onward, and the old mare plodded up the path toward the higher hill.

The day had turned hot, the air close among the trees. Beth wiped her face as she rode, hoping the folly would hold a cooler breeze.

She saw it before long, a picturesque stone building with moss on it. The flat sides had tiny windows and artfully crumbling brick. She could see why the folly had been built in that particular place, however. The view was breathtaking.

Fold after fold of land rolled away toward the flat gray sea far away. A creek gushed in a gorge that dropped from the folly's front edge.

"You're certain Fellows has nothing new?" Hart's voice rolled out of the folly, and Beth froze.

"I've said," Ian answered him.

"You haven't said anything at all. We have to talk about this. Why didn't you tell me about Lily Martin?"

"I wanted to keep her safe." There was a silence. "I didn't help her at all."

Lily Martin was the name of the woman killed in Covent Garden, Beth remembered, the night Ian had left for Paris. Fellows was convinced Ian killed her.

"Why didn't you tell me?" Hart repeated.

"To keep her safe," Ian answered with emphasis.

"From Fellows?"

"Partly."

"From whoever killed Sally Tate?" Hart asked sharply.

There was another silence, while the creek chuckled merrily away below.

"Ian, do you know?" Hart's voice went quieter, flatter.

"I know what I saw."

"Which was?" Hart asked impatiently.

"Blood. She was covered in blood; it was all over my hands. I tried to wipe it off on the walls, on the bedding. It was like paint. . . ."

"Ian. Focus on me."

Ian trailed off, the words dying away. "I know what I saw," he said quietly.

"But does Fellows know?"

Ian paused again, and when he spoke, his voice was steadier. "No."

"Then why does he want Beth?"

"I don't know. But he does, and I won't let him have her."

"Very noble of you." Hart's voice was dry.

"If she's married to me, your name protects her, too. The family of the Duke of Kilmorgan is not to be bothered by Lloyd Fellows."

"I remember."

"He tried to get her to spy against me," Ian continued.

Hart's voice turned sharp. "Did he?"

"Beth refused." Ian sounded pleased. "She saw him off. My Beth's not afraid of him."

"Are you certain she refused him?"

"I was there. But just in case . . ." Another pause, and Beth held her breath.

"Just in case?" Hart prompted.

"A wife can't go into the witness box against her husband, can she?"

Hart was silent a moment. "I apologize, Ian. Sometimes I forget how intelligent you are."

Ian didn't respond.

Hart continued. "You're right, Ian. It's best that she's on our side. But the moment she makes you unhappy, the marriage is annulled. She can be made to keep quiet for a large enough sum of money. Everyone has their price."

Beth's breath hurt, and the world seemed to ripple around her. She turned and blindly nudged Emmie forward, thankful the mare's hooves made little sound on the damp leaves.

Nausea bit her stomach. She clung to Emmie's red-brown mane, letting the mare find her way back home. Beth barely remembered the ride to Kilmorgan. She knew only that suddenly it was before her, the long mansion crouching in the valley, its windows glittering like watchful eyes.

Cameron was nowhere in sight, likely engrossed with his stallion's lost shoe, which was fine with Beth. A tall, red-haired groom appeared and took Emmie's reins, and Beth heard herself thanking him politely. The dogs ran up for her attention, but she couldn't see to pet them, and they turned and trotted back to the stables.

Somehow Beth made it into the house and up to the chamber she shared with Ian. She closed the door on the maid who'd hurried to assist her, and then she numbly undressed to her chemise and lay down on the bed.

It was late afternoon, and the sun shone through the windows with all its strength. Beth lay still, her arm across her abdomen, the absence of the corset at last allowing her to breathe. A few tears trickled down her face, then dried, leaving her eyes burning. She thought she could hear the echo of Mrs. Barrington's derisive cackle.

Beth lay still until she heard Ian coming. Then she closed her eyes, not wanting to look at him.

Chapter 16

Beth lay in the shadow of the canopy, her dark hair tangled across the pillow. Ian's gaze traced the snakes of her hair, lines of brown silk across the linen. Six strands lay straight, seven intersecting them at odd angles, and three more lay across her pale chemise. He liked the pattern and studied it for a time.

The skirt of Beth's chemise had twisted to bare her calves, muscular now from her riding lessons. He reached down and touched her skin, then started when he found it clammy and cold.

"Beth, are you ill?"

Beth's eyelids fluttered, but she didn't look at him. "No."

Ian stopped, a tiny headache threading through his brain. He always had difficulty deciphering what another person was feeling, but Beth's distress penetrated even the fog in his brain.

"Did you fall?" He sat down on the bed next to her. "Were you frightened? Tell me."

Beth sat up, her beautiful hair tumbling across her full

breasts. "Ian, please explain to me what happened that night in High Holborn."

He started shaking his head before she finished. So many people wanted to discuss it—Fellows, Hart, Beth. Hart had asked again today what Ian had done, had pried open a box in Ian's memory that he wanted to keep locked forever.

Don't make me see. . . .

Beth's fingers bit down on his. "Please. I need to know."

"You don't."

"I do. I need to understand."

"Leave it alone." His words rang harshly in the stillness. "I want you to look at me like you did when you first met me, before you knew."

"How can I? Why can't I know? I'm your wife." She let go of his hand. "You were never going to tell me, were you, until Fellows let it out? How long would you have kept silent?"

"As long as I could."

"Do you trust me so little?"

Ian looked away, his attention caught by the sharp shadow of leaves against the window shade. "With this, I trust no one."

"Except Hart."

"Especially *not* Hart." The words were grim.

"Do you think I'd tell anyone what you say to me?"

He flicked his gaze to her and then away, but not before he saw her blue eyes full of unshed tears. "Fellows asked you to."

"And you believe I would? I know you do. But Fellows can't put me on the witness stand, can he? A wife isn't considered a credible witness against her husband. I heard you explain this to Hart."

Ian's heart raced, his mind going over every single word he'd exchanged with Hart at the folly. She'd been there, she must have been riding by, she'd stopped to listen.

"Where was Cam? Was he with you? Did he hear?"

Beth's eyes widened. "No, his horse threw a shoe. I heard,

no one else. I heard you talk about her blood. I heard you tell Hart you married me to keep Fellows from using me against you. Is that true?" She bleated a short laugh. "Of course it's true. You don't know how to lie."

Memories rushed at him, hideous and vivid. Walking back into the room to see Sally's white body against the sheets, the surprise on her face, the blood soaking her limbs, her dyed red hair snaking across the pillows in patterns similar to Beth's. "I couldn't help her. I failed her."

He'd failed Lily Martin, too, the lady who'd been in the hall outside the room, terror in her eyes. She'd seen. She'd known. She couldn't be allowed to tell the constable. He'd hidden Lily away for five years, but in the end, she'd died.

And now Beth. If she knew, she'd be in danger, too.

"Help me understand," Beth pleaded. "Tell me why you're so afraid, why you'd do this to me."

"I should have known. I should have stopped it."

"Stopped what? Known what?"

Ian closed his hands on Beth's shoulders until she winced. Then he deliberately removed his grip and stood. "Cease asking me."

"Ian, I'm your wife. I promise I will not run off to Inspector Fellows to tell him everything you say. I told you that the day he asked me."

"I don't give a damn about Inspector Fellows."

She laughed, and he couldn't understand what she thought was funny. "Yet you married me to keep him from pestering me for all your secrets. What other reason would you marry a naive widow long in the tooth?"

He had no idea what she was talking about. "I married you to keep him from you. To keep idiots like Mather from you. Hart's name protects his family, so I made you family, a Mackenzie. No one touches the Mackenzies."

"Because the mighty Duke of Kilmorgan has such pull with the Home Office?"

"Yes."

Her eyes were so blue. Tears made them even more

cornflower blue, breathtakingly blue. His headache stabbed him through the temple, and he rubbed at it.

"I want to help you find out what happened," Beth said. "Help you put it to rest."

Oh, God. "No, no, no. Leave it be."

"How can I? It's tearing you apart; it's tearing me apart. If you tell me, if we think about it, maybe we can decide what really happened."

Ian jerked away. "This is not a bloody detective story."

She bit her lip, white teeth on red, and his desire rose swiftly, inconveniently. But if he made love to her, if he rode her until she couldn't breathe, she'd stop asking questions, she'd stop thinking, she'd stop looking at him.

"I lived in the East End," she was saying, her voice floating past him. "I knew game girls, and they didn't resent me—at least, most of them didn't. Perhaps some of them knew Sally Tate, knew who would follow her and strike her down, perhaps in a jealous rage. . . ."

Ian finally focused on her words. He grabbed her wrists. "No!" He stared into her eyes . . . so blue, so beautiful, like the skies in the middle of summer. . . .

He slammed his eyes closed. "Stay out of it. Leave them out of it. Why do you think Lily Martin died?"

Silence. At last Ian opened his eyes to find Beth still in front of him, her lips slightly parted. Her breasts swelled above the chemise, soft and white and inviting his touch.

"She died because she saw too much," he said. "I couldn't save her. I don't want to find you like that, too."

Beth's eyes widened. "You think he'll strike again, then?"

Ian's breath hurt his lungs. He jerked away, fists clenching until his nails creased his palms. "Leave it the hell alone. This has nothing to do with you."

"You made me your wife. It has everything to do with me."

"And as my wife, you are to obey me."

Beth put her hands on her hips, her brows rising. "You don't know much about marriage, do you?"

"I know nothing about it."

"It's sharing burdens. It's the wife helping her husband, the husband helping his wife. . . ."

"For God's sake." Ian spun away, unable to stand still. "I'm not your Thomas, your vicar. I never will be. I know you'll never look at me the way you looked at him."

She stared at him, white-faced. "What do you mean?"

He turned back. "You look at me like I'm the Mad Mackenzie. It's in the back of your mind all the time." He tapped the side of her head. "You can never forget about my madness, and you pity me for it."

Beth blinked a few times but remained silent. His Beth, who could chatter on about anything and everything, was robbed of words.

Because Ian spoke the truth. She'd been madly in love with her first husband. Ian understood about love, even if he couldn't feel it. He'd seen his brothers devastated by love and grief, and he knew Beth had been, too.

"I can never give you what he gave you." Ian's chest hurt. "You loved him, and I know that can never be between us."

"You're wrong," she whispered. "I love you, Ian."

He pressed his clenched fists to his breastbone. "There's nothing in here to love. Nothing. I *am* insane. My father knew it. Hart knows it. You can't nurse me back to health. I have my father's rages, and you can never be sure what I'll do—" He broke off, his headache beating at him. He rubbed his temple furiously, angry at the pain.

"Ian."

The rest of his body wanted Beth and couldn't understand why the anger held him back. He wanted to stop this stupid argument and spread her on the bed.

Her agitated breath lifted her breasts high, and her hair straggled across her white shoulders. If he rode her, she'd stop nattering about the murder and love. She'd just be his.

She's not a whore, something whispered in his head. *She's not a thing to be used. She's Beth.*

Ian grabbed her shoulders and dragged her up to him,

slanting his mouth over hers. He forced her lips to part, the kiss raw, brutal. Her fists on his chest softened, but she was shaking.

He hungrily took her mouth, wanting to pull her inside him, or himself inside her. If he could be part of her, everything would be all right. He would be well. The horror he kept secret would go away.

Except he knew it wouldn't. His damned memory would keep it as fresh as if it happened yesterday. And Beth would still look at him as if he were something pathetic in an East End gutter.

Her heat scalded him like the bathwater from his childhood. No one had believed him when he shrieked that it burned—they'd forced him into the water, and he'd screamed until his throat was raw, his voice broken.

Ian shoved Beth from him. She gazed up at him, her lips swollen and red, her eyes wide.

He walked away from her.

The world became very specific, the pattern on the rug pointing almost but not quite to the door. It was agony to move his feet toward the door, but he had to leave the room, and the anger and pain.

He saw Curry in the hall, no doubt having hurried up here when he heard the shouting. They all worried about him, Curry, Beth, Hart, Cam—so protective, hemming him in, his jailers. He passed Curry without a word and walked out.

"Where are you off to, guv?" Curry called behind him, but Ian didn't answer.

He moved down the hall, placing his feet precisely in line with the carpet's border. At the landing, he turned at a right angle and followed the line down the stairs.

Curry panted behind him. "I'll just go with you, then."

Ian ignored him. He walked across the black and white marble tiles below, his feet finding only the white ones, and out the back door to the garden.

Walking, walking, to the steward's house and inside to

the case containing the guns for pheasant shoots and a brace of pistols. He knew where the key was and had two pistols out before Curry, with his shorter stride, could catch up.

"Guv."

"Load these for me."

Curry raised his hands. "No."

Ian turned away. He found the bullets himself, shoved the box of them into his pocket, and walked out.

On his way through the garden, a young undergardener rose from pruning a rosebush, staring at Ian with his mouth open. Ian grabbed him by the shoulder and pulled him along with him.

The young man dropped his shears and trotted obediently alongside Ian. Curry came after them, panting. "Leave it," he snapped to the gardener. "Get back to work, you."

Ian had no idea to whom Curry was talking. He kept his grip firm on the young gardener's arm. He was a wiry lad, strong as steel.

At the end of the garden, Ian handed an empty pistol to the gardener. He withdrew the box of bullets and opened it, shoving it in the young man's open hand.

The bullets were shining, their brass casings catching the sun. Ian admired the perfect shape of them, tapered at the top, blunt on the bottom, how they fit precisely into the revolver's chamber.

"Load that one," he told the gardener.

The boy began to obey, fingers shaking hard.

"Stop," Curry commanded. "Don't do it for him."

Ian guided the young man's fingers to place the bullet in the revolver's chamber. The revolvers were Webleys, loaded by breaking the barrel forward on a hinge. "Careful," Ian said. "Don't hurt yourself."

"Put the pistol down, lad, or you're for it."

The young man sent Curry a terrified glance.

"Do as I say," Ian said.

The young man gulped. "Yes, m'lord."

Ian clicked the revolver back together, sighted down the barrel, and shot a small rock that had been resting on another rock fifty feet away. He shot again and again until his pistol clicked on an empty chamber.

He shoved the pistol at the gardener and took the second one. "Reload that," he said, and sighted down the fresh weapon.

Ian shot six more times, blowing both rocks to pieces. He took the first gun and centered it on another rock, while the young man loaded the second one again.

Dimly Ian heard Curry shouting at him, then at the gardener, but he couldn't make sense of the words. He heard others behind him. Cam. Hart.

His world narrowed to the blue steel of the pistol's barrel, the tiny explosions of rock downrange, the burst of noise as he squeezed the trigger. He felt the solid butt of the gun against his palm, screwed up his eyes at the acrid scent of burned powder, shifted his weight to take the kick.

He shot, handed off the pistol, shot again, over and over. His hands ached, his eyes watered, and he kept shooting.

"Guv," Curry yelled. "Stop, for the love of God."

Ian sighted, squeezed the trigger. His arm bucked, and he straightened it, shooting again.

Heavy hands grabbed his shoulder. Hart's voice, roaring in rage. Ian shook him off and kept firing.

Fire, hand over pistol, grab second pistol, aim, fire.

"Ian."

Beth's warm tone floated to him, and her cool hand rested on his. The world came rushing back.

It was dimmer now, twilight having taken the place of bright afternoon. The undergardener sobbed at his side, dropping the empty pistol and pressing his hands to his face.

Ian's arms ached. He slowly unclenched the pistol that Curry eased out of his hand and found his palms blistered and raw.

Beth touched his face. "Ian."

He loved how she said his name. She spoke the syllables gently, her voice always soft, caressing.

Hart loomed up behind her, but Ian dissolved into Beth. He slid his arms around her waist and buried his face in her neck.

⁓

"When he comes back and finds you gone, 'oo will he strangle?" Curry bleated. "Me, that's 'oo."

Beth handed Katie her valise and adjusted her gloves. "You told me that when he disappears like this, it's often for days and days. I'll be back before then."

Curry's mulish look said he didn't believe that.

Ian had slept with Beth, made love to her last night after Curry had bandaged his hurt hands. But when Beth had awakened, Ian had been gone, not only from their bedroom, but from the house and park around it. None of the horses was missing; no one had seen him go.

Hart was livid and demanded a search. Cameron and Curry had persuaded him to let Ian alone. Ian would come back when he was ready. Didn't he always? Hart, his look told her, blamed Beth.

"You're doing right, m'lady," Katie whispered to her as they climbed into the carriage. "I always thought he was a nutter."

"I'm not leaving him," Beth said sharply, loud enough for the coachman to hear. "I'm simply taking care of business in London."

Katie glanced at the coachman and winked at Beth. "Right you are, m'lady."

Beth snapped her mouth shut as the coachman started the horses. She felt a pang. She'd miss Kilmorgan.

The ride to the railway station proved uneventful. As the coachman lifted out the valises, Cameron's son, Daniel, suddenly rolled off the backboard, where he'd been crouching.

"Take me with you," he blurted.

Beth hadn't yet made up her mind about Daniel. He was definitely a Mackenzie, with his brown-red hair and golden eyes, but the shape of his face was different. His chin and eyes were softer, making him handsome rather than hard. His mother had been a famous beauty, according to Curry, celebrated in her day.

Just like our Lord Cameron to marry a wild one like her, Curry had said. *Anything to get under his father's skin.*

Daniel's attempt to mimic Cameron in all ways touched Beth's heart. He wanted Cameron's attention and approval, Beth could see, and Cameron didn't always respond.

"I'm not certain your father would be happy," Beth tried.

Daniel's face fell. "Please? It'll be dismal up here with Ian going to ground and Hart biting everyone's head off and Dad growling like a thunderstorm. With you gone, they'll be even worse."

Daniel would be in the middle, Beth sensed. He'd chafe and rebel, which would make Hart and Cameron harder on him.

"Very well," Beth said. "You didn't happen to pack a bag, did you?"

"Naw, but I've got clothes in Dad's house in London." Daniel ran a few steps and did a cartwheel. "I'll be good, I promise."

"Are you mad?" Katie hissed as Beth turned to the ticket window. "Why d'ya want to saddle yourself with that hellion?"

"He'll be useful, and I feel sorry for him."

Katie rolled her eyes. "He's a right nuisance, that one. His pa needs to tan his hide."

"Being a parent is complicated."

"Oh, is it? You ever been one?"

Beth hid the swift pain in her heart. "No, but I've known plenty of them." She smiled at the stationmaster as he came to the counter.

The stationmaster put Daniel's ticket on the Kilmorgan account, looking slightly surprised that Beth asked for the tickets instead of sending a servant. The idea of her ladyship purchasing anything for herself seemed to fill everyone with horror.

"I'd also like to send a telegram," she said crisply, then waited while the obliging stationmaster fetched his pencil and paper.

"Who to, m'lady?"

"Inspector Fellows," she answered. "At Scotland Yard, in London."

Chapter 17

Being alone no longer soothed him.

Ian watched the water run along the bottom of the gorge, his boots muddy, the hem of his kilt wet from the splashing stream.

At one time in his life, fishing in Abernathy's Gorge with nothing but the wind, sky, and water would have seemed like perfection to him. Today he felt drained and empty.

He wasn't strictly alone. Old Geordie fished on a rock not far from him, his pole silently dangling from his weathered hand. Long ago, Geordie had been a stable hand for Ian's father, but he'd retired and lived a reclusive existence up on the mountain, miles from anywhere. His cottage was tiny and run-down, Geordie too unsocial even to hire someone to help him keep up the place.

Not long after Ian's release from the asylum, he'd stumbled upon Geordie's retreat. Back then, Ian had been volatile and restless, easily unnerved by the scrutiny of his family and servants. He'd slipped away and wandered the wilds alone, ending up thirsty and footsore on the doorstep of a gray stone cottage. Geordie had silently opened the door, eased Ian's thirst with water and whiskey, and let him stay.

Geordie, the taciturn man who'd once taught the boy Ian to fish, had not asked any questions. Ian had helped Geordie repair a part of the roof that had peeled off, and Geordie had fed him and given him a corner to sleep in. Ian had stayed until he felt more able to cope with the world, then returned home.

It had become habit for Ian to come up here when events became too much for him. He'd help Geordie with what repairs needed to be done, and Geordie would comfort Ian with silence.

Ian had arrived early this morning. He'd stripped off his shirt and gone to work plastering the inside of Geordie's cottage to keep the wind out during the coming winter. Geordie, too feeble now to do much work, sat and smoked his pipe, saying nothing, as usual.

After Ian had finished, he and Geordie shouldered fishing poles and silently made their way to Abernathy's Gorge.

Beth would like it here.

The thought struck Ian from nowhere, but it was true. She'd like the rush of the stream, the beauty of the heather among the rocks, the sweet smell of the air. She'd smile and say she understood why Ian came here, and then she'd likely make a jest that Ian didn't understand.

Ian glanced at Geordie. The old man sat on a rock in a threadbare kilt. He held a fishing pole negligently in one hand, and had the inevitable pipe stuck between his teeth.

"I'm married," Ian told him.

Geordie's expression didn't change. He removed the pipe, said, "Oh, aye?" and shoved it back into his mouth.

"Aye." Ian fished in silence a moment. "She's a beautiful lass."

Geordie grunted. He returned his attention to his line, the conversation finished. Ian could tell that Geordie was interested, however. He'd actually spoken.

Ian fished awhile longer, but he found that the sounds of

the gorge and the calm of fishing didn't still his mind as usual. He kept replaying his scene with Beth, which had ended in his muddle with the pistols. He'd bedded her into sweet oblivion after that, but woke still troubled.

She knew the stains on his soul, the darkness in his eyes. Ian remembered how she'd gazed at him in interested innocence the night he'd met her at the opera, and he knew she'd never do so again. Everything had changed. Damn Fellows.

The afternoon turned to evening, though the Highland summer sun was still high. Beth would be readying herself for supper, though if she were sensible, she'd take it alone in her chamber. Hart's glare at the dining table could ruin an appetite.

Ian pictured her sitting at her dressing table, brushing her long, sleek hair. He loved the satiny slide of it, like warm silk on his hands.

He wanted to sleep with her against him, feel the damp warmth of her body along his. Summer air would pour through the window, and he'd breathe in its scent and hers.

Ian drew in his fishing line. "I'll be off home, then."

Geordie's head barely moved in a nod. "Goin' back t' the missus," he said around the pipe.

"Aye." Ian sent him a grin, gathered up his gear, and strode off down the gorge.

"He's here," Katie whispered. "In the drawing room."

Beth rose, peered into the mirror, smoothed a strand of hair, and left her bedroom. "Don't come with me."

"Catch me going anywhere near the man." Katie plopped down on the one chair in Beth's bedroom in the Belgrave Square house. "I'll wait."

Beth hastened out, her hands pressed to her skirts to keep them from rustling. The staircase and hall blazed with light, Beth having firmly told Mrs. Barrington's servants that she wanted to be able to see when she went up and down the stairs. The old butler had chuckled, then wheezed, but saw that it was done.

Inspector Fellows turned when she entered the drawing room. Beth thought of how she'd first met him in Isabella's drawing room in Paris, her agitation and amazement as Fellows had told her all about Ian Mackenzie. She determined to conduct this interview with a little more composure.

Fellows looked much the same as he had in their first encounter. His suit was made of cheap dark material but well-kept, his thick hair brushed back from his forehead, his mustache trimmed. Hazel eyes regarded Beth with an intensity comparable to Hart's.

"Mrs. Ackerley."

"My marriage is legal," Beth said crisply, pulling the doors shut. "So I am no longer Mrs. Ackerley. Lady Ian Mackenzie sounds strange to me, but you can address me as 'your ladyship,' if you wish."

Fellows gave her a wry smile. "Still the ferocious guardian. Why did you send for me?"

Beth raised her brows. "I might have grown up in the gutter, but I apparently learned better manners than you, Mr. Fellows. Shall we sit down?"

Fellows made a show of waiting for her to sit before he lowered himself, ill at ease, to the edge of a Belter armchair. Mrs. Barrington's horsehair furniture was hideously uncomfortable, and Beth felt a moment's glee watching Fellows shift against the chair's unyielding surface.

"Give up, Inspector; the chairs are impossible. If you don't want me to ring for tea, then I shall simply begin." She leaned forward. "I want you to tell me everything you know about the murder at the High Holborn house five years ago. Start at the beginning and leave nothing out."

Fellows looked surprised. "You are supposed to be telling me what happened."

"Well, I don't know, do I? If you explain it to me, perhaps I can share what I've learned. But you must go first."

He stared at her a moment, and then one side of his mouth turned up. "You are a harsh negotiator, Mrs. Ackerley—forgive me—Lady Ian. Do the decadent Mackenzies know what has descended among them?"

"I find the decadent Mackenzies quite gentlemanly. They care deeply about one another, have been kind to me, and love their dogs."

Fellows looked unimpressed. "Are you certain you wish to hear the story? Some bits are gruesome."

"Be remorseless, Inspector."

He had remorseless eyes, did Inspector Fellows. "Very well. Five years ago, almost to the day, I was called to investigate a crime in a private house in High Holborn. A young woman, Sally Tate, had been stabbed five times through the heart with a knife, according to the coroner. She bled some, and her blood had been smeared on the walls around her."

I tried to wipe it off on the walls, on the bedding. . . . Beth shut her eyes, trying to forget the harsh sound of Ian's voice as the words tumbled out.

Fellows continued. "It took some time to pry out of Mrs. Palmer, the owner of the house, the names of the gentlemen who'd visited there the night before. You do know that the place was once owned by Hart Mackenzie? He bought it to keep Mrs. Palmer, a famous courtesan he'd taken as his mistress. He sold her the house when his political career began to rise."

"I presume you did discover who was there?"

"Oh, yes. Five gentlemen attended Mrs. Palmer's salon the night before. Hart Mackenzie and Ian. A gentleman called Mr. Stephenson—Hart had brought him to win him to his side in some financial game. A Colonel Harrison, who was a regular guest of Mrs. Palmer and her young ladies, and his friend Major Thompkins. They apparently all managed to leave well before the murder occurred, very convenient for them. I was able to interview each man the next morning, but not Ian Mackenzie, who had been bundled off to Scotland by his brother Hart."

Beth smoothed her skirt. "You speak of them familiarly, Inspector. You say Ian and Hart, instead of 'his lordship' and 'His Grace.'"

Fellows gave her a deprecating look. "I think about the Mackenzies more often than I do my own family."

"Why, I wonder?"

His color rose. "Because they are blights on society, that's why. Rich men who spend money on women, clothes, and horses and don't do an honest day's work. They're useless. I'm surprised you take to them, you who know all about an honest day's work. They're nothing."

Bitterness rang in his words. Beth stared at him, and Fellows flushed and tried to compose himself.

"Very well," she said. "You interviewed all the gentlemen but Ian. Why don't you suspect them?"

"They were respectable," Fellows said.

"Visiting a brothel is respectable, the vicar's widow asks with her brows raised?"

"They were all bachelors. No wives breaking their hearts at home. Mr. Stephenson and the two military officers were astonished by the news of the murder and were able to account satisfactorily for their movements. None of them had gone near Sally Tate, and they'd departed the house just after midnight. Sally Tate was killed near five in the morning, according to the doctor. They left Hart and Ian Mackenzie behind. Ah, I mean, His Grace and his lordship."

"And Ian's servants swear Ian had returned home by two," Beth said, remembering what Fellows had told her before.

"But they're lying." Fellows sat forward. "What I've pieced together from their stories is this: Hart Mackenzie brings his friend Stephenson and his brother Ian to enjoy an evening with high-class courtesans. At about ten, in the parlor, the four men—Hart, Stephenson, Thompkins, and Harrison—begin a game of whist. Ian declines the invitation to play cards and reads a newspaper. According to Major Thompkins, Sally Tate sat down near Ian and started talking to him. They had a good chin-wag for about a quarter of an hour, and then she convinced him to go upstairs with her."

"*Ian* talked for a quarter of an hour?"

Fellows smiled faintly. "I imagine Sally did most of the talking."

Beth fell silent. She burned up inside, thinking of Ian leading a woman to bed, though she reminded herself that she hadn't known Ian then. He'd had no obligation to her at the time. Jealousy wasn't rational, however.

She forced herself to think over what Fellows had told her. Sally had talked to Ian for a quarter of an hour, but she couldn't have been trying to entice him upstairs all that time. Beth knew from experience that persuading Ian Mackenzie to do anything he didn't want to was an impossible task. He would have made up his mind at the start whether he wanted to bed Sally, and either gone upstairs with the woman right away or never. So, if Sally hadn't been trying to persuade him, what had they talked about?

Beth took a breath. "And then?"

"The other four gentlemen remained downstairs playing cards. None of them went upstairs, according to the ladies, the gentlemen, and the servants. Only Ian and Sally Tate."

"And everyone departed after midnight?"

"Stephenson, Harrison, and Thompkins enjoyed talking together so much that they decided to adjourn to Harrison's home. According to their statement, Hart went with them but turned back almost immediately, saying he wanted to wait for his brother."

"And did he?"

"According to Mrs. Palmer, Hart returned at about one, waited for Ian, who came down at two, and the brothers departed together." Fellows smiled. "But here we reach a snag. One of the maids declared that Hart *had* gone upstairs at some point, then rushed out later on his own. When pressed the maid got confused and couldn't swear to anything. But later, after Mrs. Palmer managed to get the girl alone, the maid changed her story and said that Hart and Ian had definitely left together at two."

Beth bit her lip. Fellows wasn't stupid, and the maid's waffling was suspicious. "What did Ian say?"

"I did not get the chance to interview your good husband until two weeks later. By that time, he couldn't remember."

A small pain began in Beth's heart. Ian remembered everything.

"Exactly," Fellows said. "I thought I had enough to pursue him, but suddenly, my chief inspector pulled me off the case and took away my notes. My chief declared that a passing tramp killed Sally, and he faked the evidence to prove it. Case swept under the rug and closed."

Beth pulled her thoughts together with effort. "What happened when Sally was found?"

Fellows sat back in the chair, his expression one of frustration. "What I was *told* happened was that a maid found her and screamed. The others came running, and Mrs. Palmer sent for the constable." Fellows paused, giving Beth a keen stare. "What I believe happened is that Ian was found in the room with Sally, Sally dead. But the ladies of that house are all loyal to the bone to Hart Mackenzie, so they sent for Hart, who cleaned Ian up and got him out of there. *Then* they shouted for the police. By the time the constable arrived, Ian was on a train to Scotland, and his servants instructed to swear up and down that he'd slept at home."

Bloody hell. Beth knew it had happened just as Fellows said. Ian had to be taken away, because he wouldn't know how to lie. He'd have told Fellows the literal truth and been arrested, perhaps hanged for a murder he didn't commit.

Then Beth might never have met Ian, never seen his golden eyes warm with his fleeting glance, never kissed his lips, never heard his voice whisper her name in the night. Her life would have been empty and shallow, and she wouldn't have known why.

"You're a pillock, Inspector," she said vehemently.

He scowled. "Respectable ladies don't use those words, Mrs. Ackerley."

"Botheration about respectable ladies. You've rubbed my background in my face, so you will receive the brunt of it. You *are* a pillock. You have been so fixed on Ian that you've let the real murderer—probably one of the other three gentlemen or Mrs. Palmer—get clean away. Hart might have told Ian to lie, but Ian can't. He doesn't see the world like the rest of us, doesn't know that people never tell the truth if they can help it. He thinks *we're* all mad, and he's right."

Fellows snorted. "Ian Mackenzie will say anything His bloody Grace tells him to, and you know it. Lies or no lies."

"You don't know the Mackenzies very well at all if you believe that. Ian doesn't obey Hart. He does as he pleases." She understood that now. "Ian helps Hart because he's grateful to Hart for releasing him from that horrible asylum."

"And will lick Hart's boots the rest of his life for it," Fellows snapped. He stood. "You are the deluded one, my lady. They're using you like they use everyone else. Why do you think the Mackenzie marriages fail? Because the wives in question finally realize they're being chewed up and spat out by the uncaring machine that is Hart and his family."

"You told me Hart's wife died bearing his child," Beth said, getting to her feet to face him. "She hardly did that on purpose."

"The woman was terrified of him, and the two barely spoke to each other, according to all gossip. His Grace was most relieved when she died."

"That's cruel, Inspector."

"But true. Hart needed a good wife for his political career. He didn't care if he never had a conversation with her, as long as she hosted his social events and gave him an heir. Which she proved she couldn't. She was better off dead."

"That's a monstrous thing to say."

"Spare me the 'oh, they are so misunderstood' speech. The Mackenzies are cold-blooded, heartless bastards, and the sooner you realize that, the better off you'll be."

Beth quivered with rage. "I think you are finished here. Please leave."

"I tell you this for your own good, Mrs. Ackerley."

"No, you tell me this so I will help you hurt them."

Fellows stopped. "You're right. They should be more than hurt. They should be destroyed."

Beth met his furious gaze. After verbally fencing with Hart Mackenzie, Inspector Fellows didn't frighten her anymore.

"Why?"

Fellows opened his mouth to reply, then abruptly closed it. His face was red, the mustache quivering.

"You're not a lady who frightens easily," he said. "And I can see you won't take my word for it. But they'll be the death of you. You mark my words." He gazed at her a moment longer, then turned away. "Good day, Mrs. Ackerley."

He marched to the door and yanked it open, and then Beth heard the front door bang behind him. She sank into a chair by the front windows, watching through swirling London fog as the inspector strode away. She sat numbly, letting all he'd said sink in.

"M'lady?" Katie stuck her head around the parlor door. "Is it safe to come in now?"

"He's gone, if that's what you mean." Beth rose, feeling exhausted. "Fetch our wraps, Katie. We're going out."

Katie sent a disparaging glance to the dark, foggy window. "Now? To where?"

"The East End."

Katie blinked. "What d'you want to go to that hellhole for? Old times' sake?"

"No," Beth answered. "To find some answers."

<p style="text-align:center">~~~~~</p>

"Gone?" Ian raised his dripping head and stared at Curry in disbelief. "Gone where?"

"To London, m'lord." Curry backed a step from Ian at the washbasin, knowing from experience how far to put his body from Ian's whenever he had to relate bad news.

Ian straightened up, water trickling from his wet hair down his bare chest. He'd been scrubbing off the plaster dust from Geordie's cottage and mud from the subsequent fishing expedition when he'd asked Curry where Beth was.

He'd expected Curry to tell him she was walking in the garden, exploring the house, or continuing riding lessons with Cameron. Not, *Well, here's the thing, m'lord. She's gone*.

"London?" Ian demanded. "Why?"

Curry shrugged. "Dunno. Shopping?"

"Why the devil should she go all the way to London to go shopping? Why didn't you stop her?"

"I couldn't stop her, could I? She's got a mind of 'er own, 'as 'er ladyship."

"Bloody idiot."

"What'd ye expect me to do?" Curry shrilled as he slapped a dry towel to Ian's chest. "Lock her in a dungeon?"

"Yes."

"She said she'd be back, guv—"

Ian cut him off. "She's not coming back, you fool. She's *gone*, and you let her go."

"Now, m'lord . . ."

Ian wasn't listening. Hollowness spread from his chest until it filled his body. Beth was gone, and the emptiness of that hurt like nothing else ever had.

Curry jumped away as Ian upended the entire dressing table, sending every knickknack and stupid toiletry to the floor. The pain in his chest was unbearable. It matched the pounding in his temple, the migraine that never went away. He struck the splintered table with his fists, the slivers of wood bloodying his hands. Beth had seen a glimpse of him at his worst—could he blame her for running away?

Ian looked at the scarlet droplets on his fingers, remembering Sally Tate's blood on them, remembering the horror of finding the ruin of her body. His mind swiftly inserted Beth in place of Sally, Beth's beautiful eyes sightless, a blade buried in her chest.

It could happen. Ian dragged in a chill breath as panic replaced his rage. He'd dragged Beth into his life, had exposed her to Inspector Fellows, had made her as vulnerable as Lily Martin.

He threw off Curry's well-meaning hands, stormed past Cameron, who'd come to see what was the matter, and raced out the door.

"Ian, where are you going?" Cameron demanded, catching up to him on the stairs.

"London. Don't tell Hart or try to stop me, or I'll thrash you."

Cameron fell into step beside him. "I'll come with you."

Yes. Ian knew that Cameron simply wanted to keep an eye on him, but Cameron would be handy. He knew how to fight and wasn't afraid of anything. Ian gave him a curt nod.

"Besides," Cameron went on, "Curry says Daniel went with her, and I'm certain he's making her life a misery."

Ian said nothing. He snatched the shirt Curry kept thrusting at him and banged out of the house for the stables, Cameron on his heels.

Chapter 18

Proper ladies did not go to the East End. Proper ladies pulled the curtains closed in their carriages and did not look out when their route took them through Shoreditch and Bethnal Green. Mrs. Barrington would turn in her grave, but Thomas . . . Thomas would have approved.

Beth's heart squeezed as her hired coach rolled past the little parish church that had been Thomas Ackerley's. The tiny building was squashed between dull brick edifices but managed to retain its dignity. Behind it, in the cramped churchyard, Thomas's body lay. A tiny square stone, all the parish and Beth could afford, marked the place.

Behind the church lay the vicarage where Beth had spent one hopeful year. Two doors past that was the hall Thomas had set up, where those forced to live on the streets could get a hot meal and a place out of the weather for a little while. The parish had not approved it, so Thomas had funded it out of his own pocket, and a philanthropic gentleman had taken it over on Thomas's death.

Beth entered the rickety building that smelled of old

meals and unwashed bodies, hoping to find her answers there. Daniel Mackenzie came behind her, towering over Katie and Beth, the lanky young man the most nervous of the three.

"Should you be here?" Daniel hissed. "My dad would tan my hide if he knew I let you come near a game girl, and God knows what Uncle Ian will do."

A tired-looking young woman sat on a hard chair with her legs stretched out, skirts hiked to her knees. As Beth rustled in, she looked up, blinked, and jumped to her feet. "Blimey, it's the missus."

Beth went to the young woman and took her hands. "Hello, Molly."

Molly grinned in delight. She had brown hair, a snub nose, freckles, and a warm smile. She smelled like tobacco and alcohol, as usual, and the faint odor of a man's cologne lingered in her clothes.

"What'cha doing 'ere, Mrs. A? I 'ear you married a right nob and live in a palace now."

"News travels fast."

"What d'you expect? An interesting bit of gab like that goes 'round." She winked at Daniel. "Did ye bring 'im so I could make a man of 'im?"

Daniel went beet red. "You watch your tongue."

"Ooh, ye scare me, little boy, ye truly do."

Beth stepped between them. "Daniel, hush. He's protecting me, Molly. The streets are dangerous."

"Are they now? I'm all amazed. So why'd ye come?"

"To ask you something."

Beth drew Molly a little way away from Daniel and Katie. She pressed a few coins into Molly's palm and asked her questions.

"I don't know much," Molly said. "Too la-di-da for me. But I have a pal I can ask. She married one of her flats and is rich and cushy now. She's a bit la-di-da, herself, but not a bad sort."

Beth brought out more coins and told Molly what she needed to know. Molly listened, then winked. "Right you are, missus." She tucked the money firmly into her corset. "You leave it to me."

~~~~~

The train down to London took far too long. Ian paced the length of it, unable to sit. Cameron hunkered into a corner of their train carriage, read sporting newspapers, and smoked cigars. Ian found the smoke cloying and spent considerable time on the back platform with one of the conductors. He watched the track unfold behind them, but the evenness of the ties and the smooth curve of the rail didn't soothe his mood.

When the train at last pulled into Euston Station, Ian leapt off and shouldered his way through the crowd and whistled for a hansom cab. He waited inside it for Cameron and Curry, closing the curtains against eyes that watched him.

He directed the coach to Belgrave Square, knowing Beth would have returned there. Mrs. Barrington's house had been a haven for her once, and Beth liked havens.

Fog swirled into the city as they reached the elegant square, dirty fog that brought darkness early. Ian had grown used to the light days of the Scottish summer, and the fog felt oily and heavy.

He pounded on the front door with gloved fists, not waiting for Curry to ring the bell. He pounded until an ancient specimen of a butler opened the door a crack and creakily asked his business.

Ian shoved the door open and strode inside. "Where is she?"

The butler shrank back. "Out. May I inquire who is calling?"

Cameron caught the door before the butler could shut it, and Curry followed with the bags.

"This is her husband," Cameron said. "Where is she out?"

The old man had to crank his head back to gaze up at them. "I heard her say the East End. There's thieves and murderers there, my lord, and she only took the lad with her."

"Daniel?" Cameron barked a laugh. "Poor woman. We'd best find her."

Ian had already left the house. Another hansom pulled up behind the one that had brought him, and before it stopped, Daniel's long body slid out of it. His narrow face took on a look of dismay when he saw Ian.

Ian pushed past him and reached into the cab for Beth. He heard her words, saying something about paying the fare, but Curry could do that. He lifted Beth out, not liking how the fog tried to snake its way around her.

"Ian," she began. "What will the neighbors say?"

Ian didn't give a damn what the neighbors said. He clamped one arm around her waist and took her inside.

Mrs. Barrington's house smelled old and musty and airless. The close odors tried to swallow Beth's lavenderlike scent, as though the house wanted to squeeze her back into the drudgery from which she'd come.

"If you are dragging me off to my bedroom," Beth said as they reached the top of the stairs, "perhaps you should ask me which one it is."

Ian didn't care which was hers, but he let her lead him. The bedchamber she took him to was small and papered in a hideous print of gigantic pansies. It had a large four-poster bed, a dresser near the window, and a wooden chair. The drapes hid any light the London day might produce. The hiss of gas lamps and their fusty odor completed the drab picture.

"This is a servant's room," Ian growled.

"I *was* a servant. A companion occupies a gray area, like a governess. Not quite a menial, not quite one of the family."

Ian lost the thread of her words. He turned the key beneath the porcelain doorknob and came to her. "The butler said you went to the East End."

"I did. I was making inquiries."

"About what?"

"About what do you think, my dear Ian?" Beth unwound the silk scarf she'd worn against the fog and stripped off her gloves.

"You sent a telegram to Fellows."

Her color rose. "Yes, I—"

"I told you to leave it. He can't be trusted."

"I wanted to know everything he knew. Perhaps he'd found something out you hadn't."

Ian's rage tasted like dust. "So you saw him. You met him."

"Yes, he came here."

"He came *here*."

"You refused to tell me anything. What could I do?"

"Don't you understand? If you find out too much, I can't protect you. You could be transported, or hanged, if you know too much."

"Why on earth would I be transported because your brother's friend Stephenson or his mistress Mrs. Palmer murdered a . . ." She trailed off, her face going still.

Ian never knew what went on behind people's expressions. Everyone else instinctively knew the signs of rage and fear, happiness or sadness in others. Ian had no idea why people burst into laughter or into tears. He had to watch, to learn to do as they did.

He seized Beth by the shoulders and shook her. "What are you thinking? Tell me. I don't know."

She looked up at him with wide blue eyes. "Oh, Ian." Instead of fearing his strength, she rested her hands gently on his arms. "You think Hart did this, don't you?"

Ian shook his head. He closed his eyes and kept shaking his head, but he held on to Beth as though he'd be torn away if he didn't. "No." The word echoed through the room, and he said it again. And again. And again.

"*Ian.*"

With effort, Ian stopped, but he kept his eyes shut tight.

"Why do you think so?" Beth's voice wrapped around him like eiderdown. "Tell me."

Ian opened his eyes, the anguish of five years trying to drown him. Sally had boasted that she knew secrets that would ruin Hart, cut him out of politics altogether. Hart loved politics, God knew why. In the middle of coitus with

Sally, she'd enraged Ian so much, going on and on how she'd blackmail Hart, that Ian had withdrawn, snatched up his clothes, and left the room. He'd felt the rage coming on, knew he had to go.

He'd walked the house, searching for whiskey, searching for Hart and not finding him, trying to calm down. Once he could think coherently again, he'd returned to Sally's room. "I opened the door and saw Hart in the bedroom. I saw him with Sally on the sofa at the end of the bed."

The images rose before Ian could stop them, every single one as coldly clear as it had been that day. Hart with Sally, her naked limbs wrapped around him. Her soft cry of joy turning to fear.

"Hart took a knife away from her—I don't know why she had it. She swore at him. He tossed the knife away. Then he pressed her throat until she quieted, and she laughed. I don't want you to know these things."

"But . . ." Beth frowned. "Sally wasn't strangled, too, was she? No one has mentioned bruises on her throat."

Ian shook his head. "Hart, he used to be . . . You wouldn't understand the terms. He owned the house. Mrs. Palmer and her women belonged to him."

"He can't own women. This is England."

For some reason, Ian wanted to laugh. "They obeyed him. They wanted to. He was everything to them, their lord and master."

Beth frowned a little longer, and then her brow cleared. "Oh." The syllable was short, pregnant with meaning.

"He did it before he married, then stopped. After his wife died he started again. He was very discreet, but we knew. He was grieving. He needed them."

"Goodness, most people make do with crepe and mourning brooches," Beth said. "But why would he try to strangle Sally Tate?"

Ian placed his hand at the base of Beth's windpipe. "When you cut off the air, the climax is deeper, more intense. That is why he had his hands on her throat."

Beth's eyes widened. "How very . . . interesting."

"And dangerous." Ian removed his hand from her neck. "Hart knows how to do it, exactly when to stop."

"You saw that," Beth said slowly. "But you didn't actually see him kill her?"

"When I saw them together, I left them to it. I knew if anyone could talk Sally out of blackmail it would be Hart. I thought to go home, but I'd left my watch on her bedside table, and I wanted it. I found a decanter of whiskey in the parlor downstairs and helped myself while I waited. Later I heard Hart rush out the front door and saw him leap into his coach. I went back upstairs for the watch and found Sally. Dead."

"Oh—" Beth broke off and bit her lip. "What does Hart say happened?"

The fact that she was still standing in front of him, talking in her cool and puzzling way, was a miracle to Ian. Beth hadn't left him in disgust, hadn't fainted in shock at all he'd revealed. She remained, still the anchor in the vast, bewildering river that was his life.

"He told me that he'd left the room once he'd got Sally bent to his will again and had his valet help him clean up and dress in another room. When he returned, he found Sally dead and ran downstairs and out of the house. He didn't see me in the parlor, he said, or he'd have insisted I come with him. He said he couldn't risk being there when the police came, because of his career." Ian shook his head. "I don't believe him. Hart wouldn't run away if he hadn't killed her. He'd have taken the house apart until he found the culprit."

"Possibly," Beth said in her slow, sure voice. "If I hadn't met Hart, I might believe he killed her and bolted. But I did meet him, and I'm confident that, if he *had* decided to kill her, he'd have made certain you were far away before he did the dreadful deed. He'd have avoided involving you, no matter what. Therefore, it couldn't have been Hart who did it."

"I know what I saw."

"Yes." Beth turned and walked away from him, but

thinking, not hysterical. "And the police would believe as you did, and a jury, and a judge. But they don't know Hart. He'd never put you in jeopardy of arrest or returning to the asylum. He never wants you locked away again."

"Because he needs me and my bloody inconvenient memory."

"No. Because he loves you."

The woman was incredibly innocent. She'd seen what she'd seen in London's slums, she'd been destitute and desperate, and yet she still looked for good in the Mackenzies. Unbelievable.

"Hart is ruthless," Ian said. "I told you I don't have the capacity for love. Neither does he, but he doesn't wonder about it as I do. He will do what he needs to, even if it's deadly, even if one of his brothers has to pay the price."

Beth shook her head, her dark hair glistening under the light. "You have to be wrong."

Ian laughed sharply. "We're all very bad at love, Beth. I told you we break whatever we touch."

"Ian, in five years, have you never put aside what you saw, thought of the thing clearly, without Hart in it? Can you pretend Hart wasn't there and decide who else might have done it?"

"Of course I have," Ian said irritably. He ran a hand through his hair. "I have run through every scenario, every possibility from beginning to end. I thought of the other men there, of Mrs. Palmer, of the other ladies in the house, an intruder breaking in. I've even worried that it was me, and I simply can't remember doing it."

"What about Lily Martin? Why did you hide her at Covent Garden?"

"She was looking into the room, watching Hart with Sally. She swore to me she never saw Hart stab her, but I couldn't tell whether she lied. I couldn't risk what she'd tell the police, so I sent Curry back to get her out of the way before the constable came. But I didn't hide her well enough."

"You think Hart found her a few weeks ago and killed her?"

"Yes."

Beth paced away from him again. "Goodness, what a mess."

"It doesn't have to be. If Fellows keeps his nose out of it, we could go on."

"No, you can't." Beth came back to him. "It's tearing you apart. It's tearing Hart apart, too, and the rest of the family. Everything you say makes perfect sense, but there's another explanation. Hart thinks *you* did it. That's why he ran out of the house, looking for you, to make sure you were gone and hadn't done it. It must have been a dreadful shock for him when he realized you were still in the house when Sally died."

Ian blinked, and for a second he met her gaze. He loved her eyes, so blue. He could drown in her.

He looked away. "Because he believes I'm mad? He does believe I'm mad, but you're wrong."

"Why are the Mackenzies so bloody stubborn? The killer must have come in and stabbed Sally while Hart was with his valet. No matter how ruthless Hart is, someone else was even more ruthless."

Memories flooded him thick and fast, memories Ian had tried to push away for two decades. The image of Hart with his hands around Sally's neck became superimposed on another man and woman. "I think it was Hart, because, Beth, he looked so much like my father."

"Your very hairy father? Hart resembles him a bit, but . . ."

He didn't hear her. The terror of the nine-year-old Ian rose up in him, memories of crouching behind the desk in his father's study when he heard his parents come in. They'd been shouting at each other, as they always did, and Ian would have been punished.

He'd watched his mother rush at his father, claws ready, and his father catch her around the neck. The duke had squeezed, then *shake*, *shake*, and she'd gone limp.

Ian's beautiful mother had crumpled to the floor in an unmoving heap, while his father stood over her, hands open, his face gray with shock.

Then had come the terrible moment when his father had looked around the desk and seen Ian. Ian had felt the watery terror in his limbs when his father had rushed at Ian and picked him up, shaking him as he'd shaken Ian's mother.

You tell no one. Do you understand me? She slipped and fell; that is what happened. You have to lie. Do you understand?

More shaking, harder, harder. *Damn you, why won't you look at me when I'm talking to you?*

Ian had been locked away in his room, and the next morning hustled into a carriage that had taken him to London and the courtroom that had condemned him as a lunatic. He'd been in the private asylum two weeks before he finally understood he'd not be allowed to go home. Ever.

Beth's palms touched his face. "Ian?"

"He killed her," Ian said. "He didn't mean to. But he had the rages, like I do."

"You mean Hart?"

Ian shook his head. "My father. He killed my mother, broke her neck with his own two hands. He told everyone she'd slipped on the rug, fell, died. My brothers didn't believe it, but they couldn't ask me, could they? I was declared mad, shut away, so no one would believe me if I told what I saw my father do."

Beth laced her arms around his waist and rested her head against his chest. "Oh, Ian, I'm so sorry."

Ian held her there a moment, taking comfort from her warmth. He had a fear inside him that one day he'd lose his mind like his father had, put his hands around the neck of the woman he loved, and kill her before he could stop himself. Beth trusted him, and Ian would die if he hurt her.

Beth lifted her head, tears wetting her lashes, and he kissed her forehead. "Hart is as ruthless as my father ever was. He doesn't rage, but he is so cold."

"I still think you're wrong. Hart sent you to Scotland after Sally's death to protect you, not keep you quiet."

Ian gave the ceiling a brief exasperated glance before he

took Beth by the shoulders and pushed her against the high bed. "I can protect you from Hart, but only if you *stop*. Forget about High Holborn, and never speak to Inspector Fellows again. He'll crush you to get what he wants, and so will Hart."

She looked at him in anguish. "You want me to go the rest of my life watching you in so much pain? Believing your brother murdered a woman? Isn't it better to find out what really happened?"

"No."

Tears swam in her eyes, and she turned her head to avoid his gaze. "I want to help you."

"You can help best by never speaking to Fellows again. And stop trying to find out what happened. Promise me."

She went silent a moment, then sighed. "Mrs. Barrington always told me curiosity was my besetting sin."

"I'll keep you safe, I promise you, my Beth."

"Very well," she whispered. "I'll stop."

Relief relaxed his body. He pulled Beth into his arms, held her tight against him. "Thank you." He kissed her hair. "Thank you."

She reached up to kiss him. As he slid his lips over hers it didn't occur to him that she'd given up a shade too easily.

Chapter 19

When Beth woke much later, Ian slept next to her, his naked body touched by lamplight, his muscles gleaming with sweat from their passion. When he'd climaxed inside her, he'd almost, almost looked at her fully again, but he'd closed his eyes at the last minute. Now he slept, and Beth lay against his warmth, her thoughts troubled.

Ian might not want to know the truth, but the truth was that Sally Tate and Lily Martin had died, lost their lives. Beth knew enough of game girls to know that unless they found a long-term relationship with a wealthy protector, their lives could be short and brutal. The wrong client could beat them senseless, even kill them, and no one would care. They were just whores.

Even if the girls managed to find a place in an elegant brothel, when they grew older and lost their looks they could be turned out, sent to live on the streets again. Those with protectors fared better, but only if the protector was kind to them.

Beth knew full well that but for the grace of God and the kindness of Thomas Ackerley and Mrs. Barrington, she could have become one of them.

Fellows didn't care that the women had died; he wanted only to destroy the Mackenzies. Ian cared—she could see his sorrow for Sally and Lily and his own mother—but what he cared most about was sparing his brother. The brother who had delivered Ian from hell.

Beth ground her teeth. Damn the dead duke for locking Ian away because Ian had seen what he wasn't supposed to see. Damn Hart Mackenzie for enmeshing Ian in his games of power. And damn Ian for his undying gratitude to Hart.

Beth hadn't understood at first why Isabella had walked away from Mac when she obviously still loved him. She understood better now. Beth wasn't certain what Mac had done to upset Isabella so much, but then he was a thick-skulled, stubborn Mackenzie. Wasn't that enough? A sweet debutante like Isabella hadn't stood a chance.

Beth rose and dressed herself. She'd learned to dress simply and hastily when she'd worked for Mrs. Barrington, having to tend the old lady any time of the day or night.

Ian didn't wake. He lay facedown, his body relaxed, eyes closed. Lamplight brushed the firm mound of his backside, the small of his back, the tight muscles of his shoulders. He was a large and beautiful man, so strong, and so very vulnerable. Hart had called him that. And yet, Hart had backed down from him.

I love you, Ian Mackenzie. Beth's heart ached.

She silently left the room and went downstairs. Glancing about to make sure she was not seen, she made for the door in the back of the main hall that led to the servants' staircase.

The cook worked busily in the kitchen, cleaning up the supper she'd just cooked for Cameron and Daniel. She beamed at Beth as Beth entered the warm kitchen, just like old times.

"It's good to see ones eat so heartily," the cook said. "They et it all straightaway and asked for more. A cook can't ask for better. Not like yourself, who didn't even come down. Can I warm something on a plate for you?"

"No, thank you, Mrs. Donnelly. I'm looking for Katie."

"You're the lady of the house now. You should 'ave rung."

"Have you seen her?" Beth asked impatiently.

"She's on the scullery stairs." The cook looked disapproving. "With one who's no better than she ought to be. I wouldn't let the likes of her in."

Beth's heart leapt. "It's all right. She's one of my charity cases."

"You're too softhearted, you are. Katie's all right, but that one she's brought is hard as nails, *and* her nose is stuck in the air. She don't need your charity."

Beth ignored Mrs. Donnelly and left through the scullery and to the stairs that ran to the street above. Katie waited on the steps, her face clouded in Irish fury. "Well, she's here, as you can see."

"Thank you, Katie. You may go in now."

"Not bloody likely. I don't trust her an inch, and I ain't leaving her alone with you."

The lady in question really did have her nose in the air, a slim, well-powdered nose. The rest of her face was well powdered, too, and rouged. Diamonds glittered on her neck and in her ears. The young woman wasn't beautiful, but she was attractive in a sensual way, and she knew it. Her red lips curved into a superior smile as she gave Beth's simple gown a once-over.

"Molly said you was a duchess," she said. "But I didn't believe it."

"You mind your manners," Katie snapped. "She's a lady."

"Hush, Katie. Your name is?"

"Sylvia. That's all you need to know."

"I am pleased to meet you, Sylvia. I'm sorry to bother you, but I want to ask you a few questions."

"Out here on the back stairs? That bitch of a cook wouldn't let me in the kitchen. I want to be sat in the parlor, and your slaveys waiting on me, or I won't talk."

"Mind your tongue," Katie snapped. "You're not fit to sit in m'lady's parlor. We stay in the shadows so no one knows she's talking to you."

Beth raised her hands. "Peace, both of you. It will only take a few minutes, Sylvia, and I know you are the right one to speak to. I imagine you know so much."

Sylvia preened under the base flattery. "You was asking about the house in High Holborn. I know all about it, and about the right old bitch who runs the place. What do you need to know?"

"Everything."

In answer to her questions, Sylvia confirmed what Fellows had said: that Mrs. Palmer had been Hart's mistress and he'd bought her the house in High Holborn.

"She met him when he was still at university, and her already long in the tooth," Sylvia said. "Didn't no one love a young man like Angelina Palmer loved *him*. She'd do anything for him, piss in her own shoes if he asked her to."

"But he sold her the house later," Beth said. "I had the idea she was no longer his mistress after that."

"Oh, he gave her the push, all right, and she turned her hand to being a businesswoman, if you take my meaning. It weren't a bad place when I was there, but me and Mrs. Palmer never rubbed on well. I left as soon as I found better prospects." She glanced fondly at her diamond rings.

"Then it truly is over between them," Beth said.

"It might have been for his part, but never hers. The duke started being high-and-mighty, hobnobbing with the queen. He'd need a young and beautiful lady, not some old biddy he had since he were twenty. I'd have been angry as anything, but Ma Palmer was most understanding. Went on loving him to pieces, though her heart was broke. If we ever said a word against the duke, we got our ears boxed."

Beth stared thoughtfully at the iron railings of the staircase. "You say she'd do anything for the duke?"

"Course she would. She's like a dewy-eyed schoolgirl with him, for all she's fifty if she's a day."

Beth's thoughts whirled. Could Mrs. Palmer have discovered that Sally wanted to blackmail Hart? Had the madam decided to shut Sally's mouth permanently? But in that case, why not wait until Ian had gone home and no Mackenzie could be implicated? Or did she not care who swung for the crime, as long as it wasn't Hart? She itched to find the woman and question her.

"When did you work in the house, Sylvia?"

"Oh, 'bout six, maybe seven years ago."

"Did you know Sally Tate?"

"That bitch? Not surprised she got herself murdered."

"You were there at the time of the murder?"

"No, I'd moved on by then. But I heard all about it. Sally had it coming, missus. She strung men along right enough, but she hated 'em. She could charm all kinds of money out of 'em. She and Ma Palmer had dustups all the time because Sally didn't want to share the takings. She had her own lady love, kept talking about the two of 'em taking a castle in the sky together and living happily ever after."

Katie glared in outrage. "That's disgusting. M'lady, you shouldn't be out here listening to such talk."

Sylvia shrugged. "Well, they get tired of men pawing at 'em, don't they? Some do, anyway. Not me, I like a handsome gentleman."

"Never mind that," Beth said impatiently. "Who was Sally Tate's lady love? Did you know her?"

"It was one of the other girls what lived there. They used to lock themselves in an upstairs bedroom and bill and coo. Sally always vowed she'd take the girl to a cottage somewhere and they'd raise roses and some nonsense. Not bloody likely, was it? Catch any respectable folk in a village letting a house to a couple of hermaphrodites what used to be whores." Sylvia tapped her lip. "Now, what was her name? Oh, I've got it. Lily. 'Cause Sally was always saying they'd have lilies in the pond on account of her. They were both daft."

"Lily Martin?" Beth asked, her voice sharp.

"That were it. Lily Martin. Now, what about me money, m'lady? I come a long way, it's damp out here, and this silk will be all ruined."

———

Ian woke when the little clock on the dresser struck ten. He stretched, his body warm and pliant, and he rolled over to wrap his arms around Beth.

He found an empty bed.

He opened his eyes in disappointment. But perhaps she'd gone down for something to eat. She'd be hungry.

Ian rubbed his hand over his face, trying to stave off the memories of their argument. He'd told her things he'd never meant to tell her, things he hadn't wanted her to know about himself and his monstrous family. But he'd at least made her understand.

Ian swung his legs out of the bed and stood up. He didn't want to wait for her to return; he needed her now. He'd find her and get Curry to bring some supper to them. He wouldn't mind seating Beth on his lap and feeding her from her plate. They'd enjoyed that at Kilmorgan, and he saw no reason not to enjoy it now.

He pulled on his trousers and shirt, remembering how Beth had helped undress him a few hours ago. Her touch had been gentle and his had been impatient; he wanted her with fierce intensity.

Ian pulled on his ankle boots and ran fingers through his mussed hair before turning to the door. He caught the china doorknob and turned it.

The door didn't budge.

He rattled the knob and pushed at the door, but nothing happened. Heart thumping, Ian crouched and put his eye to the keyhole.

No key on the other side. Someone had locked the door and taken the key away with them.

Blind panic flooded him. *Locked in, no escape, trapped, open it, please, please, please, I'll be good. . . .*

He took deep breaths, trying to banish the freezing terror.

He thought of warmth, of Beth, of the taste of her mouth, of sliding into her depths, feeling her squeeze. . . .

Beth.

He crouched down and put his mouth to the keyhole. "Beth?"

Silence. He heard noises from the street but none from the house. He yanked the bellpull beside the bed, then went back to the door.

"Curry," he shouted. He pounded on the heavy wood. "Curry, damn you."

No answer.

Ian went to the window and flung back the drapes. Mist swirled around the street lamps below. Carriages went back and forth in the square, fog enhancing the sound of hooves and rumbling wheels.

He heard footsteps in the hall and then Curry's voice at the keyhole. "M'lord? Are you in there?"

"Of course I'm in here. She's locked the door. Find a key."

Curry's voice took on a note of alarm. "Are you all right?"

"Find the blasted key."

"You're all right then." Footsteps moved away.

New fears rushed at Ian, none that had to do with being confined in a small room. Beth had gone somewhere, and she hadn't wanted him to stop her. Damn her, why couldn't she *listen*?

She'd have gone to Fellows, or to interview the men who'd been at the house five years ago, or worse, to the High Holborn house itself to talk to Mrs. Palmer. *Son of a bitch.*

"Curry!" He pounded on the door.

"Keep your shirt on. We're hunting for a key."

It took too long. Ian chafed, his temper rising. On the other side of the door, Curry swore and growled.

At last Ian heard a key in the lock, heard it turn. He yanked open the door.

Curry, Cameron, and Daniel were grouped outside with the shaky butler, the plump cook, and two wide-eyed maids.

"Where is Beth?" he demanded, striding past them.

"I don't like it, my lord." The cook folded her arms over

her ample bosom. "She will meet with the most unsavory people, always has felt too sorry for them. Why can't they get a proper job? That's what I want to know."

Her words made no sense, but Ian had the feeling they were important. "What are you saying? What people?"

"Mrs. Ackerley's charity projects. Painted tarts and whores of Babylon. One came to the kitchen door, if you can imagine, and off goes her ladyship and Miss Katie with her. In a hansom cab."

"Where?"

"I don't know, I'm sure."

Ian swung a glare on her, and the woman deflated. "I'm sorry, your lordship. I truly don't know."

"Someone must have seen," Cameron rumbled. "We'll ask on the street if someone heard what direction she gave."

"I know where she went," Ian said grimly. *Damnation. Damnation.* "Curry, fetch me a coach. *Now.*"

He pushed past the crowd and started down the stairs. Curry scrambled behind him, bleating orders in his broad Cockney.

"I'm coming with you," Cameron said.

"Me, too," Daniel said, keeping up with them.

"Like hell you are," Cameron told his son. "You're staying here, and you'll keep her here if she comes back."

"But Dad—"

"Do what I say for once, you little hellion."

Cameron snatched hat and gloves before the doddering butler could get to them. Ian didn't even bother. Daniel followed them to the door, scowling, but he stayed inside.

"How do you know where she is?" Cameron clapped on his hat and strode for the hansom rolling toward them at Curry's whistle.

Ian climbed inside, Cameron following. "High Holborn," he said to the cabbie before the vehicle careened off into traffic.

"High Holborn?" Cameron asked in alarm.

"She's gone to play detective." *Bloody little fool.* If anything happened to her . . .

Ian couldn't finish the thought, couldn't imagine how he'd feel if he found her dead, a knife in her chest, like Sally and Lily.

Cameron pressed a hand to Ian's shoulder. "We'll find her."

"Why is she so stubborn? And disobedient?"

Cameron barked a laugh. "Because Mackenzies always choose headstrong women. You didn't really expect her to *obey* you, did you? No matter what the marriage vows say?"

"I expected to keep her safe."

"She stood up to Hart. It's a rare woman who can do that."

Which showed just how foolish Beth was. Ian fell silent, willing the coach to go faster.

They rolled through thick traffic, the residents of London for some reason out in droves tonight. The cab inched up Park Lane past the house of the blasted Lyndon Mather. Ian hoped briefly that the twelve hundred pounds he'd given him for the bowl would keep the man subdued. Beth didn't need any more trouble from him.

The coach finally turned east on Oxford Street to traverse its length to High Holborn. Ian hadn't seen the house that sat innocently on High Holborn near Chancery Lane for five years. But stark memories stabbed at him as he and Cameron entered without knocking. Nothing inside had changed. Ian walked through the same vestibule with dark wood wainscoting, opened the same stained-glass door that led to the inner hall and polished walnut staircase.

The maid who admitted them was new and obviously thought Ian and Cameron were expected clients. Ian wanted to push past her and run up the stairs, but Cameron put his hand on Ian's shoulder and shook his head.

"We'll go carefully," he said into Ian's ear. "Then if they don't help us, we'll take the place apart."

Ian nodded, sweat trickling down his spine. He'd had a strange feeling of being watched as soon as he entered the house, which only grew as the maid led them up the stairs.

The maid swung the parlor door inward, and Ian walked in. He stopped so abruptly that Cameron ran into the back of him.

Hart Mackenzie sat in a plush armchair with a cheroot in one hand and a cut-crystal glass of whiskey in the other. Angelina Palmer, Hart's mistress, a dark-haired woman still beautiful in her late forties, perched on the arm of Hart's chair, one hand resting fondly on his shoulder.

"Ian," Hart said calmly. "I thought you'd arrive soon. Sit down. I want to talk to you."

~~~

Beth balled her gloved hands in her lap as the carriage wound slowly from Whitehall up to High Holborn. Lloyd Fellows glared at Beth across the cramped interior, and Katie huddled on the seat next to Beth, highly uncomfortable.

"What makes you think I didn't go through that house with a fine-toothed comb five years ago?" Fellows asked.

"You might have missed something. It's reasonable. You were in a flutter because the Mackenzies were involved."

He scowled. "I never get into a flutter. And I didn't know the Mackenzies were involved until well after I got there, did I? I wouldn't have known at all if the nervous maid hadn't let it slip."

"It seems convenient to me that she let it slip and made you focus all your efforts on Hart and Ian. I think it blurred your judgment."

Fellows's hazel eyes narrowed. "It was much more complicated than that."

"Not really. You were so pleased to have the chance to wreck the life of Hart Mackenzie that you didn't feel the need to look beyond him and Ian. I had started to feel sympathy for you, Mr. Fellows, but I've changed my mind."

Fellows spoke to the ceiling. "Dear God, where does that family find such women? Termagants, the lot of you."

"I'm not certain Lady Isabella would be flattered by that remark," Beth said. "Besides, I've heard that Hart's wife was soft-spoken and meek."

"And you see where it got her?"

"Exactly, Inspector. Therefore Isabella and I will remain outspoken."

Fellows looked out the window. "You can't save them, you know. They're beyond redemption. If they're not guilty of this murder, they're guilty of so many other things. The Mackenzies move through the world leaving wreckage behind them."

We break everything we touch.

"Perhaps I can't save them from themselves," Beth answered. "But I will try to save them from you."

Fellows pressed his lips together and looked out the window again. "Bloody women," he muttered.

~

Ian stared at Hart and Mrs. Palmer for a few seconds. "Where is Beth?" he demanded.

Hart raised his brows. "Not here."

Ian headed for the door. "Then I'm too busy to talk to you."

"It's Beth I want to talk to you about."

Ian stopped abruptly and turned back. Mrs. Palmer had risen and moved behind the sofa to pour a measure of whiskey into a clean glass, the sound like rain trickling through a gutter. Hart watched her a moment, a man comfortably studying a woman he'd bedded many times.

"Beth doesn't understand," Ian said.

"I wonder about that," Hart said. "You married a very perceptive and, if I may say it, tenacious woman. I don't know if that's good for this family or bad for it."

"Damn good, I'd say," Cameron said behind Ian. "I'll look for her," he added, then faded out the door.

Ian itched to go with him, but he knew Cameron would be thorough. Cameron could be even more terrifying than Hart when he wanted to be.

Ian gave Hart a fleeting glance and fixed his gaze on Mrs. Palmer pouring whiskey. "Whatever you think of her, Beth is my wife. That means I protect her from you."

"But who protects her from you, Ian?"

Ian's jaw hardened. Mrs. Palmer brought the glass of

whiskey to Ian, the facets of crystal catching the light. The heart of the glass held a glint of blue, like Beth's eyes, a color never seen in the crystal unless the light was right.

Ian followed the changing colors of the whiskey's amber and gold down to the blue facets. The best crystal caught light and refracted it into every color of the rainbow, but the blue always seemed to be trapped deep inside.

"Ian."

Ian jerked his gaze from the glass. Mrs. Palmer had moved back to Hart. She leaned over the back of the chair and ran her hands down the lapels of Hart's black evening coat.

"What?" Ian asked.

"I said I want to talk." Hart stretched out his long legs. His hair was the darkest red of all the brothers', and it rolled back from his forehead in a thick wave.

People called Hart Mackenzie handsome, but Ian had never thought so. He'd known that his brother's eyes could turn ice-cold, his face harden like granite. Their father had been much the same.

Hart had been the only person in the world who could calm the boy Ian's panicked reactions. When Ian had been confused, or in a thick crowd, or couldn't understand a word being babbled around him, his first instinct had been to bolt. He'd run from the family dining room table, from the schoolrooms his father tried to send him to, from the family pew in a crowded church. Hart had always found him, had always sat with him, either talking around his panic, or just sitting in silence until Ian calmed.

Ian now wanted to run through the house shouting Beth's name, but Hart's gaze told him it would be useless.

Ian sat down. He glanced uncomfortably at Mrs. Palmer.

"Leave us, love," Hart said to her. Angelina Palmer nodded, her smile practiced. She kissed Hart on his upturned lips.

"Of course," she said. "You know you only have to call if you need me."

Hart caught her hand briefly as she stood, then let his fingers drift from hers. They'd been a couple a long time, through the ups and downs of Hart's life—his brief but un-happy marriage, his inheritance of the dukedom, his rise to political power. When Hart had decided to distance himself from her, Mrs. Palmer had seemed to accept his decision without fuss.

Mrs. Palmer glanced at Ian before she left the room. Ian kept his eyes averted, but he sensed the ice-coldness of her stare and felt her . . . fear?

She turned away and was gone.

"We've never talked about this, have we?" Hart asked once the door closed softly.

Here, five years ago, four men had laughed and talked around a card table near the fireplace, while Ian had lounged in an armchair by the door, reading a newspaper. The men at the table had ignored him, which had been fine with him. And then Sally had pulled a chair next to his, leaned over the arm, and begun whispering to him.

Hart cut through Ian's thoughts. "Best to keep quiet about it, I always said."

Ian nodded. "I agreed."

"But you told Beth all about it."

Ian wondered how Hart knew that. Did he find Beth and make her tell him? Or did he have spies in Beth's house?

"If you hurt her, I'll kill you."

"I'd never hurt her, Ian. I promise you that."

"You like to hurt. To control. You like to see people at your feet, fighting for a chance to lick your boots."

Hart's gaze flickered. "You're not pulling your punches tonight, are you?"

"I always did what you told me because you took care of me."

"And I always will take care of you, Ian."

"Because it suits you to. You always do what suits you, like Father did."

Hart's brow clouded. "I don't mind you jabbing at me, but don't compare me to Father. He was a cruel son of a bitch, and I hope he's rotting in hell."

"He had rages, like the ones I get. He never learned to control them."

"And you have?" Hart asked, his voice quiet.

Ian lightly rubbed his temple. "I don't know. I don't know if I can ever control them. But I have Curry and Beth and my brothers to help me. Father had no one."

"You aren't defending him, are you?"

Even Ian heard the incredulous tone. "Hell, no. But we're his sons; it stands to reason we're all somewhat like him. Ruthless, driven. Heartless."

"I'm supposed to be having a talk with you, not you lecturing me."

"Beth is perceptive." Ian lowered his hand. "Where the devil is she?"

"Not here, as I said."

"What have you done with her?"

"Nothing." Hart dropped his cheroot into a bowl, and a thin spiral of smoke drifted upward. "I honestly don't know where she is. Why did you think she'd come here?"

"To play detective."

"Ah, of course." Hart drank his whiskey in one swift draft and clicked the glass to the table. "She wants you to be innocent. She loves you."

"No, she loves her husband."

"Which is you."

"I meant her first husband. Thomas Ackerley. She loves him, and she always will."

"I imagine so," Hart conceded. "But I've seen the way she looks at you. She loves you, and she wants to save you. You told her not to try, but am I right in thinking she didn't listen?"

Ian nodded. "Tenacious."

Hart actually smiled. "Like a terrier on the scent. If she uncovers proof of the truth, what will you do?"

"Take her away. We can live in Paris or Rome, never return to England or Scotland."

"Do you think you will be safe in Paris or Rome?"

Ian gave him a narrow look. "If you leave us be, I think so."

Hart rose again, his well-tailored coat like a second skin on his wide shoulders. "I don't want to see you hurt, Ian. I never wanted that. I'm so sorry."

Ian clenched the arms of the chair until he feared his fingers would dent the wood. "I'll not go back to the asylum. Not even for you."

"And I don't want you back there. What they did to you—" Hart broke off. "You take Beth and go far away. To New York, maybe, as far as you want. I want you safe, away from me."

"Why did you come here tonight?" Ian asked. He couldn't believe Hart had traveled all the way down from Scotland simply to drink and smoke in a house he used to own. He must have taken the train immediately after Ian's, the only one that could have gotten him here this quickly.

"Loose ends," Hart said. "I'm putting everything in order, and then all will be forgotten."

"Sally shouldn't be forgotten, or Lily. Beth is right: They died, and we should care."

Hart's voice took on an edge. "They were whores."

Ian got to his feet. "You brought me here that night so I could find out what Sally knew that might hurt your political standing. So I could tell you what she whispered to me in bed. To be your spy."

"And you found out."

"She was gleeful with it. She wanted to ruin you."

"I know," Hart said dryly. "I wouldn't let her, which made her very, very angry."

"So you did what? Made sure the dirty secrets she knew about you stayed secret?"

Hart shook his head. "If Sally wanted to prattle about me owning the house and what I did in it years before, she was welcome. Everyone knew. It even gained me a certain respect among the more stolid members of the Cabinet, if you can credit it. I did what they always dreamed of doing and didn't have the courage to do."

"Sally told me she could ruin you."

"She was dreaming."

"And then she was dead."

Hart stilled. Ian heard Cameron tramping in the rooms overhead. His gravelly baritone boomed out, then the light answers of the maid, another woman giggling.

"Oh, God, Ian," Hart said in a near whisper. "Is that why you did it?"

Chapter 20

The hansom Beth rode in drew to a halt before an incongruous house in High Holborn near Chancery Lane. The neighborhood looked respectable enough, the house in question neat and subdued.

Fellows unlatched the door of the carriage, but before he could open it, the door was ripped from his grasp and a pair of strong hands captured Beth. Beth found herself on the pavement, face-to-face with her husband. Ian's eyes were dark with rage, and without a word, he began to drag her away.

Beth resisted. "Wait. We must go in."

"No, you must go home."

Another carriage waited in the lane, this one lavish. Its curtains were drawn, the coat of arms on the door muffled.

"Whose coach is that?"

"Hart's." Ian pulled her along with him as he strode toward it. "His coachman will take you back to Belgrave Square, and you'll stay there."

"Like a good wife? Ian, listen."

Ian yanked open the door to reveal a gold interior, as opulent as any prince's sitting room. Beth put her hands on the side of the carriage. "If I go home, you must come with me."

Ian picked Beth up bodily and deposited her onto a soft seat. "Not with Inspector Fellows here."

"He's not here to arrest Hart."

Ian slammed the carriage door, and Beth lunged for it. "He's not here to arrest you, either. He's here to investigate the scene of the crime again and to question Mrs. Palmer. I asked him to."

Ian swung around. His tall bulk filled the carriage doorway, one huge hand resting on the door frame. The light was behind him, so she couldn't see his face or the glint of his eyes.

"You asked him to?"

"Yes, there are plenty of other suspects, you know. Mrs. Palmer, especially. It's her house; she'd have had the most opportunity."

"Mrs. Palmer," Ian repeated. His voice was flat, and she couldn't say what he thought.

Beth opened the door and started to climb down. "We must go inside."

She found herself against Ian's chest and his big hands holding her arms. "I'm not taking you into a bawdy house."

"My dear Ian, I grew up surrounded by game girls and courtesans. I'm not afraid of them."

"I don't care."

"Ian." Beth tried to push him away, but she had more chance of moving a brick wall.

"Go home, Beth. You've done enough." He shoved her back inside the carriage. "And stay there, for God's sake."

A scream rang out, startling and shrill.

"That's Katie." Beth gasped.

Ian melted into the darkness. Cursing, Beth clambered down and ran after him. She heard the coachman shout, but he was busy steadying the horses and couldn't run after her.

There was no lamp close to the house, and Beth hurried

through the gloom toward the door Ian had left wide open. Beth rushed inside, trying to hear where the others had gone.

The vestibule was brightly lit, but empty. She ran through to the elegant paneled hall, in which a staircase rose to the upper floors of the house. Beth heard screams and shouting beyond the first landing and farther up the stairs—Katie, Ian, Inspector Fellows. She started up toward the noise.

Someone rushed through the hall above, footsteps muffled on carpet, and then came a quiet thump of a door. Someone trying to get away, fleeing the inspector?

Beth raced up the stairs and along the passage, finding a closed door at the end of it. She opened it to a staircase leading down, the servants' stairs. Hurried footsteps sounded on it, the quarry getting away.

"Ian!" she shouted. "Inspector! Help me."

Her cries were drowned by renewed screams, male shouts, and female sobbing from above. Damn.

She gathered her skirts and plunged down the stairs. The flight took her down past the main floor, past the kitchens. Beth felt a flood of night air as an outer door was flung open. She reached the foot of the stairs in time to see a dark-haired woman dash into the squalid yard beyond.

Beth was hard on her heels. A gate led to the space between houses where the night soil men would come to collect the noisome slops. The woman fumbled at the latch, and Beth caught her.

Beth seized the woman's wrists. Her strong hands were covered with rings. Beth stared up into the face of the woman who must be Mrs. Palmer, Hart's former mistress and owner of the house. Sylvia had said Mrs. Palmer was near fifty, but she was still a beautiful woman, with dark hair and a slim body. Her brown eyes were lovely but hard as agates.

"You little fool," Mrs. Palmer hissed. "Why did you bring the inspector here? You've ruined everything."

"I'll not let him pay for a murder he didn't do," Beth cried.

"Do you think *I* will?"

"Who are you talking about?" Beth began, and then a

knife flashed in the light from the house. Before Beth could twist away, it came down.

∽

Ian, irritated, learned that Katie had screamed because she'd seen Cameron charge out of a room upstairs. It was dark, Cameron was a giant of a man with a gashed face, and Katie was easily alarmed. There was lot of shouting from the girls upstairs, more screaming from Katie, and bellowing from Cameron, until the din echoed through the house. Hart and Cameron finally helped him silence them all, and by then, Ian's head was throbbing.

"We're all here now," Inspector Fellows said testily to the three Mackenzies staring back at him. "Your good wife has a theory that Mrs. Palmer killed Lily Martin and Sally Tate, to save the hide of the duke, here."

"Angelina?" Hart asked in derision. "Where did Beth get that idea?"

Fellows answered. "Lady Ian talked to some tarts, ones she knew from her days in the slums. You really should be careful who your wife has truck with, my lord."

"Beth is an egalitarian," Hart said in a dry voice.

"What did they say?" Ian interrupted. If Beth was right— no, if they could convince Fellows that Beth was right—Fellows might turn his focus from Hart.

"They went on about how devoted Angelina Palmer is to Hart Mackenzie. How she'd do anything for him, even commit murder."

"That's ridiculous," Hart snapped. "She would have had ample opportunity to kill Sally when no one was in the house. She didn't have to do it when Ian could be accused of it."

"No?" Cameron broke in, his face stern. "She loves *you*, Hart. Why not push the blame onto Ian, and comfort you when you lose him?"

"Then why would she help me with . . ." He shot Fellows a sharp gaze.

Fellows rocked back on his heels. "Oh, I know damn well what you did, sir. You bustled your brother off to

Scotland so I couldn't interrogate him. He might tell me a few too many things, wouldn't he?"

"Why don't we get Mrs. Palmer down here and ask her?" Cameron said. "If anyone knows the truth of what goes on in this house, it's her."

"She's a hard one to crack," Fellows returned. "I've tried. Just as I've tried to break through the damned facade of your two brothers, Hart and Ian, cohorts in crime."

Cameron advanced on him. "You have trouble with respect, don't you?"

"Stop!" Ian balled his fists and stepped between them. "Cameron is right. Hart, get Mrs. Palmer. If you didn't kill Sally Tate, then she did."

"Or you did, my lord," Fellows told him, eyes glinting.

"I didn't want Sally dead. I had to leave her, she made me so furious, but I was ready to pay her off, send her to Australia or somewhere." Ian glared at Hart. "If the Palmer woman did it, she needs to admit it. She's caused us enough pain."

Hart's voice dripped with coldness. "Angelina isn't here."

"Isn't that convenient?" Fellows said. "What is she doing at this time of night? Shopping?"

Hart shrugged, and Ian's black rage rose. All these years he'd feared Hart had committed the murder, his beloved brother who'd released Ian from his prison. Ian had done his best to throw Fellows off the scent, to keep him from speaking to the one witness who could harm Hart. And all these years, Hart had believed Ian was still a madman, mad enough to stab Sally in one of his muddles. Mrs. Palmer was the one person who could clear Hart and Ian both, and now Hart protected her.

Hart was a liar. Mrs. Palmer was still in the house somewhere. And Beth was outside. . . .

Beth twisted, trying to throw Mrs. Palmer away from her at the same time. The knife skirted Beth's corset and dug its way deep into her side, just above her hip.

Beth grunted. The pain was sharp, swift, and robbed

her of breath. She dug her fingers into Mrs. Palmer's wrists
and hung on.

"Let go of me, bitch. I'll gut you."

Beth tried to scream, but her legs buckled, her body suddenly weak.

"Don't die on me, you little fool," Mrs. Palmer's hot
voice hissed in her ear. Beth felt herself being dragged out
the gate, the stench of the narrow passage gagging her.

Beth's heart pounded in panic. Mrs. Palmer was clearly
dangerous, but she was Beth's only chance to clear Ian.

"You'll make a nice hostage," Mrs. Palmer was saying
in a hard voice. "Hart tells me Ian adores his new bride. Ian
will do anything to get you back, I imagine, including let
me get out of England."

Mrs. Palmer was too strong to fight. She got Beth down
the alley to another street, Chancery Lane, if Beth had her
bearings right. But darkness swam before her eyes, and she
couldn't be sure. Her hands were so, so cold.

She heard Mrs. Palmer laughing, a loud, almost drunken
sound. But the woman hadn't been drunk, had she? Beth's
head swam with confusion as a hansom stopped for them
and Mrs. Palmer shoved Beth into it. "Bethnal Green,
love," she said to the cabbie, still laughing. "Don't worry, I
can pay. Hurry now. I have to get my sister home."

Beth slumped against the seat, and Mrs. Palmer pulled
the lap robe up over them both. The robe smelled of dust and
sweat and wet wool. Beth coughed, then groaned in pain.

"They'll come after you," Beth said hoarsely. "When
they find I'm gone, they'll look for me."

"I know that," Mrs. Palmer snapped. "You'll be well
looked after."

So a shark might say to the fish he was about to eat. Mrs.
Palmer closed her mouth tightly and refused to speak
again. Beth swam in and out of consciousness as the hansom rolled on. She dimly wondered how quickly the wound
would kill her.

"I need a doctor," she groaned

"I told you, you'll be looked after."

Beth pressed her hand against her side and closed her eyes. She was nauseous and too cold, her legs numb, sweat coating her face.

At last the hansom stopped moving. The cabbie rumbled something at Mrs. Palmer, and coins clinked into his hand. Beth hung on to the side of the hansom, but Mrs. Palmer pried her away and pulled her down the street, arm around Beth's waist.

"Hate to see two pretty ladies so drunk," Beth heard the cabbie say.

Mrs. Palmer laughed raucously, but cut it off abruptly as she dragged Beth around a corner. Lamplight shone through some windows, but little illumination penetrated the slums. The brick buildings were gray and black from years of coal smoke and dirt. Filth collected in the streets, and grime-coated people staggered drunkenly or hurried, fearful, to the nearest shelter.

Mrs. Palmer propelled Beth through alley after alley, twisting and turning. Beth realized Mrs. Palmer was trying to make her lose her bearings in the maze of streets, but Beth knew Bethnal Green like the back of her hand. She'd grown up here, had fought to stay alive here, had even once been happy here.

"Where are we?" She gasped, pretending to be confused. "Where are we going?"

"To my sister's. Stop asking questions."

"Hart will know about your sister and where she lives, won't he? And I know I won't be looked after. You'll kill me once you get me there. She'll help you kill me."

Mrs. Palmer's fingers were like iron pincers. "I'm not letting you run back to them until I'm well away. I'll send a confession of everything I've done once I'm gone, and I'll tell them where you are."

"I don't believe you," Beth sobbed, putting every bit of drama she could into her voice. "You'll let Ian hang for a crime he didn't commit."

"It's Hart I'm trying to save, you little idiot, and I don't care who hangs instead. It's always been Hart."

Again she snapped her mouth shut and kept Beth stumbling beside her. Beth's greatest fear was that Mrs. Palmer would simply leave her on the street, hurt and alone. Beth knew the denizens of this part of London would rob her blind in a minute and leave her for dead. Some kind soul might summon a constable, but perhaps too late.

"Please," she tried. "Let's find a . . . a church or something. Let me seek sanctuary there, and you can run away. I won't know where you've gone."

Mrs. Palmer growled under her breath. "I don't know why they marry such insipid women. That pale-haired creature Hart married ruined him. Stupid woman had to go and die, and it cut him up something horrible. And that bitch who jilted him before that was no better. Broke his heart. I hate them all for what they did to my lad."

Fury rang in her voice, and she gave Beth's arm an extra jerk. Beth could see what Sylvia had: that here was a woman who'd do anything for the man she loved. She'd murder for him, lie for him, risk going to the gallows for him.

Around a few more corners, that was all Beth needed. *There.* "There's a church." Beth hung heavily on to Mrs. Palmer, pointing to the gray brick of Thomas's former parish church. "Take me there, please. Don't leave me in this hellhole. I'll go mad. I know it."

Mrs. Palmer snarled something and dragged Beth toward the church. She didn't approach the front doors but tugged Beth down the narrow alley between buildings. The small churchyard opened in the back, hemmed in by the walls of buildings and the vicarage itself. In Beth's day the chapel's back door had been left unlocked, because Thomas liked to nip from vicarage to sacristy through the churchyard and always forgot his key.

Mrs. Palmer grabbed the handle and easily opened the door. She pushed Beth into the small passage that led to the sacristy. The familiar scents of candles, dust, books, and cloth assailed Beth, and transported her in her stupor back to her life as a vicar's wife. Those had been days of peace and order, of one season following the next like pearls on a string. Advent, Christmas, Epiphany, Lent, Easter, Whitsuntide, Trinity. One knew what one had to read and eat and wear, what flowers should be in the church, and what colors on the altar. Up at dawn for the joy of Easter, late to bed on Christmas Eve. No meat at Lent, a feast on Shrove Tuesday. Morning prayer, Evensong, the main service on Sundays.

There hadn't been enough money for an organ, so Thomas had blown a note on a pitch pipe, and the congregation had lurched through the hymns they knew by heart.

> *O, God our help in ages past,*
> *Our hope for years to come,*
> *Our shelter from the stormy blast,*
> *And our eternal home.*

She could hear the even rhythm of the slow tune, old Mrs. Whetherby's high-pitched warble floating out from the front row.

The church was empty. The whitewashed walls looked the same, as did the high lectern to the right of the altar. Beth wondered if the lectern door's hinges still squeaked as they had every time Thomas marched up the tiny flight of stairs and opened the half door.

The trump of doom, he called it. *Now they have to listen to the vicar preach.* When Beth suggested he have the sextant oil the hinges, Thomas replied, *Then there won't be anything to wake them up when the sermon's over.*

Everything in this narrow church spoke of Thomas and Beth's old life, the small measure of happiness she'd found here. But that was long ago, and Thomas's voice was faint and far away. Now she was hurt, alone, and feared she'd never see Ian, the man she loved with all her heart, again.

~

Ian shoved his way past Cameron and Fellows and bolted out of the room. He heard Hart behind him snap, "Stop him."

Cameron came after Ian, but Ian was faster. He was down the stairs and out the door before Cameron could catch up, and he made straight for Hart's carriage. He yanked open the door to see Katie asleep on one of the plush benches. She was alone.

Ian shook her. "Where is Beth?"

Katie blinked at him. "I dunno. I thought she was with you."

Ian's heart hammered. He slammed the door and strode to the coachman leaning on the wall near the horse's heads, chewing a plug of tobacco.

"Where is she?" Ian's voice rang out, and the horses jerked back.

"Your missus? She ran inside, guv. I thought . . ."

Ian didn't wait for the rest of his spluttered explanation. He ran back to the house, meeting Cameron halfway. His brother paused, then turned back. "Ian, what the devil?"

Ian dashed into the house, shouting Beth's name. Hart looked down from the landing, Fellows beside him. Two ladies popped out of a room on a higher floor.

"Where is she?" Ian shouted at them.

Hart and Fellows only stared, but one of the girls answered, "She ain't up here, love."

"Did you see her?"

"I saw Ma Palmer hurrying down the back stairs," another put in. "Guess she didn't want to see the good inspector."

Fear and rage narrowed Ian's focus. *Beth. Find her.*

"Ian!"

Cameron's shout came from the bottom of the back stairs, the way to the kitchens. Ian barreled down them, then through the quiet kitchen and through a back door. Cameron stood in the tiny yard behind the house with a lantern he'd snatched up from the kitchen.

Ian peered at what had Cameron's attention. A brown-red stain had splotched the bricks, new against the coal grime.

"Blood," Cameron said quietly. "And a smear here, on the gate."

Ian's heart pounded so rapidly he was nearly sick. As Fellows came out to see what was going on, Ian caught the inspector by the collar and shoved his face at the stains.

"Bloody hell, your lordship," Fellows bleated.

"Find her," Ian said. He jerked Fellows upright. "You're a detective. Detect something."

Cameron opened the gate and stepped into the alley. "Ian's right, Fellows. Do your damn job."

Hart put a hand on Ian's shoulder. "Ian."

Ian twisted away, unable to bear his touch. If Beth was dead . . .

Fellows quickly stepped away. "He's not going to have one of his mad attacks, is he?"

Ian turned his back on Hart. "No." He strode out of the gate to join Cameron, pulling Fellows by the collar with him. "Find her."

"I'm not a bloodhound, your lordships."

"Woof, woof." Cameron said, giving Fellows an evil grin. "Good dog."

Chapter 21

Beth cried out as Mrs. Palmer shoved her onto the hard wood of a pew. No one was there, not a sextant sweeping a floor or the rather doddering vicar who'd taken Thomas's place nine years before.

Beth grabbed Mrs. Palmer's wrist. "No, don't leave me."

"Don't be foolish. Someone will find you."

Beth hung on with all the strength she could muster. "Please don't leave me here alone. Wait for the vicar with me. Please. I don't want to die alone."

Her tears were genuine. The pain had increased, waves of it rolling over her. Would Ian understand where she'd gone? Would he find her? For all his obsessions with minutiae, he wasn't stupid and had a brain that could reason complex mathematical problems and memorize the intricate language of treaties. But could he fit the pieces together and come up with an answer to the puzzle?

Mrs. Palmer made a noise of exasperation but sat down in a rustle of skirts. Beth slumped against her, unable to support herself.

"Did you kill Lily Martin?" Beth asked in a whisper, too numb now to fear. If Mrs. Palmer had simply wanted to kill Beth, she would have done it by now. The woman was afraid, and Beth had the sudden feeling she was now more afraid of Hart than of being caught by Inspector Fellows. If Mrs. Palmer let Beth, the wife of Hart's beloved brother, die, Hart would never forgive her.

"Of course I killed Lily," Mrs. Palmer said viciously. "She was a witness to Sally's murder."

"Then you think Hart really did kill Sally."

"Hart was so angry with Sally. The little bitch was blackmailing him to get money so she could run off and leave me. Hart told me he would fix her, make her regret trying to play her games."

"You were angry at Sally, too."

"If Sally wanted money so much, she could have asked Hart for it. But she wanted power over him. As though she ever could control someone like Hart. He has the will to command. I saw that when I first met him, when he was all of twenty years old." Her voice dropped to fond tones. "He was a bonny lad then. All handsome and charming, before so many people hurt him."

Beth found herself with her head on Mrs. Palmer's plaid broadcloth lap, staring up at the older woman's face. Mackenzie plaid, Beth realized, blue and green with white and red thread.

"I'm sorry," Beth whispered. "You must love him so much."

"I've made no secret of that."

"It must have been hard for you to watch him marry, to start shutting you out of his life."

Not the most diplomatic thing to say, Beth thought, but she'd lost control of her words.

"I knew he'd have to marry," Mrs. Palmer said calmly. "I'm thirteen years older than he is and hardly one of his class. He needed to marry some peer's daughter to host balls and fetes and charm his colleagues. He'd never become prime minister of England tied to a woman like me."

"But plenty of lofty gentlemen have mistresses. Mrs. Barrington liked to rail about it."

"Who the hell is Mrs. Barrington?" Beth was too weary to answer, and Mrs. Palmer rambled on. "No one would mind so much Hart having a mistress, no. But it's more than that."

"Because he was your lord and master?" She remembered Ian's words, and curiosity drifted through her pain. "What exactly did he do?"

"If you know nothing of that life, you would not understand."

"I suppose not." Her attention drifted again. "I don't believe Hart killed her," Beth said, alarmed at how faint her voice had grown. "He would have waited until Ian was elsewhere. But someone else might have panicked and shoved a knife into Sally."

"Someone like me," Mrs. Palmer said. "Perhaps I killed her."

To protect Hart. Beth's eyes drifted closed. She tried to imagine the scene, Ian peering through the half-open door, Hart looming over Sally with a knife in his hand, Lily Martin in the hall outside. Something was wrong with that. If only Beth could stay awake long enough to decide what . . .

Mrs. Palmer stood up abruptly, as though she heard something, but no one came into the chapel. Beth's head bumped the hard bench, and she closed her teeth around a groan.

"You'll be fine here," Mrs. Palmer said. "Someone will find you."

"No," Beth whispered in genuine fear. She reached for the woman's hand. "Don't let me die here alone." If Beth could make Mrs. Palmer stay long enough for Ian to figure out where they were and bring the inspector along, Ian could be cleared and safe from Inspector Fellows forever.

Mrs. Palmer looked around the chapel, shivering as though a cool breeze touched her. "Why should I stay to be caught?"

"Because you didn't mean to. You thought Lily would betray Hart, and you were scared."

Mrs. Palmer bit her lip. "You're right. I went to her to find out what she knew, and she started raving that the money Ian was giving her wasn't enough anymore. The scissors were right in her basket. I picked them up. . . ."

She stared at her hand, flexing it in wonder.

"Hart will help you," Beth said.

"No, he won't. I ruined everything. Lily's death put Inspector Fellows back on the scent. Hart will never forgive me."

Beth grasped the edge of the pew, trying to stay conscious. Sleep beckoned her, sweet sleep where there was no pain. "Did you really kill Sally?"

"It doesn't matter, does it? I'll go to the gallows for Hart, and he'll understand how much I love him."

"Lily and Sally were lovers," Beth whispered. Her mind reached for something, but lights flickered on the edges of her vision.

Mrs. Palmer snorted. "Lily had a photograph of Sally in her sitting room, can you believe it? Sally had thrown her over all those years ago. I took it away with me. I didn't want to give the police any hints, but they made the connection anyway."

"Sally and Lily," Beth whispered. She closed her eyes, and the scene played again in her head. Lily staring into the room while Hart was with Sally, watching Hart leave her. Perhaps thinking that Hart had already given Sally money. Lily furious because Sally had given her the push, and she wouldn't have Sally or the money. A knife lying on the table next to the bed and Lily snatching it up. Ian watching from the parlor as Hart stormed out of the house, Ian seeing Lily in the hall, a witness, he thought, to a crime committed by his brother.

"I have to get away." Mrs. Palmer shoved her hands into the pockets of Beth's gown, snatching the drawstring bag that held Beth's coins. She grabbed Beth's hand and started working the silver ring with the diamond chip from her little finger. "I'll take this, too. I can flog it when I get to the Continent. And the earrings."

"No." Beth tried to close her fist, but her hand was ice-cold and so weak. "My first husband gave it to me."

"A small price to pay for me not killing you." Mrs. Palmer snatched the earrings out of Beth's ears, the tiny pain sharp. Isabella had given Beth the earrings in Paris when Beth had admired them. *Keep them, darling*, she'd said, careless and generous. *They suit you better than they do me.*

Mrs. Palmer stood up. She looked old in this light, a woman who'd kept herself young with paint and perseverance. Now she looked tired, weary, a woman who'd tried too hard for too long.

"I love Hart Mackenzie," she said, her voice fierce. "I have always loved him. I will make certain that little woman-loving whore Sally won't ruin him even after all these years. I made sure Lily wouldn't."

"Stay and explain to them," Beth gasped out.

In sudden rage, Mrs. Palmer hauled Beth up by the hair. Beth cried out, her side like fire.

"You had no right to go digging everything up, bringing the inspector to my house. You're as much to blame as I am." Spittle flecked her lips.

Beth couldn't fight anymore. Her whole body wanted simply to stop. She'd die here in Thomas's little church, not ten yards from the churchyard where Thomas lay.

She thought she heard the lectern door squeak, and she saw Thomas standing by it in the white cassock she'd darned so often. His dark hair was gray at the temples, his kind eyes so blue.

Be brave, my Beth, she thought he said. *It's almost over.*

"Ian."

Mrs. Palmer scanned the chapel, her fingers still gripping Beth's hair. "Who are you talking to?"

Shouting interrupted her, deep male voices, one of them Ian's. Mrs. Palmer screamed, hauling Beth in front of her like a shield. Beth groaned in agony.

Ian, his face white, eyes wild, barreled into Mrs. Palmer. He was shouting something, but Beth couldn't hear him,

couldn't understand his words. Mrs. Palmer stumbled, shriek-
ing, and Ian caught Beth as she fell.

He was beside her, warm, solid, and real. Beth tried to
reach for him, but her arms wouldn't work. He lifted her
and cradled her against him on the pew. His golden eyes
were wide as he looked straight into hers.

"Ian." Beth smiled and touched his face. She was the one
who couldn't hold the gaze, as her eyes drifted sideways.

In her peripheral vision, she saw Hart rush in, followed
by Cameron and Inspector Fellows. Mrs. Palmer stood tall
against the wall.

"I'll not hang for that slut," she said in a loud, clear voice.
Her knife gleamed in her hands, and she plunged it straight
between her breasts.

Beth heard Hart's cry, saw Mrs. Palmer's knees give and
her body slide down the wall. Hart caught her in his arms.

Mrs. Palmer looked up at Hart. "I love you."

"Don't speak," Hart said, his voice incredibly gentle.
"I'll get a doctor."

She shook her head, her smile weak. "It's all dark now.
I can't see your face." She groped blindly for him. "Hart,
hold me."

"I'm here." Hart gathered her against him, pressing a
kiss to her hair. "I'm here, love. I won't leave you."

Ian didn't even look at them. He had his eyes closed now,
rocking Beth. Beth tried to say, "I knew you'd find me," but
darkness closed on her, and her lips would no longer move.
She slid into unconsciousness just as Mrs. Palmer's last
breath rattled through her throat.

~~~~~

Ian used Hart's opulent carriage to take Beth home to the
ducal mansion on Grosvenor Square. Hart's house was always
staffed, always at the ready for any business the duke might
want to conduct in town. Ian carried Beth inside, and the
well-trained servants scrambled to obey his frantic commands.

Ian carried Beth to the bedchamber set aside for his use. A doctor came to clean Beth's wound and sew it closed, but Beth wouldn't wake up.

Cameron had stayed with Hart and Inspector Fellows at the church while Fellows fetched who he needed to fetch and tried to make sense of what happened. Ian didn't care what had happened. It was over, Mrs. Palmer was dead, and Beth had nearly died herself trying to put everything right. Fellows could do as he liked.

Beth lay in a stupor, feverish and sweating. No matter how much Ian bathed the cut in her side, it swelled and reddened, and fever set in.

Ian stayed by her all night. He heard the others return, Cameron's gruff voice and Hart's quiet replies, the deferential voices of the servants. He pressed a cool cloth to Beth's forehead, wishing he could bring the fever down by force of will.

He heard the door open behind him and Hart's heavy tread, but Ian wouldn't look up.

"How is she?" his brother asked in a low voice.

"Dying."

Hart came around the bed and looked down at Beth, unmoving on the sheets. His face was white, strained.

Beth was so hot. She groaned with it, tossing her head from side to side. She whimpered when her wound touched the bed, as if trying to find release from haunting pain.

Ian glared at Hart. "You and your fucking women. You made them your tame animals, and now they've killed Beth."

Hart flinched. "Damnation, Ian."

"You thought Beth wanted my money, our name. Why should she?"

"I did at first. I don't any longer."

"Too bloody late. She never wanted anything for herself, never demanded anything from us. You don't know what to do with people like that."

"I don't want to see her die, either."

Hart put his hand on Ian's shoulder, but Ian jerked away. "You took me to that house to be your damned spy. You used me, like you've used me for every other scheme in your life. You released me from the asylum so I could help you, but you've never believed I wasn't mad. You just needed what I could do."

"That's not entirely accurate," Hart said, tight-lipped.

"It's close enough. You thought I was insane enough to kill Sally. I did what you said because I was grateful to you, and I wanted to protect *you*. I admired you and worshiped you, just like your tame sluts."

Ian was breathing hard, but he gentled his hand to brush back Beth's hair.

"For God's sake, Ian."

"I'm finished obeying your commands. Your bloody high-handedness has killed my Beth."

Hart remained still, his eyes fixed. "I know. Let me help her."

"You can't help. She's beyond help." Ian met Hart's gaze for a fleeting moment, and for the first time in Ian's life, Hart couldn't look back at him.

"Get out," Ian said. "I don't want you here if I have to say good-bye to her."

Hart remained rigid and unmoving for a few moments, then turned around and quietly walked from the room.

Over the next week, Ian left the bedroom only to shout for Curry if the man was too slow answering the bell. Beth tossed in the bed, her face pink and sweating, groaning when anything touched her side. Ian slept on the bed next to her, or on the chair beside it when Beth became too restless. Curry tried to get Ian to sleep in the next room, to let a maid or Katie or himself nurse Beth while he rested, but Ian refused.

Ian had read every book in Hart's vast library and plenty of tomes at the private asylum, filing away every modern view of medicine in his head. He put into practice methods of nursing festering wounds, methods of bringing down fever, methods of keeping the patient quiet and fed.

The doctor brought leeches, which did help with the

swelling a little, but Ian didn't like his oils and ointments and syringes of suspicious-looking liquids. He wouldn't let the doctor near Beth with them, which led to the doctor's loud-voiced complaints to an unsympathetic Hart.

Ian washed Beth's wound every day, wiping away any evils that seeped from it. He bathed her face in cool water, fed her spoonfuls of broth, forcing them into her when she tried to turn her face away. He had Curry bring in ice, which he pressed against the cut to stop the swelling, and used more ice to cool down the water with which he bathed her forehead.

Ian wished he could move Beth from London, where coal smoke and soot seeped through every window, but he feared jarring the wound open again. He braided her hair to take the heat off her neck, fearing he'd have to cut off her beautiful tresses if the fever didn't break.

The doctor clucked his tongue and proposed experimental treatments that involved serum from monkey glands and other such wonders. He was developing them in conjunction with specialists in Switzerland, and if he could save the sister-in-law of the Duke of Kilmorgan, he said, it would make his name.

Ian ran him off with threats of violence.

By the sixth day, the fever still had not come down. Ian sat by Beth's side, his hand loosely clasping hers, and tasted fear. He was going to lose her.

"Is this what love feels like?" he whispered to her. "I don't like it, my Beth. It hurts too much."

Beth didn't respond. Her eyes were cracked open under swollen lids, a blue glitter that saw nothing. He hadn't been able to feed her today.

Ian felt sick, his stomach roiling, and he had to leave the room to vomit bile. When he returned, there was no change. Her breathing was hoarse and a struggle, her skin painfully hot.

She'd come into his life so suddenly, only a few short weeks ago, and just as suddenly, she was departing it. The sense of loss terrified him. He'd never felt it before, not even with all the loneliness and fear he'd experienced at the asylum. That fear had been self-preservation; this was an emptiness that hollowed him out from the inside.

Sitting in this dark room facing the worst brought memories back to him. Ian's perfect recall played them all clearly, little dimmed by the seven years between now and his years at the asylum. He remembered early morning baths in cold water, taking supervised walks in the garden, where a man with a long walking stick followed him about. The sheepherder, Ian had always called him, ready to beat patients back indoors if necessary.

When other physicians or distinguished guests visited, Dr. Edwards would give grand lectures, while Ian was made to sit on a chair next to the podium. Dr. Edwards would have Ian learn the name of every member of the audience and recite them back, have him listen to a conversation between two volunteers and repeat it perfectly. A blackboard would be brought out, and Ian would solve complex mathematical problems in seconds. Doctor Edwards's trained seal, Ian called himself.

His is a typical case of haughty resentment which is festering his brain. Notice how he avoids your eyes, which shows declined trust and lack of truthfulness. Note how his attention wanders when he is spoken to, how he interrupts with an inappropriate comment or question that has nothing to do with the topic at hand. This is arrogance taken to the point of hysteria—the patient can no longer connect with people he deems beneath him. Treatment: austere surroundings, cold baths, exercise, electric shock to stimulate healing. Regular beatings to suppress his rages. The treatment is effective, gentlemen. He has calmed considerably since he first came to me.

If Ian had "calmed," it was because he'd realized that if he suppressed his rages and abrupt speeches, he'd be left alone. He'd learned to become an automaton, a clockwork boy that moved and talked in a certain way. To violate the pattern meant hours locked in a small room, electric shocks through the body, beatings every night. When Ian became the clockwork young man again, his tormentors left him alone.

They at least let him read books and take lessons with a tutor. Ian's mind was restless, absorbing everything put in front of it. He mastered languages in a matter of days. He progressed from simple arithmetic to higher calculus within a year. He read a book every day and could recite huge passages from each one. He found some refuge in music and learned pieces he heard played, but never how to read music. The notes and staffs were so much black-and-white mess to him.

Ian also couldn't master subjects like logic, ethics, and philosophy. He could mouth the phrases from Aristotle, Socrates, Plato, but not understand or interpret them.

The arrogance of his class coupled with his resentment toward his family has created a blockage in his brain, Dr. Edwards would explain to his enthusiastic audiences. *He can read and remember but not understand. He also shows no interest in his father, never asks after him or writes to him even when it is suggested to him. He also makes no sign that he misses his dear, departed mother.*

Dr. Edwards never saw the boy Ian sob into his pillow at night, alone, afraid, hating the dark. Knowing that if his father came for him, it would be to kill him for what Ian had seen.

Ian's only friends were the asylum's servants, maids who smuggled him sweetmeats from the kitchen and wine from the servants' hall. They helped him hide the cheroots Mac brought him and the naughty books Cameron gave him when he came to call.

You read these, Cameron would whisper, with a wink. *You need to know which end of a woman is what, and what each is for.*

Ian had learned that at seventeen at the hands of the plump, golden-haired maid who cleaned his hearth every morning. She'd kept their secret liaison for two years, then married the coachman and moved off to a better life. Ian told Hart to make her a wedding present of several hundred guineas, but would never say why.

That was a long time ago. Ian swam back to the present, but the present was stark and terrifying. He sat in darkness, curtains cloaking the windows, while Beth struggled to live. If she died, he might as well take himself back to the asylum and lock himself in, because he'd go mad if he had to live without her.

~~~

Isabella arrived not long later. She entered the room in a faint rustle of silk, her eyes filling as she took in Beth on the bed.

"Ian, I'm so sorry."

Ian couldn't answer. Isabella looked exhausted. She caressed Beth's hand and lifted it to her lips.

"I saw the doctor downstairs," she said, her voice thick with tears. "He told me there wasn't much hope."

"The doctor is an idiot."

"She's burning up."

"I won't let her die."

Isabella sank down on the bed, still holding Beth's hand. "It happens, usually to the best people. They're taken away to teach us humility." Tears streaked down her cheeks.

"Balls."

Isabella looked up at him, her smile wan. "You're stubborn, like a Mackenzie."

"I *am* a Mackenzie." What a damn fool thing to say. "I won't let her die. I can't." Beth moved listlessly on the bed, soft sounds coming from her mouth.

"She's delirious," Isabella whispered.

Ian wet a cloth and dabbed it to Beth's tongue as she tried to talk, her voice a croak. She lapped the droplets that fell from it, whimpering.

Isabella wiped away tears as she rose from the bed and blindly made her way out.

Mac came in not long later, his face haggard.

"Any change?" he asked.

"No." Ian didn't look up from pressing a cloth filled with ice to Beth's forehead. "Did you come with Isabella?"

Mac gave a soft snort. "Hardly. Different trains, different boats, and she changed her hotel as soon as she found out I'd booked in there, too."

"You're both fools. You can't let her go."

Mac raised his brows. "It's been three years, and she isn't exactly racing back to me."

"You aren't trying hard enough to get her back," Ian said, angry. "I never thought you were this bloody stupid."

Mac looked surprised, then thoughtful. "You might have a point."

Ian returned his attention to Beth. How anyone could find love and throw it away so carelessly was beyond him.

Mac rubbed his forehead. "Speaking of bloody fools, Hart sacked that quack of a doctor. Good thing, too. I was ready to throttle him."

"Good."

Mac put his hand on Ian's shoulder, fingers squeezing. "I'm sorry. This isn't right. You of all of us deserve to be happy."

Ian didn't answer. It had nothing to do with being happy. It had everything to do with saving Beth.

Mac remained for a while, watching Beth moodily, then drifted away. He was replaced by other visitors throughout the day and into the night: Cameron, Daniel, Katie, Curry, Isabella again. They all asked the same question. "Is there any change?" Ian had to shake his head, and they went away.

In the small hours of the morning, when the house was deathly still, the gilt clock on the mantelpiece apologetically chimed twice. Beth sat straight up in bed.

"Ian!"

Her skin was bright red, her eyes glittering, pupils wide. Ian came to the bed. "I'm here."

"Ian, I'm going to die."

Ian wrapped his arms around her, held her close. "I won't let you."

She pulled away. "Ian, tell me you forgive me." She caught Ian's gaze, and he couldn't turn away.

Beth's eyes were hot blue, swimming with tears. He could look at them for hours, mesmerized by the color. He'd read that eyes were the windows to the soul, and Beth's soul was pure and sweet.

She was safe, but a monster lurked inside Ian, the same one that had lurked inside his father. He could so easily hurt her, forget himself in a rage. He couldn't let that happen—ever. "There is nothing to forgive, love."

"For going to Inspector Fellows. For raking it all up again. For killing Mrs. Palmer. She's dead, isn't she?"

"Yes."

"But if I hadn't come back to London, she'd still be alive."

"And Fellows would still believe me guilty. Or Hart. There's no forgiveness needed for finding out the truth, my Beth."

She didn't seem to hear him. "I'm so sorry," she sobbed, her voice tight with fever. She put her hand on his chest and buried her face in his shoulder.

Ian held her close, his heart thumping. When he lifted her gently to kiss her, he saw that her eyes had closed again and she'd fallen back into her stupor. Ian laid her down on the pillows, tears sliding from his eyes to scatter across her hot skin.

Chapter 22

Beth swam to wakefulness. She was soaked in sweat and sore all over, but she somehow felt, deep down inside, that the worst was over.

And she was so *hungry*.

She turned her head to see Ian in the chair beside the bed, his head back, his eyes closed. He was in shirtsleeves and trousers, his shirt open to his navel. He held her hand firmly in his, but a gentle snore issued from his mouth.

Beth squeezed Ian's hand, ready to tease him for the rumpled sprawl of his big body. Oh, for the energy to climb out of bed and curl up in his lap, letting those strong arms hold her again.

"Ian," she whispered.

At the small sound, he snapped open his eyes. The golden gaze raked over her, and then he was on the bed, a cup of water sloshing in his hand.

"Drink."

"I'd love something to eat."

"Drink the damn water."

"Yes, husband."

Beth drank slowly, liking the wetness on her parched tongue. Ian glared at her mouth the entire time. She wondered whether, if she didn't swallow fast enough for him, he'd hold her nose and dump the liquid down her throat.

"Now bread," Ian said. He broke off a tiny piece and held it to her lips.

Beth took it, unable to stop her smile. "This reminds me of when we were at Kilmorgan. You fed me breakfast."

Ian broke off more bread without answering, watching as she chewed and swallowed.

"I feel better," she said when she'd eaten several pieces for him. "Though very tired."

Ian felt her forehead and face. "The fever's broken."

"Thank heavens—"

She broke off with a squeak when his arms went hard around her. His shirt fell open, the warmth of his bare chest like a blanket.

He tried to slant a kiss across her dry lips, but she pulled back. "No, Ian, I must be disgusting. I need a bath."

Ian smoothed her hair from her forehead, his own eyes wet. "You rest first. Sleep."

"You, too."

"I was asleep," he argued.

"I mean proper sleep, in a bed. Have a maid come and change the sheets, and you can sleep in here with me." She brushed a tear from his cheek, treasuring the rare sign of his emotion. "I want you to."

"I'll change the sheets," he said. "I've been doing it."

"The upstairs maids will not be happy if you take over their job. They'll consider it not your place. Very snobbish are upstairs maids."

He shook his head. "I never understand anything you say."

"Then I must truly be better."

Ian snatched folded linens from a cupboard. In silence

he began stripping the sheets from one side of the bed. Beth tried to help, but gave up as soon as she realized she could not even pull up one corner.

Ian deftly unmade one part of the bed and tucked new sheets over it. Then he gently lifted her and laid her on the clean sheets before he repeated his actions with the other side.

"You are quite practiced at this," she observed as he tucked quilts around her. "Perhaps you could open a school of instruction for upstairs maids."

"Books."

She waited, but he only tossed the wadded-up bedding in the hall and closed the door again.

"I beg your pardon?"

"Books on how to care for the sick."

"You read them, did you?"

"I read everything." He pulled off his boots and stretched out beside her, his warmth so welcome.

Beth's thoughts went to when she'd wakened in the night, when Ian had looked straight down into her eyes. His golden gaze had been so anguished, so filled with pain. Now his gaze was evasive again, not letting her catch it.

"It's not fair that you look at me only when I'm extremely ill," Beth said. "Now that I am fully awake and feeling better, you turn away."

"Because when I look at you, I forget everything. I lose all track of what I'm saying or doing. I can see only your eyes." He laid his head on her pillow and rested his hand on her chest. "You have such beautiful eyes."

Her heart beat faster. "And then you flatter me so that I'll feel awful that I chided you."

"I've never flattered you."

Beth traced his cheek. "You do know that you are the finest man in the world, don't you?"

He didn't answer. His breath was hot on her skin. She was tired, but not so tired that she couldn't feel an agreeable tightening in the space between her legs.

More memories of the church came back to her, the awful

pain and Mrs. Palmer's desperation, overlaid with the scents of her old life. "She's dead, isn't she? Mrs. Palmer, I mean."

"Yes."

"She loved him so much, poor woman."

"She was a murderess and nearly killed you."

"Well, I'm not exactly happy about that. She didn't kill Sally, you know. Lily did."

Ian's gaze flickered. "Don't talk. You're too weak."

"I'm right, Ian Mackenzie. Sally threw Lily over and was going to keep all the blackmail money for herself. Lily must have been furious. You said she was hanging about outside the bedroom. While you were off in the parlor, and after Hart left the room, she nipped in, quarreled with Sally, and stabbed her. No wonder Lily agreed to go to that house in Covent Garden and not come out."

Ian leaned over her. "Right now, I don't give a damn who killed Sally."

Beth looked hurt. "But I solved the mystery. Tell Inspector Fellows."

"Inspector Fellows can rot in hell."

"Ian."

"He thinks he's a bloody good detective. He can find out for himself. You rest."

"But I feel better."

Ian glared at her, his eyes still not meeting hers. "I don't care."

Beth obediently settled back into the pillows, but she couldn't resist tracing his cheek. His jaw was dark and sandpaper rough, showing he hadn't shaved in a while.

"How did you find me at the church?" Beth asked. "How did you know?"

"Fellows found someone who heard Mrs. Palmer tell a cabbie to take them to Bethnal Green. Hart knew Mrs. Palmer's sister lived there. When you weren't at her house, I decided you'd try to get away from Mrs. Palmer and back to the church that had been your husband's." He looked away. "I knew you'd been happy there."

"How did you even know where it was?"

"I've explored all parts of London. I remembered."

Beth leaned into his chest, loving the clean scent of his lawn shirt. "Bless you and your memory, Ian. I'll never stand amazed at it again."

"Does it amaze you?"

"Yes, but I've been viewing it rather like a circus trick. Dear heavens, like you're a trained monkey."

"Monkey . . ."

"Never mind. Thank you for finding me, Ian Mackenzie. Thank you for not killing Sally Tate. Thank you for being so damned noble and conscientious."

"I worried sometimes." Ian rubbed his forehead in the gesture that indicated one of his troubling headaches. "Sometimes I convinced myself that it wasn't Hart; it was me in one of my rages, blocked out so I don't remember."

Beth closed her hand over his. "But you didn't. Both killers are dead, and it's over."

"You saw me try to choke the life out of Fellows. It took Curry and Mac to pull me off him."

"You must admit Inspector Fellows can be provoking," Beth said, trying to make her tone light.

"In the asylum I fought my handlers at first. I hurt more than one of them. They had to strap me down to give me my treatments."

"Handlers?" Beth started to sit up, but the pain pulled her back down. "You weren't an animal."

"Wasn't I?"

"No one should be tied down and beaten and given electric shocks."

"The headaches would come, and I'd lash out at them." His gaze slid away. "I can't always stop the rages. What if I hurt you?"

Beth's heart squeezed at the fear in his eyes. "You're not your father."

"Aren't I? He locked me away because I'd witnessed him killing my mother, but that wasn't the only reason. I couldn't convince a commission I was sane—I grew so angry I could only recite one line of poetry over and over, trying to contain myself." He caught one of her hands, brought it to his mouth. "Beth, what if I rage at you? What if I hurt you? What if I open my eyes and your body is under my hands—"

He broke off, his eyes closing tight, tight.

"No, Ian, don't leave me."

"I was so angry at Sally. And I am so strong."

"Which is why you left the room. You went out to calm yourself, and it worked." She pressed a kiss to his closed fist. "I very much need to speak to Inspector Fellows," she said.

She found herself pinned against the mattress. Ian's eyes were open again, his fear gone. But for all the strength in his hands on her wrists, he made sure his weight was far from her hurt side.

"No more conversations with Inspector Fellows. He is to leave you be."

"But—"

"No," he growled.

He stopped her next words with his lips, and Beth was not unhappy to surrender. She said no more about it, but her mind whirled with plans. She needed to have a nice long chat with Inspector Fellows, and the good inspector would know why.

~

Beth recovered swiftly from her fever, but the stab wound took far longer. She could walk fairly well after another week in bed, but the pain was still profound and tired her quickly.

She hobbled around Hart's big house, with his servants hovering, ready to bring her anything and everything. They unnerved Beth, who wasn't used to being waited on quite so intently.

She was also frustrated because after the kiss to keep her silent, Ian distanced himself from her. He told her he wanted to give her a chance to fully heal, but she knew he still worried about his anger getting away from him.

Her own father had been prone to violent rages when drunk, and he'd been free with his fists. Ian wasn't like that—he understood the need to control his anger, and he didn't try to do it with drink.

She knew her own reassurances wouldn't work. She couldn't deny that the Mackenzies had seen and caused their share of violence. But then she remembered the anguish on Hart's face as Mrs. Palmer had died. He'd held her protectively, letting her know he was there with her until the end. Ian had that same protective nature, the one that had made him openly defy Hart to protect Beth. She burned for Ian, but most nights, he stayed away from the bed altogether.

Beth had many visitors, from Isabella to Cameron's son, Daniel, all anxious about her. She'd never had a family before, never had more than one person at a time care whether she lived or died. Sometimes she'd had no one at all. The Mackenzies' acceptance warmed her. Isabella had been right that the brothers often forgot to dampen their very masculine manners for ladies, but Beth didn't mind. She liked that Mac and Cameron were comfortable enough around her to be themselves, and she knew their rough manners hid good-heartedness.

As Ian continued to insist on confining her, Beth began to feel like a prisoner in a plush palace. She had to resort to bribing Curry to do what she wanted.

"Your ladyship, 'e'll kill me," Curry said in dismay when he heard Beth's instructions.

"I only want to speak to the man. You can bring him here."

"Oh, right you are. And *then* 'is lordship will kill me. Not to mention 'Is Grace."

"Please, Curry. And I won't chide you on what I saw you and Katie getting up to on the back stairs yesterday morning."

Curry turned brilliant red. "You're a hard one, ain't ya? Does my master know what 'e's got 'imself into?"

"I grew up in the gutter, Curry, same as you. I learned to be hard."

"Not the same as me, begging your pardon, missus. We might 'ave both lived in the gutter, but you ain't *from* it. You're quality, m'lady, 'cause your mum was a gentleman's daughter. You ain't ever the same as me."

"I beg your pardon, Curry. I didn't mean to presume."

He grinned at her. "Right. Just so it doesn't 'appen again." He sobered. "Ooh, but 'e's going to kill me."

"I'll take care of that," Beth said. "You just get on with it."

Ian opened the door of Beth's bedchamber a week into Beth's healing and sidestepped as Curry rushed out. For the last few days, he'd seen Curry scuttle in and out of Beth's bedchamber, giving Ian furtive glances. He gave Ian one now.

"Where the hell are you going?" Ian asked him.

Curry didn't stop. "Things to do, things to do." He disappeared into the hall below and was gone.

Inside, Beth reclined on the chaise, her face pink, her breath quick. Ian crossed to her and put his hand on her forehead, but found no fever. He sat down on the sliver of chaise next to her, liking her body against his.

"We'll leave for Scotland next week. You should be well enough to travel by then."

"Is that an order, husband?"

Ian laced his hand through her hair. He wanted her, but was willing to forgo the pleasure of sating himself to keep from hurting her. "You will like my house in Scotland. We'll get married there."

"We're already married, I might point out."

"You can have your real wedding, with the white dress and lilies of the valley, like you told me at the opera."

Her slim brows arched. "You remember that? But of course you do. That sounds delightful."

Ian rose. "Rest until then."

Beth caught his hand. Her touch warmed his blood, made him crave her. "Ian, don't go."

He disentangled her hand from his, but she gripped it again. "Please stay. We can simply . . . talk."

"Best not to."

Tears filled her eyes. "Please."

She thought he was rejecting her. Ian leaned down swiftly, placed his fists on either side of her. "If I stay, my wife, I won't want to talk. I won't be able to stop myself from doing as I please with you."

Her eyes darkened. "I wouldn't mind."

Ian ran the backs of his fingers across her cheek. "I can protect you from everyone else, but who protects you from me?"

Beth's lip trembled as she tried to catch his gaze. He flicked it quickly away. Beth used his moment of distraction to lace her arms around his neck and kiss him full on the mouth.

Treacherous woman. He met her seeking tongue with his, her lips warm and skilled with what he'd taught her. She distracted him again by nibbling his lower lip, while her hand went straight to his hard shaft.

"No," he groaned.

Beth slid her fingers around the buttons of his trousers and popped them open one by one. "I vow I will speak to whoever designs undergarments for men and tell them that they are deuced difficult to part under certain circumstances."

Ian was so hard he hurt. Her fingers were more confident as she closed them around his cock, her thumb brushing across his tip. He clenched his teeth as she swirled her fingers around his flange, teasing his sensitive skin. Ian found himself fisting her hair, and released her before he could pull it. He closed his fingers over her shoulder, his grip biting into the thick brocade of her gown.

"Do you like that?" she whispered.

Ian couldn't answer. His hips moved, wanting to thrust.

"I like it," she said. "I love how hard your staff is, yet the skin is silken. I remember how it feels under my tongue."

She must be trying to kill him. Ian closed his eyes, clenched his teeth, willing himself to make her stop.

"It tasted warm and just a bit salty," she went on. "I remember comparing you to smooth cream." She laughed a little. "When I took your seed inside my mouth, it was the first time I'd ever done that. I wanted to swallow every bit of you."

Her voice was shy and sultry at the same time, her fingers as skilled as a courtesan's. Better than a courtesan's, because Beth wasn't doing this at his command. She was giving it as a gift.

"I am trying to learn bawdy talk," she said. "Am I doing well?"

"Yes." He grated the word. Ian tilted her face up to his and gave her a long, deep-tongued kiss. Beth opened her mouth for him, smiling at the same time.

"Will you whisper bawdy talk to me?" she asked. "I seem to like it."

Ian put his lips to her ear and told her in very explicit terms exactly what he wanted to do to her, and where and how and with what. Beth flushed a deep red, but her eyes were starry.

"How vexing that I am so feeble," she said. "We will have to save such things for when I am well."

Ian circled her ear with his tongue, finished with words. Beth squeezed his shaft, her fingers strong. She would be well very soon, and then he'd lay her down and proceed to do everything he promised.

She stroked him up and down, faster and faster, her fingers burning him. He didn't stop his thrusts now. He closed his own hand over hers and helped her stroke, helped her squeeze.

Ian threw back his head as the room spun around, and he ground out his release. His seed spilled all over her hand

and his, wet and scalding hot. "Beth," he said into her ear. "My Beth."

Beth turned to meet his lips, and their tongues tangled. He snaked his hand through her beautiful hair, kissing her over and over until her mouth was red with it.

"I take it you liked that," she said with a teasing glint in her eyes.

Ian could barely speak. His heart thumped and his breath came fast, and he was nowhere near sated. But it was beautiful. He kissed her one more time, then reached to the washbasin for a towel to clean them both up.

"Thank you," he whispered.

~~~

Someone knocked rapidly on the door. Beth gasped, but Ian calmly tossed aside the towel, fastened his trousers, and said, "Come in."

Mac walked into the room. Beth's face heated, but Ian betrayed no shame to be caught with his shirt open and his wife cradled on his lap.

"That blasted inspector is here," Mac said. "I tried to toss him out, but he insisted you sent for him."

Ian began to growl, but Beth cut in quickly, "It's all right. I invited him."

She felt the weight of Ian's glare, and Mac asked, "Haven't we had enough of him?"

"I want to ask him something," Beth said. "And since you wouldn't allow me to go out, I had to have him come to me."

Ian's eyes narrowed. "Curry helped you."

Beth started to slide off his lap. "Come down with me," she said quickly. "We'll see him together."

Ian's arms locked around her. "Send him up."

"We're hardly decent."

"He'll have to take us as he finds us. You aren't well enough to dress up for him."

Beth subsided, knowing that if Ian ordered the footmen to throw Fellows on the pavement, they'd listen to him, not her. Mac shrugged and retreated. Beth tried to straighten her hair, which had come out of the braid she'd twined it into. "I must look like a courtesan who was just with her lover."

"You are beautiful," Ian said. He held her loosely, but she knew his arms could close like a vise if she tried to rise and walk away.

The door opened again, and she heard Fellows's intake of breath. "Really, this is unseemly."

Fellows had his hands behind his back, clenching his hat. Mac stood nearby, arms folded, as though he didn't want to let Fellows out of his sight.

"I beg your pardon, Inspector, but my husband refused to let me rise and greet you like a good hostess ought to."

"Yes, well." Fellows stood uncomfortably in the middle of the room, averting his eyes. "Are you better, my lady? I was sorry to hear you were so ill."

Surprisingly, the inspector did sound sorry. "Thank you," Beth said, putting warmth into her tone. "Well?"

"I heard all about your theory. About Lily Martin." Fellows deflated. "I searched Mrs. Palmer's rooms and found the photograph of Sally Tate that Lily had kept. It was signed on the back, 'From Sally, with all my love.' There was also a letter stuck into the back of the frame."

"A letter? What did it say?"

"It was a love letter from Sally to Lily, ill spelled, but the gist was clear. Lily had slashed lines across the page and written, 'You had it coming.'"

"Is that enough?" Ian asked.

Fellows scratched his forehead. "It will have to be, won't it? Scotland Yard likes the solution, because it leaves you high-and-mighty lords out of it. But your names are all over my report for anyone to read."

Mac gave a derisive laugh. "As though anyone will amuse themselves digging through a police file."

"The journalists will make a meal of you," Fellows said.

"They always do," Ian said quietly. "They haven't stopped, and they never will."

"Writing about high-and-mighty lords always sells newspapers," Beth said. "I don't mind, as long as you know the truth, Inspector. Ian didn't do it, and neither did Hart. You've been barking up the wrong tree all this time."

She gave the inspector a sunny smile, and he scowled back at her. Being in this room made him highly uncomfortable, but Beth had no sympathy. He deserved it for all he'd put Ian through.

Fellows still couldn't look directly at Beth and Ian, so he pinned Mac with his stare. "You Mackenzies might not have done the actual murder, but you were involved up to your necks. Next time you put a foot out of line, I'll be waiting, and I'll get you. I promise you that next time, I'll pot you good."

His face was red, a vein beating behind his tight collar. Mac only raised his brows, and Ian ignored him completely, nuzzling Beth's hair.

Beth squirmed out of Ian's arms and landed on her feet. She was still a little wobbly, and put her hand on Ian's strong shoulder to steady herself. She pointed at Mac. "You two must take him seriously." Her finger switched to Fellows. "And *you* will not pot them at all. You'll leave them alone and find real criminals who are doing real harm."

Fellows finally looked at her, anger overcoming embarrassment. "Oh, I will, will I?"

"Your obsession ends now."

"Mrs. Ackerley—"

"My name is Lady Ian Mackenzie." Beth reached over and yanked the bellpull behind Ian. "And from now on, you will do exactly what I say."

Fellows went purple. "I know they've bamboozled you despite my best efforts. But give me one reason I shouldn't try to expose their wrongdoings, their exploitations, how they blatantly use their power to manipulate the highest in the land, how they—"

"Enough. I take your point. But you must stop, Inspector."

"Why should I?"

Beth smiled at him. "Because I know your secret."

Fellows's eyes narrowed. "What secret?"

"A very deep one. Ah, Katie, just bring that package I had you buy the other day, will you?"

Chapter 23

Fellows stared at her. Ian straightened from his negligent sprawl, suddenly focusing on Beth.

"What secret?" Ian demanded.

"You don't know nuffing." Fellows sounded as Cockney as Curry.

Katie waltzed back into the room carrying the package Beth had instructed her to have ready. Her eyes were full of curiosity. Beth hadn't confided in her, and she'd been very annoyed about it. "Is this the one you mean?" she said. "You going to a fancy-dress ball or something?"

Beth took the package and opened it on the table next to the chaise. Ian rose and towered over her, as curious and mystified as Katie.

Beth turned around again, holding up the package's contents. "Would you indulge me, Inspector? Put these on?"

Fellows's face drained of color, and his eyes became fixed, like those of an animal in fear. "No," he snapped.

"I think you'd better," Mac said quietly. He folded his

arms against his wide chest and stood like a wall behind Fellows.

Beth walked straight to the inspector. Fellows backed away rapidly, only to bump against Mac behind him. Ian stepped beside him to cut off any other retreat.

"Do as she says," Ian said.

Fellows went still, rigid and shaking. Beth lifted the false whiskers and beard Katie had purchased for her and held them to Fellows's face.

"Who is he?" she asked.

The room went silent with shock.

"Son of a bitch," Mac whispered.

"Blimey," Katie said. "He looks just like that bloody awful painting of that hairy man on the staircase at Kilmorgan. Gives me the creeps, that thing does. Eyes follow you everywhere."

"So there is a resemblance," Fellows said to Beth. "What of it?"

Beth lowered the pieces of hair. Fellows was sweating.

"Perhaps you should tell them," Beth said. "Or I can. My friend Molly knows your mum."

"My mother has nothing to do with tarts."

"Then how do you know Molly's a game girl?"

Fellows glared. "I'm a policeman."

"You're a detective, and Molly never worked in your beat when you were a constable. She told me."

"Who is your mother?" Mac asked in a stern voice.

"You mean to say you don't know?" Fellows swung around to face the brothers. "After all these years of taunting me, of rubbing my face in your wealth and privilege? You even almost cost me my job, damn your eyes, my only way of making a living. But you didn't care about that. Why should you care that I'm the only one that looks after my mother?"

"They truly don't know, Inspector," Beth interrupted. She wrapped up the false beard and handed the package to a smug-looking Katie. "Men often can't see what's beyond the tips of their noses."

"I'm an artist," Mac interjected. "I am supposed to be a brilliant observer, and I never saw it."

"But you paint women," Beth said. "I've seen your paintings, and if a man is in them, he's vague and in the background."

Mac conceded. "The fairer sex is much more interesting."

"When I saw the portrait of your father at Kilmorgan, the resemblance struck me." She smiled. "Inspector Fellows is your half brother."

Hart's sitting room filled with Mackenzies. Curry bustled in with them, and the other three manservants hovered in the doorway, looking worried and curious at the same time.

Beth was breathing hard, shaky from her trip down the stairs, and Ian made her sit next to him on the sofa. Why he believed he could keep Beth out of trouble, he didn't know. She was headstrong and had a will of steel. His own mother had been a victim of his father, terrified of him. Beth's mother had been a victim as well, but Beth had somehow managed to transcend the horrors of her childhood. Her troubles had made her courageous and unflinching, characteristics that had been lost on the idiotic Mather. Beth was worth saving, worth protecting, like the rarest of porcelains.

Hart entered last, his eagle gaze taking in his brothers, Beth, and Fellows. Fellows was on his feet, facing them all under the room's high ceiling.

"Who is your mother?" Hart asked him in his cool ducal voice.

Beth answered for the inspector. "Her name is Catherine Fellows, and they take rooms in a house near St. Paul's Churchyard."

Hart transferred his gaze to Fellows, looking the man up and down as though seeing him for the first time. "She'll have to be moved to better accommodation."

Fellows blustered. "Why the devil should she? Because you couldn't abide the shame if someone found out?"

"No," Hart answered. "Because she deserves better. If my father used her and abandoned her, she deserves to live in a palace."

"We should have all of it. Your houses, your carriages, your damned Kilmorgan Castle. She worked her fingers raw to keep me fed while you licked gold plates."

"No gold plates in our nursery," Cameron interrupted in a mild voice. "There was a china mug I was fond of, but it was chipped."

"You know what I mean," Fellows snarled. "You had everything we should have had."

"And if I'd known that my father had left a woman to starve and raise his child, I'd have done something much sooner," Hart said. "You should have told me."

"And come crawling to a Mackenzie?"

"It would have saved us all so much trouble."

"I had my own job, earned by my hard work, which you did your best to destroy. I'm older than you by two years, Hart Mackenzie. The dukedom should be mine."

Hart moved to the table behind a sofa and opened a humidor. "I'd give you the joy of it, but the laws of England don't work that way. My father was married to my mother legally four years before I was born. Illegitimate children can be left money, but they can't inherit the peerage."

"You wouldn't want it," Cameron put in. "More trouble than it's worth. And for God's sake, don't murder Hart or I'm next."

Fellows clenched his hands. He moved his gaze around the room, taking in the fifteen-foot-high ceiling, the portraits of Mackenzies, and Mac's painting of the five Mackenzie dogs. Mac had painted them so lifelike that Ian expected them to come loping out of the painting and start drooling on Mac's boots.

"I am not one of you," Fellows began.

"You are," Ian said. Beth smelled so good, her hair snaking over her shoulders in dark brown waves, making patterns on her gold dressing gown. "You don't want to be, because that means you're just as mad as the rest of us."

"I am not a madman," Fellows returned. "There is only one madman in this room, *my lord*."

"All of us are mad in some way," Ian said. "I have a memory that won't let go of details. Hart is obsessed with politics and money. Cameron is a genius with horses, and Mac paints like a god. You find out details on your cases that others miss. You are obsessed with justice and getting everything you think is coming to you. We all have our madness. Mine is just the most obvious."

Everyone in the room stared at Ian, including Beth. Their scrutiny made him uncomfortable, so he buried his face in Beth's hair.

After a silence, Mac said, "Proof we should always listen to the wisdom of Ian."

Fellows made an impatient noise. "So we're one big, happy family now? Will you broadcast it to the newspapers, lord it over me, make me a charity case? Long-lost son of a duke embraced? No, thank you."

Hart chose a cheroot, then struck a match and lit it. "No. The newspapers don't know what really goes on in our private lives, because they're too interested in what we do in public. But if you are family, we take care of our own."

"Are you going to buy me off then? When I should have had your upbringing and your money, you're going to dangle a bit of luxury before me to keep me quiet?"

"Oh, for heaven's sake, Inspector," Beth snapped. "If their father did wrong by you, they want to make it up to you. They won't offer false affection, but they'll at least try to do the right thing."

"We hate our father far more than you ever could," Mac put in. "He abandoned you. *We* had to live with him."

"It's their father you want to hurt," Beth said. "I don't much blame you. I'd like to have fifteen minutes alone with him, myself."

"No, you wouldn't," Cameron said. He also moved to the humidor. "Trust me."

"He's dead and gone, where he can't hurt anyone again," Beth said. "Why carry on his legacy?"

"You're trying to wrap me around your finger, my lady. You've thrown in your lot with *them*. Why should I thank you?"

Ian lifted his head again. "Because she's right. Our father is dead and gone. He caused us all misery, and we shouldn't keep letting him do it. Beth and I will have another marriage ceremony at my house in Scotland in a few weeks. We will all gather there and be finished with our father from that time on."

Beth looked at him with shining eyes. "Do you understand how much I love you, Ian Mackenzie?"

Ian had no idea why this was relevant, and he didn't answer. Everyone else started talking at once. Ian ignored them, anchoring himself with Beth. He wanted so much to leave her alone, to not hurt her, but the warmth and scent of her drove out everything else. He needed her.

"Bloody hell," Fellows said. "You're all madmen."

"And you're one of us," Hart said grimly. "Be careful what you wish for."

Cameron rumbled his big laugh. "Get the man a drink. He looks like he's about to swoon."

"You'll have a Scots accent before you know it," Mac said. "The ladies like it, Fellows."

"God, no."

Daniel chuckled. "Ye mean *'Och, noe.'*"

Mac and Cameron dissolved into raucous laughter. "I think we should celebrate," Daniel shouted. "With lots of whiskey. Don't you think so, Dad?"

⁓

A week later, Hart's coach let Ian and Beth, Curry and Katie out at Euston Station to take the train back north. The brothers and Isabella had said they would follow in their own time, promising that they'd be present for the elaborate wedding Ian would give Beth for consenting to be his wife.

The weather had turned rainy, and Ian was anxious to get back to the wide-open spaces of Scotland. At the station, while Curry rushed off to purchase tickets after settling Beth into the first-class lounge, Ian turned around to see Hart coming at him out of the rain.

The fog parted for his brother's broad shoulders, just like the rest of the world did. Travelers' heads turned as they recognized the famous and wealthy duke.

"I wanted to speak to you before you went," Hart said stiffly. "You've been avoiding me."

"Yes." Ian hadn't liked the way his rage mounted every time he found himself alone with Hart, and so he had found means to not be alone with him. Hart started to pull Ian aside, out of the crowd, but Ian remained stubbornly in the middle of the platform, the crowd snaking around them.

Hart heaved a resigned sigh. "You are right that I'm a ruthless bastard. I truly didn't know that for five years you were trying to protect me." He hesitated, his eyes sliding sideways like Ian's always did. "I'm sorry."

Ian studied the steam billowing from the train across the platform. "I regret Mrs. Palmer's death." He watched a puff of steam swell, and then dissipate. "She loved you, but you didn't love her."

"What are you talking about? She was my mistress for years. Do you think her death means nothing to me?"

"You will miss her, yes, and you cared for her. But you didn't love her." Ian looked at Hart, meeting his eyes for a brief moment. "I know the difference now."

A muscle moved in Hart's jaw. "Damn you, Ian. No, I didn't love her. Yes, I cared for her. But yes, I used her, and before you remind me, yes, I used my wife, and both of them paid the ultimate price. What do you think that's doing to me?"

"I don't know." Ian studied his brother, for the first time seeing him as something other than the stern, strong edifice of Hart Mackenzie. Hart the man looked out of his amber-colored eyes, and Hart the man was twisted in anguish.

Ian put a hand on Hart's shoulder. "I think you should have made Eleanor marry you all those years ago. Your life would have been ten times better."

"My wise little brother. Eleanor jilted me, if you remember. Forcefully."

Ian shrugged. "You should have insisted. It would have been better for both of you."

"The Queen of England I can handle, Gladstone I can tolerate, and the House of Lords I can make to dance to my tunes." Hart shook his head. "But not Lady Eleanor Ramsay."

Ian shrugged again and pulled his hand away. His thoughts moved from Hart and his troubles to Beth waiting for him in the warm lounge. "I have a train to catch."

"Wait." Hart put himself in front of Ian. They were the same height, looking straight into each other's faces, though Ian had to move his gaze to Hart's cheekbone. "One more thing. Beth, too, was completely right about me. I use you shamelessly. But with one difference." Hart put his hands on Ian's shoulders. "I love you, if I can be unmanly and say so. I didn't take you out of the asylum just so you could help me with my politics. I did it because I wanted you free from that hell and given the chance to live a normal life."

"I know," Ian said. "I don't help you because you command me to."

He saw Hart's eyes grow moist, and suddenly his brother pulled him into a bear hug. The crowd milling around them turned their heads, smiled, or raised eyebrows.

Ian held Hart close, fists pressing into his brother's back. The two released each other, but Hart kept his hands on Ian's arms.

"Take Beth home and be happy. It's over."

Ian glanced over as Curry opened the door to the waiting room, and Beth came out. She looked at Ian and smiled. "Maybe it's over for you. For me, it's just beginning."

Hart looked surprised, and then he nodded in understanding as Beth came to Ian, her hands outstretched, a warm smile on her face. Beth turned and planted a kiss on a startled Hart's cheek, then took Ian's arm and let him walk her to the train.

In the train compartment, Curry fussed about making sure they'd have everything for the long ride north, until Ian sent him off. Rain and gathering dusk darkened the sky. Beth sank to the cushions and watched Ian yank the curtains closed against the gloom.

The train's whistle hooted, the steam hissed, and the train jerked forward. Ian braced himself against the polished wall as the train rolled away from the station.

Beth leaned against the cushions, exhausted. "I could wish Curry had found a book or something for me," she said. "Or we could have stopped for my needlework."

"Why?"

"For when you go a-roaming, up and down the train. I must keep myself occupied somehow."

"I'm not going to roam the train." Ian snapped closed the lock on the door. "You are here."

"You mean you will stay alone with me? Without a chaperone?" Despite their bit of play in her bedchamber the day Fellows's secret had been revealed, Ian had again kept his distance.

"I have a question to ask you."

Beth stretched one arm across the back of the seat, hoping she looked provocative. "And what is that, husband?"

Ian leaned down, his body hemming her in. His large fists rested on the seat back behind her. "Do I love you?"

Her heart banged in her chest. "What a question."

"When you were ill, when Mrs. Palmer hurt you, I knew I'd die if you died. There would be nothing inside me, just a hole where you used to be."

"Exactly how I would have felt if Inspector Fellows had let you go to the gallows or back to the asylum," Beth said softly.

"I never understood before. It's like fear and hope, both warm and cold. All mixed together."

"I know."

He cupped his hands around her face. "But I don't want to hurt you. I never, ever want to hurt you."

"Ian, you aren't your father. From what you and your brothers have told me, you're nothing like him. You left Sally rather than hurt her. You protected Hart from Fellows, and you thought you were protecting Lily. Everything you've done is to try to help people, not harm them."

He stood silently, as though debating whether to believe her. "I have the rage inside me."

"Which you know how to control. *He* didn't. That's the difference."

"Can I ever be sure?"

"I'll make you sure. You said yourself he caused you too much misery and that you and your brothers need to be done with him. Please, Ian. Let him go."

Ian closed his eyes. Beth watched emotions flicker across his face, the uncertainty, the stubbornness, the raw pain he'd lived with for so long. He didn't always know how to express his emotions, but that didn't mean he didn't feel them deeply.

When Ian slowly opened his eyes, he guided his gaze directly to Beth's. His golden eyes shimmered and sparkled, pupils ringed with green. He held her gaze steadily, not blinking or shifting away.

"I love you," he said.

Beth caught her breath, and sudden tears blurred her vision.

"Love you," Ian repeated. His gaze bore into hers harder than Hart's ever could hope to. "Love you, love you, loveyou, loveyou, loveyouloveyouloveyou . . ."

"Ian." Beth laughed.

"Love you," he murmured against her lips, her face, against the curve of her neck. "Love you."

"I love you, too. Are you going to say it all night?"

"I'll say it until I'm in you so hard I can't speak."

"I suppose I'll have to put up with that. It might be difficult, though I wouldn't mind finding out."

He paused. "Are you joking?"

Beth laughed until she slid out of the seat, but when she landed on the floor, Ian was right beside her. "Yes. I was joking." She caught Ian's lapels in her hands. "I believe carnality is definitely called for. Perhaps we should send for Curry to pull out the bed."

Ian got to his feet, tossed the cushions onto the other bench, and unlatched the hooks that unrolled the seat into a bed. "I don't want Curry."

"I see."

Ian yanked the bed into place, then lifted Beth and laid her on it. He unlaced her boots with quick jerks, then unbuckled and unfastened every bit of her brand-new traveling clothes.

Moments later she lay back, naked in the chill air. Beth lifted one hand over her head, letting her breasts arch forward, while Ian's gaze warmed her like a blanket. She bent her knee, scooting her foot to her hip so he could see between her legs. It felt delicious and exciting to lie back for Ian Mackenzie and let him look his fill.

"Do you still love me?" she asked. "Or is it only desire?"

"Both."

Ian tossed off his jacket, cravat, collar, and waistcoat in a few smooth moves, and had his shirt unbuttoned at cuffs and throat before she could blink. She watched his vee of brown chest come into view, then his strong thighs as he kicked out of his trousers and underdrawers. The shirt came off last. Dark hair snaked down his chest, and muscles rippled as he tossed the shirt aside.

He didn't give her much time to appreciate what she saw. He climbed up to the bed, on hands and knees around her.

"Carnality?" he repeated.

Her natural instinct to joke fled her. "Yes. Now. Please."

Ian slid his fingers between her legs, swirling the moisture he found there. "Love me?"

"I do. I love you, Ian."

He withdrew his fingers, sparkling wet, and licked one clean. "The best thing I've ever tasted."

"Better than single-malt whiskey from the Mackenzie distillery?"

"I'd rather drink you than whiskey."

"And you a Scotsman? You must be in love."

"Stop."

Beth clamped her lips shut, and they trembled. Ian lowered his head and licked between her legs. He savored that, eyes closed, then began to work on her studiously. The train moved back and forth in a steady rhythm, but the room seemed to spin.

"Ian, please."

He rose on his hands and knees again, his rigid stem hanging heavily. "Spread for me."

He didn't wait, didn't go slowly. He lifted her hips with one strong hand and shoved his way inside her.

The train rocketed over a bridge. Ian moved. He rested his weight on his fists, his muscles tightening, his skin gleaming with sweat.

"Love you," he said as he thrust. "Love you, love you, love you."

"Ian." He was hard and moving fast, and she opened to him, hot, slick, and wet.

His words trailed off into grunts, and soon the sounds she made were just as incoherent. He drove his hips, pushing hard, harder.

Ian dropped onto to her, the slick sweat on his chest meeting the heat of hers. He clenched his teeth and forced his gaze to hers.

"Love. You."

The man who couldn't look anyone in the eyes was making himself do it, no matter what the pain. He was giving her a gift, the greatest one he could, straight from his heart.

Tears poured from Beth's eyes at the same time her body wrenched into hot waves of joy. "I love you, Ian Mackenzie."

One more thrust, two, and he threw his head back, the cords of his neck tight. His seed burst out of him into her, and then they were twined together, arms and legs, lips and tongues.

"My Beth," he whispered, his breath hot on her swollen lips. "Thank you."

"For what?" Beth couldn't stop crying, but she smiled, her face aching with it.

"Setting me free."

Beth knew he didn't mean from the asylum. He kissed her again, his mouth rough, bruising, then sank down to her. Their bodies fit together, hot and spent, hands caressing, cradling, touching.

"You're welcome," she said.

Epilogue

ONE MONTH LATER

Ian and Beth had another wedding at Ian's home in Scotland, a house ten miles north of Kilmorgan, under the shadow of the mountain. Ian called it a "modest" house, but it was a mansion in Beth's opinion, though it was only a quarter the size of Kilmorgan.

The wedding was held at the village church, and there Ian slid a wide band covered with sapphires onto Beth's left hand. He smiled in triumph when he kissed her.

The bride and groom and family returned to the house and garden to a wedding banquet that Curry had worked on for weeks. Everything had to be exactly right, from the flowers threaded through the arbor to the pâté to the champagne and whiskey that flowed freely to all guests.

Friends from Edinburgh and London arrived, although Beth noticed that they were Hart's, Mac's, and Cameron's friends, not Ian's. Beth, however, invited the young man called Arden Weston she'd met in the gambling hall in

Paris. He arrived accompanied by his friend Graves and Miss Weston, his sister. They enjoyed themselves, drinking and making new friends, though Graves jealously regarded any gentleman Arden spoke to.

Inspector Fellows had come and brought his mother. They still looked startled to be embraced by the family, still skittish like cats that had gone too long without a human touch. But they ate and drank with the other guests, the gulf between Fellows and the Mackenzies starting to narrow.

The family—Hart, Cameron and Daniel, Mac, and Isabella—squeezed Beth in so many hugs she thought her corset would bend and she'd never breathe again. She noted that Mac drank only lemonade and Isabella was careful never to be in the same room with him. Beth watched them, her mind whirling with plans.

Ian took Beth's hand as she watched Isabella leave a room Mac had just walked into. Ian pulled her out of the house and through the garden and walked swiftly with her until they reached a little summerhouse on a rise.

"Leave them be," he said.

Beth blinked, contriving to look innocent. "Who?"

"Mac and Isabella. They must come together themselves."

"Perhaps with a gentle nudge?"

"No." Ian leaned against the rail and pulled her to face him. Her white taffeta gown crushed the front of his formal black suit. The suit couldn't hide his fine body, the strength of his shoulders stretching the black cashmere, the hard planes of his chest behind the white shirt. Ian looked good in anything he wore, from the well-fitted suit to the frayed kilt and shirt in which he fished.

"Leave them be, Beth," Ian repeated, his voice gentle.

She sighed. "I suppose I want everyone to be as happy as I am."

Beth slid her arms around him and looked past him at the brick house and the sloping green lawn where the family and friends gathered. She loved the house already. She liked the way morning sunshine slanted into the gallery.

She loved the small room Ian had chosen as his bedroom, which was hers now, too. She loved the way the stairs squeaked, and the flagstone passage to the kitchens echoed, and how the rear doors opened to a cluttered garden filled with birds, flowers, and Ian's dogs, Ruby and Fergus, who'd come to live with them.

She tasted happiness here that she'd had only a glimpse of with Thomas. Thomas had taught the lonely, frightened Beth Villiers that she was allowed to be happy. Ian was letting her imbibe all the happiness she wanted.

"Do you like it?" Ian asked. "Up here in the wilds with me?"

"Of course I do. I believe you heard me raving about the view of the mountains, and the nice chill the butter gets in the dairy."

"It's harsh in the winter."

"I will grow used to it. I'm good at it, getting used to things. Besides, Mrs. Barrington was always stingy with the coal fires. Living with her was very much like surviving a Scottish winter."

He peered at her, then decided not to bother deciphering what she meant. He lifted his gaze to the nearby thicket of trees that smelled of pine and cool air.

"Do you mind my madness? Even if you're right that I can contain the rages, I will always be mad. I won't get better."

"I know." Beth snuggled against his chest. "It's part of the very intriguing package that is Ian Mackenzie."

"It comes and goes. Sometimes I am perfectly fine. And then a muddle comes."

"And goes away again. Curry helps you. I'll help you."

Ian cupped her chin and turned her face up to his. Then he did what he'd been practicing since the night on the train—he looked her fully in the eyes.

He couldn't always do it. Sometimes his gaze simply refused to obey, and he'd turn away with a growl. But more and more he'd been able to focus directly on her.

Ian's eyes were beautiful, even more so when his pupils

widened with desire. "Have I told you today that I love you?" he asked.

"A few dozen times. Not that I mind."

As a young woman who'd been starved for love much of her life, Beth lapped up Ian's generous outpouring of the words. He'd surprise her with them, catching her as she walked down the hall, pushing her against a wall, breathing, "I love you."

Or he'd tickle her awake and tell her he loved her while she tried to hit him with a pillow. The best was when he lay against her in the dark, fingers tracing her body. She treasured his whispered "I love you."

"I need to tell you something, Ian."

Ian blinked. His gaze tried to slide away, but he pulled it determinedly back. "Hmm?"

"I didn't want to say until I was absolutely certain, but I've seen a doctor now." She drew a breath. "Ian, you're going to be a father."

Ian kept staring at her, his gaze unmoving. He blinked again, then lightly rubbed his temple. "What did you say?"

"You're going to be a father." Beth laced her fingers through his, pulling his hand down. "I'm going to have a child. Do you hear me?"

"Yes." Ian slid his fingers down her smooth gown to rest on her abdomen. "A child." His eyes widened. "Oh, God. Will it be like me?"

"I hope so."

"Why?" He closed his fingers over the fabric, crushing the taffeta. "Why would you hope he'd be like me?"

"Well, *he* might be a *she*. And I can't think of anything better than a child who's just like his father." She let her voice go low, seductive. "Especially when that father is you."

Ian didn't look reassured. "He's a Mackenzie. He'll be mad."

"But he'll have an advantage. He'll have a father and uncles who understand." She smiled. "Or she. If it's a girl, of course, she will be perfect."

"I agree," Ian said gravely.

Beth started to explain her jest, then looked up at him in surprise. "Was that a joke, Ian Mackenzie?"

"You are teaching me." He leaned down to her. "With your spicy tongue."

Beth darted out the tongue in question. "Does it taste spicy?"

"Yes." He slid his thumb in a slow caress across her bottom lip. "But let me taste it again."

He crushed her up to him, his hands cupping her bottom. Down the hill, Isabella laughed and the Mackenzie brothers and Daniel broke into a rousing cheer.

Then sound swirled and became meaningless as Ian's mouth covered hers, and his body curved over her. She felt the firm, hard ridge of his arousal through their layers of clothes, and her heart beat with sudden heat.

Carnal pleasure, indeed, offered by the maddening Lord Ian Mackenzie.

Beth took it.

Turn the page for a preview of the second
novel in the Highland Pleasures series
by Jennifer Ashley

*Lady Isabella's
Scandalous Marriage*

Available now from Berkley Sensation!

Chapter 1

All of London was amazed to learn of the sudden marriage of Lady I— S— and Lord M— M—, brother of the Duke of K—, last evening. The lady in question had her Come-Out and her Wedding the same night, leading debutantes to plead with fathers to make their coming-out balls just as eventful.

—*From a London society newspaper, February 1875*

SEPTEMBER 1881

Isabella's footman rang the bell at the house of Lord Mac Mackenzie on Mount Street, while Isabella waited in the landau, wondering for the dozenth time since she'd set off whether this were wise.

Perhaps Mac would be out. Maybe the unpredictable man had gone off to Paris, or to Italy, where summer would linger for a time. She could investigate the matter she'd discovered by herself. Yes, that would be best.

As she opened her mouth to call back her footman, the large black door swung open, and Mac's valet, a former pugilist, peered out. Isabella's heart sank. Bellamy being here meant Mac was here, because Bellamy never strayed far from Mac's side.

Bellamy peered into the landau, and a look of undisguised astonishment crossed his scarred face. Isabella hadn't approached this house since the day she'd left it three and a half years ago. "M'lady?"

Isabella took Bellamy's beefy hand to steady herself as she descended. The best way to do this, she decided, was simply to do it.

"How is your knee, Bellamy?" she asked. "Are you still using the liniment? Is it too much to hope that my husband is at home?"

As she talked, she breezed into the house, pretending not to notice the parlor maid and a footman popping out to stare.

"The knee's much better, m'lady. Thank you. His lordship is . . ." Bellamy hesitated. "He's painting, m'lady."

"So early? There's a wonder." Isabella started up the stairs at a quick pace, not letting herself think about what she was doing. If she thought about it, she'd run far and fast, perhaps lock herself into her house and not come out. "Is he in his studio? No need to announce me. I'll go up myself."

"But m'lady." Bellamy followed her, but his damaged knee wouldn't let him move quickly, and Isabella reached the landing, three floors up, before Bellamy had mounted the second flight.

"M'lady, he said not to be disturbed," Bellamy called upward.

"I won't be long. I need only ask him a question."

"But, m'lady, he's . . ."

Isabella paused, hand on the white doorknob of the right-hand attic room. "I shall take full blame for invading his lordship's privacy, Bellamy."

She lifted her skirts as she swung open the door and walked into the room. Mac was there, all right, standing in front of a long easel, painting with fervor.

Isabella's skirts slid from her nerveless fingers, the beauty of her estranged husband striking her like a blow. Mac wore a kilt, threadbare and paint-flecked, and he was naked from the waist up. Though it was cool in the studio,

Mac's torso gleamed with sweat, his skin tanned from spending the summer on the warmer Continent. He wore a red kerchief on his head, gypsy style, to keep paint out of his hair. He'd always done that, she remembered with a pang. It made his cheekbones more prominent, emphasized the handsomeness of his face. Even the rough boots, much worn and paint-splotched, were familiar and dear.

Mac laid paint on his canvas with energy, obviously not hearing Isabella open the door. He held the palette in his left hand, arm muscles tight, while his right moved the brush in swift, jerking strokes. Mac was a stunning man, made still more attractive when absorbed in doing something he loved.

Isabella used to sit in this very studio on an old sofa strewn with cushions, simply watching him paint. Mac might not say one word to her while he worked, but she had adored watching the play of muscles on his back, the way he'd smear paint on his cheek when he'd absently rub it. After a particularly good session, he'd turn to her with a wide smile and pull her into his arms, never minding that paint now smeared all over *her* skin.

So absorbed in Mac was she that Isabella didn't notice what he painted with such intensity until she forced herself to look away from him and across the room. She barely stifled her dismay.

A young woman lay on a raised platform draped with yellow and red coverings. She was nude, which came as no surprise—Mac generally painted women who wore nothing or very little. But Isabella had never seen him paint anything so blatantly erotic. The model lay on her back with her knees bent, her legs wide apart. Her hand rested on her private place, and she was spreading herself open without shame. Mac scowled at the offering and painted with rapid brushstrokes.

Behind Isabella, Bellamy reached the top landing, puffing from exertion and distress. Mac heard him and growled but didn't look 'round.

"Damn it, Bellamy, I told you I didn't want to be disturbed this morning."

"I'm sorry, sir. I couldn't stop her."

The model raised her head, spied Isabella, and grinned. "Oh, hello, yer ladyship."

Mac glanced behind him once, twice, then his copper gaze riveted to Isabella. Paint dripped, unheeded, from his brush to the floor.

Isabella strove to keep her voice from shaking. "Hello, Molly. How is your little boy? It's all right, Bellamy, you can leave us. This won't take long, Mac. I only came to ask you a question."

Damnation.

What the hell was Bellamy playing at, letting her up here?

Isabella hadn't set foot in the Mount Street house in three and a half years, not since the day she'd left him with nothing but a short letter for explanation. Now she stood in the doorway, in hat and gloves donned for calling. Today of all days, while Mac painted Molly Bates in her spread glory. This wasn't part of his plan, the one that had made him leap onto a train to London after his brother's wedding and follow Isabella down here from Scotland. He'd call this a grievous miscalculation.

Isabella's dark blue jacket hugged her torso and cupped her full bosom, and a gray skirt of complicated ruffles spread over a small bustle. Her hat was a concoction of flowers and ribbons, her gloves a dark gray that wouldn't show London grime. The gloves outlined slender fingers he wanted to kiss, hands he longed to have slide up his back as they lay together in bed.

Isabella had always known how to dress, how to present herself in colors dear to his artist's eye. Mac had loved to help her dress in the mornings, lacing her gowns against her soft, sweet-smelling skin. He'd dismiss her maid and perform the tasks himself, though those mornings it had taken them a long time to descend for breakfast.

Now Mac drank in every inch of her, and *damn it*, grew hard. Would she see, and would she laugh?

Isabella crossed to the dressing gown Molly had left in a heap on the floor. "You'd better wrap up in this, dear," she said to the model. "It's chilly up here. You know Mac never believes in feeding the fire. Why don't you warm up downstairs with a nice cup of tea while I have a chat with my husband?"

Molly leapt to her feet, her grin wide. Molly was a beautiful female in the way many men liked—large-bosomed, round-hipped, doe-eyed. She had a mass of black hair and a perfect face, an artist's dream. But next to the glory of Isabella, Molly faded to nothing.

"Don't mind if I do," Molly said. "It's stiff work posing for naughty pictures. My fingers are that cramped."

"Some teacakes ought to loosen you again," Isabella said as Molly slid on the dressing gown. "Mac's cook always used to keep currant ones in large supply, in case of emergencies. Ask her if she still does."

Molly's dimples showed. "I've missed you, no lie, your ladyship. 'Is lordship forgets we 'ave to eat."

"It's his lordship's way," Isabella said. Molly strolled from the studio without worry, and Mac watched as though from far away as Bellamy followed Molly out and closed the door.

Isabella turned her lush green eyes to him. "You're dripping."

"What?" Mac stared at her then heard a glob of paint hit his board floor. He let out a growl, slammed the palette onto the table, and thrust the brush into a jar of oil of turpentine.

"You've begun early today," Isabella said.

Why did she keep on in that friendly, neutral voice, as though they were acquaintances at a tea party?

"The light was good." His own voice sounded stiff, harsh.

"Yes, it's a sunny morning for a change. Don't worry, I'll let you get back to it soon. I only want your opinion."

Blast her, had she come here to throw him off guard on purpose? When had she gotten so good at the game?

"My opinion on what?" he asked. "Your new hat?"

"Not my hat, although thank you for noticing. No, I want your opinion on this."

Mac found the hat in question right under his nose. Gray and blue ribbons trailed into glossy curls that beckoned to be lifted, smoothed.

The hat tilted back until he was looking into Isabella's eyes, eyes that had snared him across a ballroom so long ago. She hadn't been aware of her power then, the sweet debutante, and she didn't know it now. Her simple look of inquiry, of interest, could pin a man and give him the most erotic dreams imaginable.

"On this, Mac," she said impatiently.

She was lifting a handkerchief toward him. In the middle of its snowy whiteness lay a piece of yellow-covered canvas about an inch long and a quarter inch wide.

"What color would you say this was?" she asked.

"Yellow." Mac quirked a brow. "You drove all the way here from North Audley Street to ask me whether something is yellow?"

"Of course I know it's yellow. What kind of yellow, specifically?"

Mac peered at it. The color was vibrant, almost pulsing. "Cadmium yellow."

"More specific than that?" She wiggled the handkerchief as though the motion would reveal the mystery. "Don't you understand? It's *Mackenzie* yellow. That astonishing yellow you mix for your paintings, the secret formula known only to you."

"Yes, so it is." With Isabella standing so close to him, her heady scent in his nostrils, he didn't give a damn if the paint was Mackenzie yellow or graveyard black. "Have you been amusing yourself slicing up my pictures?"

"Don't be silly. I took this from a painting hanging in Mrs. Leigh-Waters's drawing room in Richmond."

Curiosity trickled through Mac's impatience. "I've never given a painting to Mrs. Leigh-Waters of Richmond."

"I didn't think you had. When I asked her about it, she told me she bought the picture from an art dealer in the Strand. Mr. Crane."

"The devil she did. I don't sell my paintings, especially not through Crane."

"Exactly." Isabella smiled in triumph, the red curve of her lips doing nothing to ease his arousal. "The painting is signed *Mac Mackenzie,* but you didn't paint it."

Mac looked again at the strip of brilliant yellow on the handkerchief. "How do you know I didn't paint it? Maybe some ungrateful blackguard I gave a picture to sold it to raise money to pay a debt."

"It's a scene from a hill, overlooking Rome."

"I've done many scenes overlooking Rome."

"I know that, but this wasn't one of yours. It's your style, your brushwork, your colors, but you didn't paint it."

Mac pushed the handkerchief back at her. "How do you know? Are you intimately acquainted with all my works? I've painted quite a few Rome pictures since you . . ." He couldn't bring himself to say "since you left me." He'd gone to Rome to soothe his broken heart, painting the bloody vista day after day. He'd done too damn many pictures of Rome, until he'd grown sick of the place. Then he'd moved to Venice and painted it until he never wanted to see another gondola as long as he lived.

That was when he'd still been a debauched, drunken sot. Once he'd sobered up, replacing his obsession for single-malt with one of tea, he'd retreated to Scotland and stayed put. The Mackenzies didn't view whiskey as strong drink— they viewed it as essential to life—but Mac's drink of choice had changed to oolong, which Bellamy had learned to brew like a master.

At his words, Isabella flushed, and Mac felt a flash of sudden glee. "Ah, so you *are* intimately acquainted with everything I've painted. Kind of you to take an interest."

Her blush deepened. "I see notices in art journals, is all, and people tell me."

"And you've become so familiar with each of my pictures that you know when I didn't paint one?" Mac gave her a slow smile. "This from a woman who changed her hotel when she knew I was staying in it?"

Mac hadn't thought Isabella could grow any more red. He felt the dynamics in the room change, from Isabella in a bold frontal attack to Isabella in hasty retreat.

"Don't flatter yourself. I happen to notice things, is all."

And yet she'd known straightaway that he hadn't painted what she'd seen in Mrs. Leigh-Waters's drawing room. He grinned, liking her confusion.

"What I'm trying to tell you is that someone out there is forging Mac Mackenzies," Isabella said impatiently.

"Why would anybody be fool enough to forge something by me?"

"For the money, of course. You are very popular."

"I'm popular because I'm scandalous," Mac countered. "When I die, the paintings will be worthless, except as souvenirs." He set the slice of paint and handkerchief on the table. "May I keep this? Or do you plan to restore it to Mrs. Leigh-Waters?"

"Don't be silly. I didn't tell her I was taking it."

"You left the painting on her wall with a bit sliced out, did you? Won't she notice that?"

"The picture is high up, and I did it carefully so it doesn't show." Isabella's gaze moved to the painting on his easel. "That is quite repulsive, you know. She looks like a spider."

Mac didn't give a damn about the painting, but when he glanced at it he wanted to groan. Isabella was right: It was terrible. All of his paintings were terrible these days. He hadn't been able to paint a decent stroke since he'd gone sober, and he had no idea why he'd thought this one would be any better.

He let out a frustrated roar, picked up a paint-soaked

rag, and hurled it at the canvas. The rag landed with a splat on Molly's painted abdomen, and brown-black rivulets ran down the rosy skin.

Mac turned from the picture in time to see Isabella swiftly exiting the room. He sprinted after her and caught up to her halfway down the first flight of stairs. Mac stepped around her, slamming one hand to the banister, the other to the wall. Paint smeared on the wallpaper Isabella had picked out when she'd redecorated his house six years ago.

Isabella gave him a cold look. "Do move, Mac. I have half a dozen errands to attend before luncheon, and I'm already late starting."

Mac took long breaths, trying to still his rage. "Wait. *Please.*" He made himself say the word. "Let us go down to the drawing room. I'll have Bellamy bring tea. We can talk about the paintings you think are forged." Anything to keep her here. He knew in his heart that if she walked away from this house again, she'd never return.

"There is nothing more to say about the forged paintings. I only thought you'd want to know."

Mac was aware that his entire household lurked below, listening. They wouldn't do anything so gauche as peer up the staircase, but they'd be in doorways and in the shadows, waiting to see what happened. They adored Isabella and had mourned the day she'd left them.

"Isabella," he said, pitching his voice low. "Stay."

The tightness around her eyes softened the slightest bit. Mac had hurt her, he knew it. He'd hurt her over and over again. The first step in winning her back was to stop the hurting.

Her lips parted, red and lush. Because he was two steps below her, Isabella's face was on level with his. He could close the few inches between them and kiss her if he chose, feel her mouth on his, taste her warm moisture on his tongue.

"Please," he whispered. *I need you so much.*

Molly chose that moment to climb toward them up the

stairs. "Are you ready for me again, yer lordship? You still want me sticking me fingers in me Mary Jane?"

Isabella closed her eyes, her lips thinning into a long, immobile line. Mac's temper splintered.

"Bellamy!" he shouted over the banisters. "What the devil is she doing out of the kitchen?"

Molly came closer, her smile good-natured. "Oh, her ladyship don't mind me. Do you, yer ladyship?" Molly sidled around first Mac, then Isabella, her dressing gown rustling as she headed back up to the studio.

"No, Molly," Isabella said in a cool voice. "I don't mind *you*."

Isabella lifted her skirt in her gloved hand and prepared to start around Mac. Mac reached for her.

Isabella shrank away. Not in loathing, he realized after the first frozen heartbeat, but because the hand he stretched toward her was covered in brown and black paint.

Mac slammed himself back against the stair railing. He wouldn't trap her. At least not now, with all his servants watching and listening, and Isabella looking at him in that way.

Isabella moved down the stairs around him, very carefully not touching him.

Mac strode after her. "I'll send Molly home. Stay and have luncheon. My staff can run your errands for you."

"I very much doubt that. Some of my errands are quite personal." Isabella reached the ground floor and took up the parasol she'd left on the hall tree.

Bellamy, don't you dare open that door.

Bellamy swung the door wide, letting in a wash of London's fetid air. Isabella's landau stood outside, her footman ready with the door open.

"Thank you, Bellamy," she said in a serene voice. "Good morning."

She walked out.

Mac wanted to rush after her, grab her around the waist, drag her back into the house. He could have Bellamy lock and bolt the doors so she couldn't leave again. She'd hate him at first, but she'd gradually understand that she still belonged with him. Here.

Mac made himself let Bellamy close the door. Tactics that worked for his barbaric Highland ancestors would be useless on Isabella. She'd give him that cool look from her beautiful eyes and have him on his knees. He had prostrated himself for her often enough in the past. The feeling of carpet on his knees had been worth her sudden laughter, the cool tinge leaving her voice as she said, "Oh, Mac, don't be so absurd." He'd pull her down to the carpet with him, and the forgiveness would take an interesting turn.

Mac sat down heavily on the bottom stair and put his head in his paint-stained hands. Today had been a misstep. Isabella had caught him off guard, and he'd ruined the beautiful opportunity she'd handed him.

"Oh, the painting's all spoiled." Molly hurried from the floors above in a flurry of silk. "Mind you, I think I look a bit funny in it."

"Go on home, Molly," Mac said, his voice hollow. "I'll pay you for the full day."

He expected Molly to squeal in pleasure and hurry off, but instead she sank down next to him. "Oh, poor lamb. Want me to make you feel better?"

Mac's arousal had died, and he didn't want it to rise again for anyone but Isabella. "No," he said. "Thank you."

"Suit yourself." Molly stroked slender fingers through his hair. "It's the absolute worst when they don't love you back, ain't it, me lord?"

"Yes." Mac closed his eyes, his rage and need swirling around him until he was sick with it. "You're right, it is the absolute worst."

Lord and Lady Abercrombie's hunt ball in Surrey the following night was stuffed to the rafters with fashionable people. Isabella entered the ballroom with some trepidation, expecting at any moment to see her husband, who, her maid Evans had informed her, had also received an invitation. Evans had obtained the information directly from her old crony, Bellamy.

Seeing Mac in his studio like a half-naked god yesterday had sent Isabella straight home to fling herself on her bed in tears. Her errands had never got done, because she'd spent the rest of the afternoon curled into a ball feeling sorry for herself.

Isabella had risen the next morning and made herself face facts. She had two choices—she could completely avoid Mac as she had in the past, or resign herself to encountering him about London as they lived their lives. They could be civil. They could be friends. What she ought to do was become *so* used to seeing him that his presence no longer plagued her. Grow inured to him so that her heart no longer leapt into her throat at one glimpse of his strong face or the flash of his wicked smile.

The second choice was the more unnerving, but Isabella berated herself until she stepped up to the task. She would not hide at home like a frightened rabbit. Hence, her acceptance of Lord Abercrombie's invitation, even though she knew the odds were high that Mac would attend.

Isabella bade Evans dress her in a new ball gown of blue satin moiré with yellow silk roses across her bodice and train. Maude Evans, who could boast having been a dresser to famous actresses, several opera singers, a duchess, and a courtesan, had been dressing Isabella since the morning after Isabella's scandalous elopement with Mac. Evans had arrived at Mac's house on Mount Street, where Isabella, Mac's ring heavy on her finger, had stood in her ball gown from the previous night, having no other clothes at hand. Evans had taken one look at Isabella's innocent face and become her fierce protector.

I look quite acceptable for a matron of nearly five and twenty. Isabella surveyed herself in the mirror as Evans draped diamonds across Isabella's bosom. *I have nothing to be ashamed of.*

Even so, her heart froze when she entered Lord Abercrombie's ballroom and spied a tall Mackenzie male in the supper room beyond Broad shoulders stretched a formal black coat as he rested an elbow on the fireplace mantel, his kilt Mackenzie plaid.

Isabella realized in the next heartbeat that the man was not Mac, but his older brother Cameron. Touched by relief and delight, she broke from the friends she'd arrived with, caught up her satin skirts, and sped through the crowd to him.

"Cam, what on earth are you doing here? I thought you'd be up north, frantically preparing for the St. Leger."

Cameron tossed the cigar he'd been smoking into the fire, took Isabella's hands, and leaned to kiss her cheek. He smelled of smoke and malt whiskey; he always did, though those were sometimes accompanied by the scent of horses. Cameron kept a stable full of the best racehorses in England.

The second-oldest brother, Cameron was a little larger than Mac, a little broader of shoulder and taller of stature, and a deep scar cut across his left cheekbone. Cam's unruly red-brown hair was the darkest of the four brothers', his eyes more deeply golden. He was known as the black sheep, a daunting task in a family whose exploits filled the scandal sheets. It was common knowledge that Cameron, a widower with a fifteen-year-old son, took a new mistress every six months, having his pick of famous actresses, courtesans, and highborn widows. Isabella had stopped trying to keep track of them long ago.

Cameron shrugged in answer to her question. "Not much more to do. The trainers have my instructions, and I'll meet them there before the first race."

"You're a bad liar, Cameron Mackenzie. Hart sent you, didn't he?"

Cameron didn't bother to look embarrassed. "Hart was worried when Mac raced after you following Ian's wedding. Is he making a nuisance of himself?"

"No," Isabella said quickly. She loved Mac's brothers, but they did tend to stick their noses into each other's business.

Not that she wasn't grateful to them—they could have shut her out when she'd decided to leave Mac three and a half years ago, but instead they'd rallied to her side. Hart, Cameron, and Ian had made it known that they still considered Isabella part of the family. And as she was part of the family, they tended to watch over her like protective older brothers.

"So Hart sent you down to play nanny?" she asked.

"He did," Cameron drawled, straight-faced. "You should see me in my cap and pinafore."

Isabella laughed, and Cam joined her. He had a gravelly laugh, sounding as though something had scratched away at his voice.

"Is Beth well?" she asked. "She and Ian are all right?"

"Fine when I left them. Ian is extremely pleased at the prospect of becoming a father. He mentions it only about once every five minutes."

Isabella smiled in true delight. Ian and Beth, his new wife, were so happy, and Isabella looked forward to holding their little one in her arms. The thought gave her a pang as well, which she quickly suppressed.

"And Daniel?" Isabella went on, keeping the conversation light. "Did he come with you?"

Cameron shook his head. "Daniel is lodging with an old don of mine who is to stuff his head with knowledge before Michaelmas term. I want to give Danny's tutors less cause to beat his lessons into him."

"Lessons instead of horses? I'm certain that rankles our Danny."

"Aye, but if he keeps getting poor marks, he'll never get into university."

He sounded so like a concerned father, this tall man with the dark reputation, that Isabella laughed again. "He tries to emulate you, Cam."

"Aye, he does. That's wh't worries me."

Behind Isabella, the strains of a waltz began, and couples in the ballroom glided into place. Cameron held out his broad arm. "Dance, Isabella?"

"I'd be most happy to—"

Isabella's polite acceptance was cut off when strong fingers closed over her elbow. She smelled Mac's soap and masculine scent overlaid with the faint odor of turpentine.

"This waltz is mine," Mac said in her ear. "And don't bother to tell me your card is full, my wife, because you know I'll make short work of that."

NEW FROM *USA TODAY* BESTSELLING AUTHOR

JENNIFER ASHLEY

PRIMAL BONDS

Collared and controlled, Shifters are outcast from humanity, forced to live in Shiftertowns. But waiting within are passions that no collar can contain . . .

Feline Shifter Sean Morrisey has always been a lonely man, even while surrounded by his pride. When a female Shifter comes to town seeking refuge, Sean claims the new arrival, expecting a submissive little she-wolf. Instead, he finds a beautiful woman who looks him straight in the eye without fear, stirring the mating frenzy within him.

As half-Fae, half-Shifter, Andrea Gray is used to looking out for herself. But in order to relocate to a new Shiftertown and escape an unwanted mate-claim, Andrea must accept a new mate. A Guardian seems as good a candidate as any, but Andrea's intense attraction to Sean is something she never expected—a perilous complication for a woman with a troubled past.

Now, as Andrea struggles to keep her seductive savior at arm's length, Sean is determined to turn their mating of convenience into the real thing before the frenzy they're struggling to contain burns them both—from the inside out . . .

penguin.com

THE NEW VICTORIAN HISTORICAL
ROMANCE NOVEL FROM
USA TODAY BESTSELLING AUTHOR

JENNIFER ASHLEY

Lady Isabella's Scandalous Marriage

Lady Isabella Scranton scandalized London by leaving
her husband, notorious artist Lord Mac Mackenzie, after only three turbulent years of marriage. But Mac has
a few tricks to get the lady back in his life, and more
importantly, back into his bed.

"I adore this novel."

—Eloisa James, *New York Times* bestselling author

M713T0510

From *New York Times* bestselling author
of *Sinful in Satin*

MADELINE HUNTER

Dangerous in Diamonds

Outrageously wealthy, the Duke of Castleford has little incentive to curb his profligate ways—gaming and whoring with equal abandon and enjoying his hedonistic lifestyle to the fullest. When a behest adds a small property to his vast holdings, one that houses a modest flower business known as The Rarest Blooms, Castleford sees little to interest him ... until he lays eyes on its owner. Daphne Joyes is coolly mysterious, exquisitely beautiful, and utterly scathing toward a man of Castleford's stamp—in short, an object worthy of his most calculated seduction.

Daphne has no reason to entertain Castleford's outrageous advances, and every reason to keep him as far away as possible from her eclectic household. Not only has she been sheltering young ladies who have been victims of misfortune, but she has her own closely guarded secrets. Then Daphne makes a discovery that changes everything. She and Castleford have one thing in common: a profound hatred for the Duke of Becksbridge, who just happens to be Castleford's relative.

Never before were two people less likely to form an alliance—or to fall in love ...

M848T0311

Enter the rich world of historical romance with Berkley Books . . .

Madeline Hunter

Jennifer Ashley

Joanna Bourne

Lynn Kurland

Jodi Thomas

Anne Gracie

Love is timeless.

berkleyjoveauthors.com

Penguin Group (USA) Online

What will you be reading tomorrow?

Patricia Cornwell, Nora Roberts, Catherine Coulter,
Ken Follett, John Sandford, Clive Cussler,
Tom Clancy, Laurell K. Hamilton, Charlaine Harris,
J. R. Ward, W.E.B. Griffin, William Gibson,
Robin Cook, Brian Jacques, Stephen King,
Dean Koontz, Eric Jerome Dickey, Terry McMillan,
Sue Monk Kidd, Amy Tan, Jayne Ann Krentz,
Daniel Silva, Kate Jacobs...

You'll find them all at
penguin.com

*Read excerpts and newsletters,
find tour schedules and reading group guides,
and enter contests.*

Subscribe to Penguin Group (USA) newsletters
and get an exclusive inside look
at exciting new titles and the authors you love
long before everyone else does.

PENGUIN GROUP (USA)
penguin.com